Anonymous

The Eagle

Vol. II

SALZWASSER
VERLAG

Anonymous

The Eagle

Vol. II

Reprint of the original, first published in 1861.

1st Edition 2022 | ISBN: 978-3-37505-675-9

Verlag (Publisher): Salzwasser Verlag GmbH, Zeilweg 44, 60439 Frankfurt, Deutschland
Vertretungsberechtigt (Authorized to represent): E. Roepke, Zeilweg 44, 60439 Frankfurt, Deutschland
Druck (Print): Books on Demand GmbH, In de Tarpen 42, 22848 Norderstedt, Deutschland

THE EAGLE.

THE EAGLE.

A MAGAZINE,

SUPPORTED BY

MEMBERS OF ST. JOHN'S COLLEGE.

VOL. II.

Cambridge:
PRINTED BY W. METCALFE, GREEN STREET,
FOR SUBSCRIBERS ONLY.

1861.

CONTENTS.

THE EAGLE.

A FORTNIGHT IN IRELAND.

EVER since the days of Troy travellers seem to have believed their adventures to be the most interesting topic under the sun. Whether they be justified in this belief is no matter of mine, but while Homer has deemed the wanderings of Ulysses worthy of his mighty Muse, while the travels of the pious but loquacious Æneas are known to have furnished Virgil with materials for a whole Æneid, and Dido with the means of spending a most delightful evening; I consider that the selection of my subject " A Fortnight in Ireland" needs no apology.

Our first impressions of Ireland as we neared Kingstown were most pleasing: even the tortures of ten hours sea-sickness could not blind us to the fact that we saw one of the fairest scenes of earth. On our left Wicklow Head lies basking in the morning sun, nearer to us with more sombre shade Bray Head broods, like some sea-monster, over the deep, while it shelters the peaceful and retiring bay of Killiney, called the Sorento of Ireland, as its more ambitious neighbour, " Dublin Bay," has been called " The

Irish Bay of Naples," certainly there never seemed to me a sweeter spot than Killiney, in which

> Sortiri tacitum lapidem, et sub cœspite condi.

However, the bright harbour of Kingstown lies before us, so without casting more than a glance northward, where " Ireland's Eye," the scene of the Kirwan Murder, is seen

> Like a gloomy stain
> On the emerald main.

We stagger down to the cabin, and soon reappear, carpet-bag in hand, and in ten minutes find ourselves on Irish land.   And then begins a contest to represent which would require the Muse of a Homer, or Chancellor's English Medallist, the Imagination of a " Time's Correspondent," or an " Our own Artist" of the Illustrated London News. For no sooner do we touch Irish ground than

> Juvenum manus emicat ardens.

Our carpet-bag flieth this way, our hat-box vanisheth into thin air, and when giddy from exertion after a rough passage, we gain the support of a post, we at length see our hat-box, two hundred yards distant from us in the middle of a muddy road with a small urchin seated on it, who no sooner sees us than he is on his legs shouting "dis way yer arnher—lave the jintleman alone Pat— dis way to de Erin—go bragh hotel yer arnher," meanwhile my carpet-bag has received the last strap necessary to fasten it irrevocably to an " Irish Jaunting Car," the driver of which assures me he is the owner of " The most ilighant car in the Cety Dooblin."   Of course, as my luggage has been secured, I have nothing to do but to follow it, so off we go, my erratic hat-box having been regained by the display of a sixpence, after all attempts at recapturing it by giving chase had proved useless.

As there is but little to see in Kingstown we only wait long enough to examine its grand harbour, and to have a quiet sail to Dalkey Island, which, with its martello tower and single farm-house is still, I believe, governed by its own king.   Here we make our first acquaintance with an Irish hoax in the shape of the celebrated " Rocking Stone," which is simply a large stone balancing between two ledges of rock, and worn into an oval shape by the beating of the waves.   However, the boatmen sing us songs all the way home, having previously informed us that no Irishman can sing with a dry throat, and so altogether we make a pleasant day of it; and then leave for Dublin. Though this metropolis seemed to me to be the finest city, two or three only excepted in Great Britain, I am not going to attempt a description of its churches, cathedrals, cemeteries, (in one of which the tomb of O'Connell crowned daily with fresh flowers is exposed to view); "The Phaynix," "Sackville Street," &c., must not detain my muse, for are not all these things written in the book of Black for the enlightenment of benighted tourists? My advice to my readers is to get on to an Irish Car, tell the driver to drive you to all "the points of interest"—you are safe to be in the Phaynix in ten minutes—to ask questions all day and finally to have a mighty controversy about the fare, and if you have had a dull day you may as well go home again, for it is evident that Ireland is not the country for you, in fact that you do not know what fun is.

Well do I remember the delightful feeling of being on an Irish Car for the first time, and how this pleasure was slightly diminished by my dependent legs coming into rather violent contact with a lamp-post at the first corner— how the driver turned round to point out the superiority of the Irish Car to all "Pathent Safeties;" for, said he, "Was'nt I run away wid in the Phaynix, (everything happens in 'the Phaynix') the baste being frightened by rayson of the arthillery; and when we came to the first sthrate sure did'nt the jintleman jump off and holt to the lamp-post, widout a scratch on his body. Och 'tis an ilighant vayicle intoirely, is the Oirish Car." I well remember how the rogue laughed and told me I'd make an Irishman yet, when I suggested that so active a gentleman must have been a lamp-lighter by trade—and how great a wag I believed myself, and thought I would not mind even giving an extra tip to so discriminating a driver. Still better do I remember how my scarcely quieted fears were roused to perfect horror by the company of a dragoon who was riding a "wicked baste" along side of me. How the said baste kicked out within an inch of my "dear knees." How at length he was backed close up to me by the man of war who bestrode him, that the driver might cut him across with his whip, and how relieved I felt when I saw the baste go off into a canter, the carman assuring me that "the crayture the souldier was on had more vice in her than any in Dooblin—which was saying a great deal." All this I remember, but o'er the rest fond

memory draws a veil: suffice it to say, that when I came
to pay the fare, I came to these conclusions :

(i) I am not yet an Irishman.

(ii) There is no instance known of an Irish car-driver
who has not a wife and ten—at least—gossoons to maintain.

(iii) It is rather aggravating after paying twice the right
fare, to be told in an insinuating voice that the driver
would like "to dhrink yer arnher's health in a glass of
the rale Oirish Whisky."

Will the reader be surprised to hear that after being
treated in this heartless manner I sighed for the mountains?
"There at least," cried I, "shall I find honesty ;" there,
as the Poet has it, the humble peasant

> Cheerful at morn awakes from short repose,
> Breathes the keen air, and carols as he goes :
> With patient angle trolls the finny deep ;
> And drives his venturous plough-share to the steep.
>   *   *   *   *   *   *
>
> At night returning, every labour sped,
> He sits him down, the Monarch of a shed :
>   *   *   *   *   *   *
>
> And haply too, some pilgrim thither led,
> With many a tale repays the nightly bed !

Need I add that I was the happy pilgrim, in my mind's
eye, who was to get such cheap lodgings? but alas! I found
to my cost that I might have been able to unfold one
thousand and one tales in these romantic regions, and
yet had my bill shortened not a whit in consequence.

Those who come to Ireland to enjoy the quiet of mountain
scenery should not stay at Killarney, those who are in
search of fine scenery and amusing people will find it hard
to leave the place. The day after our arrival we started
at an early hour to walk through the Gap of Dunloe to
"Lord Brandon's cottage," where a boat was to meet us
and to take us back to our hotel. We took, as guide,
a young giant, commonly called "the Baby Guide." The
first point of interest passed is "the Cave of Dunloe,"
supposed to have been an Irish Library, and interesting
no doubt to the Antiquarian. I had not heard of its
existence, and so passed by in blessed ignorance. We
then approach the Gap of Dunloe, a narrow defile, several
miles in length, running parallel to the Lakes of Killarney.

At the entrance of the Gap is Kate Kearney's Cottage: the present Kate is a tall and formidable woman in appearance: at her door the weary traveller may refresh himself with whiskey and goat's milk, an odious and headache-engendering mixture as I can testify. I merely put my lips to the cup and then put down one shilling in reward, for which I was regarded with so indignant a stare from Kate Kearney that I fled. Whether it was the smallness of my donation or of my potation that gave offence I know not. On leaving this bower of beauty our guide began to cut himself a stout stick, and on enquiry told us it was not safe to walk through the Gap without a stick to drive off the beggars. "A pretty pass we've come to," thought I; and so we had in more senses of the word than one. For the next moment we found a bugler by our side, who assured us we could not hear the echoes to advantage without his bugle. Then half-a-dozen girls with more whiskey and goat's milk; then a blind fiddler, who our guide told us was once "the best man," (*i.e.* the best *fighting* man) in Killarney—till one day he worked so hard in a potatoe field that the perspiration got into his eyes and blinded him.

Whence followed moral reflections on the hardship of having to work; our guide telling us that he got his living as a Guide in the summer months and did nothing all winter. He was interrupted by a fresh attack of some ten or twelve boys and girls, some bringing specimens of the bog-oak, others pieces of spar at the cheap price of sixpence each, which we declined to buy, as they were covering the ground on every side of us. Here our guide's stick became useful. Soon after this, as we turned a corner where the Gap grew even more narrow than before, we were saluted by a roar of artillery, and were accosted by five boys, each of whom had fired off a canon that we might hear the echoes, and each of whom said we had told him so to do, and expected remuneration. After all we managed to reach Lord Brandon's cottage, where we found our boatmen with the boat, and

> Some bread and bafe and porther,
> And some whiskey in a jar,

from which we made a capital dinner on one of those Islands in the Upper Lake, which look as if they have been just brought into existence by magic, fairer than Venus rising from the froth of the Sea, or even than the froth of Guinness's

XX, which, with thirsty lips, we were imbibing. No one I believe, will ever describe the beauty of this Upper Lake in adequate terms. I think Sir Walter Scott's description of "the Trossachs" recalls the effect then produced on me better than anything else I know—though I am not prepared to say that the description can be applied to Killarney in detail. Our boatmen were pleasant fellows, or, as some Americans who had been before us at "the Victoria," stated in the visitor's book as

Intelegant as eddycated men.

Our party consisted of Mike and Pat, two weather-beaten boatmen, and Dick, our fine young guide, who I found was a "coorting" of old Mike's daughter, and who had taken an oar in order that his future father-in-law might escape a drenching. Their notion of chaff was quite delightful. It was not perhaps expressed in those classic terms the use of which has given to the bargee of the Cam his well-earned reputation. But there was a quiet flow of humour and wit that I am afraid I cannot give my readers any idea of at second-hand. The following dialogues may be taken as specimens :—

DRAMATIS PERSONÆ.

Myself, (*Tom Pluck*); My Friend, (*Ned Plough*); *Mike, Pat,* and *Dick.*

ACT I. SCENE 1.

Pat. Och, Mike, yer was at the whiskey agin last night, else for why do yer puff so?

M. Divil a drap yer arnher have I had for sivin days, barrin no more than the tay-spoonful which I persave yer arnher is going to offer me.

P. Don't ye belave him yer arnher! Sure it's all owin to the whiskey that ye're the oogliest man in Killarney, Mike. Did yer arnher ever see as oogly a man as Mike?

T. P. O yes, I've seen an uglier man: so have you.

Pat. Divil a one have I.

T. .P Did you ever look in a looking-glass?

P. In coorse, when I shaves, or when I gets up in the mornin I have a look to see that I'm all right.

T. P. Then you must have seen an uglier man than Mike.

P. (*testily.*) Divil a one yer arnher.

Guide. (*with discernment.*) Oh! Pat the jintleman's bate yer.

Pat turns sulky and rows very hard.

SCENE 2.—" *The Long Range.*"

N. Plough. What do you call this River?

P. Sure we jist don't call it at all, it comes of itself. (*smiles again visit his countenance.*)

Guide. Does yer arnher persave the foot-prints on either side of the River?

T. P. Yes—what caused them?

Guide. Why, the O'Donoghue was comin home from a party and the Divil met him, and they fought: and the Divil bate the O'Donoghue by rayson of the liquor which he had had at sooper, and the O'Donoghue ran, and the Divil after him: till they came to the Long Range, when the O'Donoghue jumped clane over, as ye may persave by the prints of his five blessed toes. And the Divil could not cross the water.

N. P. O that's all bosh—I don't believe it.

Guide. And why not?

N. P. Why, if you or I were to jump over we should leave no marks of our feet.

Guide. Ah! but may be the rocks was young and tinder then! (*to Mike.*) Take my coat or ye'll get wet.

Pat. It's Kathleen he cares for, not you Mike.

Mike. Well, Kathleen's a good girl, and Dick's a purty fellow, and they'll suit well enough.

* * * * * * *

This sort of conversation, which it is impossible to do justice to with the pen, enlivened our way home—we reached our hotel early in the evening, where my friend Ned Plough had a speech made to him, which is as good a specimen of Irish wit and audacity as I know.

He was standing outside the hotel between two elderly maiden ladies, friends of his, and not remarkable for beauty, when his alms were solicited by an old beggar-woman; to whom he turned a deaf ear; at last she came close to him and said, in a terribly audible whisper, "God bless you sir—and ar'nt ye loike a rose atween two thistles! (*insinuatingly.*) Now then yer arnher, wo'nt ye give a poor old woman a few pence?"

But I have already tired my readers: and though at the outset I stated that I thought the selection of my subject needed no apology, I must all the same apologise for the manner in which the subject has been treated. If, however, I should be induced to believe that this Article has given any amusement, on some future occasion, with *The Eagle's* permission, I will relate more of my Irish experiences. At present I can only say with the Poet—

What is writ is writ! would it were worthier!

"T. P."

A DAY-DREAM.

I.

I DREAM'D I was a merry rivulet;
  Among tall rushes on a green hill-side
My cradle was; and without care or fret,
  Content with what the heavens might provide,
Urged from an inward source that never yet
  Had fail'd me, down the slope in joyous pride
Of my young strength, I hasten'd, day and night
Singing in ecstacies of full delight.

II.

My voice I changed in many a wayward mood:
  Now in the sunshine I would laugh and play,
Anon I murmur'd to a shady wood;
  And then in whispers soft, as I would stay,
Some hanging blossom for a kiss I woo'd,
  Then whirl'd in saucy joyousness away,
Or, muttering at a rock with feign'd annoy,
Suddenly sparkled with a flash of joy.

III.

I gush'd beneath green hedgerows where in spring
  The brown-wing'd throstle built her secret nest,
And oft above her sprightly mate would sing
  All the bright morn, and oft the glowing west,
As there at even he sat carolling,
  Pour'd its full sunshine on his speckled breast;
And then I left my covert, and bestow'd
A boon of freshness on the toilsome road.

IV.

For not in far-off moorland wilds forlorn
  I rose, sequester'd in remotest glen,
But all about the slope where I was born,
  (A high-piled slope that basks in sunshine, when
The day flows farthest from the springs of morn)
  Green farms were scatter'd, and abodes of men;
From cottage hearths blue smoke rose, morn and even,
And infant voices laugh'd to the blue heaven.

V.

And where the steep hills with a sloping base
  Ran to the valley, on a verdant plot
That turn'd to south and west its smiling face,
  Rose one fair dwelling; on a sweeter spot
Amid those vales, on which with special grace
  He bends his beams, the bright sun shinèd not,
So pleasant a retreat it was I ween
Out-peering from its nest of leafy green.

VI.

And in those bowers two sisters, exquisite
  In feature and in form, were wont to stray:
The one thro' shade and sunshine used to flit
  As light and gladsome as a breeze of May;
Agile she was, and beautifully knit,
  And free and careless-seeming, yet there lay,
Still seen beneath the laughter-lighted rose,
Calm depths of loveliness, and sweet repose.

VII.

But how may mine, nay, any verse, express
  The spiritual beauty that did move
In her fair sister, from the golden tress
  Down to the ground she trod on, and inwove
O'er all her calm and queenly stateliness
  A glory of humility and love?
Therefore, my muse, be silent, nor in vain
Stretch thy weak pinions for so high a strain.

VIII.

And fast beside those bowers, beneath the gate
　Thro' which she used to pass, my stream did slide.
O joy, if ever there she chanced to wait,
　To mirror her sweet form!　O hour of pride,
O rapture that it was, when eve was late,
　And stillness held the valley far and wide,
To think that, thro' that stillness, voice of mine
Might reach the heart of creature so divine!

IX.

And ever with sweet murmurs thro' the night,
　Sleepless, when all things slept save only me,
I strove to pour into her dreams delight,
　And soothe her slumbers with sweet melody;
But ah! my poor weak voice had little might;
　I know not that she heard, or if it be
She cared to hear me, only this I know,
For her I flow'd—and would for ever flow!

"H."

PLATO UPON POETRY.

THERE are few things which surprise us more upon a first perusal of the Republic, than the way in which Plato proposes to deal with poets and their art in his model state. We commence our study of the Platonic dialogues with vague notions of ideality and sentimentality, of Platonic love and Platonic beauty; nor are these entirely swept away as we proceed. Everywhere we meet with the most glowing rhetoric and the most gorgeous imagery, clothed in almost Homeric language and adorned with continual quotations from the great epic and lyric poets. But when we arrive at the discussion on the principles of taste, all at once Plato seems to turn round on his old friends; painting is abused as humbug, and poets are to confine themselves to hymn-writing or they will be sent about their business. This conduct was so puzzling to some of the ancient critics that they invented the theory of an original feud between philosophers and poets to account for it. Perhaps it may not be thought out of place to offer a few suggestions, first, as to the causes which led Plato thus to violate the natural constitution of his mind; and second, as to the worth of the objections which would require us to banish from our libraries our Homer and our Aristophanes.

On comparing one passage with another, we shall find this condemnation is grounded principally upon three considerations; 1st. the nature of imitation generally; 2nd. the mental condition in which poetry is produced, and to which it is addressed; 3rd. the actual effect of certain poetical writings. We shall perhaps be better able to understand the point of view from which the whole subject is treated, if we begin with the last of the three objections. Homer, Æschylus, &c., are not to be admitted into the model state, because they attribute falsehood, adultery, war, murder, and oppression to the Gods: because they terrify men with their stories of Hades, and represent their heroes as yielding to various passions without restraint. This is certainly a little remarkable. The severest of Christian moralists recommend the study of Homer and Sophocles as refining and ennobling, yet the Pagan philosopher is too fastidious to endure the sight of them. To explain the paradox, it will be necessary to refer to the general sentiments of that age. The Greek literature as every other began with poetry, which is at once the most natural organ of the warm and simple emotions of the pre-historic period, and at the same time an important aid to the memory when other means of preserving the author's productions are scanty or unknown. Poetry being thus the only form of intellectual activity, the poet was looked upon as an inspired teacher in every subject. His person was sacred, his words infallible, whether he spoke of the life of Gods above or men below, whether his song was of the past, the present, or the future. This reverence remained almost undiminished even after prose-writing had become general, and the historian and orator had put forth their rival claims to public admiration. Homer was still the Bible and the Classics of Greek boys and men. Thus, even in the dialogues of Plato, a quotation from him at once puts a stop to the discussion, or turns it away from the actual merits of the case to the interpretation of the passage, so as to suit the views of either disputant. " It was Homer," said his eulogists, " who had educated Greece, and by his directions men should regulate the whole tenour of their lives. He was acquainted, not only with all arts, but with all things human that bear on virtue and vice, and also with things divine." So a Rhapsodist is introduced in Xenophon as offering to teach a man his duties, as general, statesman, or head of a family, out of Homer ὁ σοφώτατος, who has written σχεδὸν περὶ πάντων τῶν ἀνθρωπίνων. Whatever was contrary, to the general feeling or the moral sense of the time was interpreted allegorically, to which Plato alludes in the second book of the Republic. After mentioning some of the impieties of the common mythology, he says, " It is no excuse for making these a branch of education, that they may have some deeper meaning, for even if it is possible to discover a suitable one in every instance, yet children are sure to carry away the form and miss the significance."

Such being the estimation in which the poets were held, other writers will help us to a determination of the question, whether their influence was beneficial or the contrary. Xenophanes in the sixth century B.C., complains bitterly of the wrong notions they instilled with respect to the Gods—and the comic poets of later times perpetually defend immorality by the example of Gods, as in the Nubes, the ἄδικος λόγος instances the adulteries of Zeus.

καίτοι σὺ θνητὸς ὢν θεοῦ πῶς μεῖζον ἂν δύναιο;

Similar passages might be adduced from Euripides and Terence. The fact is, the spirit of the age had become too enlightened for the traditionary religion: the result was Atheism, or a determined degradation of the moral feelings. Plato seeing the danger on the one hand of losing all reverence, on the other of losing independence of mind, assailed the poets, the prophets of the established religion, for introducing all manner of corruptions into the old pure Theism.

We now proceed to the considerations of the objections brought against imitation, in which dramatic and epic poetry are included. These may be summed up in one word, "it is false." He who imitates a bed, imitates what is itself merely an imitation, an attempt to arrive at the eternal idea of bed, from which he stands therefore at a third remove, being decidedly inferior to the carpenter. This general principle is further illustrated by the case of the painter, "who only aims at giving a thing as it appears, and therefore can paint every thing because his knowledge is only surface-knowledge," and by that of the poet, "who ventures to describe every condition of life, having himself experience of one alone." "It is clear, that he has no real acquaintance with that which he takes for the subject of his panegyric, or surely he would do what is worthy of praise, rather than sound the praises of another."

It is to be noticed in the first place with regard to this reasoning, which is found in the tenth book of the Republic, that it assumes the impossibility of rising through the real to the ideal; a doctrine utterly inconsistent with other views propounded in this very dialogue. For instance in the fifth book, Socrates asks "Do you think less of a man who has painted a beau ideal of human beauty because he cannot prove that such a man might possibly exist?" And again in the sixth book we are told that "painters fix their eyes on perfect truth as a perpetual standard of reference to be contemplated with the minutest care;" and

further on we hear of "painters who copy the divine
original." Such too is the doctrine of Aristotle, who in
his Poetics distinguishes three kinds of imitation, of things
as they are, as they ought to be, and as they are believed
to be; and approves the saying of Sophocles, "that *he*
drew men as they should be, Euripides as they were." Again
he tells us that the Tragic poet should imitate skilful portrait
painters, who while they express the particular features,
still improve upon the original: and so poetry is more philosophical than history, because it is conversant with general
truth. And while the theory of art was such, we need
only call to mind the names of Phidias and Polygnotus
to be assured that the practice was in accordance with it.
Of the former Cicero says, "When he made his statue
of Jupiter or Minerva, he did not copy any particular form
or feature, but that glorious ideal which dwelt in his mind."
And the latter is particularly distinguished by Aristotle as
painting men better than they were. If these considerations
should lead us to suppose, that Plato uses imitation in its
narrower sense, and that he is only warning us, as Ruskin
and Cousin have done, against the mindless art whose end
is merely the surprise produced by perfect deception; still
he has incautiously generalized his censure, so that true
art is condemned for the sake of the false. The same
remark will apply to his illustration of the doctrine. It
is true that painters and poets may easily fall into a superficial and conventional method of representing facts, as the
Arcadian lays of Queen Anne's time testify: but it does
not follow that the poet should confine himself to the sphere
of his own personal experience. Without being a soldier
or a king, he may judge better than they can themselves,
how the soldier or king ought to act. The mind is the
poet's province, and he may seize the secrets of this, though
the details of external life should be unknown to him. But
even supposing the knowledge requisite to the poet were
such as would enable him to enact the part he describes;
he might still deny Plato's assumption, that the fame of
one of Pindar's heroes, a Megas or Iamidas, is more enviable
than that of their panegyrist.

The remaining branch of the subject is concerned with
the condition of mind in which poetry is produced and
appreciated. The Greeks were strong believers in a poetic
frenzy or inspiration from the Muses or Dionysus or Apollo,
like that of the priestess who delivered the oracles from
the Delphic tripod. This was also the doctrine of Plato,

who complains that the poets were entirely unscientific and
incapable of giving rules for producing or judging of those
effects which proceeded from a kind of happy instinct.
Frequently he contrasts the conscious self-governed striving
of the mind after a known object, with the violent impulse
from without, which destroyed the freedom of the individual
will, and reduced the person to the level of a thing: an
argument reproduced in later times to overthrow the doctrine
of Montanus, that in prophesying "God alone wakes, man
sleeps." Still it is possible to imagine a homogeneous inspiration so to speak, which should elevate and intensify
instead of crushing the natural character of the poet.
Whether this is so in point of fact or not, is too difficult
a question to be settled off-hand; we will therefore pass
on to the safer ground of the prosaic mind, and ask how
this is affected by being brought into contact with poetry.
Plato gives the following answer—"Imitative poetry (*i.e.*
all poetry but that which is the expression of the actual
present feelings of the virtuous man) represents the violent
struggle of passion, the revolt of the appetites and affections
against the sovereign reason. It does so because exaggeration is easy both for the actor and spectator, and because
the calmness of self-control is not a field in which the poet
can exhibit the variety of his own powers, or flatter the
pruriency of popular taste. In the theatre we listen with
approbation to sentiments which we should despise and
detest in ourselves or our friends. We accustom ourselves
to look upon the dictates of passion as absolute, and stoop
to admire the coarse jests of the comedian."

No one will deny the importance of this view of the
subject; we are just as apt now as they were then, to look
upon every thing as allowable in fiction. The naturalness
of the character atones for the ugliness of it. Not that
this excellence cannot be dispensed with. Alexander Smith,
for instance, has exaggeration in as high a degree as the
other faults mentioned by Plato. Nor is our age without
instances of indecency made fashionable by an elegant wit
or musical rhythm or beauty of form or colour. A writer
in "Meliora," himself a working man, asserts that the immorality of the lower orders in London is chiefly encouraged
by the exclusive acquaintance with such writings as those
of Sue and Ainsworth and Reynolds. Plato's denunciation
is fairly applicable to imitation of this kind, but again his
too sweeping condemnation requires to be limited by the
teaching of his pupil. There *is* tragedy which purifies the

affections by pity and terror, raising the veil of ordinary life and bringing to light the internal struggle of good and evil, leading us to sympathize in the varied fortunes and ultimate triumph of the former, but not aspiring to that peaceful contemplation which may find a place in the philosopher's Utopia, but which was as little suited to the fourth century before, as to the nineteenth century after Christ.

DAS KIND DER SORGE.

(*The Child of Sorrow.*)

ONCE, where a brook with gentle murmur flowed,
　Whose crystal stream the sleeping pebbles shewed
Care, deeply musing on a bank reclined
Thought after thought revolving in her mind,
At last, the work of many a toilsome day
She fashioned with her hands a form of clay,
Yet still some wish appeared to give her pain,
Pensive she sat, nor wished she long in vain;
"What dost thou seek," said Jove approaching near,
"What are these sighs, these wishes that I hear?"
"Jove" spake the goddess then, "This form behold,
Framed by my hands, and framed of mortal mould;
O let Life's flame through each cold member spring
Whirl the hot blood, the nervous muscles string,
Through the frail fabric breathe the vital air;"
'Let it have life,' spake Jove—and Life was there;
Then said the god, "Mine let this creature be;"
"Nay," answered Care, "Leave it, great Lord, to me,
This hand hath made it, and these fingers formed,"
'But I' said Jove 'with heavenly fire have warmed
Its senseless body, and have given it life'—
While thus with words they lengthen out the strife,
Tellus approaching speaks, 'The thing is mine,
What from the earth she took, let Care to earth resign.'
Their causes thus with partial words they plead,
Each urged his claim, of judgment there was need;
When, lo, his face o'er seamed with many a scar,
Saturn they see, approaching from afar,
O'er his grey head had years unnumbered rolled,
His birth in Chaos hid, immeasureably old,
Unpitying Age had closed his weary wing.'
In his left hand he bore the serpent ring;

To him at once the Deities apply,
And thus they hail him as he paces by:
" O, Saturn, arbiter among the Gods,
Supreme Seneschal of their bright abodes,
Thus stands the case, decide between us three,
An equal judge, a just assessor be,"—
They paused, and now while each attention pays,
Thus Saturn speaks, the God of many days,
" All have it, all,—so wills high Fates decree,
It, while life lasts, belongs, O Care, to thee;
Soon o'er his head Time's wasting blast shall blow,
Wrinkle the brow and tinge the hair with snow;
Then ye the justice of the Fates shall learn,
Jove gave him life, life shall to Jove return;
When to Death's stroke he bends his drooping head,
Earth shall contain him, numbered with the dead.
Thus shall each claimant have an equal share,
This is the judgment which the Fates declare.

The Child of Sorrow thus his course began,
Care gave her work its name and called it Man,
She holds his life,—when life his body leaves,
Earth takes his bones, and God his soul receives.

" οὔτις."

CHESS AND MATHEMATICS.

"YOU play at chess, of course," remarked a Swiss gentleman, with whom I had been for a short time acquainted,
and who had gathered that I was reading for Mathematical
honors, "all Mathematicians are Chess-men on the Continent." He was right in his assumption: and this set me
thinking to discover what connection there is between the
science and the game. Between the science and the game;
for with all deference to the great name of Leibnitz, who
declared Chess to be a science, and accounting for his
dictum by supposing him to be fresh from the contemplation
of some brilliant catastrophe six moves deep, I must humbly
dissent from the definition, but, at the same time, would
express my ready acquiescence in its being the most
scientific game.

Undoubtedly a deep connection exists between the two
subjects, a connection which rests upon a wider basis than
the fact that it requires computation to establish such a
truth as that a Knight can cover the sixty-four squares of
the board in sixty-four moves. The man, who can make
such a computation, is not necessarily more of a Chess-player
than the boy who can solve the historical arithmetical
question of the nails in the horse-shoe, is a horse-jockey.
The principles of thought are, as far as they go side by
side, the same; nevertheless they do not coincide, for,
although a mathematician ought to make a good Chess-
player, the converse of the proposition does not hold—
Philidor's brain might have been a segment of Sir Isaac
Newton's, but it could not have been similar to it as a whole.

Chess is indeed very analogous to solving a problem
in the quick and brilliant way that makes a high man in
the Tripos; but, as was ably observed in the Athenæum,
in an Article upon the death of Dean Peacock, this problem-
solving draws not more upon Mathematical talent than
upon ready ingenuity, or "knack."

Solving problems in this manner is attacking the solution; and, as in attacking the King, we have to branch off from the main object to remove Pawns, and resolve other difficulties, keeping fully in mind the plot at issue; so, in getting at our result in the aforesaid question, we have to solve equations, and prepare the way for our grand assault.

In these problems the solution is invariably, so to speak, castled behind some equations, and the attack is only varied by combination, and is never of different elements.

Again, it is well known in Chess how much success depends upon a spirited onward course; upon your being altogether abstracted in that one view of the matter, and not entertaining at the same time dim visions of another way of going to work. A divided mind fails equally to check-mate, or to solve a problem. Perfect abstraction begets in the mind a potent spiritual feeling which avails alike to accomplish any mental work, and is the παμμήτωρ of arts, sciences, and games.

Though the analysis of a gambit is an entirely different thing from the analysis of a problem, yet it will be found that mathematical analysis—the working backwards from the result to the data—is in constant operation in Chess, more especially at the close of the game.

A mate, or a position, is conceived, the next step noticed, and so the materials are squared to be in readiness. In the openings of games this seems more difficult (though perhaps it is not impossible to such players as Staunton, Morphy, or Anderssen), and the way in which an ordinary player at least proceeds is in fact the trial and error system. If Philidor could really see a check-mate in the placing a pawn at the fourth move, of course the analytical method was open to him at the beginning.

The fact of their being two sides in the game of Chess, but only one in Mathematics, is of no weight in the case of good players. For, a position being given, your opponent may be altogether ignored; you allowing the best move possible to be made, and winning from the nature of the position: in fact doing as all good players do, playing, in your forward calculations, your right-hand against your left.

In both the science and the game there is a considerable amount of book-work. The Gambits should be well known, as to investigate all the consequences of moving the second Pawn, during the game, would be like making your own table of logarithms to solve a problem.

I have said that Mathematics involves Chess, and

something more; I except however the poetry and metaphysics of Chess. That Chess has its poetry is seen from Walker's treatise on the subject, where he talks of a Pawn being "enshrined" in a square, and like ultra-Tennysonian expressions; and that Chess has its metaphysics is to be inferred, a priorí, from the fact of the numerous German works on the subject, and a posteriorí from an inspection of their works, where the investigator will find a heap of rubbish or metaphysics, perhaps no one knows which.

In conclusion, it is to be regretted that Chess is not universally known throughout the College; for, whatever may be thought of the relation in principles between Mathematics and Chess, it is certain, that in the intricate combinations, and perplexed involutions of the game, there is ample material for the composition of some of those tremendous equations that rejoice in the number seven.

" DIONYSIUS."

"THE COMING OF THE EQUINOX."

THREE huge clouds trail through Heaven's black height,
   And a little one drifts below,
There's red where the sun was last in sight;
It's going to be a gusty night,
And the caps of the waves are getting white
   As the wind comes on to blow.

There was a rainbow this afternoon,
   And the Grey Mare's Tails in the sky,
Never man saw them together, but soon
The wind would awaken and pipe his tune,
And to-night will be rising the Harvest Moon
   To carry the waters high.

Upward a mighty cloud comes with the storm,
   High upward out of the west,
Lo, it is like to a warrior's form,
   Hard by the enemy prest;
And he drives like a torrent along the red sky,
As if he from a flaming town did fly,
Yet withal is he drawing his sword from his thigh,
   To die in doing his best.

There's Hesperus sits where the sun sat before,
   And calmly he doth shine,
Though the oak tree's rocking upon the shore,
   And on the hills the pine;
And every wave has now got a crest,
   Yet the wind through the mountains calls,
And more clouds are coming up out of the west,
   So, my friends, look out for squalls!

" οὔτις."

ADVICE TO A YOUNG CURATE.

THE type of a bad English clergyman of the last century is not difficult to construct. We can easily picture to ourselves the country parson, stout, passionate, and sensual, shooting, hunting and drinking with the squire, inexorable in the exaction of tithes, a very Rhadamanthus to poachers, elsewhere jovial and rubicund, the sole duty and annoyance of whose life was that every seventh day he had to read two services and preach a sermon. But when our times have passed away, when the age of Queen Victoria has become subject for history, and when our manners and thoughts are discussed by an impartial and inquisitive posterity, what then will be the type of an English curate of the nineteenth century? Will he not be represented as a mild and inoffensive creature, mediæval amidst modernism, full of impracticable and inoffensive theories, skilled in church architecture, cunning in curious altar cloths, in stained glass and brasses, a man of strange vestments and many genu-flections, whose most striking characteristics are a white neck-cloth and unlimited capability of painful blushing? And yet, such as this creature may be, it was not hatched without some pains: many nurses in the shape of grammar-schools, tutors, private or otherwise, fostered it, brought it to Alma Mater; and she, the kind mother, nurtured it for three years and more in her bosom; why then should our cygnet turn out an ugly-piping-goose? Oh future curate, the question is too hard for me, I cannot answer it, merely would I desire to give you a little useful advice. Do you want to be considered a practical man, to be looked up to in your parish, to obtain the esteem of all the respectable and well-to-do part of your flock, to have influence, full congregations, unresisted church-rates and praise from all men? If so, haste, come on board: Eureka! I have found the breeze which will waft you to the haven of your desires. Who says, " woe unto you when all men speak well of you ?" We know better than that now-a-days.

Let us then imagine a youthful curate, as yet unhatched, studying, we will suppose, at one of the universities and anxiously looking forward to the time when his name shall be highly exalted in the annals of the church of which he is a member; what should be his course of proceeding? In the first place our curate will avoid all that false and useless prestige which arises from taking a high place in the classical or mathematical tripos: he will content himself with the more modest but solid honors of the poll, and will devote his spare time to the study of elocution, and the other preparations for the ministry. By so doing, he will avoid two evils; firstly, a high degree will not confer upon him that reputation for unpracticableness which is its invariable accompaniment; and secondly, he will be freed from the danger of injuring his chance of church advancement, which, it is well known, varies directly as the power of a man's voice, and inversely as his learning and ability. After taking his degree, our curate will pass the voluntary examination, and immediately enter upon his field of duty, if possible, in some town where he will have the opportunity of frequent preaching. And here let me pause, while I solemnly warn my reader at this crisis of his life to divest himself of every idea derived from the university and freely to give himself to the surrounding influences of his parish. He has been accustomed perhaps to regard forms and ceremonies as things indifferent in themselves, createable or destructible at the will of men, and therefore matters of comparatively slight importance. This is wrong. Never was there a greater mistake than that of supposing the laity to be indifferent to forms. They attach more weight to forms than did Laud himself, with this difference, that, while the latter insisted upon their employment, the former still more vehemently insist upon their omission, not so much because they imagine them to be useless, as out of a secret dread of a mysterious necromantic power supposed to be inherent in them. A bow at the name of the Saviour has ere now brought a young clergyman's ministrations to an untimely end, and if, in ignorance of his congregation's habits, an unfortunate curate turn toward the East at the creed, his name will form the single subject of conversation for the crowds who stream from the church-doors at the conclusion of the service, and he will probably overhear that 'he has shewn the cloven foot already.' Our pupil therefore must give up without a murmur any old forms to which his parishioners may be averse; he must not, for a few genu-flections more or less, ruin his chance of influencing his flock for good. Nor is this all; these are merely the requirements of plain common sense; some further sacrifice is necessary, if we would propitiate success. For example, if chance should conduct our successful curate to some rural parish, he should not be tyrannously earnest in overthrowing those ancient little baize-lined houses, called pews, in which, ever since the reformation, the chief family of the village has been allowed to sleep with impunity; he must not shew too outspoken a desire of innovation if he see an eighteenth century parallelogrammic window foisted into old Norman architecture: if the churchwardens like to make the church look like a large green-grocer's shop at Christmas-time, if the choir sing out of tune, and prefer so to sing, or if they rapturously cling to their old virginals in place of a new organ, why in the name of success, so let it be! In all things of this nature he must " let well alone," or rather, if need be, 'let very bad alone'. "Quieta non movere" will be the rising curate's best motto.

But these are minor points. I pass now to the pulpit, the battle-field, if I may so express it, of our protégé: the scene of all his triumphs, where alone if anywhere he must achieve his future eminence. Now though there undoubtedly are many districts in which a written sermon may be read with impunity, still, on many accounts, I lay down this rule that our curate's sermons be "*ex tempore.*" In the first place, the late government appointments cannot but have some influence on our determination in this matter: again, there are parts of England, particularly in some of the south-west counties, in which a written sermon argues want of faith and fervour, and the reader, as soon as the fluttering of the first leaf has made his congregation conscious of his crime, is in a solemn conclave of whispering bonnets declared to be 'not a gospel minister.' Lastly, his own convenience, if nothing else, should dictate this step. A written sermon takes a considerable time: a man cannot commit words to paper without thinking a little, though sometimes a very little, about them, and the mere labour of writing is no trifling one. But an extemporaneous sermon, that is, such a one as is likely to please his audience, will take no time or trouble at all. Nor will our curate be deterred by any foolish nervousness or fear of failing before the face of so many hearers. Paul preached extempore, why should not he? For fear however he be not quite persuaded by this argument, and persist in entertaining a suspicion that perhaps the circumstances in which he is placed may in some respects differ from those of the Apostle of the Gentiles, and may consequently require some corresponding difference of conduct, it will be well to remove any such lingering objections by a hint on the subject of extemporaneous preaching. A good extemporaneous, or, to speak more correctly, a good spoken sermon, in which deep thought, sound reasoning, and much learning, are set off by beauty of diction and appropriate gesticulation, is one of the highest efforts of human genius, such as I live in the hopes of some day witnessing—but let not our preacher imagine that any such model is to be placed before *him.* His task is of a different nature. His " ex tempore" sermon should consist of as many texts of scripture as can possibly be strung together with the smallest possible compound of original matter, the less the better. In this way the least offence will be given, and the least suspicion of heterodoxy will be aroused, a point in which he will do well to be very careful. Whatever cementing matter he may employ should be, as far as he can contrive, composed of Scripture-phrases. In fact, I should recommend every young curate to learn by heart daily a certain number of verses from the Epistles of Paul, solely with a view to this object: thus will he acquire the faculty of delivering at a moment's notice a sermon of any conceivable length on any conceivable subject, and that too without giving room for any censorious expressions, since he can truly assert that every word of his discourse is taken from the Scriptures. Nothing can be more ill-judged and misplaced than words and phrases which remind his congregation of every-day life. A broad line of demarcation, it cannot be too broad, should be drawn between the Sabbath and the six unsanctified days of work, between the church and the world, and this difference should be expressed by an appropriate difference of language.

Now, as for the subject of his sermon, as long as he remembers the rule I have just laid down, and strictly avoids secular and, above all, political subjects, our curate may be left to his own devices. During the present state of religious feeling in England, a sermon on the Errors of Popery (provided that the influence or numbers of that sect in your parish be not so large as to produce inconvenient consequences) will not be inacceptable about once in three or four months; the heresy of the Unitarians will furnish a telling topic though more rarely, and if our friend be of a tolerant or liberal disposition, he will be careful to control himself, at least so far as to avoid saying anything which might be construed to signify that he felt any unorthodox hopes of the possibility of the future salvation of any member of either of these sects. Different audiences will no doubt have different tastes; and the great business of our curate's life will be to develope and improve, if I may so say, a theological cuisine, an art whereby he may be enabled to adapt his discourses to the palates and requirements of his parishioners. General rules would here therefore be out of place: our pupil must in this matter be left to his own ingenuity. One piece of advice, however, may not be altogether useless. Be technical. Only let the preacher confine himself to technicalities and all will be well. You may tell your congregation that they are not in a state of grace, and they will go out of the church thanking you for your gospel-sermon, and thinking you pious yourself in proportion to the fervour of your condemnation of them, but beware, as you love respectability and desire success, beware of telling them that they are leading an unjust and dishonest life. Is your congregation a congregation of tradesmen? Warn them not against that covetousness which leads to the defrauding of the exchequer, the adulteration of their goods. Have you whole pews full of stout prospering farmers? Talk not to them of farm-labourers starving on ten shillings a-week, but tell them about their souls and how to save them, and presume not to desecrate that holy place and the sanctity of the Sabbath by allusion to the things of this world. "What has grace to do with earthly things?" has been very properly asked by a learned judge in his place on the bench, and hundreds of English congregations will answer in deed if not in word—"nothing." A place for everything and everything in its place: the proper place to talk about the Bible and religion and our souls is the church, and the proper day is the Sabbath: and on the other days, and in other places we are to devote ourselves to secular occupations. I insist the more earnestly on this point, not only because in it lies the whole secret of our pupil's success, but also because there has lately arisen a set of misguided young men who utterly ignore the line between religious and secular life, and are continually confusing together sacred and worldly things. These men talk about the Bible as though it concerned us on week-days as much as on the Sabbath, they profess to see in the narrative of the Holy Scriptures events which have occurred once and are occurring now, not merely to be read of, but also to be acted on; they imagine there are at this day English false gods, English false prophets, aye, even English Pharisees, as well as English Publicans and Sinners! They talk about men being just and honest and true, instead of " in a state of salvation," and use ugly words, such as covetousness, injustice, and hypocrisy, than which expressions none can be conceived more unscriptural or more utterly destructive of that good feeling which should exist between a pastor and his flock. But now mark the unhappy fate of these infatuated men, and compare it with the career of our rising curate. The latter, admired and even idolized by the respectable part of his congregation, a popular preacher, and a practical man, finds in this life a bishopric and after death an epitaph. But if any man hanker after joining the ranks of these erring schismatics, let him not do so unwarned. Blasted by the withering denunciations of the Record, styled infidel by one party, derided as visionary by another, attacked unsparingly by all, clogged on every side by an indistinct suspicion of unorthodoxy, the more injurious because indistinct, he must expect neither friendship nor sympathy from the great mass of his parishioners: the high places of the church are closed against him: he will die, as he has lived, a curate, with no other consolation than the weak-minded regrets of a few visionary men, and such pitiful satisfaction as he may be able to derive from the imagination that he has done his duty.

THE HAVERN HUNT.

WHAT was the reason that there was such a dearth of Latin and Greek Grammars, and where did all Dr. Colenso's valuable educational productions go to, were questions that presented themselves forcibly to the mind of every new boy, in Havern School, during the last week of one September not so long ago. Various were the answers the "old fellows" gave, according as they estimated the amount of gullibility each querist had, but that the hunting season was coming on, seemed the solution that was most general, though the connection of the two was not so obvious.

Friday solved the new boy's doubts, since they found themselves, together with a good many old boys, "douled" to tear scent in No. 8.

To No. 8 Study let us then adjourn ; very barren indeed we find it, for the inhabitants, not having at any time much furniture, have removed all but the tables, to make room for the numbers who throng in. Soon the huntsman and his attendant satellites the whips appear, laden with old books, papers and such like, begged, borrowed or — appropriated, (not to speak harshly); these they distribute to the multitude, with instructions to tear them to small fragments. While this is proceeding, we may as well explain the constitution of the hunt. The original rank of every member is that of a "hound," when he has attached to him an appropriate name, to which he must answer.

Promotion, which is acquired by one's head, as well as by one's heels, that is by merit, scholastic as well as pedestrian, is to the rank of gentlemen, involving the privileges of sporting pink during a run, carrying a " hound-stick" (a short stick with a hook at one end, by which to assist a lagging hound, or pull the owner over a fence), and the more doubtful one of contributing to the expences. From the gentlemen are chosen the huntsman and whips.

Let us now return to No. 8, where we find the hounds tearing scent into their square caps, a few gentlemen lounging in to take a turn, and the officials watching narrowly that the scent is of the proper size, and not torn double, that is, so that two pieces stick together. Towards the end of the proceedings, it transpires that the run for to-morrow is the one thro' Annesley Chase, one of the most popular, but one of the hardest.

Great is the excitement next morning; new made gentlemen buy their hound-sticks, the knowing ones grease their boots, or rather make their "douls" do it, get out their oldest bags, to run in; Music despairingly seeks for someone to tell him it is not so hard; Songstress to improve his wind takes two raw eggs, and so is ill, and cannot go; Little Dairymaid persuades that big good natured gentleman with the very ancient hunting costume to promise to help him if he is hard up; the huntsman and the two foxes for the occasion consult the map, and maliciously contrive to include the Annesley Brook; the scent is stored into a bag, and all due preparations are made for the run; and uncommon little for second lesson, after which the event comes off.

Well, second lesson is said, and we stroll down to the old barn in Fumigator's Lane, where we find the two foxes just started, one with the scent-bag hung on his back from which his brother fox ever and anon distributes handfuls of the paper fragments, as guides for the pack to follow.

Meanwhile one whip couples the hounds, the other makes an insane row on his bugle, an ancient party of drunken aspect and Irish origin, produces a basket in which to carry superfluous clothes to run in. Belts are tightened, caps jammed hard on. "The hounds are coupled, Mr. Huntsman," announces the whip to that dignified individual, who thereupon condescends to put himself at their head, and to say "Gently For'ard," which does not mean "Gently For'ard," for the pace is fast, the grass long and wet; down the hill merrily we go, the huntsman first, round him the hounds, a whip on either side, while the gentlemen follow through the gate at the bottom, jump the little ditch, cross a small field or two, through one stiff hedge, and then up a long, long expanse of turnips and mud; little cares Mr. Huntsman, on he goes, not so the gentlemen, who prefer going round a little to escape this, except one or two extra plucky ones;

while the hounds, who must follow, set at nought the whips, endeavours to keep them together, but drop into a long line, from the rear of which one has a vision of heads and shoulders bobbing up and down in most eccentric methods.

Every one is pleased when a jump over the stile brings us into Farmer Hammond's stubble fields, along which we go merrily, to the great disgust of that plethoric and wrathful man, who, attended by two rustics, armed with pickets, fondly hopes to stop us. Ah! fond man, there is never a rustic in hobnails and a smock frock, who can come near us. "Dang ye," he cries, and "dang ye" all the echoing woods resound. On we go, hurling at him "winged words," careless of the deep black plough we now run over, tho' one or two hounds want assistance, and not a few have got purls over the last two or three fences to the great detriment of their appearance.

But now the pace is slackened for an instant to gather up the stragglers, or leave them all together, silence is enjoined, for now we have to run through the drives of Annesley Park, long green alleys cut through the plantations, sacred alone to pheasants; and dire would be the wrath of old Annesley, should he see the invasion, for the first of October is nigh, and all Havern boys rank as poachers in his mind, and perhaps he may have some reason for thinking so.

The services of the gentlemen are now required, to pull along those of the hounds who are done up: go along they must, three miles through these drives without a stop: very pleasant is it tho', for there is good turf below, and the trees arch over head, still laden with the rain drops of the morning which shine like pearls in the Sun; whirr—goes some old cock pheasant disturbed by the tramp of many feet.

At length we emerge by the Havern's side, whose waters are swollen, and keep along its banks for a short way, then turn through a plantation into the Annesley Park, past the front of the Hall, over the sunk fence, round the old Chapel to the astonishment and amusement of some young ladies drawing the same, who do not often see sixty fellows in such attire, or hear such noise as the junior whip gets out of his bugle. Tramp, tramp, on we go past Farmer Goughs, who gives us a cheer, for didn't we save his stacks from fire not so long ago. "Gentlemen forward," cries the huntsman; off they go and race in, to where the foxes stand as judges of the race; and then the hounds race in for the last hundred yards; Champion first, Venus second, Rattler third;

and thus the Annesley Run was done; nine miles in almost no time.

The rest of the day being a holiday is spent in talking it over again, how well Champion ran, how hard the Senior whip tipped the silk to all who lagged, how little Dairymaid was pulled all the way, while the smaller Tiny would not be helped at all; these, and all these, are they not written in the Chronicles of the R. H. H?

A WORD ON UNIVERSITY STUDIES.

A STRANGER to our University can hardly look over the Mathematical Honor lists in the Calendar, without feeling some surprise that so few names are distinguished by the *a*, *β* or *γ* which indicate a man who has also taken Classical Honors. To a stranger, I say, this must be a subject of surprise, but to ourselves of regret; regret that so few among us are found capable of distinguishing themselves in more than one branch of study, that so few are willing to give their minds that generality of education which alone can furnish them with sound judgment, or fit them to achieve really great works. To me it seems, that for a man to give up the years he is here, the years in which his mind is most impressible, most capable of being expanded by a generous education, the years, one might almost say, in which his mind *is formed*, to give these up to *one* study alone, whether it be Classics or Mathematics, is a course as preposterous as to give the body meat and refuse it drink, or to give it drink and refuse it meat. But I will not trespass upon these pages to shew that this system is bad, for I am persuaded that there is not a man in this College who does not feel that a Senior Wrangler who knows nothing but Mathematics, is by no means so well educated as a man of very much lower place in that Tripos, who is well informed on most subjects, and whose name also appears moderately high in the Classical Tripos. Indeed, if a man's education has been confined to Mathematics, and let him be acquainted ever so well with this science, what is he fit for? Perhaps he is unwilling or unable to teach, (for it does not follow that a man who is thoroughly acquainted with a subject is able to convey his ideas with perspicuity to others,—one must be *born* a teacher,) and he is scarcely fit to take holy orders and be entrusted with the care of souls; what can he do? If you would see this question answered, pass with me into a certain office in the West of England, where you may see a Senior

Wrangler engaged in the somewhat unintellectual occupation of marking down the weights of loads of coal, and exciting within us no better hopes than that, *as he was a Senior Wrangler, he will be able to add up the rows of figures correctly!*

Assuming then that this one-sided and partial education is bad, let us with a view to its remedy, investigate its origin. I think its origin is Prejudice, a two-fold prejudice. In the first place there is a prejudice very prevalent in the University that our course here is very short, and that we have not time to pursue in it more than one study to any effect. This prejudice makes the expectant of Mathematical honors shrink from reading even the Classical subjects of our College Examinations: it makes the Classic rejoice when his Little-Go is past, that he needs no more mathematics, and with joy dispose of his Arithmetic and Algebra as useless acquirements which he may now cast away for ever. It is this same prejudice which causes men to say that they would be very glad to avail themselves of the advantages which would be derived from writing for our College Magazine, but they have no time. It was this that caused so many to refuse the pleasure and the improvement afforded in the Long Vacation by our Debating Society, saying, that it would doubtless do them a great deal of good, but they really could not take an hour a week from the time they had set apart for Mathematics. I have called this a *prejudice* for I believe it is nothing more. I feel confident that any one who will try the experiment will find that if his chief attention be directed suppose to Mathematics, his progress in that science will not be less, or less satisfactory, at the end of a term, if he has been devoting two or three or four hours a day during that term to Classics. The one study will be relaxation after the other; to turn the mind wearied with any one pursuit to a different pursuit is a better rest for it than to leave it unemployed to wander where it will. Thus by dividing our attention between different studies we are enabled to work longer without fatigue and not only longer but with greater application, for every one who is accustomed to reading must know that after he has been engaged for some time at a subject he finds it difficult to apply himself as thoroughly as at first to that subject although he could easily give up his mind entirely to any other. And here I may be allowed to introduce an observation which scarcely belongs to my argument, but which may be useful to some reader. A very great number of the

Undergraduates at this College purpose taking holy orders.
I would suggest to them that they will find it very desirable
in interpreting the Old Testament Scriptures to have a knowledge of Hebrew and that here there are unusual advantages
offered to them of studying that language ; I think that
if they at all agree with the remarks I have been making,
.they will have no fear that their progress in other studies
would be interfered with by their attendance at the Hebrew
lectures.

But there is a second prejudice which induces the evil
of which I speak. Mathematical men, as they are called,
tell us that they *cannot* read Classics because they are mathematical and not classical. And similarly, and I believe to
a much greater degree, Classical men object that they cannot
do mathematics. Perhaps I am rather bold in calling this a
prejudice, but I am not without reason for supposing that
in many cases, if not in every case, it is so. Among children
brought up in the same circumstances, we find one early
acquiring an idea of number and loving to count, while
another exhibits no such precocity, though in other respects
he may appear the cleverer of the two. We observe this
difference, and not perceiving anything external to account
for it, we say that the difference is *innate*, and that the one
child is *naturally* mathematical and the other is *not*. But
I think that where children and older persons exhibit this
apparent incapacity for acquiring one subject and aptitude
for another, it is often the result of prejudice contracted perhaps in mere infancy. At a very early age children are
put to learn reading and arithmetic. One of these subjects
is brought before a child we may suppose in a more pleasing
form than the other : or disagreeable associations of punishment perhaps accompany one more than the other. And
similarly when they begin Latin : they find difficulty in a
lesson of Latin Grammar, and are glad to be allowed to do
some arithmetic instead, or they are puzzled in their sums
and look on the Latin as a relief. Prejudices thus arise and
grow, and are afterwards regarded as capabilities and in-
capabilities, natural it is thought to the child, but certainly
hindering the man most grievously in his education.

And if we are right in deciding that in most cases what a
man calls his inability to read Mathematics is indeed merely
prejudice, (though perhaps of very long standing,) surely an
effort should be made that this prejudice do not stand in the
way of his usefulness and advancement in life. It is *not*
probable that he would ever take to Mathematics with the

delight that he now derives from Classics, but without interfering with his Classical reading, he may doubtless make such progress in the science as will expand his mind and enlarge his ideas, and have no mean effect on his success in life.

But I would not have it supposed from what I have said, that I think all men or most men should attempt to take double honors; I think more should do so than do at present, but my chief object in writing this paper is to urge those who are reading for honors, in either tripos, not to neglect their other studies for the sake of the one they have chosen, but to let their reading be extensive, even though their honors are single. My object is to combat that idea so prevalent in our College and especially among ambitious and impetuous freshmen, viz. that if they are reading Mathematics it is waste of time to read a Latin author, it is waste of time to attend a Classical lecture; history and poetry are snares to take their attention from Euclid and Conics; newspapers and novels are incompatible with Dynamics and Newton. These men should remember that they came up to Cambridge not to be made into calculating machines, but to be educated, and Education is a lady who cannot be won by a *single* attraction. Let them be Senior Wranglers if they can, but by all means let them be educated.

I conclude with the hope that future numbers of *The Eagle* may contain opinions on this subject from abler heads and more fluent pens than mine, for it is a subject of importance to all of us, it is a question admitting of profitable discussion, and one upon which our readers may pronounce the verdict, applicable indeed to most questions, that " much may be said upon both sides."

" NE QUID NIMIS."

ATTICA.

(A Translation from Sophocles.)

"εὐίππου, ξένε τᾶσδε χώρας."—
Soph. Œd. Col. 668.

MIGHTY is the land, O Stranger,
Which thy wandering footsteps tread;
It shall shelter thee from danger,
It shall guard thine aged head;
Here Colonos' woods of sable
Shade her chalk-cliffs as a crest,
Here the steed may find a stable,
And the nightingale a nest,
Deep within her ivy cover
Circled by no fettering bars,
She, lamenting like a lover,
Pours her music to the stars:
O'er this valley's verdant bosom
Venus guides her golden rein;
Here Narcissus spreads his blossom,
Crown of the immortals twain;
Bacchus, round whose brow supernal
Wreathes the grape in purple twine,
Roves amid these groves eternal
With his nurses, nymphs divine;

Here, scarce seen 'mid trees which hide it,
Roams Cephisus' sleepless stream,
And the Muses roam beside it
Through the groves of Academe;
Aye the cool green slopes he presses
Of the hills which gave him birth,
Shadowy hills, whose fond caresses
Clasp him to the breast of Earth,
Dew divine supplies that river
And he fails not from the land,
But he rolls his wave for ever
'Twixt the sunlight and the sand,
And the crocus round him blazing
Lifts to heaven its golden eye,
He, upon its beauty gazing,
Wonders as he wanders by;
But a tree this region blesses
Favoured most by Pallas' smile,
Such nor Asia's land possesses,
Nor as yet the Dorian isle;
By no human hand 'twas planted,
'Twas no mortal sowed the seed,
'Twas the gift a goddess granted
To supply a nation's need:
Young and old revered its beauty
And to smite its trunk forbore,
Still the Olive held its duty
As the guardian of the door;
Ne'er was tree so blest before it,
Never fruit so famous grew,
Zeus the guardian watches o'er it,
Watch Minerva's eyes of blue;
Nor alone the Olive's clusters
Raise this region o'er the rest,
Yet another boast she musters
By another gift is blest;
God-given gifts they ne'er shall perish,
Skilled to rear the steed is she,
Skilled the tender foals to cherish,
Skilled to rule the foaming sea.

Hail! O God, Poseidon hoary!
'Twas thy voice the mandate gave
That her sons should ride to glory
On the War-Horse and the Wave!
Through thy gift the bark swift sliding
Shoots the buoyant wave along,
While the Nereids round it gliding
Cheer its passage with their song.

" ουτις."

THE BOATING MANIA.

ST. JOHN'S is a very respectable old-established institution—there can be no doubt of that—and a Johnian, as every one knows, is the very type of sobriety, regularity and grind; yet there are times, regularly recurring in their appointed course,—for St. John's, we speak not of the other Colleges, is regular and systematic, even in its irregularity, there is a method in its madness,—we say there are times when St. John's lays aside the gravity and sedateness which become its years, the regularity and order which befit its character; and, entering into some pursuit, some phantom chase, with all the zest and earnestness, the vigour and the fun of its more youthful, more frolicsome brethren, shows that the sober robe of age but covers the warm, enthusiastic heart of youth, and that, though increased in size, it has not grown unwieldy: in fact it allows itself to be possessed by a mania.

We are not about to enter into a scientific discussion of the diagnosis of a 'mania'; we believe manias to be almost characteristic of Englishmen, and we have our own opinion that the world gets on by manias, and that, from the manias of the schoolboy to the manias of the nation, the step is not so great as elderly gentlemen who believe themselves to constitute the nation, are in the habit of supposing. These however are questions into which we do not propose to enter. We speak but of St. John's, and we think we shall be understood when we say that the three Johnian Manias are the Examination Mania, the Boating Mania, and the Tripos Mania—of these the first is the most frequent, the second is the most contagious, and the third the most important. Each has its peculiar priesthood, its established ritual, its periodical literature, its zealous votaries; and from each some few stand apart, in pitiable isolation and futile opposition, professing to object on principle—and hereof we note a

D*

curious law—that he who avoids the third has generally
opposed and often suffered from the first has in fact been
operated upon by its doctors, or in their technical phraseology
been 'plucked'; and that he who opposes the second, the
first and third seem to have possessed to a frightful and even
dangerous extent—we say 'seem' for the instances are rare,
and, from their confinement, necessitated by the disease, not
easily studied—these are they who scoff at the uselessness
of pulling bits of painted wood about, as if the true Johnian,
who studies con amore the abstract truths of Mathematics,
cared for mere utility.

Gladly, did opportunity allow, would we linger here to
touch, however lightly, the whole subject of the Johnian
manias—to recall to the minds of our readers the wannish
light of the. midnight lamp which marks unerringly the
windows of one class of maniacs,—their consumption of
pens and paper, their absence from the social gatherings,
the monomaniac tendencies of their conversation, all finally
culminating in the orgies celebrated in their high hall—
the hooded priests attending—hour after hour, day after
day; and contrast with them the regular attendance at the
college chapel suspiciously synchronizing with the approaching races and causing joy in the heart of a guileless dean—
the early hours—the healthy look and voice—the consumption of beef and beer—the sanguinary costumes about the
college courts which characterize another mania; we must
however pass on. We have a word or two to say of the
boating mania alone—or rather of its boat-clubs. Not in
the way of defence: those few who, born with no more
muscle than suffices to hold open and turn the trembling
leaf, or who, blessed with so sound and lasting a stock of
health that they can dispense with all exercise except the
regular Trumpington grind, cannot understand the use of
boating and will not recognize its position as a true Johnian
mania; such, I think, our fellows have recently taught by
their very marked and liberal encouragement of other out-
door sports as well as boating, that they at least do not
think and do not wish us to think that the Chapel and the
Hall, the Dean and the Coach alone sum up our College
Education, but that spirit, mind and body must all according
to their nature receive careful cultivation and development.

Setting aside then, because we cannot understand, those
abnormal beings who either think or act as if boating or the
Tripos were the end and aim of College Life, we suppose
there are few who will deny that boating shares with cricket

the honour of being the finest physical exercise that a hard-reading undergraduate can regularly take. But a boat-club does somewhat more than afford facility for boating, more than merely circulate the blood and develope the muscles of its members. Every pursuit which draws men together must do good in ways and to an extent that we with our yard-measures and mathematical formulæ can neither understand nor explain—and of boating especially do we believe this to be true. Let any captain of a racing crew, whether near the top or the bottom of the racing list, give his evidence; let him tell frankly, but without exaggeration, of the petty jealousy, the selfishness, obstinacy, conceit, discontent and frivolity which he had continually to witness and control; let any member of a racing-crew tell his story of the dog-headed, senseless tyranny and favouritism displayed by some captains; of the discord, bad management and confusion that prevailed in the boat, until all hope and chance of success seemed alike gone; and then let them both tell how, in some mysterious way and almost imperceptibly, through all these opposing differences, through pains of temper and pains of body the crew did fight its way to something like union and oneness; how day after day, as the stroke became steadier and the swing surer, a feeling of unity and the forgetfulness. of self did seem to spring up in the boat, until all felt like one man, that whatever might happen, whether they gained or lost they would one and all do their duty to the boat and pull their best and hardest. Was nothing gained here but good exercise? Was this time wasted? Would the extra hours stolen from the hard grained muses of the cube and square have been more profitably devoted to problems or bookwork? We think not. This is not however the only direction in which we can see that the boat-club works for good

The dandy pensioner, candidate for an easy, gentlemanly poll, environed by the splendour of a glossy coat, and leaving scent of perfume and odours of tobacco behind him as he goes, looks down with scorn upon the careless figure robed in academicals, which shabby by use, but not tattered by ill-use, covers perhaps a still shabbier coat, as papers in hand he hurries to his coach; but let them get into a boat together and the mathematics will soon find that the back before him is not merely an average specimen of Sartorian architecture, worth only the value of its decorations, but that it owns a pair of brawny arms, and that the captain has found real solid stuff and got good work where tutors could only find a vacuum, and have recourse to gates; while our would-be swell finds that his friend behind is as earnest though perhaps not so skilful in the boat as at his desk, and that he handles an oar even better than he does his pen, so each respects the other more and himself less.

We all have our fancies about men and manners, and very foolish ones they are sometimes. This man talks too much, another too little, one is untidy, another too particular, and so on through all the various combinations and forms of expressions of individual character. They annoy you, disturb the true and even balance of your temper—foolish fellow. See them in their Margaret or Somerset jersey, get into a boat with them, and you'll find half the peculiars have vanished; that they give fairish backs and can pull with a will which wins your heart, before you have half reached the Plough. Laugh as you may, and explain it as you can, there is a fellowship about true work which overrides all these petty, superficial differences, and which makes you feel what a mine of good there is in many a man whom previously you had shrunk from and almost loathed.

ON THE ADVANTAGES OF BEING IN THE WRONG.

I HAVE always hated "accurate people!" They are ever the dread of the theorist; they are even a sad clog on the measures of the practical man. Void of imagination themselves as they almost invariably are, they are a wet blanket upon the imagination of others, to the prejudice of all poetry and all that approaches romance.

Why *should* we be accurate? Is nature always strict, invariable, precise? Is it not the charm of the world around us that it greets us with endless surprises? that no billow on the ocean is like its brother wave, and no bud upon the briar the counterpart of that which is bursting beside it?

You can't reckon on nature being accurate, except in a very general way indeed, and I for one am particularly glad that it is so. Think of the dreadfulness of looking at the Mediterranean through a Showman's tube, and being able to tell exactly how the ridges run along the water. For my own part I had very much rather not know the exact height of *any* wave at all. I object to Dr. Scoresby and his profane attempts at prying into the secrets of the ocean, and I shall hail with joy the day which will demonstrate the fallacy of that great man's conclusions, always provided it do not bring with it the establishment of other irrefragable ones in their room. No! 'Give me an irregular universe', say I! It was with a deep insight that the poets feigned a hell where the damned spirits were doomed to gaze on thick ribbed ice for ever. A crystallized world seems to me a not unmeet picture of what the infernal regions ought to be. Meanwhile, I love an inaccurate Nature— Nature with puzzles and flaws and storms and anomalies— Nature wild, unkempt, ragged, just as often wrong as right!

Yes! Mr. Senior Wrangler! Just as often! My notion of 'right' is when things turn out exactly as I expect and desire them to turn out, and that being my premise, dispute my conclusion if you can!

Nature is inaccurate, you hear. Then why shouldn't
I be? "Sequere naturam!" I desire to meditate upon the
advantages of inaccuracy, upon the positive good to myself,
and you and all the world of being downright wrong. Wrong
in our practice, wrong in our principles, wrong in our heads!
Take the matter on its lowest grounds! Consider for a
moment how shocking it would be if we all had correct
taste! Taste in dress let us instance. Shall it be brown
now? or 'mauve'? You know it WAS 'mauve' last year!
Imagine the dreariness of a brown concert, everybody in
brown, and dull brown, because it was 'right' in the vulgar
acceptation. Imagine the sombre sadness of a world where
ALL were Quakers—or worse still, where all the gentlemen
went dressed like the maniac in the diary of a late Physician,
with an ostrich feather in their heads, and the rest of the
person enveloped in green baize, fitting tight to the skin!
Now these things are inevitable, if nobody is wrong-headed
in the matter of taste. You would have one dreary monotony
of apparel, sodden, solemn, flaring perhaps or painful, but
unvaried; instead of which, now we have duchesses in yellow
and ladies in crimson; dowagers in velvet and damsels in
muslin; bachelors in peg-tops and divines in cassocks; the
marshall in his cockt hat, and the flunky in his blazes!
And be it remembered, the very diversity in the shapes and
colours and materials and arrangement are necessarily inse-
parably bound up with much that is faulty, ugly, and objec-
tionable in the highest degree!

Do you wish to do away with this wholesome variety; do
you wish to correct all the 'mistakes'. I protest, good
reader, you are an idiot, and most perversely and deservedly
and ridiculously WRONG!

But consider the delight of being MORALLY WRONG.
I take it you have never been convicted of Felony! Well!
I don't exactly recommend you to try it, because I suppose
a Felon has done something wicked, and that sounds very
bad! But imagine yourself a Felon, and look at the bright
side of the matter. Surely there is a bright side! Surely
it must be very gratifying to reflect, how much money you
have made change hands. Trace the history of a Felon from
the apprehension of the rascal to the period of his ultimate
release. We'll give him seven years of it! What a useful
career! The constable, the lawyer, the barrister, the jailors,
the chaplain, the Judge, the jury, the—the—Heaven knows
how many more, and all *paid*, all living a fair average comfortable life for the behoof of felons only. How many hun-

dred operations did we hear the Enfield rifle has to submit
to? Bah! your Felon beats it hollow. Who shall say he is
not an eminently useful member of society?

But contemplate all the machinery for the morally wrong
in other directions,—the reformatories, the Bethlehems, the
Magdalens, the refuges, and what not. The positive advantage to the wrong doers is often incalculable, to the commu-
nity at large scarcely less extensive.

I pass over the advantages of being religiously wrong;
but I'm very sure if New Zealand had been a Christian
land, it would not have been noticed as it has; and but for
the big Patagonian's pulling off Captain Gardiner's boots as
he lay shivering with the scurvy, few would have cared
to visit that gloomy stygian shore!

Think of the quarter of a million (which nobody grudges,
God forbid!) spent by our Missionary Societies. Who
would give twopence to teach a Tartar a faith which he
knew as well as you?

Then again, you and I brother know what it is to be
physically wrong. That favorite corn you know! or that
particularly inconvenient stomach-ache. Whew! The delight of getting rid of the one or the other! Then the
petting you get when you're out of sorts! Adolphus comes
home thoroughly emaciated after the hideous toils of the
May term. Is there no Cecilia at home to pity him? His
nervous system has received a shock indeed, but Clara's
sympathy! Ah! what value for a sensitive nature in the
sound of that voice, in the touch of that hand, in the look of
that eye, that says so softly in most musical glances, " Poor
fellow, how sad!" I often think, with a kind of awe, of that
rough fusileer at Balaklavah, who swore with a coarse oath
he'd be wounded every day of his life to have such a kind
" nuss" to hold his head!

And is there no joy in being *commercially wrong* too?
Crede experto, you never know your friends till you've become " rather embarrassed." But then you do! Aye! it is
a horrible annoyance to find yourself really in debt. And
Great Britain (and I've no doubt I may include Ireland too)
highly resents a state of insolvency in men, women, or
children. Yet, mark you! if you want to see how many
friends you have, get royally into debt and see who sticks to
you. Take my word for it, you won't find a British trader
who will stand that test. No! " Wholesale retail and for ex-
portation" holdeth in abhorrence a paucity of funds. But
it is a joy which has few equals in delight, to find one staunch

B 2

true man in the hour of trial, who will fight your battles, and give you the hand of fellowship, and never shirk nor waver, who will nail his colours to the mast, and take as his motto at such a time, ' No surrender' ! and—better than all—put his hand in his pocket and not draw it out empty !

I think you will not expect me to dilate upon the advantages of being *intellectually wrong*—they are *too* obvious! Why! Humboldt wrote his Cosmos for those who stood in need of correction, not for the miserable creatures who had nothing to learn ! I always did think Milton's picture of the devils' imperfect knowledge, their wranglings and disputes and glorious arguments one with the other, was a far higher, and nobler picture than that other of a learned seraph who talked so very correctly beside Adam in paradise. All literature that deserves the name goes upon the assumption, that the reading public are astray on some subject or other. All progress in knowledge is built upon our past mistakes, all worthy instruction is based upon the rectifying of our errors. The man who never says a foolish thing, is pretty certain never to do a wise one!

I am not wholly unversed in the instruction of youth, and I never knew yet a precocious boy who made no blunders do anything brilliant. A good, stirring, rattling, false quantity, for instance, is such a wholesome stimulant. To be sure *that is* rather vulgar ! But the making Alexander a rival of Caractacus in the affections of Zenobia, or the multiplying certain powerful x's by multiplying their indices, these are instructive misdemeanours, from which a man learns more than by a year's dogged persistence in a course of humdrum accuracy.

Take comfort then my fellow blunderers, we are on the right side of the hedge after all. WE are alive, "the other party" are mere machines—wind 'em up and they 'll go! We can't! We sometimes go wrong! All the better! I would not wear a chronometer in my fob habitually, no! not for the world ! I regard a man who gives fifty guineas for a time-piece that never loses a second, in the light of a monomaniac! I greatly enjoy that pulling out of watches, all differing (only *one* unhappy one right you 'll observe!) and all affording a pleasant topic for conversation. I honour the man who despises Greenwich time and sticks to the longitude. For me, I never had a good watch, and never intend to have until some infatuated people give me a Testimonial, and then I shall take it to pieces to insure it's going not over well for the future. It is so *very* dull to know precisely the time of day, and to have no margin allowed you!

  *   *   *   *   *   *

 Of course you expect a conclusion. Is it quite the correct thing ?—Pish !

" A."

SONG.

SHE cometh in dreams of Summer days,
 With the chirping of Summer birds—
With a faint sweet scent of new-mown hay
 And the lowing of distant herds.
And tearful eyes look down on me
 And a sad face haunts my mind—
But I only hear the plash of the wave,
 And the breath of the Summer wind!

She cometh to me in the gray, gray dawn,
 With a sadness on her brow,
With a tremulous glimmer of golden hair,
 And a voice that speaks not now.—
She bringeth a mem'ry of pale, pale cheeks,
 And the grass of a quiet grave,—
But I only hear the breath of the wind,
 And the plash of the Summer wave!

" F. V."

AUTOBIOGRAPHY OF A GOOSEQUILL.

TEMPORA quam mutantur! eram pars anseris olim:
  Nunc sum penna brevis, mox resecanda minor.
De patre rostrato sine glorier ante, recidar
  Quam brevior. Princeps ille cohortis erat.
Nunc longa cervice minax et sibilus ore
  Currebat per humum: nunc dubitante gradu
Et capite obstipo steterat similisque putanti
  Quo sol deficeret tempore quaque tenus.
Sæpe anatum mediocre genus brevioraque risit
  Colla suis, risit rostra canora minus.
Et quoties risit, concordes nos quoque pennæ
  Risimus, atque alæ concrepuere pares.
"Stranguler atque coquar," stridebat gutture ovanti,
  "Ni crepat horridius, quam strepit anser, anas.
"Dem jecur in•lances, in pulvinaria plumas,
  "Ansere si melius cantat anhelus olor."
Hæc et plura quidem croceo dabat ore cachinnans.
  Galle, cachinnanti territa terga dabas.
Flave pedes, flave ora parens, alia omnia candens,
  Multicolor pavo te bicolore minus
(Hoc quoque jactabas) nivei splendoris habebat.
  Nec rostro exciderat vox ea vana tuo.
Ah quem portabas ventrem et quam varicus ibas,
  Altiliumque timor deliciæque coqui!
Ah quoties tecum lætabar, sive biremis
  Liventem per aquam candida vela dares;
Sive volaturum graviter te passa levaret
  Ala, ministerio proficiente meo!
Ah stagni decus! Ah ranarum gurges et horror!
  Ah desiderium vulpis, opime pater;
Sol medium (memini) conscenderat æthera, dumque
  Derides anatum colla minora tuis,
Efflaras: Taratalla coquus tibi guttura longa
  Fregerat elidens, excsideratque jecur.
Hæc, pater albe, tui memor heu non alba litura
  Flens cadit in chartam. Nunc mea fata sequar.

Vellor, et aligenæ velluntur rite sorores ;
　Mox patior morsus, culter acerbe, tuos.
Rasa cavor dorsum ; tum fissa cacuminor ima :
　Est mihi lingua ; loquar : sunt mihi labra ; bibam.
Atramenta bibo : novus adfluit halitus : arai
　Currere sub digitis et sine voce loqui !
O ubi terrarùm loquar ? O ubi nuncia mentis
　Audiar in Græcis stridere literulis ?
Musarum domus est : piger adluit amnis ; agerque
　Collibus, ut flumen mobilitate, caret.
Camum Castaliâ Polyhymnia, Pallas Athenis
　Mutavit Grantam : quo coiere pares.
Me quoque fors devexit eo : diagrammata duco ;
　Scribere versiculos conor : utrumque decet.
Terra, tuos sequor errores, dum volveris inter
　Quæ fugiunt solem flumina* quæque petunt.
Tum lapidis jacti curvum signare tenorem
　Instruar an doceam, quis scit ? Utrumque puto.
Pons sacer est, asinorum infamia : sæpe per illum
　Ivit inoffensus, me duce, discipulus.
Tandem, prætrepidans orbem quadrare, cucurri
　Noctes atque dies irrequieta duos.
Futilis ille labor quanto stetit atramento !
　Vana quot inscriptis signa voluminibus !
Me tunc, dum toties in gyrum volvor, adorta est
　Vertigo capitis : dissiluere genæ :
Succubui, excideramque manu, ni prensa tenerer :
　Tam grave quadrando vulnus ab orbe tuli.
Non sum qualis eram : fio maculosa : fatisco :
　Varica, rostrati more parentis, eo.
Arent labra siti : cessat facundia linguæ :
　Dirigui : careo mobilitate meâ.
Lector, in hoc (maculis veniam da) carmine, nostræ
　Quidquid erat reliquum garrulitatis, habes.
Hæc memor in nostro sit scalpta querela sepulcro,
　" Penna, levi chartis sit tibi terra levis."

　　　　　* Magnesia flumina saxi.—LUCRET.

　　　　　　　　　　　　　　　　" T. S. E."

RUGBY, *March*, 1858.

A WORD MORE ON UNIVERSITY STUDIES.

THE article on this subject in the last number of the *Eagle*
was, with one exception, to me by far the most interesting.
Not that it is new or profound, witty or logical, but that it
says precisely what I should have said three years ago.
I have the strongest sympathy with the unknown writer of
it, and cannot better express it than by disputing most of
his inferences. An hour's conversation would, I have no
doubt, leave us thoroughly agreed at bottom; let me briefly
indicate the line I should adopt.

You speak, Sir, of the worthlessness of this one-sided and
partial Education that a man obtains, if he reads nothing at
College but mathematics, even though he attain the highest
honours in that branch of study.

I do; supposing him, as I said, to be ignorant of other
things.

Just so; but here you virtually ignore all early training
(assuredly no unimportant part of education), all his boyhood
at home, and all his years at school. From ten years old to
nineteen what was he doing? The greater part of that time
was spent in Latin and Greek. He has already devoted in
some way or other nine years to language, and what he did
at all he is likely to have done in earnest; on your own
theory he ought now to turn to science.

Yes; but those seven or eight years, for I will not grant
you more, are years in which comparatively little progress is
made; his mind was not captivated by his work; it was done
perfunctorily; and with what effect let the Little-Go examiners tell.

I think their evidence could not help us much just now.
But you have no right to say that the work was done perfunctorily; and less still to estimate the value of a training
by the quantum of producible knowledge it has given. Even
if he can barely translate Virgil and Homer, and such cases
are rare, the amount of labour, (and that is an item never to
be lost sight of in estimating the value of a branch of educa-

tion) that must have been bestowed in the acquisition of that
ability is very apt to be under-estimated. I consider it as of
great importance.

Well, it's worth something; we can't quite define how
much.

Therefore, Sir, you have greatly overstated your case in
speaking of a Senior Wrangler who knows nothing but
mathematics. You should have said, who knows nothing
better than the generality of educated (I mean University)
men, except mathematics.

I grant you this; if you think it is worth having.

I do ; it is the first concession I wanted, and fatal to your
remarks on Educated men *v.* Calculating machines. I shall
now go on to the next point. You complain that he should
give three whole years to mathematics, and get so full of
them, while he is comparatively ignorant of other things.
But he knows very little of mathematics. He is much further
behind Adams and Stokes (not to go out of Cambridge) than
a senior classic is behind Shilleto and Donaldson. Is there
any man in Cambridge who could give an opinion on the
subjects on which Adams is understood (or not understood)
to be engaged? I have heard not. In fact your hero knows
about as much mathematics as a clever fourth-form boy
knows of classics, of whom you can say that he may perhaps
turn out a pretty scholar if he works well. In discussing a
University Matriculation Examination, some Classical and
Mathematical men agreed that the students should be expected to shew a competent knowledge of the rudiments of
both branches of education. But how would our schools
have opened their thousand eyes had they heard a worthy
Cambridge Professor fix as a minimum (so runs the tale) that
a man should be able to *differentiate freely!* Therefore it
appears that there is no such great disproportion in his at-
tainments, even if his classics are those of the third form ;
and we observe a disproportion rather in the Classical Senior
Optime who is still in his *hic, haec, hoc* of mathematics.

There is some plausibility about this; but the proof of
the pudding is in the eating; tell me what mainly occupies
the mind of the mathematical student! Is it well balanced ?

You take strong ground. I trust that while he is at
work at Mathematics he thinks of them, and of them only.
The strong mind will throw them aside entirely, and say,
' Lie there, Todhunter' when he puts off his shabby old coat
for Thurlbourn and Holden's new one, and turns out at
2 P.M. The weaker mind, the reserved or unsociable man,

cannot get rid of the phantom page, except in longer rests, or by artificial divertisement; he sees triangles in the landscape, and finds Gog and Magog invaluable as vertices. But we are not talking of such men.

No: but your strong man thinks of x and y for three years—

Only for seven hours a-day, remember—

And then—

—Goes down and blissfully forgets them all in a year's time; or begins to study them in right earnest; or takes pupils. He can please himself. In a year's time he is well balanced enough, even if he were as top-heavy at the time of the Tripos as most men are: if it is his profession to teach Mathematics, he has his pupils and pen before him for not so many hours as a shoemaker has his leather and awl, and his poking and punching and proging entitle him to no more compassion. They are sometimes very happy pleasant fellows, whom you would never suspect of differentiation; and that though their Latin Prose would be intolerable. What I wish to call your attention to is that, as Mrs. Poyser might say, " Folks as grind axes may expect to have their teeth set on edge," but when you stop the stone, and hack away, your teeth are all right again. In fact, as I said before, my teeth *have been* on edge, I *have* squeaked, I have passed clean through your stage and come out on the other side; and I say the single-minded (I mean the single reading) man is in the right of it. Let him do one thing well, at least as well as ever he can. It is not the first four, or the first six hours of reading that are *morally* worth much to the man, but the *last*; when his attention wanders, and all the power of his will is strained in fixing it; when his head aches and his hand trembles, and he won't give in yet: when his heart is sick, and he bates not one jot. The moral value of a high degree is far greater than its intellectual value; here is no dilettante, but a man of firm will, which has conquered the feebleness of his body. You would lose all that, and just when his work is absolutely priceless in value to him—bah! you would let him off and take up his Horace !

You ruin the elasticity of his body and mind for the sake of this unheard of morality.

I don't. Experto crede. Of course he is tired at the time, it may be unutterably wearied. It is right that it should be so; the weariness is transient. What events of your life are worth remembering except occasions of danger or fatigue, of trouble, of self-denial: when did you grow sensibly except

then, when every nerve was strained. Man is made to look
back with pleasure, not forsooth on a change of work (which
is no better than play) but on intense and perhaps continuous
efforts. How we recal with pleasure that tug up the soft
yielding snow slope 13000 feet high in Switzerland; that
forty mile walk, with three passes, we took in the lakes; was
there no pleasure in the aching numbed arms before a Trinity
boat up the Long Reach?

Would you have him read mathematics alone?

I should reply as Demosthenes did. First, second and
third—Mathematics.

But what should the poor fellow do in his intervals of
lucidity?

In his intervals of lucidity as you are pleased to call them,
let him read anything in the wide world except classics and
novels.

You barbarian to yoke them thus!

I stick to it. Classics pay in examinations, and unless he
is a shocking bad hand, may beguile him into being plucked
for the Classical Tripos; novels will ruin him. Experto crede.

That's the way. Experto crede, that's the way old fogies
come down on young moralists. Novels ruin him!

I don't mean to argue that now, and I believe you take
up novels because I would put them down. At this stage of
an argument one grows contradictory.

Possibly: at least I thought so a minute ago. But what
a shame to spend thus *the three best years of his life.* He
ought to develope himself more generally.

I smell a little cant here (cant with a *c*, not cant with a *k*)
that developement is an ugly word, we don't either of us quite
know what we mean by it. But I will maintain that my plan
developes him naturally.

How? how *naturally?*

By his taking the studies in their *natural* order: and
their natural order is clearly indicated to us by history.
Mathematics have followed Language in the historical developement of the human mind. The splendid and rapid
growth of the Greek mind made them models in eloquence,
in history, in poetry; even in philosophy they were at once
brilliant and profound: but not in mathematics; and they failed
still more signally in natural science, and that was not for
want of trying. They require the maturer mind, as of the
world, so of the individual. They are altogether of later
growth.

I grant it. But one-sidedness, want of sympathy with

other pursuits, are not these great evils and also characteristic of wranglers?

They are great evils; they are not characteristic of wranglers. A very few men, whom we are both thinking of are—I won't call them names—but as a class far from it. You remember the one-sidedness was shewn to be temporary.

I remember—temporary insanity. But about the other reading; I am specially interested in that. Don't you think it rather (just a little) likely to slip out of the fourth place?

Not the least: the harder the regular work, the stiffer must be the cement to bind it all together. In those terribly long mornings of the Long Vacation (I wonder whether other men long for interrupting visitors as I did) I have known men catch the Carlylian and Coleridgian fevers, and have them severely too without their other work suffering. I have known a man Mill'ed mildly in his third Long; and bitten all over with German philosophy in his last term of all times. Terrible stiff cement that. I am sure it is the same with you.

I am sure you talk a great deal faster than I do.

Of course I do. Ain't I writing the dialogue?

Good Day. I hope we shall finish our talk some day.

[The writer begs to apologize to his fellow disputant for the freedom of the tone adopted in conversation with a stranger.]

A VISION.

As hard at work I trimmed the midnight lamp,
   Yfilling of mine head with classic lore,
Mine hands firm clasped upon my temples damp,
   Methought I heard a tapping at the door;
'Come in', I cried, with most unearthly roar,
   Fearing a horrid Dun or Don to see,
Or Tomkins that unmitigated bore,
   Whom I love not, but who alas! loves me,
And cometh oft unbid and drinketh of my tea.

'Come in', I roared; when suddenly there rose
   A magick form before my dazzled eyes:
'Or do I wake', I asked myself 'or doze'?
   Or hath an angel come in mortal guise'?
So wondered I: but nothing mote surmise;
   Only I gazed upon that lovely face,
In reverence yblent with mute surprise:
   Sure never yet was seen such wondrous grace,
Since Adam first began to run his earthlie race.

Her hands were folded on her bosom meek;
   Her sweet blue eyes were lifted t'ward the skie.
Her lips were parted, yet she did not speak;
   Only at times she sighed, or seem'd to sigh:
In all her 'haviour was there nought of shy;
   Yet well I wis no Son of Earth would dare,
To look with love upon that lofty eye;
   For in her beauty there was somewhat rare,
A something that repell'd an ordinary stare.

Then did she straight a snowy cloth disclose
   Of Samite, which she placed upon a chair:
Then smiling like a freshly-budding rose,
   She gazed on me with a witching air;
As mote a Cynic anchorite ensnare.
   Eftsoons, as though her thoughts she could not smother,
She hasted thus her mission to declare:—
   'Please, these is your clean things I've brought instead
     of brother,
'And if you'll pay the bill you'll much oblige my mother.'

"Ψ."

SCRAPS FROM THE NOTEBOOK OF PERCIVAL OAKLEY.

READER, do you keep a diary? if you don't, and never have, I should certainly advise you not to begin. The amount of hours I have wasted over mine, (first in writing it, then in reading and admiring it when written,) would, if better employed, have qualified me to be Senior Wrangler at least, not to say a first class in Classics into the bargain. Despite these unavailing regrets I gaze with justifiable pride on the series of manuscript volumes filled with interesting records of my past existence. There is one for each year; all are beautifully bound; the paper exquisite cream-laid; each provided with a lock to screen their contents from eyes profane; and the locks so very superior that whenever I lose the key (which happens on an average about once a month) I am obliged to take or send the volume of the current year to town in order to have it opened. But the contents! they are indeed beyond all praise. Every day of the week has no less than ten pages devoted to itself. First and foremost comes a list of the reading I intend to do in the sixteen hours of waking life: (this list is always peculiarly large); immediately below stands a list of the reading I actually accomplish: (this list is always peculiarly small.) A minute account of my personal proceedings follows, beginning with my first waking action (which is generally to abuse the person who has disturbed my slumbers) and ending with my last drowsy reflection (which is generally on the pleasures of an eight o'clock lecture next morning). Such details *may* occupy space, but their value is of course more than an equivalent compensation. The remaining pages are devoted to an abstract of the news of the day, a philosophic essay, and some slight offering to the muse. Can you imagine anything more delightful in conception, more perfect in execution, more interesting in perusal?

Possibly from reading the above you may infer that I am a conceited person; my friends have done so ever so long;

they say to my face that I have too good an opinion of myself, and behind my back that I am a fool and a puppy. Charming is the judgement of friends; it resembles an astronomical telescope devoid of correcting eye-piece, and sees your very merits the wrong side uppermost. *Virtutes ipsas invertitis.* That I have a high opinion of myself I do not deny, that it is too high I beg leave respectfully to doubt.

However, for the present, enough of egotism—let me commend to your notice a small passage from one of my most recent diaries, put into historical form, which I entitle—

Scrap Sentimental.

It matters very little what took me down, a summer or two since, to the fashionable watering place of Weremouth. Suppose Seraphina Maria *was* staying with her maiden aunt at No. 1, St. Aubyn Terrace; what is that to the purpose? [Seraphina is now Mrs. John Tugg, and mother of a diminutive Tugg female. Have you, reader, never happened to love a dear gazelle, &c. &c. ?] Perhaps I went there to read; what spot is so favourable to study as a lively sea-side town? Perhaps for the good of my health; isn't being plucked twice for Little-Go, a trial to the strongest constitutions?

The rail (in its usual obliging way) set me down about a mile from my destination, whereupon I became the lawful spoil and pillage to the bus-driver of the Royal hotel; my modest amount of luggage pitilessly hurled on the roof, and myself, despite all resistance, stowed in the stifling interior, a pull of twenty minutes up a perpendicular hill landed me at the door of the Royal. The view was rather superior, I suppose, by moonlight, for two pages of the volume are devoted to describing the same, but as one sea-side place is just like another, you may all imagine the scenery for yourselves. A moment's reverie rudely broken by a stern demand from my plunderer for " one and a tizzy," and I turned into the hotel. A figure standing at the bar instantly caught my attention, and simultaneously I settled that it must be a fellow Cantab: it was young Cambridge all over; the marvellous head-cover, (for I cannot bring myself to call it either hat or cap) the turn-down collars, the elaborate scarf and pin, the shortest of coats, the most peg-top of trowsers, the patentest leathered of boots, and, as if anything was wanting to clinch the matter, that tankard of beer, and that everlasting pipe of meerschaum. On hearing my step he

turned, and 'this murmur broke the stillness of the air',
"Oakley, my pippin, what the deuce brings you down to
this infernal hole?" Sure enough it was Henry Saville of
Unity College in the year below myself, and with whom
I had spent days pleasant at least, if not profitable, at Alcester
School. Being at different colleges we had not seen much
of one another at the University, but the old *esprit d' école*
had knit us together once and for good. It was a case of
"Waiter—supper for two directly—chops of defunct sheep,
if you please, for the murdered cow at dinner was not satisfactory; likewise a quart of bitter, and *don't* draw it mild,
for it's flat enough without." [Such was Saville's wit, and
in his own College they *actually* thought him an amusing
fellow!]

A good long chat we had over the supper and the pipes
that followed; discourse of the season in town, with its
theatres and exhibitions, fêtes and concerts, casinos and
saloons; of Henley Regatta whereon, as both were boating
men, our talk threatened to become interminable, specially
when we diverged from the waters of Thamesis to father
Camus, and discussed the merits of every boat in the least
degree meritorious, including the second crews whereof we
had severally been members. However a happy turn in the
conversation led to the proceedings of our common friends—
old Whitechapel was off for the continent with (startling
announcement) a pony in his pocket, and had vowed to spend
the Long in Russia with an eye to ices. Fluker the senior
classic in embryo had joined a reading-party in a four down
the Main, whereas Potter, the sucking Senior Wrangler was
up at Cambridge reading subjects so extremely high, that
they would only keep till January following in the best
ventilated of minds. And so on, and so on, nor am I going
to specify our number of glasses of "cold with", or what
the clock struck when we considered it fairly "the hour of
retiring."

If my head ached at breakfast next morning, I pretty
soon forgot all about that. From where I sat I could see St.
Aubyn Terrace plain enough, could see the door of No. 1
open, and a bewitching figure in a straw hat and white
brown holland dress trimmed with blue, trip down to the
bathing machines. By the time she reappeared on the
esplanade, with her magnificent hair all hanging loose for
the sun to dry, I was strolling (quite by accident) in the
same direction, and need scarcely say that I saw no more of
Saville, save once *en passant* till six that evening, the hour
we had fixed for dinner.

About a quarter past that hour (I like to be minute in particulars) I found Saville staring out of the large bow-window that had a view down on the Marina. " Look here," he exclaimed, as I entered, and truly there was something worth looking at.

A marvellously handsome girl, tall and dark, with the most brilliant complexion, and most astonishing eyes and hair; eyes of no " misty depths" or " luminous darkness," but sparkling and pleasantly audacious to behold, hair done up in such a rich coronal, that the net seemed scarcely equal to keeping it in order; the nose Grecian, and the mouth " with an underlip you may call it, a little too ripe, too full"; the head small and beautifully set on the neck (in a curve, whose equation ought to appear in Analytical Geometry, if mathematicians' hearts were only human); her very perfect figure was dressed in what was then the height of the fashion, a light summer muslin of delicate and indescribable colour, with a scarf of the same hanging loose from her shoulders; a Spanish hat and feather, without any invidious fall of lace, completed her costume. *Parfaitement chausée* and *parfaitement gantée*, she walked

> A form of life and light
> That seen, became a part of sight.

A veteran officer (her father apparently from the age) with tanned complexion and grizzled moustache, was her only companion, a striking looking man enough, in spite of an unmistakeable air of " has-been-fast-once" which there was about him: it was no wonder that they attracted the eyes of all spectators then idling on the promenade. We had front seats however for the spectacle, for from the position of the window they faced us as they walked; and of course, just as they were close to the hotel, the *donzella alletévole* — (you know how it always happens— magnetic influence and so forth) raised her eyes for the space of a flash of lightning to where that moon-struck Saville was standing.—Short as the look was, I read in it both a decided degree of recognition and a slight touch of approbation. They passed out of sight: the mooning one drew a long breath; and I was just going to ask him for an explanation, when in comes the waiter with dinner, and Saville, himself again, be-gins volubly to abuse Weremouth in general for a dull provin-cial end of the earth, and the hotel in particular, for a vile uncleanly abyss. I don't report his conversation at full, for it was peculiar to his class of Undergraduates; few of the words he used would be found in Webster's Dictionary, and he gar-

F

nished his sentences with too many "deuceds," "infernals," and (I regret to say) stronger expletives still, to make it pleasant to read.—Such as his talk was, there was plenty of it; in a vein of happy audacity he enquired after the health of the ladies he had seen me walking with, profanely called one of them "a serene tip," offered congratulations, and expressed a hope I should send him cards. Then explained his reasons for having left town in such a hurry, to wit, because if he had not he should have "been in quod" at the present moment; two individuals of Caucasian extraction, instigated by a much-enduring but exasperated shoe-maker, had waylaid him at his lodgings in St. James' Street, and he had only escaped by the timely warning of one of his inti-mates, a Hansom cabby by profession; the latter had driven him with all speed to the Great Western station, whence he had taken a ticket to the first place he could think of, and so arrived only the night before myself—"that was all" he said, and quite enough too, in all conscience.

I asked him what he meant to do, and whether his guardian wouldn't help him down from the "tree" as he called it. He said he was expecting remittances shortly, but didn't know whether they were due that month, or next, or perhaps the month after that, meanwhile he had enough to carry on the war, but not sufficient to satisfy Mr. Solomon Heelam's "little account"—so what was the odds as long as he was happy, to which new and original sentiment he drank a glass of hock.

But as we were prowling along by the sea, in the cool of the evening, and adding a touch of Havannah to the general fragrance of nature, more disclosures appeared. He had met with an adventure—(he was one of those men who have always been meeting with an adventure; there is a lady generally in the case of high rank, and great personal attractions, who has declared her affection for the narrator unmistakeably, only unfortunately he has never been able to speak to her, or even see her, except on the other side the street): however the present case was a degree more tangible —he had seen the Veteran and his daughter at Paddington, had heard them take their ticket for Weremouth, and intended to travel in the same carriage by way of improving (?) his acquaintance; had however found their carriage full and not set eyes on them again till that morning, when he had not only discovered their lodgings, but had been able to take rooms for himself in the same house, where was another bedroom for me if I liked to join him. What did I care where my earthly tenement resided while my soul was always with Seraphina in ideal conversation—I censured his cheek, expressed my opinion there would be a row at no remote period, and consented to partaking the rooms, the more especially as they were in St. Aubyn Terrace. So we lounged up and down, but the beatific vision appeared no more, and S. M. had gone with her Aunt "quite in a friendly way" to spend the evening at the Tuggs (horrid cotton spinning people devoted to Mammon) where she would have a lively tea-fight, singing duets with that oppressively plain Eliza T. and playing chess with dear John, no doubt.— Under the circumstances Saville and I relieved our feelings by a quiet game at billiards on a shockingly bad table, and turned in early.

Before the next day we were installed in our rooms at No. 6, and the evening after that Saville was positively sitting in the first floor drawing-room listening to some of old Colonel St. Croix's campaigns, and exchanging intelligent looks with Miss Eugenie St. C. At the same hour Mr. Solomon Heelam was giving further instructions *in re* Ernest Saville, Esq. to the two Caucasians. At the same hour Fluker was raving against the authorities at Würzburg because the whole of his Long Vacation library had somehow got lost between that and Ratisbon, except an index to Sophocles which he luckily had in his pocket. At the same hour Potter was wrestling for life with Lunatic Theory, and Regular Stolids, while a demon in the rooms underneath him was playing the Satanella Valses, and a legion of fiends opposite were trying the "Shriek" chorus in "Moloch." At the same hour I, Percival Oakley, was at Miss Veriblue's lodgings playing piquet with her adorable niece, and suggesting how pleasant the air must be on the balcony, and other people were there, and Mrs. Tugg was regretting the absence of "her John who had gone to Blackwall to look for a ship": whence she proceeded to denounce the folly of early marriage (scowling malignantly at our secluded corner) and the heinousness of limited means, instancing as melancholy examples, a young clergyman and his wife then passing their honeymoon at Weremouth, "who have positively nothing, my dear, except what he makes by teaching at Oxford College, and who look so happy and thoughtless it is quite lamentable to see them." To which Miss V. responded that "she for her part was no advocate for matrimony." Well, matrimony at any rate had been no advocate for her.

"P. O."

F 2

TYPHŒUS.

Typhœus.	Sun, moon, and stars, hid in a night of pain; Blacker than midnight here with rolling smoke, And fume of pitch; and livid-licking flame About my eyes, that flashes in my face With mocking laugh, as if my strength at last Were shorn away, and I no Titan were; And this dead weight,— Typhœus, shake it off!
Spirits of the Flames.	Yes, shake it off, Typhœus.
Typh.	Who are ye, That keep a triumph in your laughing mock; And rail at me?
Spirits of the Flames.	Typhœus, shake it off!
Typh.	If I could catch ye in these writhing hands, Then I would stop your railing. Who are ye? If ye be spirits of Zeus, that think ye have His might in you, O come a little close, And let me feel you. I would stop your mock, If I could catch you creeping near me now. I have a strength hid in this heart somewhere, That will come soon.
Spirits of Pain.	We will subdue thy strength, Typhœus.
Spirits of the Flames.	If thou could'st catch us now? Can'st thou not feel us licking in thine ears, And kissing thy large hands, as if we loved To toy with strength? Typhœus, shake it off, If the weight press thee.
Typh.	O ye eternal Fates!

Watchers.　He will not say terrific Zeus does this;
　　　　　But only Fate.　How horrible he is!

Typh.　If I could shake this horrid mountain off;
　　　　If I could but a little time grow calm,
　　　　And gather my cowed strength; or grasp the flames
　　　　Shrivelling in these hands, and put them out;
　　　　If I could get a little my lost strength;
　　　　Or turn upon my side, and roll away
　　　　The grinding rocks—

Watchers.　　　　　　　　See how he writhes in pain!
　　　　If he can but do what he thinks, and turn
　　　　His weary side; if he roll off the mass
　　　　Of lava-livid mountain in the deep;
　　　　Zeus in his citadel may shake for fear.
　　　　If he can open those shut eyes, and see
　　　　The blessed stars, and stand upon his feet,
　　　　And breathe himself, he will heap up again
　　　　Pelion upon Ossa.

Spirits.　　　　　　　　Thou art bound
　　　　With subtle links of pain: the flame has thee.
　　　　It will not loose thee any more, Typhœus.

Watchers.　He will not shake it off; the rock holds firm:
　　　　Rolling on him again, to keep him down;
　　　　Tho' all the earth shudders to feel him move.
　　　　He grows a little calm, and speaks low words;
　　　　As if he prayed to mother Earth for help.

Typh.　It will come back again: it fails me now.
　　　　It grew upon me in my youth, this strength,
　　　　A mighty joy.　Even a little child,
　　　　I tore the pines out of the rocks with ease.
　　　　It does forsake me now.　It will come back.

Spirits.　It will come back, Typhœus.

Typh.　　　　　　　　　It was a sight
　　　　To make the Fates relent:—Enceladus,
　　　　By terror-flashing bolt of Zeus struck dead,
　　　　A massy blacken'd corpse, lie many a rood,
　　　　Along the wreck of lands where battle swept,
　　　　And all the rest of them.　I hear the deep
　　　　Rocking about the bases of the isle;
　　　　And in its hollow caverns under me
　　　　Moaning for ruth, and hissing with the flame.
　　　　May be an age shall pass before this strength
　　　　Grow what it was.

Spirits of the Flames.	We will subdue thy strength. It is but weak already. We will scorch Thy sinews into wires, and crack the bones Thou trustest in to help thee. We shall dry The blood up in thy heart ere long, Typhœus.
Spirits of Pain.	We will subdue thee soon.
Watchers.	How great he is! Making himself a greater than himself With his proud calm. The gods get little praise. He makes himself mightier than the gods.
Typh.	If it be in the wisdom of the Fates To make him stronger for a little time, Let him not think I fear his puny pains. Lashes of flames, and molten chains of rocks, And liquid livid flowing of these ores, That melt about my limbs, and lick the flesh To sores and boils, and run in little streams, Thro' cavern glooms, into the sea beneath,— It is not these Typhœus fears to meet. For I will lie beneath the weight, and shut My lids for calm, and curse him in my heart; Knowing the ancient strength will come sometime. It may be days, or years, or ages hence: But time is little to eternal life; And strength will come.—I, lying here till then, Will rest at ease as on a meadow couch; Turning upon my side sometimes for change.
Watchers.	How terrible he is! The spirits cease Their taunts, to wonder at him.
Typh.	It is not The writhing pain and flame that trouble me; And not so much my strength awhile subdued, Or base defeat; but in my clouded thought A little doubt.
Watchers.	What can his doubt be, then?
Typh.	If it be writ in Fates that Zeus be King, Is any heart so bold, or hand so strong, That it may cut it from the scroll of Fates? If it be so, who is Typhœus then? If it be written, as I think it is, What is it in the Future can bring help, Tho' year by year the ages roll away?

Spirits.　　What is it in the Future can bring help?
Tell us, Typhœus.　It is little need
To wait for ages: why not burst free now?

Watchers.　How his eyes stare into the hollow gloom!
As if the dark were thick with beckoning hands!
As if he saw the battle raging fierce
Again, and sudden terror of the gods!

Typh.　　Then if Enceladus, a blasted trunk
Of Titan ruin and wreck, were no more so;
And rose up strong, not rotting on the meads:
And if the ancient strength grew up again
In all of us, and with it dire revenge;
Cottus and Gyes and Briareus,
And I Typheus and Porphyrion;
And if we gather'd in a brotherhood
About Olympus proud, and held close siege
To Zeus and all his brood of weakling girls;
And all his nymphs, and goddesses of youth,
And petty queens of beauty died of fear;
If we pluck'd up Olympus by the roots,
And if we hurl'd his sun from his high seat,
And shrinking moon, and pull'd his stars on him;
And plotted for his hundred realms such dread,
And such confusion in his fastnesses,
With our mere force; would it avail us much?
If he be writ in Fates supreme, and be
For ever shielded of the Destinies?
It would be little better in the end.
For somehow we should fail, and it would all
End in our ruin, as before it did.

Watchers.　Now he would seem to work it out in thought.
He shuts the sear'd lids over his fierce eyes.
The mocking spirits echo him:—

Spirits.　　　　　　　　　　　　　　Would all
End in your ruin.

Watchers.　　　　　　　　See, he has it now!

Typh.　　This it is, then;—what is 'twere best to bear.
It is not I would ever yield to Fate.
Because Fate strove to crush and make me yield:
It is not I would give Zeus place, because
This hand could not displace him:—I would strive
Ever and ever thro' eternal time,

And thwart his aims and plague and trouble him;
Till his god-life were mostly wretched made ;
With such continual terror of his foes.
But this it is,—what is 'twere best to bear.

Watchers.

How leisurely he thinks, thought after thought,
His knotty problem out!   Look at his eyes!
The visage of the dead were not more calm.
As if this were a meadow-couch indeed!
As if the flame lick'd not his bare limbs now!

Typh.

To bear it, not of terror, but of will.
If I for fear obey the Destinies;
Then I no better were than unsoul'd clay,
Or sorry beast, or leopard of the hills.
If I for fear echo to his behest;
And lay aside, but at the will of Zeus,
My unused strength; I little better were
Than unskill'd slave, that supples at the whip,
And gets a slow reprieve by cringing prayers.
That were to make myself a less than he.
But if I bear that which there is to bear,
Not of constraint, but of my own proud will;
If I put on an energy to keep
My heart content, and suffer willingly;
Then I say not I suffer any more,
But call it triumph: it is victory:
Victory, not of Zeus, but I myself
Subdue myself: so then I am a god:
So then I am a greater than myself.
There is no greatness any greater left,
Than willingly to bear what must be borne.
And ever more the agony shall be
The sealing of my greatness: all the pain
Be changed from pain, and evermore be joy.
The running of the melted ores shall hiss,
As melody of triumph after fight:
The flaming flame as flag of victory,
Over my head waved after tug of strife:
And ever under-murmur of the sea
Be murmur'd sound of one that is content.
Ever I am a greater than Typhœus.
He was a giant in those days of storm ;
And mighty in a meaner strength, that is
Put off from him :—he has subdued himself.
And Zeus supreme over Typhœus is:
I greater am,—o'er Zeus and him supreme.

Watchers.　　　This is a soul that is a king of soul.
　　　　　　　This is a godhead o'er immortal thought.
　　　　　　　This is a better kingdom than to sit
　　　　　　　Throned on Olympus: this is greater far
　　　　　　　Than any sceptre over things and men.

"T. ASHE."

BEVERTON HALL,

A Tale.

THE Pagets were a great family at Beverton some hundred years ago, and used to own all the land for miles round, and the chancel of the church into the bargain. But their family has long since gone to decay, and the old chancel has fallen in, where they used to sit in their laced coats and high collars, and listen to the preaching of some Rector also long gone and forgotten.

Yes, the good old Paget family have long ceased to exist, and there is but little known of them.

Some old women tell stories which they heard, when they were children, about the last of the family.

They say he was a stern fierce man, with a fair sorrowful wife, much younger than himself, who always seemed afraid of him. They tell many a tale of her goodness and of his wickedness, but I forget them now, and probably there is no more truth in them, than in the story of his wife's ghost, who is said to wander about the church-yard.

But there was such a man as Sir Hugh Paget, we all know, for his tomb is in the chancel, with large iron rails round it, and some years since any one who understood Latin, could read the inscription, and learn his many *virtues ;* but the ivy has grown over the tablet now, and formed a sort of triumphal crown round the old rusted helmet, which is still fixed to the walls.

If we were to open the old vaults under the chancel, we should know more about the Pagets. I dare say their names are all written on the gilded coffins. One after another they were all laid in that dark cold vault.

The flag stone which covers them may still be seen, though upon it the wild violet grows, looking pretty, and blue as the sea, which shines through the ruined windows.

If you walk a quarter-of-a-mile from the church along the cliffs, and then turn sharp to the left and through that little plantation, where there are so many primroses and wood anemones and violets in spring, as soon as you reach the top of the mound where there is that curious oak tree (which you must have observed if you have been in those parts), you will see some old chimneys. You can't help observing them, and thinking the next wind would send them over, they look so tall and thin and old. They looked just as they do now sixty years ago. Some how or other those old chimneys never have come down, though part of the house has fallen in, as you will see when you get into the court-yard, where the old Peacock, the crest of the Paget family, still keeps guard on the top of the gate.

A very dim dusty old Peacock it is to be sure, and no wonder, for it has been watching up there through all weather, ever since old Sir Ralph Paget placed it there more than one hundred and fifty years ago. Most of the house still stands, though one entire gable fell in some years since, during the awful storm of 1840. It was the newest part of the house which tumbled down and was built at the same time as the gateway with the old Peacock. The old part is still standing, and I dare say would stand for another century if they do not pull it down as they talk of doing.

It is a rambling curious old place. The hall is by far the most ancient part, (said to be built in the time of Edward the Second) the other parts being added at different times.

There are some curious old pieces of armour hanging even now in the hall, they are very rusty, and look much the same colour as the old stags' heads that grin all round the walls, with their large round senseless eyes.

Ask the old woman who takes charge of the house to shew you over, she'll tell you all sorts of strange stories, it was she who first told me of the Ghost in the church-yard.

The old women say Dame Groats was very beautiful once, though it is hard to believe it. They say they have heard many strange stories about that shrivelled old woman. One old woman in the Almshouse says, that she can remember her as bonny a lass as ever she saw, driving about with the old Sir Hugh (whose lady is under the stone in the chancel) after the death of his wife, from a broken heart, caused by her husband's cruelty and unfaithfulness, but it was a very confused tale the old woman told me.

All that I could make out was, that Bessy was very lovely once, and that Sir Hugh thought so too, and though he never made her his wife he intended leaving her almost every thing, and would have done so had he not been accidentally killed one night, by one of his wild friends, who used to live with him, and make the old dining-hall echo with their drunken orgies. A wild lot they must have been in those days though Bessy won't often speak of them or of Sir Hugh.

Once I remember taking a friend of mine to see the old hall, who was much delighted with the quaint old house, its odd corners, rambling passages, and many stair-cases. There is only one picture in the house, and that is let into the wall over the fire-place in the great dining-room, it is a pretty picture of a fair, handsome, open-looking boy of eighteen. "That is a portrait of Sir Hugh, the last of the family who ever lived in the hall," said old Bessy, looking up at it, with something like a tear in her eye.

"Bless my soul," said my friend, "you don't mean to say that wicked old Sir Hugh was ever such a nice, honest looking fellow as that?"

"Yes he was," said the old woman, "and I don't know who you are young gentleman, to call Sir Hugh wicked, I wish there were many more like him in the world. No, young gentleman, it is not for you to speak of those who are gone like that, nor for me to listen to you, so if ye wish to see over the house Mr. Hartley must take you, for I speak to ye no more!" so saying, the old woman hobbled out of the room.

"What an extraordinary old hag!" said my companion. "She *is* a curious old woman," I said, "and at times even dangerous. I believe she has known better days, I don't know much about her, but I fancy she has had the charge of this house for fifty or sixty years, and has effectually managed to keep it all to herself, but come and see the other rooms, I know my way about the place almost as well as Bessy."

So we went all over the dismal old place, and saw the great bedstead, where Queen Elizabeth (I think it was) once slept, and has not been slept in but once since, and no wonder, for one seldom sees such a great funereal thing, with its dusky plumes and old embroidered curtains. I should have been sorry to have passed a night in it as did Captain Dickens to his cost.

The drawing-room was up the old carved staircase,

and was a long gloomy room hung with tapestry, worked by the deceased Lady Pagets. There was one piece close to the door, worked by poor Lady Flora, Sir Hugh's wife. I dare say that old dry piece of canvass had been wet with many a hot tear. The bottom of the horse's leg, as you will at once notice, is not finished, the poor lady died before she had finished the knee. As there was no one else to finish it, it was hung up just as it was, and after all, it looks as well as the other pieces. There is a little dark spot on it which looks as if it might be any thing, they say it is a drop of Sir Hugh's blood, he fell close at the foot of that piece of work, when the sword of his friend pierced his body.

But it is gloomy work, looking over a dusty old place, and so my friend thought, so we went out into the garden; my friend having first endeavoured to appease Bessy with half-a-crown, which the old woman refused with the greatest scorn.

"No," said she, "I'll take nothing from such as you— you're more charitable with your money than with your words, and I'll not take a penny from ye—no, not if I were starving—starving;—and did ye look on that spot on the canvass?" said the old woman with a hideous laugh. "D'ye know what it is? ye'll see some more of it on the floor if ye turn up the rug—it'll not come out, though years ago I scrubbed at it for hours every day."

"It's a nice room, is it not?" said she, suddenly changing her tone, "very nice, the room is so pretty; I'm sorry Sir Hugh's not at home, though I'm expecting him every minute, we shall be married soon, and then I hope you'll come and see us—good morning!" and the old hag bent her shrivelled body and bowed us out of the room.

The garden was much pleasanter than the house, which smelt like a charnel-house. A very pretty old garden it was, with its terraces, broad gravel walks, and fish-ponds. In the spring many flowers used to come up, such as are seldom seen now, they must have been planted years ago, and still come up fresh and beautiful, though the hand which planted them has long turned to clay.

"By the bye," said my friend, "tell me the tale of the ghost Captain Dickens saw. I have heard part of it, but could never make out the true story."

"Well," said I, as we sat down in the arbour at the end of the quaint yew walk, "I have heard it so often I can tell it as well as the Captain himself, who did not

recover the fright he got for more than a year. I don't
believe in ghosts myself, though certainly if you could
hear him tell the tale, it is almost enough to make you
a confirmed ghost believer for the rest of your life.

About four years ago, the Captain was riding home
late one evening, and as he was passing the church had a
fall from his horse, and strained his ankle considerably.
He tried to ride on, but found it gave him so much pain,
that he determined to try and get a night's rest at the
Hall, which was the only house within two miles. The
house was quite dark all but one window, where Bessy's
rushlight was burning dimly, and throwing out a faint light
into the dark night.

"By George," said the Captain, who had never been
in the neighbourhood before, "it seems a gloomy old place,
and not kept up much, I can see an old woman through
the window, I hope she's not the only one in the house."

"May I come in?" said he, as the old woman opened
the door, "I've hurt my leg, and want to know if your
Master will give me a bed."

"My Master!" said the old woman, "he does'nt live
here, he's been lying in the chancel for more than sixty
years, and you'd better spend the night with him, for it's
no bed you'll get here to night," and she began to close
the old oak door.

"Well," said the Captain, "you're very kind, but to
tell you the truth I'd prefer sleeping here, and I'll pay
you handsomely if you'll give me a bed—come, I'm sure
you won't refuse a poor fellow with a hurt leg, I couldn't
ride another half-mile to save my life."

"If you must come then, you must come, so put up
your horse and come in, though you'll not find much
accommodation here."

After some time the Captain managed to tie up his
horse in the ruinous old stables. When he reached the
room where he saw the candle burning, which was at the
end of a dreary long corridor, where his footsteps echoed
as he walked, he found the old lady seated in what was
formerly the saloon, opposite to a tiny bit of fire, which was
feebly burning in the huge grate, which in the good days
of yore used to blaze up so merrily.

The room was large and long, and very scantily furnished
with faded torn velvet with gilt borders, remnants of former
grandeur.

In the few minutes the Captain had been tying up his

horse, the old woman had changed her dress, and now appeared in an ancient brocade dress, and a curious old head-dress like a cheese, which used to be worn by ladies some sixty or seventy years ago.

As the Captain entered she pointed to a chair, and then resumed her work, knitting stockings—not heeding the Captain's remarks on his late accident.—

" Quaint old woman," said the Captain to himself—who at last gave up all hope of getting the old lady to open her mouth,—"curious house very, wonder where I shall have to sleep, the sooner I turn in the better, for it's not cheerful sitting opposite that old hag, with that old picture staring at one out of the dusty frame with Sir Hugh written under, as if he were offended at my coming, without his having asked me. I wonder who Sir Hugh was? I say Mistress, excuse me," said the Captain, pulling out his pipe, "you don't mind a little smoke I dare say, perhaps you'll take a pipe yourself, t'aint bad 'bacca, I can tell ye."

" Sir Hugh never used to smoke in the saloon," said the old lady raising her eyes for a minute from her knitting, " and would be angered if he caught us, but he's gone out, so I will not refuse your offer young man."

" Here's a pipe Mistress," said the Captain producing one of the many he always carried about with him, " and now tell us all about Sir Hugh."

And so the old woman did, and a fearful story she made of it, all about his death and the ghosts which haunted the house,—smoking the pipe all the time, and a wondrous figure she looked with her brocade, head-dress and pipe.

" Enough of that," said the Captain, "if you tell me any more of these stories, I sha'n't be able to get to sleep all night, will you shew me my room madam?"

" I'll ring the bell for the servants," said the old lady, pulling the bell rope, and making the whole house echo with the peal. " Dear me," said she after some time, "they must be all in bed, I'll shew you your room, though Sir Hugh wouldn't like it if he knew."

" I wonder what the old beldame will do with me?" said the Captain to himself; as he took the bit of dipt candle, and followed her up the oak staircase broad enough to drive two hearses abreast—"What an old tumbled down place it is to be sure—how one's steps echo along."

" You must see the drawing-room before you go to bed, if I had known you were coming I'd have had the fire and lamps lit. Look here," said the old woman, pointing to the stain of blood, "that's part of him—it came from his heart! Lady Flora worked that, but they shut her up in her coffin before she had time to finish it. Oh such a grand coffin it was too, white and gold, I saw her put in it, she slept in the room which opens through yours; she was a pretty putty and rose faced girl, but not so pretty as I was, and Sir Hugh and I didn't cry much when she died; here's some blood here, but I keep it covered up."

"Hang the blood!" said the Captain, "I'm awfully tired, for heaven's sake shew me my room old woman!"

"Do you know who you are talking to?" said Bessy, giving him an indignant glance, and leading down another long passage, till she came to the great state bed-room where Queen Elizabeth slept.

"Good heavens! what an awful room,—can't you give me a smaller one?—I shall never be able to sleep here," cried the Captain.

"Lady Flora slept through that door, and Sir Hugh and his father before him both lay in state on this bed for two nights and days,—with long candles and watchers. You'll find the bed comfortable. The great Queen Elizabeth slept here once,"—and the old woman closed the door and left the Captain to his thoughts, which were anything but pleasant.

"What an awful place this is," said he as he took off his boots, "I'd sooner ride forty miles than sleep in that bed, but what can't be cured must be endured, and the sooner I get to sleep the better." So saying the Captain threw himself *on* the bed, moths and damp forbad his getting *in*, leaving the candle burning on the carved oak chimney-piece, as he did not relish the idea of being quite in the dark.

"It's all very well trying to get to sleep, but hang me if I can, I've been more than an hour turning about on this fusty old bed. I'd get up if that infernal bit of rushlight was not nearly burnt out. How gloomy and ghostlike the old place is. I wonder what the time is?" and the Captain struck his repeater—"twelve o'clock, I declare, hang the watch, yes it was plain enough!"

The watch had scarcely ceased striking, when an invisible clock began slowly and solemnly to strike the hour of midnight.

In less than a minute, a long, long arm was stretched out,—it seemed to come from under the bed, though the Captain said he could never quite make it out—anyhow, it caught hold of the rushlight, which now flared up into a blue livid flame, and applied it to the fire, which soon flamed up into a high crackling blaze, which lit up every crevice of the room.

" Mercy on me," said the Captain, who sat up trembling on the bed. " I wonder what will come next! I suppose that it's no use making a bolt for it. Goodness! how the bells ring!"

Ring! I should just about say they did ring! peal after peal; one old fashioned bell in the corner seemed possessed it kicked itself up in such a crazy manner.

After some time the bells ceased, and the long thin arm came from under the bed and placed two chairs by the fire. They were curious high backed oaken chairs, (such as we don't see now a days) and threw their long shadows behind them.

In another moment the bells began to ring wilder than ever; and the wind that had got up during the last four hours banged against the shutters, as if anxious to know what all the disturbance could be about.

The bells did not ring more than a few seconds though it seemed a long time to the Captain.

After they had ceased, there was a sound of treading and distant music, as if some fifty people were dancing in another part of the house.

Nearer and nearer the footsteps seemed to come, and the Captain heard sounds like the rustling of a silk gown, in lady Flora's room, which was just on his right.

At last the door flew open, and a tall white figure, in a silk gown, walked very slowly into the room and sat down on the chair farthest from the bed. It was a handsome face, but deadly pale. The eyes shone as brightly as the great diamond that glistened on her forehead. She did not speak but bent down, and held up her long damp hands before the fire.

She had not sat there long, when there was a furious knocking at the chief entrance door, and a figure entered, dressed in the costume of the last century. There was blood all over his face, and a deep wound in his side; so deep that as the fire light shone on it you could almost see through him.

After having walked round the room without noticing the Captain, who in his fright had crawled under the clothes to the foot of the bed, where he was peeping out at the extraordinary scene, the apparition seated himself opposite the white figure, and a violent altercation seemed to com-

G

mence, judging from their gesticulations, though nothing could be heard.

This continued for some time, till the male figure rose and rang the bell, which set all the other bells in the house ringing more violently than ever.

After a time there was silence, and the invisible clock chimed the half-hour. As the clock ceased both faces seemed fearfully agitated, and the lady arose and folded her shawl around her as she was wont to do in former days while waiting for her carriage.

The faces of both grew thinner and thinner, till after a time they were nothing but grinning skulls, though the hair still remained. The white silk of the lady had meanwhile been undergoing an extraordinary change, but so gradually that it could scarcely be preceived,—the silk had changed to a long winding-sheet, and the bright diamond on her forehead to a piece of charcoal.

The fire had burned up to a still brighter flame which threw a lurid colour round the room, and lighted up the ghastly skeleton of the man, who was still garbed in his former gay clothes, though the knee breeches hung loosely over the bones of the legs as they rattled horribly whenever he moved.

His hands had grown to an enormous length as he knelt down and held the trembling finger bones to the fire. There was a sound outside which seemed to make them both shudder. The long arm then threw open the door, and louder and louder grew the noise on the oaken staircase.

It was not long in coming up,—and a hugh dark velvet coffin on four fiery wheels, slowly entered the room drawn by invisible agents. Nothing could be seen, though the stamp of horses' feet, and the crack of a coachman's whip was clearly perceptible.

The arm threw open the lid, and the figures throwing their arms over their heads, as if in mortal anguish, sprang into the coffin. Then there was a click, click, as the lid closed, and the melancholy carriage left the room, as a sepulchral voice cried out " Drive to the Chancel!"

The bells clashed, as the doors banged, and the rattling was again heard upon the staircase. It was not long however before the noise ceased indoors, the wind outside burst through the shutters and extinguished the candle and flames, and as the clock struck one, there was a sound of hurrying footsteps all over the house, and the Captain was left in silence and darkness!

Any one may believe this story or not as he likes. I have told the tale as it was told to me. Whether he really saw this or not, it is impossible to say. All that I know is, that he was found next morning in a violent fever which he attributes partly to his injured leg, but far more to the fright he had undergone.

"P. R."

MARCH 5TH,

MDCCCLX.

———

THERE'S a clash of martial music through the ancient college comes,
There's a flourish loud of trumpets and a muttered roll of drums,
St. Mary's bells are pealing on, and flags are waving free,
And there's crowding on the King's Parade, a sight of sights to see;
For thick along yon narrow street a serried line appears,
'Tis Alma Mater's trusty sons, the RIFLE VOLUNTEERS.

There's many a stout athletic frame amid that gallant corps,
There's many a slashing cricketer, and many a stalwart oar,
There's many a swell who loves to lounge and smoke the idle weed,
And many a man who flees a wine and sports his oak to read,
And beardless freshmen march in rank with dons of high degree,
One spirit in six hundred hearts, one true fraternity.

Why let the prosing pedant chide, the lazy idler sneer,
The sinews of our English land, its youth and prime are here:
Service, forsooth, they'll never see! Your pointless taunt unsay!
What higher service can be theirs, than they have paid to-day?
The noblest works for man assigned since first the earth he trod,
Allegiance to his country's Queen, and worship to his God.

And should the cloud, that threatens yet, e'er burst upon our shore,
And fierce invaders on the strand their eager myriads pour,
When round the Island, beacon-lit, fast flies the warning word,
To draw "for Altar and for Hearth," the bayonet and the sword,
To lay the foeman in the dust, to break invasion's brunt,
God speed our gallant Riflemen, and CAMBRIDGE TO THE FRONT!

"P. O."

A COINCIDENCE.

I.

THERE is an old and particularly wise saying to be found somewhere (probably in Tupper), that "no fox can be caught twice in the same trap." Now, some of my readers may possibly remember the disagreeable issue of my sojourn at the delightful village of Purbridge: how, with an imperfect pen, but with strict historical fidelity, it was related in a former number of *The Eagle*. Well, without laying claim to any superhuman sagacity, by a simple mental process I came to the conclusion that my misfortune there was owing to two circumstances, one social, and the other geographical;—in the first place that I had gone there alone, and secondly that I had gone there at all. So when the sun in the course of his usual duties had supplied the requisite number of days and nights to bring round another vacation, I duly made arrangements with my two friends Smith and Robinson to spend our Easter three-weeks together. The minor matters of locality and lodgings were left to my discretion; my colleagues however, like the tribunes of old, reserved the right of pronouncing a veto on any measure of mine they might deem unadvisable. I accordingly took down a large map of England, and stood over it in helpless bewilderment for some time; for, since we were not ubiquitous by nature, it was necessary to fix on some one place for some one given time. We read of lofty-minded astronomers being lost in the immensity of the telescopic universe, of thoughtful sages being perplexed to the uttermost in the windings of some philosophic speculation, of hardy travellers benighted and bewildered in the centre of a mighty prairie; but neither astronomer, nor philosopher, nor traveller will ever appreciate perplexity in its fulness, view its length, breadth, and thickness, till they gaze on an ordnance map of England to select one spot out of so many myriads in which to pitch their tent.

I had looked earnestly at the ceiling, paced up and down the room, bitten my lips, poked the fire with vehemence, and taken all the other usual steps to emerge from a difficulty,—but to no purpose. The postman, when he brought me my letters, found me still in this state, and looked as though he would have pitied me had he not been pressed for time. The letters were a relief at any rate. One was a circular from a tobacconist, the second a tract on profane swearing sent by an anonymous friend. These I laid quietly aside, seeing I neither smoke nor swear, and took up the third which was excessively damp; so much so that I thought it only common prudence to dry it carefully before reading it. The penmanship was an indifferent attempt at Gothic epistolary architecture; it was in the early pointed style, smacking more or less of the perpendicular. The letter itself came hoping to find me in good health, as it left the thankful writer at the time of its composition. It further stated, that the writer had had a melancholy time of it during the absence of her husband on "government business," but that such events must occur in this vale of tears; that after Mr. Biggs left she had moved to the fashionable town of Stockleton, where she kept furnished apartments for single gentlemen; and lastly, that she hoped she might have the pleasure of seeing my "honour" an occupant of these said apartments, after our "breaking-up" at College. Some further remarks were obliterated by two large round drops of colourless fluid, out of which emerged, like the sun from a cloud, the well known name of my lacrymose landlady, "Niobe Trout." I conferred with my two friends, and, after ventilating the matter, we resolved to close a bargain with Mrs. Trout, and that I should forthwith repair to Stockleton; the rest promising to follow in a few days.

While portmanteaus are being packed and exeats procured, I may perhaps just say a word or so on my two friends, as I had known them before the vacation began. Smith was a good-looking fellow, with black curly hair and fine grey eyes. He was possessed of a great amount of information on various subjects, though he had a decided failing in favour of romance literature. He was a strong admirer of Byron, and fierce in vindication of the age of chivalry; withal he was an agreeable companion, and possessed the fee simple of a genuine good heart. Robinson on the other hand was fair in the matter of hair and eyes, somewhat negligent in person, brilliant and witty in conversation, impulsive, but still a steady going industrious fellow, one in whom you could place implicit trust for sincerity and kindness. Smith and Robinson, though both friends of mine, were not acquainted with each other at the time I write of; they agreed to my scheme however, each well satisfied with my description of the other, and were anxious to institute a mutual friendship.

Such was the state of things, when one morning I offered up my person and luggage to the Eastern Counties Railway, and, after the preliminary rites had been performed, was duly sacrificed in a second-class carriage of that rapid and luxurious line. After travelling with praiseworthy caution through numberless corn-fields, in the middle of some of which we stopped for passengers, I alighted at a junction to change into a Stockleton train. I was walking along the platform looking for an eligible seat, when my eyes were suddenly arrested by a pair of tarred trousers which stood conspicuous in an open carriage door. I followed up the trousers till my eyes reached a familiar pea-coat, then a tie, and finally the storm-beaten face of Mr. Trout of cigar-importing memory.

"How's yer honor?" said he, as I jumped into his carriage, "you see, sir, they have taken up the hatches and here I am on deck again." I congratulated him on his release; and after enquiring, to the great apparent interest of a fat man in the corner of the carriage, if any "notes or papers" had been sent to Stockleton for me, proceeded to gain some information about our destination. Stockleton, it appeared, was about ten miles from Purbridge, a town just beginning to bud into a fashionable resort for quiet notabilities. I moreover heard how Mrs. Trout had nothing short of a splendid mansion awaiting our arrival; how very sorry the worthy couple were for the unfortunate conclusion of my last stay with them; and how such a thing could not happen again, since the unsuccessful smuggler had turned shipwright. Meanwhile our fellow-passenger had been eyeing me in a most suspicious manner, so much so that I asked Trout *sotto voce* if he knew who he was. "He's a hinformer agoing down to Stockleton, after a couple of runaway forgers," whispered he; adding, that it was expected that the Government would come down handsome for convicting evidence. The fact was,—as I afterwards learned,—that this man was an importation from Yankeedom, who had succeeded in obtaining a situation in the London Police Force. Being of a tolerably acute nature, he was in time promoted to the exalted rank of an occasional Detective, and had undertaken this mission to Stockleton with the avowed intention of " showing the Britishers a thing or two." From a glance at *The Hue and Cry* he had in his hand, which I obtained before I left the carriage, I found the two forgers described as both tall, one of them fair, " dandified and fantastic in dress," with light curly hair parted in the middle; the other conspicuous for large collars turned down, for negligence of dress, and meditative air. The description went on to say that they usually travelled separately, and,—though for the most part living together,—were seldom to be seen walking out in each other's company. I scarcely noted these things at the time, but subsequent events called them up afterwards strongly to my recollection.

The object of our kind interest, seeing we observed him, turned away and composed himself to sleep. And a particularly successful composition it was, for in a very few minutes he commenced to edify us with a musical entertainment of a mixed character, partly vocal and partly nasal. His bass notes were rendered with such accuracy of time and volume of sound, that they after a while disturbed, and finally woke him. He started, looked sheepishly round, and remarked to me that he " guessed he was very nearly asleep."

I had only time to observe that I believed he was not far from it, when a relapse took place, and his incomplete Sonata was continued. Trout appeared much amused, and assuming a philosophic air addressed me :—

" I don't know whether yer honour ever observed the fact, but there are three werry innocent birds as everybody is ashamed of having caught in his rigging."

I told him I could not exactly see the force of his remark.

" Well, yer honour," continued he, " the birds be, taking a snooze, awriting of potry, and afeelin' spoony on a pretty gal. And still, sir, when a chap's sleepy there's no harm in a nap; and when a man's a genus and has no honest smuggling to do, he might as well make potry as anything else; and as to being sweet on a peticklar nice gal, why, yer honour, a man can't help it unless he got a cowcumber by mistake for a heart."

I mention this remark as it has some bearing on what follows.

At last we arrived. Mrs. Trout received me with much emotion. She at first carefully extracted a tear with a corner of her apron from one eye, then one to match from the other. This done, she expressed a hope that I should find everything comfortable, and I, of course, had no doubt whatever I should. Then, I was very good to think so well of her; and the right eye wept a few skirmishing tears. These were followed up by a few sobs from below, while the left eye went on duty and turned out whole regiments of tears, which were duly received into a piece of linen vestment held in readiness for that purpose. Trout stood by hitching up his trousers; at last, suggesting to his spouse that she had "swabbed her decks" enough for all practical purposes, he shouldered my portmanteau and led the way to our snuggery.

Next morning, down came Smith. But what a change did I behold in my friend! He had turned down his collar *à la* Byron, and assumed great negligence of dress and abstraction of air. His eyes had forsaken the plane of the horizon, and were directed sometimes to zenith, sometimes to nadir. Robinson too, when he arrived in the evening, was quite metamorphosed. Instead of his wonted carelessness, he was dressed in a most scrupulous and fanciful manner. He had his hair parted in the middle, and his long curls hanging over his shoulders. His vivacious countenance had assumed a cast of sentimental melancholy, and tropes and metaphors flowed from his lips with unwonted facility. Here then were my two friends whom I had so warmly admired, and from whose sociability and hearty good-feeling I had anticipated so much pleasure;—here they were, changed most unaccountably in two short days into human anomalies. Affectation had superseded honesty, and their good sense had abdicated in favour of ridiculous sentimentality. For one moment a vision of *The Hue and Cry* flashed across my mind, but for one moment only.

I never was so puzzled in my life. I introduced the two men to each other, and then I speculated on this strange state of things till I went to bed, silent, thoughtful, and disappointed.

II.

Yes, I was disappointed; for I consider it no mawkishness to confess that I do enjoy the society of those I regard, that I do value the happy hours I innocently spend with friends after my own heart, that I do consider it one of the sweetest thoughts to think how, perhaps, in after life intimacies begun and increased here at Alma Mater may ripen into lifelong ties. It is an old tale to tell of warm hearts and generous impulses, how man is drawn towards man, and soul communes with soul, but I dare say once again that there is a reality and truth in friendship, and that that man cannot be too deeply pitied who has not this visitor at the fireside of his heart. But I am moralising.

Time did not mend my trouble. Instead of merry rambles together, and rural expeditions of discovery,— after a breakfast seasoned by deep remarks from Smith on the general misery of mankind, and the hollow groaning of the ocean by night; or by light sketchy rhymes on the moonlight from Robinson,—the one would draw a slouched sort of cap over his brow, the other, clothe his fingers with delicate kids, and then both sally forth in opposite directions, leaving me to melancholy and Trout. It was a rare thing for me to get a stroll with them; nor, to my grief, did that ready intimacy spring up between my two comrades which I wished and had imagined might be. They were distant and polite to each other; they never sought one another's company save at meals, for though they went out every day, still it was a separate affair for each; and, to the best of my belief, Smith had his fixed round in one direction, and Robinson his in the other. Meanwhile my mind went through various stages. Perhaps the first was disgust, next succeeded hope, then despair; out of despair, phœnix-like, hope began to spring again, and over and through all there floated a strong feeling of curiosity as to the cause of this metamorphosis.

Such was my state when Trout in great trouble confided to me the fact that "the hinformer" had taken lodgings just the opposite side of the street, and appeared to be keeping a kind and attentive watch over him and his family.

"Now, yer honour knows," said he appealingly, "that I am an honest shipwright, and though it certainly ain't as haristocratic a callin' as smuggling, still it's all above deck, as legal and straightforward as a handspike. What then can that aire hinformer want a keepin' sich a look-out on our port-holes?"

I assured Mr. Trout his vocation was a highly respectable one, and that though it was natural for him to feel great mortification of spirit at leaving the chivalrous paths of cigar-importing for the humble life he now led, still his honesty would be its own recompense; and I begged him not to disturb himself at the worthy gentleman opposite, since his present location was doubtless accidental. Trout shook his head at this, not half satisfied, and I sallied out for a walk, leaving him in this state of doubt and distrust.

I bent my steps towards a ruined castle, some two or three miles from the town. It was a noble specimen of the grandeur of days gone by; its antique arches and ivy-clad windows, its vast proportions, and commanding situation impressed me with a strong and perhaps somewhat romantic feeling of admiration. I climbed the grassy slope, and entered the principal gateway. The sun was setting, and its parting rays were gilding the hills in the distance. The scene was pretty, and, to command a better view, I scaled a crumbled portion of the castle wall, and seated myself among the ivy branches in one of the old windows. From this point of observation I looked away to east and west, and took in the whole landscape with all the pleasure orthodox on such occasions. On bringing my gaze round to closer objects, I preceived for the first time that another individual in the next window, perched just as I was, appeared to be enjoying the scene equally with myself. Our eyes met, and I recognised my companion as the fat gentleman in search of the forgers. I would willingly have got out of the way unobserved, but it was too late, for the Detective turned the full light of his well fed countenance upon me, and, by way of being agreeable, remarked,

"I reckon I'm a pretty considerable judge of scenery, I am, yes sir;" and he nodded at me as well as his precarious position in the ivy would allow him. I felt bound to return the nod, but I made it so minute as to be scarcely observable with the naked eye.

"Yes sir," continued my friend, "and I guess that is a perquisitely enchanting sun-set, viewing it you see as a brother hartist, yes sir."

"Really, sir," I said with some trepidation, "I have not that pleasure."

"Not a brother hartist, hey? yes sir, that won't do neither sir. Not fond of copying the old masters, hey?"

"Never did such a thing in my life, I assure you," I replied with vehemence.

"Come now," said the fat man persuasively, pointing to the grassy slope beneath, "I know as how you and that party there do something in the miniature line. Britannia on water-marked paper is a neat little design for rising hartists, yes sir."

In less time than any system of notation yet invented will enable me to express, I followed his look till I saw

Smith pacing pensively the grass below, and then I scrambled down to *terra firma.* I was just able to seize the Detective's legs, so, with a movement composed of equal parts of cork-screw and pump handle, I rolled and pulled his portly person till he lay well be-walled and be-ivied at my feet.

"You impertinent scoundrel," I exclaimed, "what do you mean?"

"Well, well, now," he gasped forth, "I reckon you are no hand at a joke. But if you queer fellows are all so very innocent, that party outside, I suppose, would not object to my knowing his name?"

"Certainly not," I said, "you or anybody else. That gentleman's name is Smith."

"Yes sir," said the other pulling out his pocket book, "and the other?"

"Robinson," I replied. He paused, leered incredulously at me, placed one finger on the side of his nose, made an allusion to a man Walker, and referred me to a fabulous battalion of her Majesty's troops. In a few minutes I was beside Smith, and had told him how his movements were watched. He received my account with profound silence: at last, under the most solemn promise of secrecy, I was let into the cause of his abstraction. He was writing a prize poem;—at least a poem which would get the prize if the adjudicators were men of sufficient poetic feeling to agree with my friend on the merits of the composition.

As we walked home he recited what he had written, and discussed with me each simile and idea. Before we parted I had to reiterate my promise not to divulge his pursuit, particularly to Robinson, under any circumstances whatever short of an earthquake or a monsoon.

Robinson was at home when we returned, and he wished a few words with me in private. He was very much ashamed to confess, but confess he supposed he must, that he was actually writing a prize poem. He would not have it known, no not for the entire world with Uranus, Neptune, and five or six asteroids thrown in with it, but he didn't much mind telling me, seeing I was not on any account to mention it to anybody, especially not to Smith. He had meant to tell me from the first, and now a little difficulty induced him to ask my aid. Of course I was ready to do anything I could.

" Well," continued Robinson, " I have usually meditated on my poem in the further end of that park behind the Town, which I always understood was open to the public.

I used to walk up and down thinking, and when I came upon anything fine I noted it in my pocket-book. Now, this morning, just as I was dotting down a most brilliant thought, a gamekeeper seized me, and before I could collect my senses to give a satisfactory explanation, I was conveyed to the Squire's house, and charged in good round terms by that irascible gentleman with being a ' sentimental humbug', and haunting his premises with matrimonial designs on his daughter (a damsel I never knew existed till that moment), who it seems is an heiress in her own right. I was, of course, ashamed to tell him my occupation, but I protested over and over again that I knew nothing whatever of the young lady; and that, though I did not wish to say any thing un-gallant, still I certainly should not feel any deep amount of anguish, if she were located at that very moment in the distant climes of China or Peru. After a very stormy inter-view, which ended by his kindly threatening to horsewhip me, 'if ever I came poking about his park again,' I left; and now I want you to visit this irate Papa, and to appease his wrath by explaining things as far as you think necessary."

I promised to go in the morning on this errand. Then he read me his poem as far as he had gone, and we chatted over it, and discussed its points. He thanked me for my observa-tions and hints, which he took down to embody in his poem; and it was not till afterwards, in thinking over the matter, that I discovered I had by piecemeal recited Smith's lines in a most unintentional manner. Nor was this all the mischief done, for by some means or other I let out Robinson's to Smith, and then again Smith's to Robinson, and so on; so that the materials, nay words, of one were in time in the possession of the other. All this was almost entirely acci-dental; I may just possibly have indulged in the minutest amount of mischief, but beyond a doubt, the greater quantity of lines was wormed out of me by one or the other, who then appropriated them, little thinking where they really came from.

III.

Thus the poems progressed by this new species of literary partnership. I was almost as unconscious of what was going on as my two friends were. I felt indeed that my whole spirit was fast becoming imbued with strange and fantastic notions on Slavery (for this was the theme on which they sang); I felt that these notions had a local habitation and a name within the limits of my mental kingdom, still I never stopped to consider whether they were native aborigines, or nomad tribes of ideas, which, having left the Smithian or Robinsonian territories, had settled for a time in the agreeable pastures of my own mind. I fear the latter was the case; but if want of reflection was my fault, want of generosity was not likewise my failing. What I had so freely received in the way of Slavery notions, I must say, in all justice to myself, I as freely dispensed. If it so happened that I dispensed them in a manner which entailed awkward results, this was misfortune, not malice. On one day Smith would consult me on the domestic arrangements of the interior of Africa; on another Robinson, on the slave population of America. At one time we discussed the length and weight of the chain required to curtail the movements of a muscular though respectable negro. At another time the character of a slave-dealer underwent the blackening process at our righteously indignant hands. No wonder, 'mid such a variety of thoughts, that confusion got the better of memory; no wonder I imparted the right idea to the wrong man, and handed over Smith's most exquisite lines to Robinson, and Robinson's to Smith. This was just the sort of case, which must have first called into being, in some deep philosophic mind, the well-known social doctrine, that natural contingencies of a disagreeable character may occur within the circumference of the best regulated domestic circle.

Prize poems are finite;—that is to say, in actual material length, they are finite. A few days passed and the two compositions were concluded simultaneously, and I was asked by each author to copy his for the Vice-Chancellor. I would willingly have declined the honour; but reflecting that a copy in their own handwriting would not be received, and that the choice of an amanuensis lay between me and Trout, I assented, and set to work. To secure privacy I copied them in my bedroom. I first got through Smith's, and then, somewhat fatigued, commenced my attack on Robinson's. What was my horror and surprise to find his almost line for line the same as Smith's! I looked again; could I possibly have taken up by mistake the one I had just copied? No; here lay the poem with Robinson's name attached, and there lay Smith's. I was completely perplexed, and in a highly puzzled state I adjourned to the sitting-room with the papers in my hand.

The two poets were talking amicably together when I entered, and both simultaneously started to see their productions thus publicly exposed in my hand.

" My good fellow," said Smith turning round to Robinson, " is it possible that you too — ?"

" Yes, yes," replied Robinson, " but I had no idea that you—."

" How very odd !" exclaimed the two in chorus.

" Well," said Smith, " I propose now that our scribe reads both. I shall be delighted to hear yours." Robinson expressed himself as highly honoured, and quite agreeable to the arrangement. I was looking on meanwhile, with rather a blank face. " Very well," I said at last, " if you wish it, I shall be very happy to do so." So clearing my throat with stoical determination, I commenced. I read one line, when Smith cried out, " Stop, not mine ; I vote for Robinson's first." Robinson's brow darkened, " That *is* mine," he said angrily. " Yours !" ejaculated Smith, as I went on, " you must be dreaming." " And you must be mad, Smith. I say again, those are the two opening lines of my poem," said the other. I could stand it no longer. I laid down the papers on the table, and remarked, " It does not much matter, gentlemen ; they are both well nigh line for line the same." To describe the astonishment of my two friends at this announcement would be simply impossible. Let the reader take equal quantities of amazement and despair ; add to these a little of disgust, a sprinkling of amusement, and a pinch or two of sheepishness. Mix these well together, and apply the compound to the countenances of your ideals of Messrs. Smith and Robinson, and you will have a faint, a very faint representation of how they looked at each other, at things in general, and at me.

Just at this critical moment a little scuffle was heard outside, and, directly after, a knock at the door. Trout appeared grasping the Detective in not exactly an affectionate manner by the coat collar.

" Is this here party a peticklar friend of yours, gem'l'm ?" asked my landlord.

" Quite the contrary, I assure you," I replied.

" Because," continued Trout, " he is peticklar fond of your conwersation, which he thinks it is none the worse for coming through a key-hole in a deal door."

" I guess," interposed the offending individual, " that I was only admiring the painting on the door panel as a work of hart."

" Vell then," replied the other, " as you looks at pictures vith your ears, perhaps you'll kindly see the vay down stairs with your nose. I suppose gem'l'm I may show this party down ?"

Without waiting for a reply, Trout commenced to assist the Yankee down stairs, in a manner more impulsive than is generally allowed by the rules of society.

This was the last we saw of our friend the Detective. Report however says, that the real forgers escaped while his attention was so keenly fixed on us, and that he himself, overpowered by the ridicule of his comrades, left the Force in disgust, and ended his days in the quiet retirement of a Turnpike Toll-house.

In a few minutes Trout returned with his wife, and pulling a lock of his hair in front, said respectfully, "I hopes, gem'l'm, you'll hexcuse me, but I hope everything's above board and proper here. I has been in with Government once, and having sich an unkimmon affectionate old woman," (he winked and pointed with his thumb to Mrs. Trout, who was weeping intensely) "I think I'd rather not go in again."

"It's all right, Trout," I said, "that fellow may dog us about if he likes, but we are quite correct in our conduct I assure you."

"No whiskey?" inquired Trout, looking under the sofa. I shook my head. "Nor cigars?" he continued, I shook my head again. He still seemed dissatisfied, and looked suspiciously at the papers on the table. I followed his glance, and taking up the poems remarked that my friends, I doubted not, would have no objection to my showing him these. Hereupon a fierce discussion arose. Smith disclaimed having any thing to do with them; there was no poem of his there, he said. Similarly Robinson disowned his offspring; and each declared in the strongest possible manner that *the* poem should not go in with his name attached. At last I quieted them, and read the production, to Trout's great satisfaction. Mrs. Trout was fearfully affected by the pathetic parts. The description of a slave being flogged, judiciously brought in towards the end, brought on a climax. She wept like an April cloud, till there was not a dry thing about her; at last she seized my great coat behind the door, and mopped up her tears with wild enthusiasm.

"Am I to understand, yer honour," said her husband solemnly, when I concluded, "that at Cambridge they serve out rations of meddles for that sort of sarvice?"

I told him there was one such medal given every year by our Chancellor, for the best poem.

"Vell, Sir, these here gem'l'm don't seem over willin'" to stand by their guns, so if 'twill be any advantage to your honours in the way of meddles, I shall have no hobjection to put my epitaph to the potry and send it in to the commodore, duly promising to hand over the prize-money, perwided you come down with hextra grog to the wolunteers, that is, me and my old woman here."

This speech was received with a shout of laughter. Smith and Robinson forgot their chagrin, and joined in it heartily; and before the smoke cleared off to the tune of Rule Britannia, Trout and his wife (yes, Mrs. Trout laughed!) joined too. Meanwhile, Smith turned up his shirt collar, and Robinson disarranged his hair and tore two buttons off his waistcoat.

And how can I tell my readers how pleasant a week we had after this? my friends became their dear old selves once more, and lonely walks and dismal meditations were exchanged for laughing, happy, sociable rambles, with the merry round of jest or tale. The days flew by as only days of innocent healthy enjoyment can. The grand old sea-waves scattered spray which sparkled as it never did before; the merry children on the sands laughed with a music we had till then overlooked; the bright open sky beamed upon us with a smile so genial and so warm, that we wondered what we had been about for the last fortnight, to have thus missed the glories of Nature around us, and neglected the sunny influence of friendship's sweet communion.

Does my reader ask, " And what of *the* poem ?" Let him take down from his shelf the well-worn volume, in which our venerable Alma Mater loves to record the great deeds of her sons; let him refer to that part which contains the list of Prize Poems, and the following will strike his gaze;—" 1857. None adjudged."

" λαβυρίνθειός τις."

SPRING AND AUTUMN.

SPRING.

SWEET is the April morn: the birds call loud in the woods,
 The larks overflow with song in the cope of a dappled sky;
The larch in the little copse grows green with its swelling buds,
 And the rill o'er its rocky path goes joyfully purling by.

AUTUMN.

O Time! that beautiful Spring is dead, and the larks are dumb,
 And the willow-leaves clog the brook that gurgles, swollen with
     rain;
And a sad thought lies at my heart, and will not be overcome,
 That a Spring as happy as *that* may never come to me again!

Why not? it was but a thought by the sorrowful season bred,
 Which now that the time is past, I am half-ashamed to tell—
Shall I fling the fresh rose away, because it may sometime be dead?
 I will live in hope, and be happy, and trust that all will be well!

DEBATING SOCIETIES.

READER! do you belong to a Debating Society? You
don't! you never heard of such a thing! Listen a few
minutes then, while I endeavour to enlighten you. Imagine
yourself in a tolerably large room with about fifty other men
of every standing, from the bachelor whose strings have not
yet drawn him away from old memories, to the freshman
nervously meditating his maiden speech in yonder corner.
The President, who sits at the upper end of the room supported on either side by the Vice-President and Secretary,
commences the evening's proceedings, by calling on the latter
to read the minutes of the previous meeting. The other
private business of the Society is then transacted, such as the
balloting for new members (supposing that odious and unnecessary system to exist) or alterations in the rules. The
discussions on these points are often most amusing. I
remember one which ensued on a motion proposing the
repair of a dilapidated box, which was used to contain the
voting balls. I believe nearly every member in the room
got up to say something—an amendment was introduced in
the form of a new box; the treasurer came forward and
presented a lamentable statement of the Society's finances,
and finally the original motion was thrown out by a majority
of 1. When the private business is over, the subject of
the evening's Debate is introduced by a member previously
named. It may be a political question, or an historical question, or perhaps a question deep in the chaos of metaphysics.
Another member rises to respond, and the rest take part or
not according as they please, speaking alternately for and
against the motion. At the conclusion, the first two speakers
having the right of reply, the question is put to the vote,
after a discussion which usually lasts about a couple of hours.
  " And a couple of hours very unprofitably spent—literally
wasted," says the Reader; " what! men meet to talk about

mending a ballot-box, to talk merely for the sake of talking ! Why it's almost as bad as writing for *The Eagle*." And consequently almost the same argument will suffice to defend these institutions. That men who pass their days and nights in gorging themselves with knowledge, should be accused of cultivating the *cacoethes loquendi*, or of unprofitably spending their time when they meet to talk for a couple of hours every week, seems an astounding paradox; inasmuch as the whole tenor of our University course aims at the expansion of the mind or the inculcation of new ideas, while the expression of those ideas is entirely left to ourselves. I will not pretend to say that the educational system, as pursued here, is in any way insufficient; but I have sometimes wondered whether it has ever occurred to the University Commissioners to appoint in their new Statutes, a Professor of Rhetoric and Elocution to preside for the term of his natural life at the Union, Port Latin, and other Debating Societies in the University. Amid their sweeping reforms we hardly know what to expect, but perhaps the institution of such a Professorship would not be the worst thing they might do. For if there is any line of study which is neglected here, it is the art of putting our ideas into words. Coming as many amongst us do from public schools, where Latin Themes indeed are rife, but where the name of English Essay is scarce heard once a-year, we often find a difficulty, when our education is supposed to be completed, in clothing our thoughts with suitable language. A man may acquire logical accuracy by the aid of Mathematics, or that refinement of mind which is derived from the study of the Classics, but it will be of little avail to the world that he has laboured under Parkinson, or is thoroughly saturated with Shilleto, if at the same time he is unable to impart his knowledge to others. Yet it seems to me that this is forgotten, and that with our Examination mania and the Tripos mania, we, of this respectable and old-established institution of St. John's College, are peculiarly liable to neglect everything else to secure a first-class in the May. Such ought not to be the case. The nineteenth century is an eminently practical age; when a man must be able to shew his learning, if he would have it appreciated.

Scire tuum nihil est, nisi te scire hoc sciat alter

was never truer than at the present day. And for a place of education like this, whose members will be called for the most part to the church or the bar, and some of whom may one day be guarding the interests of England in her Parliament—for such a school to neglect the study of elocution, surely is a great mistake. True it is that a certain M.P. of editorial celebrity was returned at the last election through employing substitutes to address his constituents. Still when our turn comes, we may not be so happy in the choice of a substitute. I say when our turn comes, for although we may not covet his enviable title, who is there among us that can say that he will never have to undergo the ordeal of public speaking? It was only the other day that a late fellow of this College said to me, in speaking of the scene of his parochial labours, "Nothing can be done here without a meeting and a speech: and such a place for lectures!" And it has always appeared to me a lamentable disgrace to the learning of our clergy, when one of its members is seen—perhaps not heard—muttering a few incoherent sentences on Church Missions—as we discover from the placards,—and at length compelled to sit down in confusion.

To remedy this evil Debating Societies have been instituted, where by being pitted against one another in honest debate, we may learn to say what we mean, and practise those powers of elocution, which are requisite in almost every profession. And I would humbly recommend my brother students not to neglect this means of education, but while they are reading to become full men, and writing to become accurate, to complete the Baconian precept by speaking at these debates to make themselves ready men. They may find difficulties at first, but let them only persevere, though it be at the expense of their auditory, and I will guarantee that they will become, I do not say orators, but at least respectable speakers. Oratorical qualities there are, which must be to a certain extent innate ; ἔστι φύσεως τὸ ὑποκριτικὸν εἶναι καὶ ἀτεχνότερον suggests a friend who is just going in for the Voluntary Classical. But at the same time any one possessing these qualities in a moderate degree, may by perseverance become a good debater. Who does not remember the admirable parallel to this point, which Macaulay has drawn between Pitt and Fox? "Poeta nascitur, orator fit," is certainly no less true than the usual reading, under certain restrictions of the meaning of orator— and it may be laid down as a rule that, while the true poet is naturally endowed with the gift of poesy, it is by long practice and application that a man becomes a great debater. How laborious must have been the pebble-process of that chief—that *facile princeps* of orators! How tedious the tracing of those complex characters on the polished roll! I can imagine Demosthenes sitting up all night to write out the Midias or the De Corona; or perhaps addressing invisible gentlemen of the jury whom he has to face to-morrow morning, and rehearsing the orthodox action of his hands as he watches the trickling of the water-clock. And when I recollect that Sheridan and others of England's greatest orators have established their claim to eminence, owing to their custom of preparing their speeches, I am convinced that it is chiefly by practice, and perhaps after repeated failures, that a man becomes eminent in debate. And no one can, without great injustice to himself, despair of learning to speak fluently.

Studied speeches, if known to be such, are generally regarded with aversion; as whatever is the offspring of genius appears more striking and brilliant than the result of patient industry. There are times, however, when a set speech is more applicable, and does more credit to the speaker than any display of oratorical talent. And for practice in this style, as well as to learn to speak on the spur of the moment, it is equally advantageous to join a debating society. For there a speech must depend to a certain extent on the remarks of the previous speaker, and a clever repartee is often called forth by what has only been uttered the minute before. Thus, though the generality of speeches are delivered ex tempore, the opening speech and that of the chief opposer are (or if not, shame on the speakers!) studied harangues. An opening speech in a debate should contain all the arguments and statistics which can be brought forward to support the motion, while the opposer should adduce all the evidence on the opposite side.

And herein lies the advantage of having a stated leader of the opposition, as in our Long Vacation Debating Society; for besides the pain of hearing the president, after a vain inquiry for an opposer, driven to ask if any honorable member will speak on either side of the question, I have observed that when this is not the case, the opposer often is content to ward off the attack of his adversary without bringing forward any positive proofs himself; and thus it happens that a whole debate is carried on without a single direct argument being adduced in favour of the opposition. For half the men who speak, speak I may venture to say on no further knowledge of the subject than they may glean from the two opening speeches, and if these speeches are deficient in matter, the succeeding speakers will be content to carp at the language of their predecessors, and twist their words often into what they never meant, and perhaps never could mean. On these grounds then the Committees of Debating Societies, if they wish to have really good debates, will always provide an opposer of the motion ; and let the opposer thus selected not care so much to repel the enemy's attack, as to adduce all the evidence he can in his own case, and he will have the satisfaction of making a far more interesting debate.

  But a serious charge has been brought against these Societies by no less a personage that the Archbishop of Dublin. It is his opinion that they tend to foster a spirit of pride and dogmatism. It may be a bold act to question the Archbishop's sayings, nor should I wish to do so, were he alone in his opinion. But as I have heard among ourselves remarks to the same effect, my few hints would be altogether incomplete, if I did not attempt to answer the difficulty.

  Undeterred then by great names, I venture to assert that so far from promoting a spirit of dogmatism, the debates, as carried on in these Societies, have the natural effect of shewing that there are two sides to every question, and generally much to be said on both. If a Society were con- stituted to uphold the tenets of a particular party, designated by its watchword, and admitting no one who was not professedly attached to that party, I can well understand that the debates would not only lose much of their naïveté, but would foster the spirit Dr. Whately complains of. But considering the constitution of these Societies generally, I cannot conceive that they have such a lamentable effect. For putting out of the question those men, who are deeply imbued with prejudice before they enter the room, and whom therefore the debate will not affect, the rest will probably gain much additional knowledge about the matter in question, and if they do give a hasty verdict on the spot, they nevertheless have a spirit of enquiry aroused within them, which will not rest till they have further investigated the subject to their entire satisfaction. And even supposing they did not pursue such an investigation, but felt satisfied with their previous knowledge, I am not quite sure that a fixed opinion, even when incorrect, is not more desirable than utter ignorance or perpetual vacillation. But I am inclined to believe, somewhat perhaps paradoxically, that while debates compel men to reflect, the verdict passed at the conclusion does not represent the result of that reflection. Nay, so far from this being the case, I have known instances where the introducer of the motion has confessed, that the very evidence by which he hoped to maintain his cause, has satisfactorily convinced him that his own is not the right side of the case, and although by the laws of the Society he is compelled to support that side, the ultimate result is his conversion to the other.

These Societies then not only are peculiarly adapted for the exercise of innate oratorical talent, but they present the means whereby a man may secure fluency of speech, and make his tongue in very truth the interpreter of his mind. You classical men! are you ever at a loss in your translations for the particular word which will exactly suit the case? Here is your remedy. And you mathematical men, who do not get up your book-work by heart! do not you sometimes find a difficulty in expressing your meaning in good English? Here then is your remedy. By speaking at the debates you will gain power over your native tongue, and learn to express in plain good sense, what before cost you so much labour and was so unintelligible after all. And there is another advantage they present, which should also be taken into consideration. I mean the incentive to the investigation of truth. It often requires considerable reading and research to make a good speech, and if the debater is thereby induced to extend his knowledge of our literature, he may reap no slight benefit. Let him only bind himself never to make an assertion against his better judgment. Let him beware of inconsistency, and of speaking without sufficient knowledge of the subject. Let him not be discouraged at a few failures, but let him endeavour to speak at every debate, remembering what Fox used to say: "During five whole sessions, I spoke every night but one, and I regret only that I did not speak on that night too."

OUR EMIGRANT.

IT is a windy, rainy day—cold withal; a little boat is putting off from the pier at Gravesend, and making for a ship that is lying moored in the middle of the river; therein are some half-dozen passengers and a lot of heterogeneous looking luggage—among the passengers and owner of some of the most heterogeneous of the heterogeneous luggage is myself. The ship is an emigrant ship, and I am an emigrant.

On having clambered over the ship's side and found myself on deck, I was somewhat taken aback with the apparently inextricable confusion of everything on board—the slush upon the decks, the crying, the kissing, the mustering of the passengers, the stowing away of baggage still left upon the decks, the rain and the gloomy sky created a kind of half amusing, half distressing bewilderment, which I could plainly see to be participated in by most of the other landsmen on board—honest country agriculturists and their wives looking as though they wondered what it would end in—some sitting on their boxes and making a show of reading tracts which were being presented to them by a methodistical looking gentleman in a white tie; but all day long they only had perused the first page, at least I saw none turn over the second.

And so the afternoon wore on, wet, cold, and comfortless —no dinner served on account of the general confusion— fortunately I was able to seize upon some biscuits. The emigration commissioner was taking a final survey of the ship and shaking hands with this, that, and the other of the passengers—fresh arrivals kept continually creating a little additional excitement—these were of saloon passengers who were alone permitted to join the ship at Gravesend. By and by a couple of policemen made their appearance and arrested one of the passengers, a London cabman, for debt. He had a large family and a subscription was soon started to pay the sum he owed. Subsequently a much larger subscription would have been made in order to have him taken away by any body or anything—I, who at the time was not a subscriber, not knowing that a subscription was on foot, have often congratulated myself since, that New Zealand has not got to blame me in any way for the emigration of Mr. G—.

Little by little the confusion subsided. The emigration commissioner left; at six we were at last allowed some victuals—unpacking my books and arranging them in my cabin filled up the remainder of the evening, save the time devoted to a couple of meditative pipes—the emigrants went to bed—and when at about ten o'clock I went up for a little time upon the poop, I heard no sound save the clanging of the clocks from the various churches of Gravesend, the pattering of rain upon the decks, and the rushing sound of the river as it gurgled against the ship's side.

Early next morning the cocks began to crow vociferously. We had about sixty couple of the oldest inhabitants of the hen-roost on board, which were destined for the consumption of the saloon passengers—a destiny which they have since fulfilled: young fowls die on shipboard, only old ones standing the weather about the line—besides this the pigs began grunting and the sheep gave vent to an occasional feeble bleat, the only expression of surprise or discontent which I heard them utter during the remainder of their existence, for now alas! they are no more. I remember dreaming I was in a farm-yard and woke as soon as it was light. Rising immediately I went on deck and found the morning calm and sulky—no rain, but everything very wet and very grey. There was Tilbury fort so different from Stanfield's dashing picture. There was Gravesend which but a year before I had passed on my way to Antwerp with so little notion that I should ever leave it thus.—Musing in this way and taking a last look at the green fields of old England, soaking with rain and comfortless though they then looked, I soon became aware that we had weighed anchor, and that a small steam-tug which had been getting her steam up for some little time had already begun to subtract a mite of the distance between ourselves and New Zealand. And so, early in the morning of Saturday, October 1st, 1859, we started on our voyage.

Here I must make a digression and once for all fairly apologize to the reader. Let me put him in my own position.

The thermometer shall be 45° Fahrenheit in his cabin, although it is the begining of January, and he is in Lat. 47° South; that is to say, though he is in Paris at the beginning of July. He shall be clad in full winter plumage, moreover he shall have a great coat on, and a comforter round his neck. Yet the continuance of the cold many days, or rather weeks, with insufficient means of exercise, shall have covered his fingers with chilblains and almost chilled his toes off. He shall be so wedged between his washing-stand, his bunk and a box, that he can just manage to write without being capsized every other minute, outside he shall have a furious S.W. gale blowing. His ship shall be under nothing but a closed reefed main-top-sail, close reefed fore-top-sail, reefed fore-sail and top-mast-stay-sail, shall have been as near on her beam ends twice already within the last hour as she could well be—he shall every now and then feel a tremendous thump and see the water pouring over the little glass pane let into the roof of his cabin, thus becoming cognizant of the fact that a heavy sea has broken right over the poop— and then he shall be required to be coherent, grammatical, and to write that pure and elegant style of English for which *The Eagle* is so justly celebrated. It cannot be done. Yet if I don't write now I shall not write at all, for we are nearing New Zealand, and I foresee that as soon as I get ashore I shall have but little time for writing.

To resume then—we were at last fairly off. The river widened out hour by hour. Soon our little steam-tug left us. A fair wind sprung up and at two o'clock or thereabouts we found ourselves off Ramsgate. Here we anchored and waited till the next tide, early next morning. This took us to Deal, off which we again remained a whole day at anchor. On Monday morning we weighed anchor and since then we have had it on the forecastle, and trust we may have no further occasion for it until we arrive at New Zealand.

I will not waste time and space by describing the horrible sea sickness of most of the passengers, a misery which I did not myself experience, nor yet will I prolong the narrative of our voyage down the channel; it was short and eventless. The Captain says there is more danger between Gravesend and the Start Point (where we lost sight of land,) than all the way between there and New Zealand. Fogs are so frequent and collisions occur so often. Our own passage was free from adventure. In the Bay of Biscay the water assumed a deep blue hue, of almost incredible depth; there

moreover we had our first touch of a gale—not that it
deserved to be called a gale in comparison with what we
have since had—still we learnt what double reefs meant.
After this the wind fell very light and continued so for
a few days. On referring to my diary I preceive that on the
10th of October, we had only got as far South as the
forty-first parallel of Latitude. And late on that night
a heavy squall coming up from the S.W. brought a foul
wind with it. It soon freshened and by two o'clock in
the morning the noise of the flapping sails as the men
were reefing them and of the wind roaring through the
rigging was deafening. All next day we lay hove to
under a close reefed main-top-sail—which being interpreted
means that the only sail set was the main-top-sail and
that that was close reefed, moreover that the ship was
laid at right angles to the wind and the yards braced sharp
up. Thus a ship drifts very slowly, and remains steadier
than she would otherwise, she ships few or no seas, and
though she rolls a good deal is much more easy and safe
than when running at all near the wind. Next day we
drifted due north, and on the third day the fury of the
gale having somewhat moderated we resumed—not our
course but a course only four points off it. The next
several days we were baffled by foul winds, jammed down
on the coast of Portugal; and then we had another gale
from the south, not such a one as the last, but still enough
to drive us many miles out of our course, and then it fell
calm which was almost worse, for when the wind fell the
sea rose and we were tossed about in such a manner as
would have forbidden even Morpheus himself to sleep:
and so we crawled on till on the morning of the 24th of
October, by which time if we had had anything like luck
we should have been close on the line, we found ourselves
about thirty miles from the Peak of Teneriffe becalmed.
This was a long way out of our course which lay three
or four degrees to the westward at the very least, but
the sight of the Peak was a great treat, almost compensating
for past misfortunes. The island of Teneriffe lies in Lat-
titude 28°, Longitude 16°. It is about sixty miles long,
towards the southern extremity of the island the Peak
towers upwards to a height of 12,300 feet, far above
the other land of the island, though that too is very elevated
and rugged. Our telescopes revealed serrated gullies upon
the mountain sides, and showed us the fastnesses of the
island in a manner that made us long to explore them:

we deceived ourselves with the hope that some speculative fisherman might come out to us with oranges and grapes for sale. He would have realised a handsome sum if he had, but unfortunately none was aware of the advantages offered and so we looked and longed in vain. The other islands were Palma, Gomera, and Ferro, all of them lofty, especially Palma; all of them beautiful; on the sea board of Palma we could detect houses innumerable, it seemed to be very thickly inhabited and carefully cultivated. The calm continuing three days, we took stock of the islands pretty minutely, clear as they were, and rarely obscured even by a passing cloud; the weather was blazing hot but beneath the awning it was very delicious; a calm however is a monotonous thing even when an island like Teneriffe is in view, and we soon tired both of it and of the gambols of the Blackfish (a species of whale), and the operations on board an American vessel hard by.

On the evening of the third day a light air sprung up and we watched the islands gradually retire into the distance. Next morning they were faint and shrunken, and by mid-day they were gone. The wind was the commencement of the north-east trades. On the next day (Thursday, October 27th, Lat. 27° 40′) the cook was boiling some fat in a large saucepan, when the bottom burnt through and the fat fell out over the fire, got lighted, and then ran about the whole galley blazing and flaming as though it would set the place on fire, whereat an alarm of fire was raised, the effect of which was electrical: there was no real danger about the affair, for a fire is easily extinguishable on a ship when only above aboard—it is when it breaks out in the hold—is unperceived—gains strength—and finally bursts its prison, that it becomes a serious matter to extinguish it: this was quenched in five minutes, but the faces of the female steerage passengers were awful. I noticed about one and all a peculiar contraction and elevation of one eyebrow, which I had never seen before on the living human face though often in pictures: I don't mean to say that all the faces of all the saloon passengers were void of any emotion whatever.

The trades carried us down to Lat. 9°. They were but light while they lasted and left us soon. There is no wind more agreeable than the N.E. trades. The sun keeps the air deliciously warm, the breeze deliciously fresh—the vessel sits bolt upright, steering a S.S.W. course, with the wind nearly aft: she glides along with scarcely any perceptible motion, sometimes in the cabin one would fancy one must be on dry land, the sky is of a greyish blue, and the sea silver grey, with a very slight haze round the horizon. The sea is very smooth, even with a wind which would elsewhere raise a considerable sea. In Lat. 19° Long. 25° I find we first fell in with flying fish. One generally sees most of these in a morning—they are usually in flocks—they fly a great way and very well, not with the kind of jump which a fish generally takes when springing out of the water, but with a *bonâ fide* flight, sometimes close to the water, sometimes some feet above it during the same flight. One flew on board, and measured roughly eighteen inches between the tips of its wings. On Saturday, November 5th, the trades left us suddenly after a thunder storm which gave us an opportunity of seeing chain lightning, a sight that I only remember to have seen once in England. As soon as the storm was over, we perceived that the wind was gone and knew that we had entered that unhappy region of calms which extends over a belt of some five degrees rather to the north of the line.

We knew that the weather about the line was often calm, but had pictured to ourselves a gorgeous sun, golden sunsets, cloudless sky, and sea of the deepest blue. On the contrary such weather is never known there, or only by mistake. It is a gloomy region. Sombre sky and sombre sea,—large cauliflower headed masses of dazzling cumulus towering in front of a background of lavender coloured satin,—every shape and size of cloud—the sails idly flapping as the sea rises and falls with a heavy regular but windless swell, creaking yards and groaning rudder lamenting that they cannot get on—the horizon hard and black save when blent softly into the sky upon one quarter or another by a rapidly approaching squall,—a puff of wind—"square the yards"—the ship steers again—another—she moves slowly onward—she slips through it—it blows—she runs—it blows hard—very hard,—she flies—a drop of rain—the wind lulls, three or four more of the size of half-a-crown—it falls very light—it rains hard, and then the wind is dead—whereon the rain comes down in a torrent which those must see who would believe. The air is so highly charged with moisture that any damp thing remains damp and any dry thing dampens: the decks are always wet. Mould springs up anywhere, even on the very boots which one is wearing, the atmosphere is like that

of a vapour bath, and the dense clouds seem to ward off
the light, but not the heat of the sun. The dreary monotony of such weather affects the spirits of all and
even the health of some, one poor girl who had long
been consumptive but who till then had picked up much
during the voyage, seemed to give way suddenly as soon
as we had been a day in this belt of calms, and four
days after we lowered her over the ship's sides into the
deep.

One day we had a little excitement in capturing a shark,
whose triangular black fin had been veering about above
water for some time at a little distance from the ship.
I will not detail a process that has so often been described,
but will content myself with saying that he did not die
unavenged, inasmuch as he administered a series of cuffs
and blows to any one that was near him which would have
done credit to a prize-fighter, and several of the men
got severe handling or, I should rather say, "tailing"
from him. He was accompanied by two beautifully
striped pilot fish,—the never failing attendant of the
shark.

One day during this calm we fell in with a current—
the aspect of the sea was completely changed. It resembled
a furiously rushing river—and had the sound belonging
to a strong stream only much intensified. The empty
flour casks drifted ahead of us and to one side; it was
impossible to look at the sea without noticing its very
singular appearance—soon a wind springing up raised the
waves and obliterated the more manifest features of the
current, but for two or three days afterwards we could
perceive it more or less. There is always at this time
of year a strong westerly set here. The wind was the
commencement of the S.E. trades and was welcomed by
all with the greatest pleasure—in two days more we reached
the Line.

We crossed the line in Long. 31° 6', far too much to the
west, after a very long passage of nearly seven weeks—
such a passage as the Captain says he never remembers
to have made; fine winds however now began to favour us,
and in another week we got out of the tropics having had
the sun vertically over heads, so as to have no shadow,
on the preceding day. Strange to say the weather was
never at all oppressively hot after Lat. 2° north or thereabouts. A fine wind or even a light wind at sea removes
all unpleasant heat even of the hottest and most per-

pendicular sun. The only time that we suffered any
inconvenience at all from heat was during the belt of calms;
when the sun was vertically over our heads it felt no hotter
than an ordinary summer day. · Immediately however
upon leaving the tropics the cold increases sensibly, and
in Lat. 27° 8' I find that I was not warm once all day. Since
then we have none of us ever been warm save when taking
exercise and in bed—when the thermometer is up at 50°.
I think it very high, and call it warm. The reason of the
much greater cold of the Southern than the Northern hemisphere is that there is so much less land in the Southern.
I have not seen the thermometer below 42° in my cabin,
but am sure that outside it is often very much lower. We
have almost all got chilblains, and wonder much what the
January of this hemisphere must be like if this is its July:
I believe however that as soon as we get off the coast of
Australia, which I hope we may do in a couple of days, we
shall feel a very sensible rise in the thermometer at once.
Had we known what was coming we should have prepared
better against it, but we were most of us under the
impression that it would be warm summer weather all
the way. No doubt we feel it more than we should otherwise, on account of our having so lately crossed the line.

The great feature of the Southern seas is the multitude of
birds which inhabit it. Huge Albatrosses, Molimorks (a
smaller albatross) Cape Hens, Cape Pigeons, Parsons, Boobies,
Whale Birds, Mutton Birds, and many more wheel continually about the ship's stern, sometimes there must be
many dozens, or many scores, always a good many. If
a person takes two pieces of pork and ties them together,
leaving perhaps a yard of string between the two pieces,
and then throws them into the sea, one Albatross will catch
hold of one end, and another of the other—each bolts his
own end and then tugs and fights with the other Albatross
till one or other has to disgorge his prize: we have not
however succeeded in catching any, neither have we tried
the above experiment ourselves. Albatrosses are not white;
they are grey, or brown with a white streak down the back,
and spreading a little into the wings. The under part of
the bird is a bluish white. They remain without moving
the wing a longer time than any bird that I have ever seen,
but some suppose that each individual feather is vibrated
rapidly though in very small space without any motion being
imparted to the main pinions of the wing. I am informed
that there is a strong muscle attached to each of the large

plumes in their wings. It certainly is strange how so large
a bird should be able to travel so far and so fast without any
motion of the wing. Albatrosses are often entirely brown,
but further south, and when old, I am told they become
sometimes quite white. The stars of the Southern hemisphere
are lauded by some : I cannot see that they surpass or equal
those of the Northern. Some of course are the same.
The Southern Cross is a very great delusion. It isn't
a cross. It is a kite, a kite upside down, an irregular
kite upside down, with only three respectable stars and
one very poor and very much out of place. Near it however
is a truly mysterious and interesting object called the
Coal Sack : it is a black patch in the sky distinctly darker
than all the rest of the Heavens. No star shines through it.
The proper name for it is the black Magellan cloud.

We reached the Cape passing about six degrees south of
it, in twenty-five days after crossing the line, a very fair
passage—and since the Cape we have done well until a
week ago when after a series of very fine rains, and during
as fair a breeze as one would wish to see, we were some
of us astonished to see the Captain giving orders to reef
top-sails. The royals were stowed, so were the top gallant
sails, topsails close reefed, mainsail reefed, — and just at
10. 45. p. m. as I was going to bed I heard the Captain give
the order take a reef in the foresail and furl the mainsail—
but before I was in bed a quarter of an hour afterwards
a blast of wind came up like a wall, and all night it blew
a regular hurricane. The glass, which had dropped very
fast all day, and fallen lower than the Captain had ever seen
it in the southern hemisphere, had given him warning what
was coming, and he had prepared for it. That night we ran
away before it to the North, next day we lay hove to
till evening—and two days afterwards when I was commencing this letter we had just such another only much
worse. The Captain says he never saw an uglier sea in his
life, but he was all ready for it, and a ship if she is a good
sea boat may laugh at any winds or any waves provided she
be prepared. The danger is when a ship has got all sail set
and one of these bursts of wind are shot out at her. Then
her masts go over board in no time. Sailors generally
estimate a gale of wind by the amount of damage it does—
if they don't lose a mast or get their bulwarks washed away
or at any rate carry away a few sails they don't call it
a gale, but a stiff breeze : if however they are caught even
by a very comparatively inferior squall and lose something

they call it a gale. The Captain assured us that the sea never assumes a much grander or more imposing aspect than that which it wore on the evening of the day on which I commenced this letter. He called me to look at it between two and three in the morning when it was at its worst; it was certainly very grand, and made a tremendous noise, and the wind would scarcely let one stand, and made such a noise in the rigging as I never heard: but there was not that terrific appearance that I had expected. It did'nt suggest any ideas to one's mind about the possibility of anything happening to one. It was excessively unpleasant to be rolled hither and thither, and I never felt the force of gravity such a nuisance before; one's soup at dinner would face one at angle of 45° with the horizon, it would look as though immoveable on a steep inclined plane, and it required the nicest handling to keep the plane truly horizontal. So with one's tea which would alternately rush forward to be drank and fly as though one were a Tantalus, so with all one's goods which would be seized with the most erratic propensities,—still we were unable to imagine ourselves in any danger, save one flaxen headed youth of two-and-twenty, who kept waking up his companion for the purpose of saying to him at intervals during the night, "I say N— is'nt it awful", till finally N—silenced him with a boot. While on the subject of storms I may add that a Captain, if at all a scientific man, can tell whether he is in a cyclone, (as we were) or not, and if he is in a cyclone, he can tell in what part of it he is, and how he must steer so as to get out of it; a cyclone is a storm that moves in a circle round a calm of greater or less diameter, the calm moves forward in the centre of the body of the cyclone at the rate of from one or two to thirty miles an hour. A large one 500 miles in diameter, rushing furiously round its centre at a very great pace, will still advance in a right line only very slowly indeed. A small one 50 or 60 miles across will progress more rapidly. One vessel sailed for five days going at 12, 13, and 14 knots an hour round one of these cyclones before the wind all the time, still in the five days she had made only one hundred and eighty-seven miles in a straight line. I tell this tale as it was told to me, but have not studied the subject myself. Whatever saloon passengers may think about a gale of wind, I am sure that the poor sailors who have to go aloft in it and reef topsails cannot like it much.

I think I have now mentioned the principal physical

phenomena that I have noticed so far: I will now add a few
words about the preparations, which I should recommend
any one to make who felt inclined to take a long sea voyage
like myself; and give him some idea of the kind of life he
will have on ship-board.

First and foremost—he *must* have a cabin to himself unless
he is provided with a companion whom he knows and can
trust. I have shuddered to think what I should have done
had I been an inmate of the same cabin with certain of my
fellow passengers, men with whom one can be on very good
terms when not compelled to be too much with them, but
whom the propinquity of the same cabin would render, when
sober, a nuisance—when drunk, madly drunk, as often
happens, simply intolerable. Neither again would it have
been agreeable to have been awoke up during a hardly
captured wink of sleep to be asked whether it was not
awful—that however would be a minor inconvenience.
Believe me no one will repent paying a few pounds more
for a cabin to himself, who has seen the inconvenience that
others have been put to by having a drunken or disagreeable
companion in so confined a space. It is not even like a large
room. Comfort is a great thing. And when a man can
fairly have it, he is surely reprehensible if he does'nt. On
a sea voyage comfort makes more difference than it does on
land. A man who is uncomfortable is almost sure to begin
longing for the end of the voyage: he becomes impatient,
and an impatient man is no good at all. If he is unoccupied,
he is worse: if occupied, whatever he is doing, the idea
that it is still so much, or that it is only so long to the end of
the voyage is perpetually presenting itself to him. He can't
fix his attention, and so three months of valuable time are
protracted into a dreary year, often because provision has been
neglected for a few little comforts which a man might easily
have. Most men are slaves to something. By slaves I mean
they don't like going without it whatever it may be—
though they will forego every thing else and rush through
fire and water without a murmur, provided it be left; Galton
tells us that the Cape servant is a slave to a biscuit and cup
of coffee—that on this you may do anything with him and
lead him up to death's door—that if you stop it for three
days he is ripe for mutiny. Assuredly however bad it may
be to be a slave to any such thing, ship-board is not the place
to commence leaving it off. Have it, if you can honestly.
Have plenty of books of all sorts: solid and light. Have
a folding arm-chair—this is a very great comfort and very

cheap, what I should have done in the hot weather without it I don't know, and in the bush it will still come in handy. Have a little table and common chair—these I have found the greatest luxury possible: those who have tried to write or seen others try to write from a low arm-chair at a washing-stand won't differ from me; besides no man can read a hard book in an arm-chair, and give it the attention it merits. Have a disinfecting charcoal filter, a small one will do. Ship's water is often bad, and the ship's filter may be old and defective. My filter has secured me and others during the voyage a supply of pure and sweet tasting water when we could not drink the water supplied us by the ship. Take a bottle or two of raspberry vinegar with you, about the line this will be a very great luxury. By the aid of these means and appliances I have succeeded in making myself exceedingly comfortable; I should like to have had a small chest of drawers instead of keeping my clothes in a couple of boxes, and should recommend another to get one; a small swinging tray would be very nice. The other cabin fittings are matters of course—bed, bedding, washing-stand, looking-glass, bookshelves, lamp, and piece of carpet. A ten-pound note will do the whole well, including the chest of drawers. The bunk should not be too wide—one rolls so in rough weather; of course the bunk should not be athwartships if avoidable. No one in his right mind will go second class, if he can by any hook or crook whatsoever raise money enough to go first.

On the whole I should consider that the discomforts of a sea voyage have been very much overrated. I have enjoyed the passage exceedingly so far and feel that I have added a larger stock of ideas to my previous ones than I ever did before in so short a time—one's geography improves apace, numberless incidents occur pregnant with interest to a landsman; moreover there are so many on board who have travelled far and wide that one gains a very great deal of information about all sorts of races and places— one finds things becoming familiar to one as household words, which one had hitherto regarded afar off as having no possible connection with oneself—which books had to do with—but which would never be impressed upon one's own mind, by the evidence of one's own senses. A very great many prejudices are done away with, and little by little one feels the boundaries of the mind enlarging. My chief study has been Gibbon's History of the Decline and fall of the Roman Empire—a book which I cannot sufficiently recommend to those who like myself have been intimidated from commencing before owing to its large extent. The second and third volumes have I think pleased me most. I should say these two volumes would be especially useful to those who are thinking of taking orders. That portion I mean commencing with the progress of the Christian religion and ending with the accession of Marcian. One effect of a sea voyage is perhaps pernicious, but it will very likely soon wear off on land. It awakens an adventurous spirit and kindles a very strong desire to visit almost every spot upon the face of the globe. The Captain yarns about California, and the China Seas. The doctor about Valparaiso and the Andes,—another raves about Owyhee and the islands of the Pacific, while a fourth will compare nothing with Japan. The world begins to feel very small when one finds that one can get half round it in three months, and one mentally determines that one will visit all these places before one comes back again, not to mention a good many more.

As I have already extended this letter to a considerable length, I will close it here, and send the remainder of our adventures with my first impressions of New Zealand as soon as ever I can find time to put them on paper after my arrival. We are all rather downhearted at present, for ever since the last gale, now a week ago, it has been either dead calm, or the next thing to it, and there are now less signs of wind than ever. I suppose however that like all other things the voyage will come to an end sometime—somehow.

PAST AND FUTURE.

Oh present moment, priceless point of time!
  Shall ever mortal learn to know thy worth?
In gazing on the pageantry sublime
  Of future scenes that Fancy shadows forth,
Or brooding on the past, how seldom seen
The chain of golden moments hung between!

Pondering thus, I had a dream
  On the Old Year's dying day,
Methought I arose with the morning beam
And wandered by a lonely stream
  On the moorlands far away.

I gazed around, and a dismal sight
  Before my eyes was spread,
The sun shone out with a lurid light,
But the earth below was dark as night
  As though the world were dead.

Through blackened rocks and weedy slime
  I sped my fated way,
And methought I heard a voice sublime—
"This is the land where the tyrant Time
  Can never use his sway."

Away and away like a restless wave,
  Till the wind began to blow,
And I came at last to a gloomy cave
As the sun sank suddenly into the grave
  Of the chaos spread below.

The night was rough, my feet were sore,
  I entered the cavern vast,
Careless I sank on the slimy floor,
Near to a massy dungeon door
  That echoed the howling blast.

But soon I was roused, for a stranger sound
  Saluted my weary ear,
Of iron hoofs on a stony ground
And clanking chains, I looked around,
  For the sound came loud and near.

I gazed through the seething and driving storm
  Of sleet in its frantic speed,
And boding thoughts began to swarm
As I saw advance the dusky form
  Of a man on a duskier steed.

Of an aged man with armour black,
  And a beard as white as snow,
The weight of time had bent his back,
In hollow voice he cried—" alack
  And alas for my year of woe."

And on he came with the iron clank
  Of his steed of dusky hue,
Till he came to the dungeon dark and dank,
Where poisonous weeds and creepers rank
  In wild profusion grew.

Then slowly opened the dungeon door,
  And a dismal groan it gave,
As the savage blast through the cavern tore
The horse and his rider were borne before
  And closed in their gloomy grave.

I fell asleep,—and many a dream
  Of the year that had passed away
Flowed through my mind like the lonely stream,
Till morning came, and the sun's glad beam
  Illumined the New Year's day.

I hastened forth, for the earth was bright
  And sadness was changed to glee,
Woodlands were teeming with life and light,
The rocks were white, and the glorious sight
  Had wrapped me in ecstacy.

And gaily on the morning air
  The sound of music flew,
The bugle strains of the coming year,
And now a vision bright and fair
  Arose to my dazzled view.

A Spirit on a shining steed
 Rose up from the cavern's rocks,
With a swell of his trumpet, o'er mount and mead
Away he soared with the lightning's speed,
 And scattered his golden locks.

Then a voice from the cavern I heard exclaim—
 "Oh mortal why wait you here?
Fly, fly to the country from whence you came,
Joy, wealth and prosperity, wisdom and fame,
 Must be asked from the *Future* Year."

"Go, follow him now while his powers are rife,
 Ere ever this year be sped
His brow will be darkened with sorrow and strife,
And armour be donned for the battle of life,
 And Time will have silvered his head."

"For he is the Present and I am the Past—
 The ghost of the Year that is dead,
Then seize on the Present and follow him fast,
And all his bright glories may bless you at last
 When others have vanished and fled."

"S. Y."

THE SUNBEAM.

THIRTY years ago Wilfred Hall was standing. Time, if left to himself, will soon crumble an old hall into common dust with that beneath it; yet, scarcely in thirty years. So that if Wilfred Hall had not been burnt, the curious reader might have gone to look at it—if I had given him much clue to its locality; in which case I should have been very careful to keep the secret, for reasons known to myself. As it is, it is little matter. For twenty years ago Wilfred Hall was burnt; causing no regret, as far as I could hear, save only to one solitary artist, who had half finished a sketch of it. Had the sketch been finished, it might have stood at the head of this tale of a sunbeam; but now I shall have to describe the old hall.

A mile away was a little town. Through a long line of cottages ran the main road, climbing a wooded hill; on the hill stood the church. Then the road descended the hill again, at the other side, winding through the woods; and led away to a distant city. Here and there, as it went on, quiet picturesque lanes branched off along the hill sides, or down the valleys. At the entrance of one of these lanes might have been sometime a hall gate. For there stood two mouldering neglected gate pillars, with armorial bearings; a stag at gaze, looking stiffly from a shield, disfigured by time and vagrant hands; and on the top of each pillar a hooded hawk; but no gate to swing now even on rusty hinges. Wandering down the lane, where no vehicle seemed to have travelled for a century,—for the grass grew rich as pasture fields, and the hedgerows were wild and neglected— you came, after ten minutes stroll, in sight of a lonely hall, set low in the hollow of a hill with woods climbing up behind it, and level lands in front:—the very hall I tell you of.

Weeds grew in the gravel walks and had grown there many a year. Weeds grew on the door steps, in cracks and

K

crevices: in every window niche flourished rare green moss:
and the hundred-eyed lichen spread its yellow plates on the
hollow broken roofs. The steps were black and sunk; and
the porch, to say the least, was dangerous. The windows
seemed dirtied by design, to keep out as much light as
possible. Even the large oriel, of coloured glass, which had
once lighted the main hall, was stuffed here and there
with rubbish in broken panes, to keep out the wandering
wind.

Who should live here but the old bookworm, Sir Wilfred
Wilfred! Here he lived, and continued to live, or rather
perhaps to die; with a solitary servant, and one other inmate;
hid in dusty tomes, sapping continually. Few guests had
he. Many who came were not so welcome. Warily the
servant's face reconnoitred if you knocked: and little chance
of admittance had you, if you looked like a creditor. For
the wealth Sir Wilfred possessed was not coin of the realm.
But if you came with an old book, or a musty parchment,
then the good gentleman was at home; and you a welcome
guest, to stay as long as you liked.

From four or five in the morning to the same hour in the
evening Sir Wilfred slept. Little joy had he in the sunshine
and singing birds. He never went to lie on a summer day,
plucking bits of grass. He never went to watch the lady-bird
on a sprig of may, and teaze it to split its scaly coat, and
spread the wings of gauze. For his heart was dried up.

From four or five in the evening to the same time next
day he pored over strange books. He sat in slippers and a
morning gown, which was never worn in a morning; and the
gown was tightened about his lean shapeless waist with
something like a rope; as if his study were a monk's cell,
and this his fasting costume. He wore large oval spectacles
over his little bat eyes; and he smoked a foreign weed,
horrid man! not to the annoyance of many ladies though, for
he saw but one; who got used to it in time.

His study, though containing nothing but what was old,
including his worthy self, was yet a novelty. From the
mouse-eaten wainscot to the somewhat lofty roof books were
piled in shelves. In one corner stood a crazy ladder, up
which Sir Wilfred climbed, at the risk of breaking his neck.
Long cases of books lay about the carpetless oak floor; made
so as to be removed with the greatest possible convenience;
though the fire found them in that same place, when it
laughed and leaped to burn them. Heaps of books tumbled
about on each side the comfortless hearth. His very chair

was a layer of folios : and his only table was a huge packing-case, in which many curious manuscripts were stowed away. There he sat, with a greasy lamp, hour after hour, an unwashed, benighted mortal; rooting up treasured things, like old coins, out of heaps of Dryasdust; and burying them as a miser would, in the dull earth of his human brain. Not till streaks of dawn quickened the blackbird's heart did he seek the needful sleep. Then, when the windows glimmered, and his lamp grew dim with the better-shining light, he would leave his study; to thread his way up the crazy stairs, through layers of dust-covered folios, from the great hall to the second landing. Sir Wilfred Wilfred, with his meaningless, withered face. Once he had been a boy. How his life had slipped away! he had become a phantom of humanity; going and doing to day as yesterday; the grey twilight of the house. But there was a sunbeam.

How I seem to slip back through the mazes of thirty years. Take a look at the hall. Branching antlers, and rust-eaten arms: coats of steel, and spears. But chiefly books. Shelves of labelled volumes stretched from side to side; with jutting unetherial wings here and there, to gain more room : till the place was quite a labyrinth, where the thoughtless bride of old might have concealed herself as effectually as in a certain oak chest. And there, at a little table, on which the morning sun through the painted window played with crimsoned light; dreaming over some romance; whiling away, as best she could, the companionless weary hours; the sunbeam might have been seen :—his daughter, of course.

Her blue dreaming eyes looked as if they knew little of what was going on in the world. Her hair fell in half neglected ringlets, bright and thick; and was as golden as I dare make it now, when it is no longer fashion to go *flavis oapillis*. Had these been the days of Horace, I should have spoken the whole truth without concealment; and told you that her hair was as golden-bright as a sunset bar of gold; yellow as the fabled sands which Tagus river used to flow over, but has long since washed away. Her face was sweet and sad; like such a face as Sir Calidore the Courteous would have delighted to rescue; pained in his gracious heart to see it, looking beseeching to him across some imprisoning moat. Her blushed cheek would lean on her white blue-veined hand, many a weary morning; as she sat in a silken gown, white, with threads of gold, that wound into sapless flowers, about the golden belt; a treasure Sir Wilfred had purchased for its quaintness and antiquity.

K 2

As when a little mist forms about a brook, in a valley with closing hills; and by and by widens and widens, and thickens and gathers strength, and fills the valley at last with a grey dreamy haze; so in the valley of time, about her little brook of life, had gathered the love-longing. Now it throbbed with its intensity, and the valley of time was widened by it into a mysterious void. In vain she had tried to satisfy it by loving the old repugnant man. The yearning had grown and grown. She read of knights and dreamed of knights. She had nothing to call her back to realities; and wandering desolate and cold about the desolate rooms, like a sunbeam that gilds a heath, she grew to live on dreams.

Then it was a stranger came. He was a student. He designed to spend the main energy of his life in producing an edition of Shakspere worthy of the immortal subject: and as Sir Wilfred possessed several rare editions of old plays, and was always willing to entertain a stranger on such an errand, he came to collate or copy them. Day after day he copied and stayed, and the bookworm saw little of him, in truth almost forgot him. Week after week he copied. But copying cannot last for ever. How precious the books must have been that it lasted so long!

His face was a long white intelligent face. Lines of thought were drawn along it, and made the mouth fine and delicate. The eyes were clear, flashing and dark; keen with a resolute resolve not to let life slip away unused: and over a broad high forehead fell black thick lustrous hair. The face was a striking face, and the sunbeam loved to linger on it.

For he copied in the hall. He used a small table, partly facing hers, screened a little by an angle of bookshelf. All the morning his busy pen went on—somehow not the slightest sound or stir he made escaped her—and when it was still awhile, she durst not look, though indeed sometimes she did; and when she did the mist grew restless. It was no wonder her fancy should dwell on him. It was no wonder that every day he puzzled her more and more. Living caged up there, like a rich-feathered foreign bird, thinking how her life was meaningless; somehow fancying, out of books, that a woman's life had meaning; having read in some dangerous modern dream-book that a fireside, and household duties, fitted a. woman in these days; thinking that her knight was long in coming; sometimes, in less dreamy moods, remembering that there were no knights now, but only men; liking the thoughtful mouth, and the speaking eyes; not feeling that looking at them wearied her; finding that the books and shelves and the painted window vanished if she met his glance; what wonder that the mist grew bright and restless, as if the sun had broken in upon it over time's hills.

At first they scarcely spoke, but by and by grew friendly. Many a close page was copied before her shyness left her. I cannot pretend to relate every little incident. One morning he leaned over her shoulder, and her hair brushed his face. "What might my fellow-student be poring over so earnestly?" said he, with elegant sweetness:—(his voice was the sweetest sound she had ever heard.) She leaned to let him see, and looked up laughing. "Mort D'Arthure, surely. And what is this morning's lesson about? maidenless Sir Galahad?"

"Not that saintly wanderer, student, but one almost as luckless," she answered, with an arch laugh. "For the poor Sir Palomide was just leaning against a tree, with his arms sorrowfully crossed, and tears in his knightly eyes, weeping for the lost Iseult."

"Happy man Sir Palomide had been, could fair Iseult have been his," said he; and went his way to the old Plays. What could he mean by that?

Every word of his was turned over and over; and many things he said perplexed her. Half unconsciously, half consciously, she got to mix him up with the longing. That morning, when he left his books, she stole to his little table. Her eyes wandered to his open manuscript. What is that graceful sketch, trailing down the side of the page? a figure leaning on its hand, in a long gown with a belt. Herself! it must be. Here he comes! quick! quick! But he caught her slipping away. And whether something in her look justified his conduct, I will not presume to guess; but after that he called her "Iseult."

Day after day passed: the copying went on still. So did the friendly talk. Things grew on apace. "This copying is tiresome work: hear how the thrushes sing. See how the sun smiles at us through the oriels. Will Iseult stroll out awhile?" why should Iseult refuse to stroll out, feeling no unwillingness?

That morning the brook we spoke of ran as merrily as a brook can. How fresh the sunshine was! and the grass was a richer carpet than any in the desolate house. The flowers about the fields had in them more delight than those

which crept in formal gold round the pages of " Sir Tristrem."
How the doves cooed in the old woods ! And they found
a nest of new-fledged birds—quite curious in its way.   And
what wonderful things he talked about ! He talked of life and
the busy world.   He told her of the women that lived in it.
He told her of a home he had, with a fireside warm and
snug, but no one to sit by it.   And a great many things
besides.   And he said " if you were Iseult, would you let
Sir Palomide stand weeping, with his arms so sorrowfully
crossed ?" and she said " no !" and blushed.

How her soul widened to take in the fulness of a woman's
soul, as he talked of noble women ; how the knights seemed
to go away after questing beasts, and make room for women
and men, in that dreaming fancy of hers ; how things grew ;
how fancies took form ; this were all too long to tell : here
is the upshot at once.

The copying ended suddenly one fine summer morning.
It ended all at once, when Sir Wilfred Wilfred might have
been asleep some two hours or more.   At any rate he was
fast asleep when the copying ended.   Why should the
student take his packet of manuscripts in his morning stroll
with her ? Perhaps a mere whim.   Away they went on the
usual walk, through the usual woods.   But they did not
linger as usual to examine the leaves and trees.   And after
a while they turned off.   As they crossed over the fields
Wilfred Hall was lost sight off : so that, of course, any
one in Wilfred Hall would lose sight of them.   Now they
enter the grass-grown lane.   They pass rather quickly,
perhaps, along the great road that goes to the little town.
They laugh merrily as they climb the hill.   Why, that
must be the church.   And the door is open too.   Did you
ever find an open village church door without going in ?
not you : nor did they.   But what can the priest mean,
standing there, inside the altar-rails, in his robes of office
white ? as the bride is not forthcoming, and a pity it would
be the priest should lose his fees,—no ! no ! no deceit ! it
is all arranged before.   Listen, as they kneel, what the
priest's words are :—" If any one see any just cause or
impediment, &c. &c."   But no one does.   At least, no
one comes to " declare it," if he does.   So the priest goes
on :—" let him hereafter for ever hold his peace."

And so, frowning readers, you hold yours.   It is all
right enough.   Sweet birds should not be kept in cages
at the pleasure of selfish men.   Let them fly away to their
proper homes, and find their mates.   Only many a smoky

volume went up in a certain study, before the old bookworm returned to his feast of books with zest: and many and many a weary day crumbled Wilfred Hall, before Sir Wilfred Wilfred found the same delight in the buried coins he dug up.

"O. B."

A WORD FOR WANDERERS.

"The man that hath no music in himself
Nor is not moved with concord of sweet sounds,
Is fit for treasons, stratagems, and spoils,
The motions of his spirit are dull as night.
And his affections dark as Erebus.
Let no such man be trusted."

ALLOW me to inform you, ladies and gentlemen, that a champion has at last arisen for the persecuted organ-grinders—one who fearlessly enters the lists against nervous old gentlemen, cross old ladies, invalids, policemen, studious men and lovers of peace generally. What though Mr. Nervus Phidgetts be at this moment helplessly wrapping his bald head in the bed-clothes and muttering smothered imprecations, ("Pop goes the weasel," every now and then cheerfully sounding below him, cruelly merry and livelily torturous, while a wandering dewdrop of cold perspiration trickles down the side of his imbedded nose):—what though Mr. Weakly Everill has just awoke from a short sleep snatched from departing night, with a bad head-ache, to the joys and sorrows of a suburb morning, and catches, faintly borne upon the breeze, the well-known strains of "Bobbing around," half a street away, but coming on surely and slowly, like the spider on the ceiling walking leisurely down the web to his prey as if meditating some slow torture for the victim-blue-bottle, and what though the papoosed watch at the back of the invalid's pillow already anticipates the coming melody, by ticking with devilish glee to the tune that is slowly approaching:—what though the studious Mr. Reading Jones, fists on ears and elbows on table, shuts his senses to the music and his heart to the upturned eye of the expectant grinder, and desperately reads pages and pages of his book, to find in the end that he remembers not one word of what he has been reading. For

"His heart was otherwhere,
While the organ shook the air,"

as the City Poet hath it:—and what though Mr. Punch himself, driven to despair, represents in his next number a persistent musician defying the policeman's command to move on, and so endeavours to urge the imbecile authorities to more effective steps:—what though all this be true, still I repeat, ladies and gentlemen, that a champion has at last arisen for the persecuted organ-grinders—I, a quondam grinder, am that champion.

But before I begin to defend my musical brethren, it becomes me to return the thanks and blessings of them and myself to our unprejudiced patrons, those of the public who have enjoyed and supported, or at least endured patiently our serenades; especially to him who, taking an interest in me, and I hope I may say without conceit, considering that I had a soul above organs, has lifted me from my low estate and given me education and honourable employment,—in fact has made me what I am.

Now, in the first place, I mean to say that our street music is generally in itself agreeable.—Be not prejudiced, ye lodgers who look down from above and lodging-house-keepers who look up, from kitchens below, at that olive-faced, brown-eyed, laughing Italian boy who gives you music at so small a charge.—Be not prejudiced, but open your hearts and ears to the melody, and ten to one you will enjoy it, a hundred to one you will not dislike it so much, as if you treat the boy harshly and fidget and annoy yourselves. Ulysses scarcely deafen'd his ears to the siren-songs more obstinately than you do to street music, or, more correctly, his companions' ears, for he seemed not to dislike the music himself, and listened attentively to the performance on the beach, though for safety he spliced himself to a mast, for fear the melody should be too much for his feelings and entice him overboard, as it had former voyagers, who,

> " By these prevailing voices now
> Lured, evermore drew nearer to the land,
> Nor saw the wrecks of many a goodly prow,
> That strewed that fatal strand;
>
> " Or seeing, feared not—warning taking none
> From the plain doom of all who went before,
> Whose bones lay bleaching in the wind and sun,
> And whitened all the shore."

No, take yon smiling baby in his nurse's arms for your example—see how the little fellow stretches forth his tiny arms and croaks with delight; while you, determined to make yourselves miserable, draw in your sensitive horns like insulted snails.

I, on the other hand, in my suburban abode, in the extreme confines of the suburbs where the town meets the country, twilight as it were, am charmed, as I sit in my shady little lawn this beautiful June afternoon, by an organ fragment floating from afar, louder and lower as the changeful breeze rises and falls—what with the bright blue sky, the sunlight shadow-chequered on the grass, flowers, a wandering butterfly or two, a light wind playing with the leaves of an open book, and a cigar whence thin blue smoke wreaths slowly ascend and vanish,—the effect is quite fairy-like and mystic.

In the second place, as to the construction of barrel-organs, though it be objected that turning a handle round and round is too automaton-like, artificial and ungraceful, yet there is certainly this advantage in it, namely that correct time is pretty sure to be kept—and if we have the music what matter how it is produced? it sounds well and in moderation is quite enjoyable; witness yonder nursery window crowded with juvenile faces eager to buy with a copper or two the music-ware of the approaching organ-man: he will unstrap his burden and grind any amount for the money, and then seek some more rural scene, rural enough at least to supply a hedge and bank, where he will rest awhile to eat his bread and cheese, and, meeting perchance with some similarly burdened companion, will gleefully gabble in his native tongue.

It might perhaps be a good thing if these young Italians could be formed into regiments and sent home as soldiers, especially in the present state of European affairs.* A certain amount of endurance they must have acquired by their rough wandering life here,—and they would find it less labour to carry military knapsacks and arms, used as they are to the weight of something like a young piano strapped on their backs. And, as for marching, many of them, from being so long accustomed to no other conveyance than their feet, would probably without much difficulty march any army off its legs, so to speak, in a few days.

But what induced me more than anything to say a word for my companions, was, because I have really been often struck by the great beauty of the music, and think that it

---

* This was written last long vacation, 1859.

is unjustly and with prejudice accused of being unbearable and inharmonious. Climb up Primrose hill some fine day and sit down on one of the benches, whence you may enjoy an extensive view, rows of houses, streets crossing each other, trees, lamp-posts, palisading, men, horses, and vehicles. From some spot in this panorama extending from Hampstead road to Primrose hill and the regions about Regent's park, you will probably hear one or more strains of wind-borne music, anon pausing and again arising in some nearer or more remote locality, approaching or retreating. If you are in a good humour and open to soothing influences of sunlight, bright skies, fleecy fleets of sailing clouds, and that fresh hilarity of spirits which results from a lofty situation, you will find that the effect is not bad.

I could relate many queer anecdotes, aye and affecting romances of organ-grinders, if it were worth while to do so and if space permitted, and I shall be glad to continue my subject, which is a very extensive one, in future numbers of *The Eagle*, if what I have now written meets with any approbation from its readers.

"F. V."

HOME FROM THE EASTER "VOLUNTARY."

I.

HAMMER, hammer, hammer; rattle, rattle, rattle over the flinty pavements of Cambridge; away from the frowning Senate-House, the old familiar colleges, staring shopfronts and often-trod streets. Away, away from the hazy atmosphere of learning and levity, with its mirage prospect of future fame or present pleasure; away from lectures and examinations, away from boating and cricket, away from congenial companions of every shade of opinion, of every degree of mental calibre; away at last and for ever from dear old Cambridge, severe, exacting old Cambridge, from Cambridge that I have so often pettishly regarded as an "injusta noverca," but whom I now feel to be an "alma mater."

On we jolt past Parker's Piece, and I hear the well-known sound of "ball, Sir" "thank you, Sir," "thank you, Sir, ball," and instinctively look around to see if there are not half a dozen balls of all colours dodging with all velocities about my bewildered head. Then as I lean back dozing on the cushion, I seem to hear above the rattle of the wheels and buzz of the town, a mysterious cry like the shouts of a far off nation, ringing through the air, and fancy catches the sound of "well rowed John's!" The buss bumps a stone, and on the action-and-reaction-are-equal principle I am bumped off the seat, and my reverie bumped out of my brain. Again I doze, and now the cheers of the Senate-House din my ears as the Senior Wrangler makes his debut with his young laurels.

I tumble into the railway carriage and coil myself up to doze again. I feel my fingers ache, and this reminds me that I have performed a great deal of writing in the last four days, far more than will "pay;" and this reminds me of a very good resolution I formed, not to make any "random shots," but to consider well what I was about, and use common sense as much as memory in my answers. And this

again reminds me that every good resolution of mine passes
through my brain twice and twice only, viz. when it is made,
and when I make the sage reflection "pity I did not think
of it at the time."

But here we are at Bedford with two hours to lionize.
I am going to make the best of the time, and if you choose
to accompany me, do not be offended if I indulge a little
" that forward delusive faculty, ever obtruding beyond its
sphere; of some assistance indeed to apprehension......—
but you do not want Butler in Bedford.

The first thing that strikes me is that here, in the very
centre of Saxondom, the appearance of the people is decidedly
Celtic. It is market-day, and I have scrutinized some hundreds of faces, town and country, and have seen but one
raw-beef visaged, indubitable Saxon. Perhaps the local
historian can account for the fact, for fact I believe it to
be, that the Bedfordians are decidedly Celts.

The gates of the great churchyard are locked, and I wend
my way towards a lovely little district church, standing on
a flowery mound of a churchyard, and conferring life and
beauty on a part of the town otherwise dull and uninviting.

"What is the name of this church"? I ask a passer-
by.

"I cannot tell you so much about that church, Sir, as
about this chapel on your right; this chapel is built on the
spot where the immortal John Bunyan used to preach, and it
is called Bunyan's Chapel." "Of the which John Bunyan,"
I said to myself, "you may add that you are a worshipper."
But why should I feel anything like anger at a stranger
who meant to be civil? or why should I feel taken aback
at suddenly finding myself in the presence as it were of the
shade of Bunyan the tinker and rabid dissenter? I may
meet his living self hereafter, and find that he has shuffled
off together with his mortal coil, his character of contumacy
and kettle-mending, as parts of the costume in which he
performed on this world's stage—this costume being no part
of the aforesaid John Bunyan. For it is as easy to conceive
that he might exist out of the costume he then wore (viz.
that of a factious tinker) as in it, that he might have animated a costume of a totally different grade and effect from that
he then wore, and that he might afterwards animate the same
or some new costume variously modified and organized, as
to conceive how he did animate his own costume. And
lastly, his getting out of all these several costumes would
have no more conceivable tendency to destroy the living

being, John Bunyan, than his getting out of the walls of
Bedford gaol.

But you are looking squeamish, what is the matter?

"You think Butler a very good thing *when it is asked for*
in the hall at St. John's or the Senate-House. Also you prefer the unadulterated article,— Butler without Bunyan."

Well, come along. What is here? We are in a land
of celebrities. Next door to Bunyan's chapel is another with
the inscription :

> "Erected by John Howard, the Philanthropist.
> He trod an open and unfrequented path to glory......"

So far the inscription, which is in fact an epitaph, is a most
happy one. Some dozen artless words tell of a good man's life,
death and glorious hope : and pass an honest censure on a
heartless world. There is no adulation in the former part, no
bitterness in the latter. They do what every epitaph on a good
man should do, they so inform us of his deeds as to raise in
us a just respect for the dead, and a hearty intention to follow
his example. It is the fault of our language and not of
the epitaph, that a nasty Greek word and a long Latin one
are used. They could not be avoided. No form of words
I think could be more pregnant, pithy and pointed than the
part quoted of the inscription. But when it goes on into
the details of the philanthropist's life and doings, thus allowing it to be supposed that Howard's fame was not universal,
the whole thing is weakened and debased. There should
not have been another word save the two lines,

> "Born at ——, in the County of ——, A.D.,
> Died at Cherson in Russia, A.D."

The contrast between a sunny nook of rich green England,
and the bleak cold Cherson plains would convey the intended
idea more perfectly and more forcibly than many words.

The church doors are fortunately open, and the sexton is
eager to shew the neat and well-arranged interior. He points
out what he says is the "only partic'lar thing" to be seen,
and certainly is rather "partic'lar." It is a tablet to the
memory of a young man who "when two years old hurt one
of his kidneys, from which he suffered great pain, and strange
to say when twenty years of age he hurt the same kidney,
from which he suffered a great deal more pain, and then
strange to say he died!"

There is another evidence of a Celtic origin,—each grave
is a flower-bed. The Irish deck the graves of their relatives
with cut flowers on Palm Sunday ; this is also done on the

borders of Wales. The Welsh plant the graves with flowers
and small shrubs, and tend them carefully. The custom
arose no one knows when, and it will probably never die, for
it is agreeable to the turn of mind of the people, which is
retentive, reflective, and pleasingly melancholy.

Usages with regard to the disposal of the dead are
perhaps less liable to change than any other. A man would
be thought unfeeling and even profane, who tried to force
his own notions respecting sepulture, &c., on the friends
of a deceased person, even when existing customs are absurd. Mankind generally wish to be " laid with their
fathers," and after death relatives are disposed to give that
wish its fullest possible meaning, and bury them as their
fathers were buried. The existence here, isolated, of this
pious and beautiful custom of planting the graves with
flowers, seems to intimate that the people here have a
common origin with the Celts, among whom the same custom
obtains.

Again I am in the train, now speeding away to Oxford,
the " City of Palaces." How strange it will be to wake
up in the morning and hear the tinkling of the chapel bells,
and the solemn toll of Great St. Mary's, in a University
where every face will be strange and myself an unrecognised
wanderer ! At every station University men get in ; our
carriage is full of Queens' men, Merton men, Balliol men,
and now comes in an All-souls man.

Here is the Oxford Station and here the Mitre " buss."
It is towards midnight, and the buss, being almost the
only vehicle, is overcrowded. Away it goes ! one feels as
though he were dragged along in a basket over a shingly
beach by some grinning lightning-footed imp of darkness,
while his Master makes congenial music by lashing simultaneously with his tail 101 deranged piano-fortes. That
man must have brains at least of granite who can endure
all this poetry of motion without inhaling enough of the
spirit of the " Vinum Dæmonium," to applaud (as my poor
bones are now madly doing) that expressive expression of
Coleridge's—

> " Pavements fang'd with murderous stones."

If any man desire to write a Prize Poem containing
very many such lines as this, or a few degrees stronger,
let him seek the inspiration resulting from half an hour's
pounding in a buss, over the shingly lanes of Oxford.

Where *is* Jehu driving to, that he has not got to the

Mitre yet? Alas! alas! Jehu lives at the Mitre, (likewise
Tiger and the Buss) where he has faithfully promised to
put me down "all snug." To the more effectual doing of
which he thinks it proper to see all his other passengers
safe home first. Meanwhile he generously drives me, seeing
I am a stranger, all round Oxford, without any extra charge!

II.

I cannot conceive of circumstances better suited to calm and
elevate the spirit, then to awake on a sunny Sunday morning
and find the early May breezes laden with incense pressing
for admission at the window, and then when you throw
open the casement and drink in the balmy breath of a
glorious morning, to hear the rich sound of bells answering bells filling the heavens with music, to feel that the day
is a holy day of rest for body and mind, and to see the
glad world turn out in its best array to do it honour.

I was sitting at breakfast at the Mitre when a heavy
" dong" thrilled through the air,

> " Swinging slow with solemn roar,"

as though it were the great sum and substance of steeple
music, and the merry chimes of the small bells were but
ancillary accompaniments.—It was plain that as I wished
to attend the service at St. Mary's I must hasten.

I shall not commit the folly of attempting to describe
the outside or the inside of this beautiful building. The
seats of the Heads, Fellows and M.A's (that is to say our
"Golgotha" and "Pit") are all on the ground-floor. They
and the Undergraduates' benches in the gallery were at
least half full. Many of the Undergraduates took notes.

The Bampton Lecturer was the preacher. Although
I had heard so many similar sermons at Cambridge, I could
not help being struck with the scholastic and apparently
secular nature of the discourse. After three years and
a half of University life, I still felt very much as Verdant
Green felt when he heard his first Oxford sermon. How
I thought all my non-University friends would stare to hear
a chapter of Persian history delivered from the pulpit on
a Sunday morning, and that too by a great teacher and
pattern of young parsons! How they would rub their eyes
and look again and again to see if they were in a Church
while they heard Xerxes proved (and greatly to the speaker's
satisfaction, whatever it might be to theirs,) identical with
somebody else; and were told that they could not suppose

Esther to be all her life-time Queen-regnant without doing grievous and irreparable wrong to some profane historian! (*" Profane!*—Why then be so tender of him? Well, really, we did expect to meet a little Puseyism at Oxford, and almost hoped or feared we should detect disguised Romanism,—but this Godless sermon, this insinuating sympathy with a profane man.")

After service I made my way to the Martyrs' Memorial. What a lovely little pile it is! Before coming close to it, I perceived this advantage of its hexagonal form, that thereby the figures of the three martyrs, having each a vacant space on either side, stand out with a cleanness and boldness characteristic of the men.

I looked at Cranmer first. He wears his archiepiscopal robes, has a cap on his head, and the pall on his shoulders: his right hand is slightly extended, in the left he bears his Bible, and he is in the act of walking forward with a resolute air. Beneath him is sculptured the pelican, the mystic bird that feeds its young with its own blood. I should have been glad to see (though perhaps it would appear too theatrical) *under his feet* a crumpled scroll representing his recantation.

Of the three martyrs, I have always felt my sympathies inclining most towards Latimer, that aged servant of God, too aged to argue or answer subtle argument, too aged to lay again, and therefore declining to disturb the foundation of faith, which, when his intellect was in full vigour, and with God for his helper, he had carefully and strongly laid. Too honest to mould his conscience into conformity with an uncongenial state of things, he would have done himself more violence than his enemies could inflict, had he done other than compose himself in the faggots and make his prophetic remark to " Master Ridley." I looked at the carved work about this figure, but did not discover torch, or candle, or any thing emblematic of " a burning and a shining light."

Ridley " explained all the authorities advanced against him of the spiritual presence only." The artist has represented Ridley with a countenance indicative of refined intellect and gentleness, shaped to a sweet triumphant smile, and looking up to heaven. This heavenward look is of the English style, I mean that Ridley is not represented, as most Madonnas are, with neck strained painfully backwards, and eye-balls almost hidden under the forehead, but with a natural and easily-sustained look a little above the hori-

L

zon, just enough to shew that it was directed beyond earth.

As I leaned over the railing, scrutinizing the figures and spelling the inscription, (it would have been more in keeping with the men, though perhaps not with the monument, if the letters were in plain English, that he who runs may read,) I thought, what a suitable place for such a martyrdom! In the very centre of England, in this great fountain of learning, whose motto is " Dominus illuminatio mea," close to the walls of Balliol, under the eyes of the Martyr who looks down from over the gateway of St. John's.—I said to myself " have not we of the Church of England, saints of our own flesh and blood? and can it be wrong, is it indeed anything but justice to give the title of "holy one" to those who by their faith and works and sufferings have shewn that it belongs to them? And might not this church close to the memorial, be as well called the " Martyrs' Church" as " Magdalene ?"

I turned towards St. John's. The time-worn statue of the Patron Saint looked down upon me—

> " O would some power the giftie gie us
> To see ourselves as others see us,
> It would from many a blunder free us,
> And foolish notion !"

Here was I idolizing men who resisted, even unto blood, Idolatry's first and gentlest approaches ; who through disgrace and torture made their way to death, and at the altar there flaming on this very spot, offered up all they had, even their precious lives, to the intent that we, knowing the sacrifice, might also learn the danger.

" M."

AN AUTUMN NIGHT.

The night is wild: the winds arise
    In gusts that make amid the corn
    A seething rustle; eastward borne
The clouds are roll'd across the skies;

And far away amid the night
    Upon those heavy folds on high
    The furnace-fires flash luridly,
And smoke-wreaths wave along in light

That ever varies: where the cloud
    Cleaves, now and then a star looks forth,
    As yonder, in the glimmering north,
Like pale-face peering from a shroud.

I pass along the village street:
    On one side with a gurgling low
    The brooklet's darken'd waters flow,
And from the lone hearth's smouldering heat

The merry cricket loudly sings:
    All else, beside the wind, is still.
        Thro' many a world of thought I range,
        And fancies, fetcht from far, and strange,
    Crowd round me as I mount the hill,
Beneath the dark night's wizard wings.

SCRAPS FROM THE NOTE-BOOK OF PERCIVAL OAKLEY.

SCRAP SENTIMENTAL.*

"YOUR affair in the last number was a great failure"—
such was the kind remark that recently hailed my
gratified ears—"a very great failure; not heavy, you know;
but feeble and slow in the extreme—evidently written in a
tremendous hurry, and with a desperate though most unsuccessful effort to be amusing. You're going on with the
trash, are you? well! I'm sorry for the subscribers; but
with such a beginning no one can accuse you of falling off
in the continuation."

Now, if there is anything thoroughly agreeable, it is
candid criticism; and if there is anything thoroughly satisfactory, it is to find one's arrow gone home to the mark—
Feeble and slow? just what I intended it to be! When
you are writing a thing in parts, it is *the* weakest proceeding
to make the first number a good one: you should begin
piano and *maestoso;* then introduce a gradual *crescendo;*
and wind up with an amazing *fortissimo.* I'm not going to
say through how many numbers this 'Scrap Sentimental'
will "drag its slow length along"—of course that rests
entirely with the discriminating Editors; but, if about
the middle of the said Scrap you don't find it highly interesting and entertaining,—why, I shall consider you a very
obtuse person, and request you never more to be Quarterly
reviewer of mine.

But among numerous other base insinuations thrust upon
me, one was of that glaring nature which must be at once
refuted. It implied that my precious diary, my *præsidium,*
yea! my *dulce decus,* had absolutely no existence whatever,
and was only alluded to in order to fill up space, and give

* *Continued from Vol.* II. *page* 63.

scope to a vapid self-laudation. To overwhelm the abominable miscreant who started such an idiotic notion, I am compelled to give a very brief extract from the valuable register in question.

EXTRACT, Vol. IX. p. 2041.[*]

July 24th.—Middle of the night. Dreaming hard, but far from comfortable. Have I a headache? no! it's Seraphina who is hammering a nail into my temples—rap, tap, tap—how she lays it on—look at Tugg standing by with a huge mallet to administer the final clinch—rap, tap, tap—well it's through my head now and well into the pillow—couldn't move if I were paid for it. "Don't, oh! please don't—" Hollo! whadsaay—pasnineclock—boosanhotwarr—no! no! drop it! drop it! dro-o-o—"

Somewhat later.—Agreeable change of vision—invasion the prominent idea. The French are come, are they? well, tell the coast-guard to go and help 'em to land. Get up? I'll see you further first—my word! just hear the cannon—bang, bang—they must be bombarding the house—bang, bang, bang.

"Now, Saville, I won't stand this; I've only just closed my eyes and I am not going to be disturbed for *you*. Dressed this half-hour? you know you've nothing on but a Barabbas and boots, and I wonder you're not ashamed of yourself. Going to a picnic? I won't go—make my excuses and say I've got typhus fever, then perhaps those blessed Tuggs won't bother me with another invitation. You won't leave off till I get up—well, to be rid of your loathsome presence I can make any sacrifice—you just be off, and make the tea, —no! I won't look sharp about it. I shall be three-quarters of an hour at least. Now, none of your coarse language—Vanish!"

* * * * *

[*] For a gentleman who owns to having "been twice plucked for Little-Go," Mr. Oakley's mathematical accuracy is rather surprising. In the previous description of his diary he mentions "one volume for each year and ten pages for every day"—from which *data* any of our readers may find that 2041 would really be *almost* the right number of page for July 24th, in any current year.—[EDITOR.]

11. 15 a.m. *Scene, the breakfast room—splendid morning —fresh breeze through the windows, which are doors, by the way, and both wide open. View on to the bay with Saint Symeon's Mount in the distance. Ernest Saville, Esq. in the chair, sans collar, tie, or waistcoat—his feet encased in embroidered slippers—ah! how changed from that Saville, who yesterday was pacing the esplanade with Eugenie St. Croix— to him enter his fellow lodger.*

S. Morning, my ancient: how about coppers, eh? rate of exchange rather considerable, I reckon.

O. Well, *you* needn't talk, after the state of mops and brooms you were found in last night.

S. Who wanted to fight the native in the billiard-room, because he wouldn't take points off you? A swell native too, who could have given you five-and-twenty and licked your head off.

O. Who wanted to embrace the Bobby, and addressed him familiarly as 'Robert, toi que j'aime!'

S. Who tried to put out the lamp, and was so screwed he couldn't swarm half-way up the post?

O. You'd better shut up, unless you want your ugly nose flattened.

S. Well, which of us began? oh! that's right, say it was me, do!

O. Put some of that grill in your calumnious chops, and then hand it over here.

S. Thank you; I an't got a jaded palate and a ruined digestion like some people; you may eat it all yourself, and more cayenne to your liver! The idea of a fellow at your age wanting stimulants in the morning!

And here Saville put a wine-glass full of brandy into his tea, by way of illustrating his own theory.

&c., &c.   *   *   *   *   *

Well! I won't bore you with any more of this, gentle Subscribers; we had been three weeks at Weremouth when it was chronicled as above, and had been passing our time extremely agreeably for many and various reasons.

First, as regards myself, I had by persevering sieges and blockades, so softened the adamantine heart of Miss Veriblue, that she not only allowed me to come in and out of their lodgings whenever I pleased, 'tame-cat fashion,' as the Colonel used to call it, but even regarded the aspirations of my doting and infatuated heart with a benignant eye. As

I mused on the difference this made to my personal comfort
I used often to catch myself quoting—

> Quem tu, Miss Veriblue, semel
> Intrantem placido lumine videris—

and so on. They liked going on the sea, both aunt and niece;
of course I had a sailing-boat constantly at their service: they
liked parties, concerts, dances and the like; I wearied myself
to get introductions and tickets, invitations and bouquets.
Seraphina liked trifling with amateur German—precious
little did this child know on the subject, but it was pleasant
enough to spend an hour of the sultry afternoon fancying
we were translating Schiller's Ballads, or that everlasting
" Die Piccolomini"—then she could play and sing like an
angel, and I could manage a feeble tenor enough for an easy
duett or two; she sketched in pencil and water-colours,
and delighted especially in attempting the same from nature;
I couldn't draw a stroke, but could cut pencils to perfection,
fill the little cup with spring-water, lie at her feet and bestow admiring criticism rather on the verge of flattery.
Altogether we found sundry congenial occupations, and
" happily the days of Thalaba went by." I had never
' spoken', thinking it judicious to wait for the right moment;
but everybody in the place regarded it as a settled thing, and
used to favour us with intelligent grins as they passed us
upon the Esplanade. By Jove, how handsome she used to
look in her plain straw hat and light muslin dress, with the
loose jacket over the same affecting nautical buttons; how
delicious in her ball-room attire when she stepped into the
carriage, with her blue opera-cloak drawn closely round her
neck, and the wreath on her sunny hair. Yes! I *am* a fool,
I know, to be dwelling thus on " hours of pleasure, past and
o'er;" but the Seraphina of my youthful days, and the present Mrs. T. are two quite distinct personages, nor am I
going to do myself out of a jolly reminiscence or two just
because she chose to be an Alice Grey of the most perfidious
description, and to earn from society at large the appellation
of an extremely sensible girl.

Now, as regards Ernest Saville, *he* had not been playing
his cards badly by any means: he was a man who never did,
whether they were the tangible cards of crafty whist and
reckless loo, or the metaphorical hand of the world's chances
and frantic flirtation. He got on well with the Colonel, who,
I fear, had been a sad reprobate once, and never undergone
a thorough reform of his anciept ways. Saville used to play

a good deal of billiards with him, and took good care to win but rarely; he would listen to the old boy's yarns, and give him a supply of new jokes and anecdotes, adapt himself with pernicious facility to all the ways of a *ci-devant jeune homme*, and in fact, make himself generally necessary to St. Croix's notions of comfort—so he was pretty well domiciled in their rooms, or else with them when out; and Eugenie and he very soon came to an understanding. Poor Eugenie! she had the material of a splendid creature, but foreign life and unsettled ways had done much to spoil her, nor was her father exactly the man to bring her up properly. Had her mother been living she would probably have been a different being; as it was, she was as thorough a flirt as she was perfectly beautiful. In the strange circumstances that followed, in which I myself was so helplessly floored (I can use no weaker expression), her nature underwent the most total change, and when I met her again a month or two since, I hardly knew her for the same person.

Ernest had a curious way of making odd acquaintances; he could be hand and glove with any one at the shortest notice, and was particularly fond of cultivating the 'plebeian order' as he loved to call them. At Weremouth he was great among the coast-guard, fishermen, and smugglers, between which three classes much amity and sociability appeared to subsist; one day I met him walking along the beach with a disreputable old ruffian in a pilot-coat and sou'-wester, the very bargee of nautical adventure, whom he afterwards described to me as captain of the spanking schooner Nancy, better known to the Revenue cruisers as Fly-by-Night, and the fastest craft in the channel. My acquaintance with the said ruffian was eventually promoted vastly beyond my own desires; but of that anon, for I shrink as long as possible from the details of our catastrophe.

Suppose we proceed at once to the picnic—it was a small affair; the Tuggs came in their open carriage, Mrs. T., I mean, and the charming Eliza, Miss Veriblue reclined in the same vehicle, Eugenie and the Colonel were on horseback, so were Seraphina, and Saville, and myself. A pleasant canter along the sands, emerging into a bridle-road across an open common, over which the breeze was sweeping in all its freshness, a friendly farm-house where our steeds were stabled, a scramble down the slippery side of Fairbeacon Slopes, and there we were in the scene of action. Sir John Trevegan's estate stretches along by the coast for many a mile; the leafy covers grow right down to the edges of the cliffs, and are intersected with sundry labyrinthine paths, all issuing into a most lovely glen, where the Wishing Well bubbles and sparkles for ever and a day, and then scatters bright brook and streamlets downward to the ocean ; a scene that should be consecrated to the Dryads and Naiads of the spot, or penetrated only by reverential visits of poet and artist—instead whereof it was constantly profaned by the ringing of laughter and the popping of champagne corks, and its sacred precincts defiled by unhallowed crumbs from Weremuthian picnics.

The carriage party arrived hot and dusty from the road, but the provisions came with them, which was certainly their sole redeeming point. After a slight refection, Seraphina of course was anxious to immortalise in water-colour a particular view, and no one but myself could shew her the exact site for such operation. Ernest and Eugenie went to hunt for sea anemonies, the Colonel lighted a cigar and sat making talk for the three ladies who were averse to locomotion. So you see all was peculiarly serene.

As for the seraph and myself, after losing our way once or twice, we emerged on a snug corner out of the breeze, where she immediately sat down and took an angel's-eye view of Fairbeacon woods, a bit of grey cliff beyond, a roof of a coast-guard station just visible above the trees, with a union-jack flying from the flagstaff, and a fishing-boat quite convenient in the distance, evidently the exact scene for an amateur pencil.

I lay at her feet serenely and lazily happy, talking and chaffing about any trifles that came uppermost, regretting John T.'s protracted absence, and indulging in flattering encomia on his mother. And I heartily wished that one could go on for ever as we had been for the last three weeks, without a thought of care to dim the brightness of those summer hours—but I knew that before long both Ernest and myself must be on the route again, and move from our pleasant quarters, so I gradually brought our talk round in this direction, taking for my ground-work that very new motto " all that's bright must fade," and hinted that in a week's time, or very little over, these " days would be no more."

" In a week's time ?" she exclaimed, pausing in a thorough wash which the refractory sea of her drawing had been doomed to undergo: "in a week's time ?" and she let her hazel eyes rest on mine till I thought they must be reading my inmost wishes.

" Yes, Miss Hawthorn, we have but little time to spare, and idling is a luxury neither Saville or I can well afford at present."

"And what's to become of my German? and our duetts? and the drawing lessons? and those delicious sails on the bay? and—oh! Mr. Oakley, we cannot spare you so soon."

"I fear," quoth I sententiously, "that I am more an interruption than a help to any of the virtuous practices in question, or at any rate my duties are so lightly insisted on, that you'll very easily find another to fill my place to admiration."

No answer; the washing out of the stubborn billows resumed with a vengeance.

" Mr. Tugg will be back at Weremouth next Friday, and I'm sure he is a most congenial companion," said I.

Still no reply, but by a slight mistake the brush has been dipped into the carmine, and the waves get suddenly " incarnardined."

"And a fellow who's getting on so well in his profession:" I added: "those naval men always carry everything before them, especially ladies' hearts, and it's always pleasant being consoled."

She was desperately angry now, and wouldn't lift her face: but all the same there fell a great big drop on the paper, a drop which was neither water nor colours; and I instantly felt myself a fiend in human form.

"Miss Hawthorn," I began, (as people in novels always do) "Seraphina, dearest Seraphina, dare I think that my presence gives you a moment of pleasure, (here I smiled an ineffable smile) or my absence will cause you a moment of pain, (here gloom the most profound overspread my visage) dare I think that to all my devotion you are otherwise than cold and—

"Cold!" said another voice, very different to those melodious accents I longed for; "cold! I should just think she must be: where's your shawl, child? Mr. Saville how could you let her sit there running the risk of bronchitis and toothache, and ticdoloureux, and I don't know what all!"

Miss Veriblue was the speaker, and indeed there was some truth in her remarks, but I was past thinking or feeling at the moment, except for a dull sickening sense of hope deferred. "Haw! haw!" said the Colonel, on whose arm Miss V. was leaning, "vewy—ar—domestic sort of corner—fwaid we're wather de twop pewhaps—"

He was a monster.

How we got home I hardly remember. Seraphina came in the carriage I believe, but I made some excuse for taking myself off, seeing that at the moment I was past talking also. So I rushed towards the farm-house, but, in passing up the glen, caught a glimpse of two very well known figures, a lady and a gentleman, sitting on the stump of an old oak tree, duly moss-covered, and there was an unmistakeable arm round an unmistakeable waist, and a straw-hat very close to a Spanish plume, and more in my haste I saw not—they had their backs to me and why should I disturb them? In five more minutes I was on Black Prince's back, and galloping him promiscuously home to his stables, in a style I should fancy he had never been ridden before along those Fairbeacon tracks.

"P. O."

BORES.

MANY and startling have been the theories advanced by botanists, naturalists and geologists, to account for the existence and propagation of the numberless species of animals and plants which are spread over the surface of our globe, but none of them are sufficiently comprehensive to account for the infinite diversities in the species of the genus "bore", and for their wide spread distribution :— to do this aright would perhaps require a genius greater than that of Darwin, and theories more universal in their application than those of development, or natural selection. We find bores everywhere;—we doubt not but that the African traveller, the Arctic voyager, and the Johnian under-graduate are equally pestered by them;—we have bores taciturn, bores talkative, bores social and bores political, besides a multitude of others whom it would be difficult to class, but who still belong to that numerous and disagree-able set of men, to whom we all at times feel inclined to say—

> "Stand not upon the order of your going,
> But go at once."

It is bad enough to have to spend an evening with the taciturn bore, to receive monosyllabic replies to all your questions, and to have your most witty remarks on things or persons, answered by a mere nod or shrug of the shoulders;—it is still worse, perhaps, to have to endure the volubility of the talkative bore;—but worst of all is the bore with a decided tendency to monomania, who can only talk of his pet subject, and that a disagreeable one. There's Jones, for example, otherwise a worthy pleasant fellow, who mars everything by his insane passion for mathematics;—(it is my firm conviction that he always carries a rigid rod instead of a walking-stick, and runs round the parallelogram mainly because it is a geometrical figure); when submitting to the infliction of a walk with him, and wishing, as is my wont, to admire the calm beauties of nature,—the stupendous scenery of the Gogs, the pellucid stream in Grantchester meadows, or the spreading forests of Madingley,—the incorrigible Jones dilates upon the beauties of the subject he is reading, puzzles my brains with mysterious allusions to Zenith and Nadir, and puts me into a fit of by no means easy reflection on the incomprehensible technicalities of mathematics.

Watkins, on the other hand, makes a point of visiting me just when I am most absorbed in the study of the treatises of Phear or Barrett, or most busy in digging for the roots of those fearfully irregular words, which I meet with in our Greek subject;—his talk is of boats and boating, and while I sit writhing under the infliction, I hear how 'two' screwed, 'three' did no work, 'four' did not keep time, 'five' caught three crabs, 'six' splashed, 'seven' was worse than useless, while 'stroke' was no better than he should be;—Watkins himself being the immaculate 'bow', who neither caught crabs, nor splashed, nor screwed. All things however have an end, so even Watkins' eloquence is finally exhausted, and he departs, leaving me to the pleasant reflection, that though he may be thought by some to be an agreeable companion, yet to me he is indeed " an unmitigated bore," and one whose step I dread to hear ascending my staircase.

Not only, however, are we bored by our firesides, and in our walks, but we can hardly attend a public meeting, or a debate in the House of Commons, without being bored by some would-be orator, who reminds us of nothing so much as of Moore's Comparison of Castlereagh with a pump—

> " Because it is an empty thing of wood,
> Which up and down its awkward arm doth sway,
> And coolly spout, and spout, and spout away,
> In one weak, washy, everlasting flood."

Instead, however, of going into further detail with respect to the different classes of bores, it will be as well to devote a little space to the consideration of the other side of the subject; for we must grant that bores are often exceedingly useful members of society.

We are indeed often too apt to stigmatize by the name of bore, any one who has some object, which he rightly feels to be an important one, in view, and who perseveres in his endeavours to attain it, in a way which tends in some slight degree, to the diminution of our personal luxury or comfort. It has been well observed that in these modern days of cheap

literature, the many read, but few think; there seems indeed
to be in the people at large, a spirit of indolence, (except of
course with regard to money matters,) which recoils from
a contact with unpalatable facts, and detests trouble of any
sort;—if not, how is it that in a debate, for example, the man
who gets up his case thoroughly, and is armed with figures
and statistics wherewith to defend his opinions, is generally
looked upon as a bore and coughed down accordingly?

Again, in the House of Commons, how wonderfully thin
is the attendance, when Indian affairs are to be discussed;—
it is true the subject may be of the highest importance,
the welfare of an Empire perhaps depends upon it; but, alas,
honourable members think it too great a bore to hear Col.—
or Mr.— speak on Indian difficulties, or British misgovern-
ment.

If we review the history of the world, we shall find
that many of the men whose names are now most illustrious
for their discoveries in science or art, or for the good which
they have, in other ways, done to their fellow men were
considered by their contemporaries as bores of the worst
order.

Was not this, think you, the feeling of many of the sages
and people of Greece and Rome, with respect to those who
strove to arouse them from a vain philosophy, or from
a listless ignorance;—was not this the feeling of the Papal
dignitaries, when Galileo exposed the errors of Aristotle,
or when Luther thundered against the Vatican;—were not
those considered bores, who, at a later period, clamoured
for a free press, and free institutions; and, lastly, was it
not by a system of laudable boredom, that Clarkson, Wilberforce, and their supporters in parliament, won the glorious
victory of humanity over Slavery?

In short, wherever any great and beneficial public act
has been accomplished, we find that it has generally been
effected by a consistent course of action, tending to one end,
by perseverance under difficulties, and by keeping the subject
continually before the people; and this mode of procedure,
although it may earn for its authors the unenviable appellation of bores, yet has its own reward in success, and should
tend to make us more thankful to that much maligned, and
insufficiently appreciated class of men.

"Q."

CORRESPONDENCE.

[We have been favoured with the following from a former Correspondent. We fear that he considers his censure or his approbation a matter of more importance than it is to Aquila or its contributors.]

Peace and goodwill to this fair meeting!
I come not with hostility, but greeting,
    Not *Eaglelike* to scream, but dovelike coo it.
        PETER PINDAR's *Ode to y*^e *Royal Academicians.*

J. to the Editors, Contributors, and Subscribers, greeting:

YES, my brethren, I am that J. who, in a past number of your highly esteemed periodical, favoured you with my gentle impressions regarding your powers of writing and your judicious application of the same. But, as my motto has already informed you, I have no intention of repeating the dose: no idea of answering that very pleasant fellow (an 'Earnest Grubber' I think he called himself) who sat upon me so effectually last time. If ever we meet, won't I 'overlay him with classicalities,' won't I 'look at him hazily through a pewter,' and puff smoke in his eye? Truly I am rejoiced that you have not taken in that extra touch of ballast which he seemed to recommend; but I meditate no further specimens of 'abusive criticism.' Fear not therefore, ye budding Dickenses, fear not ye incipient but feeble Thackerays, above all fear not, *irritabile genus poetarum.* Your first volume reposes on my shelves bound in calf and highly gilt, and with a most respectable accumulation of dust on its upper surface.

My present object is merely to send a line or two of congratulation to the ancient College and Domina Margareta ('on her knees in the hall' or otherwise). Three cheers for your wranglers of this year: plenty of them, not to say the highest BAR ONE: if trees coming down in the grounds have anything to do with it, you'll have a dozen sucking Newtons bracketed at the top next time! Three cheers for the Classics too, and more power to your youthful champion for next year's Tripos! Sorry to see none of you sharing in the Aquatic laurels at Putney, but you've pulled the old ship up to second on the river, which looks more natural ; and I understand there will be plenty of you to help in taking the shine out of Granta's sister next month at Lord's. So here's good luck to the Questionists and wishing them well through it, though fancying a man reading in the May term makes me fit to be knocked down with a straw.

I was up myself the other day, and the taste of Classic air moved me to write as above : and I went to the flower-show at two o'clock, and saw many flowers of the *genus* Eve, all in bewildering dresses and distracting bonnets : then I dined in hall, and thought the Lady Margaret table were a noisier lot than ever : then I returned to Trinity grounds and came to the conclusion that it was a crisis for the police to interfere : wound up the evening with the C. U. M. S. concert, where as usual the thermometer was 'riz,' and swearing at the same strictly prohibited : heard for the hundred and first time that a new Town hall was sadly wanted, and fancied there might have been a *little* less instrumental music ; where, oh ! where, was there any one to sing a tenor *solo* ?

My pipe is out, " and grace fearing of quarrels prohibits me to touch above three" sherry cobblers—so we bid you heartily farewell and much satisfaction out of the Long Vacation. Shall be right glad to see any of you that happen to be passing through Town next week. If you want my address enquire at the Butteries.

"J."

LIST OF BOAT RACES.

UNIVERSITY EIGHT-OAR RACES.

THURSDAY, May 10, (Second Division).

20	Caius 2	33	Trinity Hall 3
21	Lady Somerset 1	34	Catherine
22	1st Trinity 4	35	Jesus 2
23	Clare 1	36	Lady Somerset 2
24	3rd Trinity 2	37	Caius 3
25	Emmanuel 3	38	Christ's 3
26	Corpus 2	39	1st Trinity 5
27	Pembroke	40	1st Trinity 6
28	Queens' 1	41	Caius 4
29	Christ's 2	42	Corpus 3
30	Lady Margaret 3	43	Lady Somerset 3
31	2nd Trinity 3	44	Clare 2
32	King's	45	Queens' 2

FRIDAY, May 11, (Second Division).

20	Lady Somerset 1	34	Trinity Hall 3
21	Caius 2	35	Lady Somerset 2
22	Clare 1	36	Jesus 2
23	1st Trinity 4	37	Christ's 3
24	3rd Trinity 2	38	Caius 3
25	Corpus 2	39	1st Trin. 5
26	Emmanuel 3	40	Caius 4
27	Queens' 1	41	1st Trin. 5
28	Pembroke	42	Corpus 3
29	Christ's 2	43	Lady Somerset 3
30	Lady Margaret 3	44	Queen's 2
31	King's	45	Clare 2
32	2nd Trinity 3		
33	Catherine		

SATURDAY, May 12, (Second Division).

20	Emmanuel 2	33	2nd Trin. 3
21	Clare 1	34	Lady Somerset 2
22	Caius 2	35	Trinity Hall 3
23	1st Trinity 4	36	Jesus 2
24	3rd Trinity 2	37	Caius 3
25	Corpus 2	38	Christ's 3
26	Queens' 1	39	Caius 4
27	Emm. 3	40	1st Trin. 5
28	Pembroke	41	Corpus 3
29	Christ's 2	42	Queens' 2
30	King's	43	Lady Somerset 3
31	Lady Margaret	44	Clare 2
32	Catherine's		

WEDNESDAY, May 16, (Second Division).

20	Clare 1	32	Lady Margaret 3
21	Emmanuel 2	33	Lady Somerset 2
22	Caius 2	34	2nd Trinity 3
23	1st Trinity 4	35	Jesus 2
24	3rd Trinity 2	36	Trinity Hall 3
25	Queens' 1	37	Christ's 3
26	Corpus 2	38	Caius 3
27	Pembroke	39	Caius 4
28	Emmanuel 3	40	Corpus 3
29	King's	41	Queens' 2
30	Christ's 2	42	Clare 2
31	Catherine	43	Lady Somerset 3

THURSDAY, May 17, (Second Division.)

20	2nd Trinity 2	32	Lady Somerset 2
21	Caius 2	33	Lady Margaret 3
22	Emmanuel 2	34	2nd Trinity 3
23	1st Trinity 4	35	Caius 3
24	Queens' 1	36	Christ's 3
25	3rd Trinity 2	37	Trinity Hall 3
26	Pembroke	38	Jesus 2
27	Corpus 2	39	Corpus 3
28	King's	40	Caius 4
29	Emmanuel 3	41	Clare 2
30	Christ's 2	42	Queens' 2
31	Catherine	43	Lady Somerset 3

THURSDAY, May 10, (First Division).

1	3rd Trinity 1	11	Jesus 1
2	1st Trinity 1	12	Lady Margaret 2
3	Lady Margaret 1	13	Trinity Hall 2
4	Trinity Hall 1	14	Peterhouse
5	2nd Trinity 1	15	2nd Trinity 2
6	Magdalene	16	Emmanuel 2
7	Caius 1	17	Sidney
8	Emmanuel 1	18	Corpus 1
9	Christ's 1	19	1st Trinity 3
10	1st Trinity 2	20	Lady Somerset 1

FRIDAY, May 11, (First Division).

1	1st Trinity 1	11	Peterhouse
2	3rd Trinity 1	12	Trinity Hall 2
3	Lady Margaret 1	13	Lady Margaret 2
4	Trinity Hall 1	14	Jesus 1
5	2nd Trinity 1	15	Corpus 1
6	Caius 1	16	Sidney
7	Magdalene	17	Emmanuel 2
8	Emmanuel 1	18	2nd Trinity 2
9	Christ's 1	19	1st Trinity 3
10	1st Trinity 2	20	Lady Somerset 1

SATURDAY, May 12, (First Division).

1	1st Trinity 1	11	Trinity Hall 2
2	3rd Trinity 1	12	Peterhouse
3	Lady Margaret 1	13	Lady Margaret 2
4	Trinity Hall 1	14	Corpus 1
5	Caius 1	15	Jesus 1
6	2nd Trinity 1	16	Sidney
7	Emmanuel 1	17	Lady Somerset 1
8	Magdalene	18	1st Trinity 3
9	Christ's 1	19	2nd Trinity 2
10	1st Trinity 2	20	Clare 1

WEDNESDAY, May 16, (First Division).

1	1st Trinity 1	11	Trinity Hall 2
2	3rd Trinity 1	12	Peterhouse
3	Lady Margaret 1	13	Sidney
4	Caius 1	14	Jesus 1
5	Trinity Hall 1	15	Corpus 1
6	Emmanuel 1	16	Lady Margaret 2
7	2nd Trinity 1	17	Lady Somerset 1
8	Christ's 1	18	1st Trinity 3
9	Magdalene	19	2nd Trinity 2
10	1st Trinity 2	20	Clare 1

THURSDAY, May 17, (First Division.)

1	1st Trinity 1	11	Trinity Hall 2
2	Lady Margaret 1	12	Peterhouse
3	3rd Trinity 1	13	Sidney
4	Caius 1	14	Corpus 2
5	Trinity Hall 1	15	Jesus 1
6	Emmanuel 1	16	Lady Somerset 1
7	2nd Trinity 1	17	Lady Margaret 2
8	Christ's 1	18	1st Trinity 3
9	Magdalene	19	Clare 1
10	1st Trinity 2	20	Caius 2

FRIDAY, May 18, (First Division).

1	1st Trinity 1	12	Peterhouse
2	Lady Margaret 1	13	Corpus
3	3rd Trinity 1	14	Sidney
4	Caius 1	15	Lady Somerset 1
5	Trinity Hall 1	16	Jesus 1
6	Emmanuel 1	17	1st Trinity 3
7	2nd Trinity 1	18	Lady Margaret 2
8	Christ's	19	Clare 1
9	1st Trinity 2	20	Caius 2
10	Magdalene		
11	Trinity Hall 2		

OUR EMIGRANT.

Part II.

WE had had some difficulty in crossing the Rakaia, having been detained there two days before even the punt could cross; on the third day they commenced crossing in the punt, behind which we swam our horses; since then the clouds had hung unceasingly upon the mountain ranges, and though much of what had fallen would be in all probability snow, we could not doubt but that the Rangitata would afford us some trouble, nor were we even certain about the Ashburton, a river which, though partly glacier-fed, is generally easily crossed anywhere. We found the Ashburton high, but lower than it had been in one or two of the eleven crossing places between our afternoon and evening resting places; we were wet up to the saddle flaps— still we were able to proceed without any real difficulty— that night it snowed—and the next morning we started amid a heavy rain, being anxious, if possible, to make my own place that night.

Soon after we started the rain ceased, and the clouds slowly lifting themselves from the mountain sides enabled my companion to perceive the landmarks, which, in the absence of any kind of track, serve to direct the traveller from Mr. Phillips's house to the spot where I hope my own may be before this meets the eye of any but myself.

We kept on the right-hand side of a long and open valley, the bottom of which consisted of a large swamp, from which rose terrace after terrace up the mountains on either side; the country is, as it were, crumpled up in an extraordinary manner, so that it is full of small ponds or lagoons—sometimes dry—sometimes merely swampy— now as full of water as they could be. The number of these

M

is great; they do not however attract the eye, being hidden
by the hillocks with which each is more or less surrounded;
they vary in extent from a few square feet or yards to
perhaps an acre or two, while one or two attain the
dimensions of a considerable lake. There is no timber in
this valley, and accordingly the scenery, though on a large
scale, is neither impressive nor pleasing; the mountains
are large swelling hummocks, grassed up to the summit,
and though steeply declivitous, entirely destitute of precipice.

It must be understood that I am speaking of the valley
in question through which we were travelling, and not
of the general aspect of the country: on the other side
the Rangitata the mountains rise much higher, and looking
up the gorge many summits meet the eye, on which the
snow rests all the year round, and on whose sides lie miles
and miles of iced-plum-cake-looking glacier; these are a
continuation of the range which culminates in Mount Cook,
a glorious fellow, between thirteen and fourteen thousand
feet high, and shaped most sublimely.

Before I describe the river, I may as well say a word
on the nature of back country travelling in the Canterbury
settlement. It is so hard for an Englishman to rid himself
not only of hedges and ditches and cuttings and bridges,
but of fields, of houses, of all signs of human care and
attention, that I can hardly hope to give any adequate idea
of the effect it produces upon a stranger. That effect is
ceasing rapidly upon myself: indeed I feel as if I had never
been accustomed to anything else—so soon does a person
adapt himself to the situation in which he finds himself
placed.

Suppose you were to ask your way from Mr. Phillips's
station to mine, I should direct you thus:—"Work your
way towards yonder mountain—pass underneath it between
it and the lake, having the mountain on your right hand
and the lake on your left—if you come upon any swamps
go round them, or if you think you can, go through them;
if you get stuck up by any creeks, (a creek is the colonial
term for a stream) you'll very likely see cattle marks, by
following the creek up and down; but there is nothing
there that ought to stick you up if you keep out of the
big swamp at the bottom of the valley; after passing that
mountain, follow the lake till it ends, keeping well on
the hill side above it, and make the end of the valley,
where you will come upon a high terrace above a large
gully, with a very strong creek at the bottom of it—get

down the terrace, where you'll see a patch of burnt ground, and follow down the river bed till it opens on to a flat; turn to your left and keep down the mountain sides that run along the Rangitata; keep well near them, and so avoid the swamps; cross the Rangitata opposite where you see a large river bed coming into it from the other side, and follow this river bed till you see my hut some eight miles up it." Perhaps I have thus been better able to describe the nature of the travelling than by any other—if one can get anything that can be manufactured into a feature and be dignified with a name once in five or six miles, one is very lucky.

Well—we had followed these directions for some way, as far in fact as the terrace, when the river coming into full view, I saw that the Rangitata was very high; worse than that I saw Mr. Phillips and a party of men who were taking a dray over to a run just on the other side the river, and who had been prevented from crossing for ten days by the state of the water. Among them, to my horror, I recognised my cadet whom I had left behind me with beef which he was to have taken over to my place a week and more back; whereon my mind misgave me that a poor Irishman who had been left alone at my place, might be in a sore plight, having been left with no meat and no human being within reach for a period of ten days. I don't think I should have attempted crossing the river, but for this; under the circumstances, however, I determined at once on making a push for it, and accordingly taking my two cadets with me, and the unfortunate beef that was already putrescent, (it had lain on the ground in a sack all the time) we started along under the hills and got opposite the place where I intended crossing by about three o'clock. I had climbed the mountain side and surveyed the river from thence before approaching the river itself. At last we were by the water's edge—of course I led the way, being as it were, patronus of the expedition, and having been out some four months longer than either of my companions—still, having never crossed any of the rivers on horseback in a fresh, having never seen the Rangitata in a fresh, and being utterly unable to guess how deep any stream would take me, it may be imagined that I felt a certain amount of caution to be necessary, and accordingly folding my watch in my pocket-handkerchief and tying it round my neck in case of having to swim for it unexpectedly, I strictly forbade the other

two to stir from the bank until they saw me safely on the
other side.

Not that I intended to let my horse swim: in fact I
had made up my mind to let the old Irishman wait a little
longer rather than deliberately swim for it; my two companions were worse mounted than I was, and the rushing
water might only too probably affect their heads; though
mine had already become quite indifferent to it—it had
not been so at first—these two men, however, had been
only in the settlement a week, and I should have deemed
myself highly culpable had I allowed them to swim a river
on horseback, though I am sure both would have been ready
enough to do so if occasion required.

As I said before, at last we were on the water's edge;
a rushing stream some sixty yards wide was the first in-
stalment of our passage—it was about the colour and consistency of cream and soot, and how deep? I had not
the remotest idea, the only thing for it was to go in and
see; so choosing a spot just above a spit and a rapid—
at such spots there is sure to be a ford, if there is a ford
anywhere—I walked my mare quickly into it, having perfect
confidence in her, and, I believe, she having more confidence
in me than some who have known me in England might
suppose: in we went—in the middle of the stream the
water was only a little over her belly, (she is sixteen hands
high); a little further, by sitting back on my saddle and
lifting my feet up, I might have avoided getting them
wet, had I cared to do so—but I was more intent on having
the mare well in hand, and on studying the appearance
of the remainder of the stream, than on thinking of my
own feet just then; after that the water grew shallower
rapidly, and I soon had the felicity of landing my mare
on the shelving shingle of the opposite bank. So far so
good—I beckoned to my companions, who speedily followed,
and we all three proceeded down the spit in search of
a good crossing place over the next stream. We were
soon beside it, and very ugly it looked. It must have been
at least a hundred yards broad—I think more—but water
is so deceptive that I dare not affix any certain width. I
was soon in it—advancing very slowly above a slightly darker
line in the water, which assured me of its being shallow
for some little way—this failing, I soon found myself descending into deeper water—first over my boots for some
yards—then over the top of my gaiters for some yards
more—this continued so long that I was in hopes of being

able to get entirely over, when suddenly the knee against which the stream came was entirely wet, and the water was rushing so furiously past me that my poor mare was leaning over tremendously—already she had begun to snort, as horses do when they are swimming, and I knew well that my companions would have to swim for it even though I myself might have got through, so I very gently turned her head round down stream and quietly made back again for the bank which I had left; she had got nearly to the shore, and I could again detect a darker line in the water, which was now not over her knees, when all of a sudden down she went up to her belly in a quicksand, in which she began floundering about in fine style. I was off her back and into the water that she had left in less time than it takes to write this. I should not have thought of leaving her back unless sure of my ground, for it is a canon in river crossing to stick to your horse. I pulled her gently out, and followed up the dark line to the shore where my two friends were only too glad to receive me. By the way, all this time I had had a companion in the shape of a cat in a bag, which I was taking over to my place as an antidote to the rats, which were most unpleasantly abundant there. I nursed her on the pommel of my saddle all through this last stream, and save in the episode of the quicksand she had not been in the least wet; then, however, she did drop in for a sousing, and mewed in a manner that went to my heart. I am very fond of cats, and this one is a particularly favourable specimen: it was with great pleasure that I heard her purring through the bag, as soon as I was again mounted, and had her in front of me as before.

So I failed to cross this stream there, but determined, if possible, to get across the river and see whether my Irishman was alive or dead, we turned higher up the stream, and by and by found a place where it divided; by carefully selecting a spot I was able to cross the first stream without the waters getting higher than my saddle-flaps, and the second scarcely over the horse's belly; after that there were two streams somewhat similar to the first, and then the dangers of the passage of the river might be considered as accomplished; the dangers—but not the difficulties—these consisted in the sluggish creeks and swampy ground thickly overgrown with Irishman snow-grass and Spaniard, which extend on either side the river for half-a-mile and more—but to cut a long story short, we got over these too, and then we were on the shingly river bed which leads up to the spot on which my hut is made, and my house making; this river was now a brawling torrent, hardly less dangerous to cross than the Rangitata itself, though containing not a tithe of the water; the boulders are so large and the water so powerful—in its ordinary condition it is little more than a large brook; now, though not absolutely fresh, it was as unpleasant a place to put a horse into as one need wish; there was nothing for it, however, and we crossed and recrossed it four times without misadventure, and finally, with great pleasure I perceived a twinkling light on the terrace where the hut was, which assured me at once that the old Irishman was still in the land of the living. Two or three vigorous "coo-eys" brought him down to the side of the creek which bounds my run upon one side.

I will now return to the subject of wild Irishman and wild Spaniard. The former is a thorny tree growing with ungainly unmanageable boughs, sometimes as large as our own hawthorn trees, generally about the size of a gooseberry bush; he does not appear to me to have a single redeeming feature, being neither pleasant to the eye nor good for food; he is highly inflammable when dry, and a single match, judiciously applied, will burn acres and acres of him. I myself being up the Waimakiriri one afternoon, far beyond the possibility of doing any mischief, (a very easy matter when burning country) stuck a match into a forest of Ogygian Irishmen that had lain battening upon a rich alluvial flat for years. I camped down upon the other side the river, and waking at constant intervals during the night, was treated with the grandest conflagration that I have ever seen. I could hear the crackling of thorns above the rushing of the river, while the smoke glaring and lurid was rising up to heaven in volumes awfully grand and quite indescribable; next morning there was nothing left but the awkward gnarled trunks, naked and desolate, rising from the blackened soil; a few years would rot these too away, and rich grass would spring up, where before its growth had been prevented by the overshadowing of its more powerful neighbours.

A match is the first step in the subjugation of any large tract of new country; thence date *tabulæ novæ*, as it were; the match had better be applied in spring; such at least is the general opinion out here, and I think the right one, though I was at first inclined to think that autumn must be better. The fire dries up many swamps—at least many disappear after country has been once or twice burnt; the water moves more freely, unimpeded by the tangled and decaying vegetation which accumulates round it during the lapse of centuries, and the sun gets freer access to the ground; cattle do much also—they form tracks through swamps, and trample country down, and make it harder and firmer; sheep do much—they convey the seeds of the best grass in their dung, and tread it into the ground: the difference between country that has been fed upon by any live stock even for a single year, and country which has never yet been stocked is very noticeable: country that has been stocked any length of time is assuming quite a different appearance to that which unstocked country originally similar now wears.

I will mention a few facts connected with firing country, which may perhaps be not generally known in England: first and foremost, that the most furious fire of grass may be crossed with impunity on horseback; it is never more than a strip some four or five feet broad, and a man either on foot or on horseback can almost always rush through it without being in the least burnt. Secondly, that it does'nt often *kill* sheep, it burns their wool, it often spoils their feet, and sometimes burns their bellies so as to cause death; a gentleman however of my acquaintance had four hundred sheep burnt the other day, but only forty of them have died, and the rest are all expected to recover. Thirdly, that sheep will run towards smoke and have no notion of getting out of the way of fire, and fourthly, that they may be smothered by the smoke of a fire some two or three miles off them; under peculiar circumstances I have been told this, but have been unable to verify it.

Now to return to wild Spaniard—Irishman was a nuisance, but Spaniard is simply detestable—he is sometimes called spear-grass, and grows to about the size of a mole-hill; all over the back country everywhere as thick as mole-hills in a very mole-hilly field at home. His blossom is attached to a high spike bristling with spears pointed every way and very acutely; each leaf is pointed with a strong spear, and so firm is it, that if you come within its reach, no amount of clothing about the legs will prevent you from feeling the effects of his displeasure: I have had my legs marked all over by it. Horses hate the Spaniard—and no wonder—in the back country when travelling without a track, it is impossible to keep your horse from yawing

about this way and that to dodge him, and if he gets
stuck up by three or four growing close together, he will
jump them or do anything rather than walk through them.
The leaf is something in growth and consistency like a
large samphire, and has, when bruised, a very powerful
smell, something between aniseed and samphire, (a great
deal of samphire) and the capsules, which may be purchased
at Pain the chemist's for two shillings, or at Deck's for
three; a kind of white wax exudes during early autumn
from this leaf; a careless observer might not, however, notice
this; the whole plant burns with great brilliancy, giving
a peculiarly bright light, and lasting for a long time; if, when
camping out, I had laid anything down on the grass and
was unable to find it, (the most natural thing in the world
to do, and the most annoying when you have done it) a
Spaniard laid on the fire would throw an illumination on
the subject which no amount of sticks would do; his root
is capable of supporting human life for a long time, but
the taste is so very strong that I should be excessively
loth to eat it myself upon any consideration; if, when
camping out, you stir your tea with a small portion of a
single leaf, it will make the whole pannikin taste of it.
So much for Spaniard. Coronita is a pretty little evergreen,
which reminded me at once of the bushes in a piece of
worsted work: any one who saw it would say the same
in a minute.

If, however, I were to go on yarning about the plants,
I should never have done. I think Spaniard and Irishman
are the two deserving of most notice, but on the whole
the Canterbury flora is neither extensive nor anything approaching in beauty to that of Switzerland or Italy, the
countries which in general aspect this more nearly resembles
than any other that I have yet seen. It lacks, however,
the charm of association; there is such a jumble of old
things and new; the old things seem all to have got here
by mistake, and the new things are so painfully and glaringly
new, and predominate so largely over the old ones, that
it is hard to believe that Canterbury ever had existed before
the pilgrims came there in eighteen hundred and fifty.
A person would understand the almost oppressive feeling
of newness about everything, were he to enter into a colonial
slab hut, and see an old carved oak chest in the corner
marked with a date early in the seventeenth century; the
effect is about as incongruous and about as startling as it
would be to a geologist to discover the backbone of an

icthyosaurus in the cone of Vesuvius, or to an antiquary
to find a beadle's cocked hat and staff in the ruins of
Pœstum.

Not but that even this place has some old things belonging to it! but they are rapidly passing away. I saw a
Maori woman standing near the market-place in Christ church
the day before I left it last—her petticoat was of dark green,
and the upper part of her dress was scarlet; a kerchief was
folded not ungracefully about her head, and she was smoking a short black cutty-pipe, splendidly coloured. There
she stood, staring vacantly at the sky in the middle of the
street; her face not unpleasing, with a gentle, patient expression, rather resembling that of an amiable, good-tempered
animal, than an intelligent being; her stature wonderfully
tall, so much so, as to have won for her the appellation
among her kindred, of "Mary in the clouds;" her proper
dwelling-place is on the west coast, on the other side the
Hurunui; but then she happened to be in Christ church,
the tribe being on one of its yearly or half-yearly migrations.
My eyes were rivetted at once by a figure so new and so
picturesque, and the same sensation of what a jumble it all
was came over me, as I noticed that the name of the person
against whose shop she stood was "Turnbull"—Turnbull—
and "Mary in the clouds,"—there was no doubt, however,
whose star was in the ascendant. The Maories in this island are
rapidly becoming extinct, one scarcely ever sees a child
among them. European diseases, measles, scarlet fever, &c.,
&c. carry them off wholesale, and I am told that according to the best calculations, another fifty years will have
swept them away from among the nations of the earth. In
the north I hear that the race is much finer, and that these
are a miserable remnant of tribes expelled thence.

I will now touch briefly upon the birds of the place—
will then describe the "coo-ey," and finally bring the reader
safely home to my hut. With regard to the birds, the first
thing that strikes one is their great scarcity: save an ubiquitous lark exactly like our English lark, except that it does
not sing, and has two white feathers in the tail, one sees no
birds at all; by and by however, one finds out that there are
several more, and after travelling in the back country, one
begins almost to believe that Canterbury is not much more
deficient in birds than our own island at home. The plains
are entirely destitute of timber, so that they find no shelter,
and are forced to take up their abode in the dense forests of
the inner and western portions of the settlement. The

next thing that strikes one after having found out that there
are birds, is, that they are wonderfully similar to our own;
most of our English birds are represented, the lark is nearly
identical—the quail is the same—the hawk the same, the
robin has its counterpart here in a bird with a slate coloured
head and throat, and a canary coloured breast, to all intents
and purposes it is a robin for all that; it is much tamer than
our robin at home, so much so, that you can kill as many
of them with a stick as you please—that is, if you have a
mind to do so. All the wild birds here are much tamer than
they are in England. I have seen the rarest kind of mountain duck swimming within five yards of me, as unconcernedly
as though I had no soul for roast duck or seasoning. There
are several ducks: the paradise duck, not a duck proper
but a goose, is the commonest; the male bird when flying
appears nearly black—the female black, with a white head,
a nun-like looking bird; the male bird says " whiz—whiz—
whiz," very much in his throat, and dwelling, a long time
on the *z*; the female screams like Bryant's waterfowl was
supposed to be shortly about to scream at the time that he
addressed her; see these birds on the ground, and their
plumage appears very beautiful indeed—the moment they
take wing they resume their sable habiliments. Then there
are the grey duck and the mountain duck—rarer, less striking in their personal appearance, and better eating. The
wren, and the tomtit, and the thrush, all are represented
quite as nearly or even more so than the robin, save that the
tomtit is black-headed with a yellow breast; besides these,
there is a kind of parrot called the kaka, of a dusky green and
a dirty red plumage, and a very pretty little parroquet, bright
green with a little blue and yellow. The parson bird is as
big as a starling, with a glossy, starling looking appearance,
save that from his throat projects a cravat-like tuft of white
feathers, whence his name. This bird sings very sweetly,
as do the others generally, and can be taught to talk very
well. The wood-hen is wingless, and marked not wholly
unlike a hen pheasant, but with a short bobtail instead of a
long one; it walks round about your fire when you are
camping out with imperturbable gravity—it will eat everything and anything—it has the reputation of being a very
foul feeder; when stewed however for a good long time, it
is considered very good eating. It is generally very fat, and
the oil that is extracted from it is reckoned sovereign for
wounds and for hair, and for greasing boots; and in fact is
supposed to be one of the finest animal oils known. It comes

to anything red, and is very easily caught; every step it takes it pokes its head forward, and bobs its tail up and down, which gives it a Paul Pry sort of look that is rather ludicrous. There is a large and very beautiful pigeon—and besides these I should add the "more pork," a night bird which is supposed to say these words. The laughing jackass is unlike the well-behaved boy, inasmuch, as the latter is seen and not heard, the former is heard but has never yet been seen; I should never have supposed it to resemble a laughing jackass, never having heard a jackass laugh, unless I had been told that it did so; but the parties who stood sponsors for the bird, doubtless knew what they were about, and I might be highly culpable were I to style them fanciful or misinformed.

So much for the birds—not that I have enumerated all by any means, and a more intimate acquaintance with peculiar localities will doubtless enable me to extend my list. With regard to the gigantic extinct bird the moa or dinornis, I may mention that its bones are constantly found, and that near each is always a small heap of round smoothly polished agate, or flint, or cornelian stones, from the size of a bantam's egg downwards. These, however remarkable it may appear, were the gizzard stones of the individual.

Now for the "coo-ey." This corresponds to our English hoy! halloa! but is infinitely more puzzling, for the hoy and the halloa are generally but preludes to an explicit expression in plain English of the wishes of the hoyer or the halloer, to the hoyee or halloee respectively. Coo-ey however is far more extended in its signification, and is often expected to convey that signification in itself. Coo-ey can be heard for a very very long way—the "coo" is dwelt on for some time, and the "ey" is brought out sharp and quick in high relief from the "coo," and at an unnaturally high pitch. It requires some courage to give vent to a coo-ey at first; the first attempts are generally abortive, not to say rather doleful and somewhat ludicrous; by and bye one gains confidence, and one's coo-eys are more successful; my own at present is quite unimpeachable, though in England nothing would have induced me to give utterance to such a noise.

The butcher-boy is coming up with the meat. He coo-eys a long way off, and by the time he has got up to the house the door is opened to receive the meat, and he goes on his way rejoicing. A man comes to the Rakaia, and finds it bank to bank; seeing Dunford's accommodation-

house on the other side the river, he coo-eys some three
or four times to it. At Dunford's accommodation-house
they see the river bank to bank, and the man on the other
side of it; they hear him coo-ey, by which he means, " come
over and help me—and they coo-ey back again, which
means, " its no earthly use your stopping there, you fool;
the river's bank to bank, and no human being can cross."
Coo-ey means breakfast's ready—dinner's ready—I'm coming
—bring the ferry-boat—mind your eye—come here—get
out of the way there—where are you?—I'm here!—in fact
anything and everything; the remaining interpretations to
be discovered, as the classics have it, "inter legendum."
The worst of the sound is, that the moment any one coo-eys,
all within ear-shot interpret it differently, and consider it to
have been personally addressed to themselves.

So like Herodotus, whose authority I must plead for this
discursive style of narration, (although the real excuse must be
made on the ground of the excessively adverse circumstances
under which I am writing), I have brought the reader safely
back to the side of the stream which divides my run from
that of one of my next neighbours, whose house, however,
is more than thirty miles off. There I coo-eyed, and the
Irishman came down the terrace and met us. He had given
us up for lost, and had seen my ghost appearing to him and
telling him where I lay. Then we went up the terrace
and commenced taking the swag off our horses.

Apropos of swag, I may as well mention here, that
travellers are always accustomed to carry their blankets
with them; in the back country there are very few stations
where blankets are provided for more than the actual in-
mates of the house or hut; besides which a person might
easily be benighted, and have to camp down before arriving
at his destination. My swag generally is as follows:—A
mackintosh sheet, two blankets, one rough pea-jacket, saddle-
bags, and a tether rope round my horse's neck; if I meditate
camping out beforehand, I take a pannikin for making tea,
and a little axe for cutting fire-wood—it is very handy and
very easily carried—but I must not digress further.

When I reached the place which I suppose I must almost
now begin to call "home," it was already dark, and a cold
drizzling rain had set in for an hour and more; it had rained
nearly continuously in the ten days interval of my absence
at Christ Church, and accordingly I need not say that
matters here had not improved. We had had lovely weather
when I was up before, and had taken advantage of it to

put up a V hut, in which I had slept the night before I left.

A V hut is a roof in shape like the letter V set down, without any walls, upon the ground; mine is 12 feet long by 8 feet broad; it does not commonly possess a fireplace, but I had left space for one in mine as I daily expected winter to set in in earnest, and having been informed that my hut is not, at the lowest computation, under two thousand feet above the level of the sea, I did not relish the idea of taking all my meals *al fresco* in all weathers. No signs of winter, however, had set in by the twenty-first of May, in which month I left; the nights, it is true, were frosty, but the days serene, calm, and most enjoyable; now, however, the wet weather had fairly commenced, and matters looked very different. The snow that was before upon the tops of the mountains had crept a long way down their flanks; the higher mountains were deeply clothed, and gave me the impression of not being about to part with their icy mantle ere the return of summer. It is wonderful, however, how much of it is now melted.

The hut—now fully complete, and for its size wonderfully comfortable (I have written all this in it)—was discovered to be neither air tight, nor water tight; the floor, or rather the ground, was soaked and soppy with mud; the nice warm snow-grass on which I had lain so comfortably the night before I left, was muddy and wet; altogether, there being no fire, the place was as revolting looking an affair as one would wish to see; coming wet and cold off a journey, we had hoped for better things. There was nothing for it but to make the best of it, so we had tea, and fried some of the beef—the smell of which was anything but agreeable— and then we sat in our great coats, on four stones, round the fire, and smoked; then I baked and one of the cadets washed up—unorthodox—but I think on the whole preferable to leaving everything unwashed from day to day; and then we arranged our blankets as best we could, and were soon asleep, alike unconscious of the dripping rain, which came through the roof of the hut, and of the cold raw atmosphere which was insinuating itself through the numerous crevices of the thatch.

We will awake to a new chapter.

CHAPTER II.

I slept in all my wet things—boots and all—how could I dry them? how change them? I have done so often since I have been in New Zealand, and cannot say that I have ever felt the least harm from it, though I would always change if I could. I have been much more particular, however, about another kind of damp, I mean that which rises from even the dryest ground, and which will search through any amount of blankets. I have always been careful to make a layer of small broken boughs, and cutting snow-grass or tussock-grass with the little axe, to spread a covering of this upon it, with my mackintosh sheet laid over all, no damp can penetrate—it is the wet from below that I fear, not the wet from above. I have not had a cold, or the ghost of a cold, since I have been in New Zealand.

Rising with the first faint light of early morning, I crossed the creek—a rushing mountain stream which runs down the valley in which my hut now is, and over which by taking it in two streams you can find two or three crossing places in a hundred yards, where you can get over dry shod without any difficulty. I crossed this creek and went to look at the horses; there is no feed on this side the creek at present; it was all burnt in early autumn, and the grass will not grow again till spring; on the other side there is splendid feed, so we turn our horses on to that; we kept one on the tether—tethered to a tussock of grass by a peculiar kind of New Zealand knot—and let the others loose; they will always keep together and are sure not to leave the one that is tethered far off—that is, if they know the horse. The nuisance of keeping a horse tethered is that he is pretty sure to tie himself up as it is called. New Zealand grass is not a sward like English grass, but it consists chiefly of large yellow tussocks of a very stiff, tough, hard grass, which neither horses, nor cattle, nor anything else will eat, except when it is springing up tender and green, after having been just burnt. So tough is it that when you tether your horse to it, he may pull all night but cannot get away, unless you have selected a very weak one, and he pulls it up root and all out of the ground. Well, the horse advances cropping the tender grasses that spring up between and underneath the tussocks; he then turns round, and of course turns the rope too; the rope then may very probably be detained round either a Spaniard, or a burnt tussock, or a small piece of Irishman, or what not; the horse goes on cropping the grass, and winds his rope round this just like the picture of the hare in Cruikshank's illustration of the waggish musician. Sometimes he may be doubly or trebly tied up, and of course he may have contrived to do this within half-an-hour of the time when he was first tethered out: it is a very annoying thing to go to your horse the first thing in the morning and find him tied up, and so of course unable to feed, when you have been wanting him to fill his belly against a long day's journey; there are few places where a horse does not stand a pretty good chance of getting tied up, (it is astonishing how small a thing will answer the purpose); but on the whole I prefer tethering a horse to putting a pair of hobbles on him, so do almost all here. Of course the last care of a considerate traveller before going to bed, and his first care before even washing in the morning, is to look at his horse.

Well, I went to look at the horses, the creek was high—too high to get over dry shod—but very crossable; I changed the horse that was on the tether, one of my cadet's, and tethered my own mare on as nice a spot as I could find. I then returned and had breakfast—it was still raining, as indeed it had been all night—and breakfast was not much more comfortable than tea had been the night before. Then we all set to work at the hut, completed the chimney, and made the thatch secure by laying thin sods over the rafters and putting the thatch (of which we could not readily get any more, all the snow-grass on my side of the creek being burnt) over these sods, as secure and warm a covering as can be possibly imagined; in the evening we lighted our first fire inside the hut, and none but those who have been in similar conditions can realise the pleasure with which we began, ere bed time, to feel ourselves again quite warm and almost dry. It rained all day—had we not got over the Rangitata when we did, we should have assuredly been detained another week—it rained, I say, all day, and the creek got very high indeed; it has a river bed some three or four hundred yards wide opposite my hut, and precipices or very like them descend on it upon either side as you go higher up: I climbed the terrace just above the hut from time to time, and could see the mare on the other side still with her head down to the ground quietly feeding. "You may stop there all night," said I to myself, for I did not relish crossing the creek in its then condition: we could hear the boulders thump, thump, thump beneath the roaring of the waters, and the colour of the stream was bright ochre and as thick as pea-soup. Next morning, the rain having continued all night, matters were worse, and worse still; the mare was not feeding, she was evidently tied up—the only wonder being that she had not tied herself up before— matters seemed less likely to improve than to deteriorate, so I determined to cross the creek at once and release her.

Each stream was a furious torrent, more resembling a continued cascade, or series of very strong rapids, than any thing else; the thumping and clattering of the boulders beneath the water was perfectly horrid; divesting myself how- ever of my coat, trowsers, and stockings, and retaining my boots, shirt, and waist-coat, I advanced very gently into the first and least formidable of the two streams. I did keep my footing, and that was all; in the second I got carried off my legs a few yards, and pretty severely knocked about by boulders as big as my head, which were being carried down the stream like pebbles. I then released the mare, tethered another horse, the risk of losing all the horses being too great for me, to allow them to run loose while still new to the place, (we let them all run now) and then I found my way back to the side of the larger stream; this time I was hardly in before my legs were knocked from under me and down I went helter, skelter, willy, nilly—of course quite unable to regain my lost footing. I lay on my back at once and did not resist the stream a bit, kicked out with my legs and made the bank I wanted before I had been carried down fifty yards,—to try to swim would have been absurd,—I knew perfectly well what I was doing and was out of the water in less time than it has taken me to write this; the next stream I got over all right and was soon in the hut before the now blazing and comfortable fire.

Oh! what fires we made!—how soon the snow-grass dried!—how soon the floor, though even now damp, ceased to be slushy!—then we humped in three stones for seats, on one of which I am sitting writing, while the others are at work upon the house,—then we confined the snow-grass within certain limits by means of a couple of poles laid upon the ground and fixed into their places with pegs,—then we put up several slings to hang our saddle-bags, tea, sugar, salt, bundles, &c.—then we made a horse for the saddles, four riding saddles; and a pack saddle—underneath this go our tools at one end, and our culinary utensils, limited but very effective at the other. And now for some time this part has been so neatly packed in the first instance, and every thing has been so neatly kept ever since, that when we come into it of a night it wears an aspect of comfort quite domestic, even to the cat which sits and licks my face of a night and purrs, coming in always just after we are in bed by means of a hole under our thatched door which we have left for her especial benefit. We were recommended by all means to tether her out for a day or two until she got used to the place, but the idea struck me as so excessively absurd that I did not put it in practice. Joking apart, however, it is a thing constantly done.

Rats are either indigenous to New Zealand, or have naturalised themselves here with great success; they would come round us while we were sitting round the fire and steal the meat in the coolest manner, and run over us while asleep in the tent, before we had put the hut up; now however we seem entirely free from them, and bless the cat night and day.

I said I would take an early opportunity of describing the process of camping out.

It should be commenced if possible one hour before full dark; twilight is very short here! I never found it out so much as when crossing the Rangitata the other day, not the occasion to which I have alluded above; but since then, opposite Mount Peel, some thirty miles lower down; there it is all one stream, of which more anon. Well, it was daylight when I got into the stream, and dark when I got out, and allowing for a slight mistake which I made in the ford at first, I don't suppose I was more than seven or eight minutes in the water.

An hour before dark is not too much to allow of all preparations being made in comfortable daylight; of course the first thing to look out for in choosing a spot wherein to camp is food for the horse, that it may feed well against the next day's journey; the next is water for yourself, and the third is firewood, and, if possible, shelter;—feed—water—and fire-wood. On having found a spot possessing these requisites— no easy matter in but too many places—first unswag the horse, either tether him out, or let him run according to the propensity of the animal; in nine cases out of ten a horse may be safely trusted not to wander many hundred yards from one's camp-fire, and if there be two or three horses, to tether one is quite sufficient; then kindle a fire,—in wet weather a matter often involving considerable delay. The secret of successfully kind-ling a fire lies in having plenty of very small wood ready beforehand; dry wood, even though wet, can soon be taught to light, when green wood, though comparatively dry, will

N

do nothing but smoke and smoulder, and make the eye to smart, and weary the lungs with blowing: blowing is generally the refuge of the incompetent; a few puffs may sometimes help a lame dog over the style, but if a fire wants more than this, it is usually a sign that it has been badly laid, or that the wood has been badly selected. White men, when camping out, generally make a very large fire; the Maori makes a little one: he says, "the white man a fool—he makes a large fire, and then has to sit away from it." I have generally myself followed the example of my own colour. Then set on a pannikin of water to boil; when it boils throw in a handful of tea, and let it simmer: sweeten to taste; fish out your bread and meat, and by the time you have commenced feeding, you will commonly find that dark has begun to descend upon the scene. You must be careful to avoid laying anything down without knowing where to find it again, or you will rue it: lay every thing down in one place, close by your saddle. After tea—at which you will have had plenty of companions in the shape of robins and other small birds, with perhaps a woodhen or two, all of whom will watch your proceedings with the greatest interest—smoke a pipe, and then cut up black birch boughs, or tussock-grass, or snow-grass, or all three, and make yourself a deep warm bed, if not too tired, and then lay your saddle on its back; spread the mackintosh sheet, with the blankets on the top of it; heap up a good fire, and lie down to rest; use the hollow of the saddle as a pillow, (it's astonishing what a comfortable pillow it makes); don't take off any of your clothes, except your boots and coat (not that I ever take off the former of these myself); strap the mackintosh sheet, blankets, and all round your body, and I don't think that there is any fear of your catching or even feeling cold. I have slept very warm and comfortable thus, and in the morning found the remains of the tea frozen in my pannikin, my sponge hard and unmanageable, and my blankets covered with frozen dew.

I will now return to the V hut for a little while. It is about eight miles up a river bed that comes down into the Rangitata on the south side, not in my opinion very far from the source of that river. Some think that the source of the river lies many miles higher, and that it works its way yet a long way back into the mountains; but as I look up the river bed, I see two large and gloomy gorges, at the end of each of which are huge glaciers, distinctly visible to the naked eye, but through the telescope resolvable into tumbled masses of blue ice, exact counterparts of the Swiss and Italian glaciers.

I consider these enough to account for even a larger body of water than is found in the Rangitata, and have not the smallest intention of going higher up the river to look for country.

My river bed flows into the main stream of the Rangitata, a good way lower down; on either side of it rise high mountains—the spurs and abutments of the great range; from these again descend into my river bed numerous streams, each through a grassy valley, the upper part of which is bare and shingly, and is now (June 28) covered with snow, though a good deal less thickly than I could have expected. The largest of these tributary streams flows into the river bed; from the eastern side, about eight miles up it; and at the confluence of the two streams I have built my hut. A beautiful wood, large, but not too large, clothes a portion of the lower side of the mountains close down to the junction of two streams; affording alike shelter, and fire-wood, and timber: the mountains embosom my hut upon all sides, save that the open valley in front allows me the full benefit of the whole day's sun, or nearly so. The climate of New Zealand is notoriously windy, but so sheltered and secluded is this spot, that I have scarcely had a breath of wind ever since I have been up there; though on getting down to the main valley of the Rangitata, I have generally found it blowing up or down (chiefly down) the river bed with great violence: from the terrace just above my hut, I can see a small triangular patch of the Rangitata in the distance, and have often noticed the clouds of sand blowing down the river when no air is stirring at my own place: the wind blows up and down the main river, and does not reach up my river bed, for above three or four miles. Thus whether, there be a sou'-wester blowing, or a nor'-wester, if I feel either at all, they come from the north east.

I have about five thousand acres up this valley, and about ten or twelve thousand more adjoining it, but divided from it by a mountain ridge, with three or four good high passes over it. People meet me whenever I come down to church, and ask me if I am frozen out yet, and pity me for having buried myself, as they call it, in such an out-of-the-way place: all I can tell them is, that I have not had a flake of snow yet; that whenever I go down to my neighbours' fire, and twenty miles off, I find that they have been having much colder and more unpleasant weather than myself; that the rain I have alluded to above, was alike felt and alike commented upon all over the plains and back country, and considered everywhere to have been some of the vilest weather known in the settlement; and that the very people who most profess to pity me, are those who were laughed at in exactly the same manner themselves for taking up the country adjoining my own, than which nothing can have turned out better, and that in my opinion their pity is principally dictated by a regret that, as they were about it, they did not go a little further, and get the country of which I am now only too well content to call myself the possessor. A few years hence, when people have taken up the glaciers beyond me, I am sure I shall find myself doing exactly the same thing; so invariably has it happened here that even the most despised country has turned out well; and so many cases have there been of people taking up country, and then absolutely refusing to have anything to do with it, and of others quietly stepping into it free gratis, and for nothing, and selling it at the rate of one hundred pounds for the thousand acres, the novel price paid for country, that I have not the smallest doubt that after I have completed my stay here during the winter, finished the house, brought a dray up, and put up a yard or two, I may be a thousand pounds in pocket, the reward of my adventures. But I most emphatically express my belief that there is no more available country left in this province untaken up. It may appear absurd to suppose myself the last fortunate individual who has succeeded in procuring country without buying it; but I must urge that I have followed up the Hurunui, the Waimakirivi, the Rakaia, and the Rangitata, and have only been successful in the case of the last-named river; that the Waitangi, the largest of all, is notoriously explored, and that much more country has been taken up in that district than actually exists, and that I should go on exploring myself, were I not strongly of opinion that I should make nothing by my motion.

True—the west coast remains, the tower in which the slumbering princess lies, whom none can rescue but the fated prince—but we know that the great Alpine range descends almost perpendicularly into the sea, upon that side the island, and that its sides are covered with dense impenetrable forests of primeval growth. Here and there at the mouths of the rivers a few flats may exist, or rather do exist; but over these rolls upwards to the snow line a heaving mass of timber. I do not say but that my own curiosity concerning the west coast is excited, and that I do not, if all is well, intend to verify or disprove the reports of others with my own eyes; but I have little faith in the success of the undertaking, and should go more as a traveller and an explorer, than as intending to make any money by the expedition.

I have yet much to write:—I should like to describe the general features of the New Zealand rivers, or rather of the Canterbury rivers, the remarkable nor'-west winds, the south-west winds, the character of the plains, and the peculiarities of the inhabitants; but, for the present, I have trespassed sufficiently upon the patience of the reader.

Flax and cabbage trees belong more to the front country; they are not so characteristic of the back: the forests too, upon the front side of the mountains, are well worthy of a description, but these things I will reserve for the present. The departure of the mail is at hand, and I must arise from my stone in my V-hut, and take these papers down to Christ Church. Let the reader be set to write under similar circumstances, occasionally getting up to turn a damper, or to assist in carrying a heavy log of timber from the bush to the scene of the building operations, and he might perhaps write English neither better nor more coherent than I have done. On these grounds, claiming his indulgence for the present, I bid him a hearty farewell.

PHILOCTETES IN LEMNOS.

Again the day is dying down the west
And I yet here, and thus nine summer times
Have pass'd, with nine harsh winters, and again
The tenth spring-tide hath found me still alone,
And tortured with this ever-growing wound
Which day by day consumes me; woe is me!
  O mighty cliffs, O dark steep rocks, O seas
That ever plunge and roar upon the coasts
Of this wild isle, O listen to my voice,
For thro' these years of suffering ye have been
My sole companions, hear my tale of wrongs!
  Would I had never left my native hills
To join in Aulis them that went to Troy,
Or that the snake whose poison caused this wound
Had slain me, so the crafty, cruel kings
Had never seized me as amid the camp
Helpless I lay and groaning, nor the ship
Had brought me hither, leaving me to die.
  O mountains, how ye echoed to my cries
When from my sleep awaking, while the night
Was filling silently the sky with stars,
I saw no vessel in the heaving bay,
Nor heard or voice or sound, save faint and low,
The breakers dying on the yellow sand;
And loud I cried "Odysseus," and the rocks
Mocked me, and cried "Odysseus" far away
Until my voice was weary, and I sat
Hopeless as some poor shipwreck'd mariner
Who waking from his stupor on the sands
Where the great waves have cast him, sees the cliffs
Piled round him, so that there is no escape,
And feels death creeping nearer in each wave.
  But when at last the slowly-moving morn
Was risen, in the cave I found my bow
And these famed arrows, which from day to day
Have slain me bird or beast to serve my need;

And, dragging on this wounded foot with pain,
I gather broken wood and fallen leaves
Wherewith to feed the fire that from the flints
I force with labour, and the dewy spring
Here by the cave supplies my thirst, tho' oft
Frozen, when winter strips this sea-girt isle.

And thus I live, if to exist in pain
Be life, and whether parch'd by summer noons
When all the shore lies steaming in the sun,
Or drench'd with dews that fall on summer nights,
I lie exposed; and all the winter long
The harsh frost bites me, and I hear from far,
From the dark hollows, voices of the wolves
Ring to the keen-eyed stars: woe, woe is me!
Yet, when from west to east the setting sun
Bridges with golden light the purple seas,
And airs blow cool about me, sometimes comes
Some little calmness o'er me as I sit
And watch the sea-gull sporting on the wave,
And, high amid the rosy-tinted air,
The eagle sailing towards his rocky home.
I hear in spirit, dying far away,
The torrent streams of Œta, and behold
The snowy peaks, the hollows of the hills,
And the green meadows, haunt of grazing herds
Thro' which Spercheius wanders to the sea,—
My ancient home—and there methinks I see
My father coming homeward from the chase
With all his dogs about him, and the youths,
Their weapons gleaming in the falling dew.
O is he yet alive, or does he lie
Sepulchred with his fathers? for whene'er
A ship hath chanced to touch upon this isle,
I have besought the mariners with tears
To tell him of my lot, that he might send
And fetch me, but no ship hath ever come,
And so I fear that all who loved me there
Are with their fathers; would that I might lie
Among them, but my bones, alas! the sport
Of every wind and wave, when all the birds
Have feasted off them, on these sands must bleach
Unburied, and unwet with any tears.

O often, as in dreams, I seem to hear
The din of battle, and I long to know
How fares the war, and if it rages still
Beside the reedy banks of Simois,
Or up divine Scamander's whirling stream,
And on the lotos-bearing meads that stretch

Beneath the breezy battlements of Troy;
Or if the fair broad-streeted city yet
Hath fallen, or the noble Hector died;
For there went many thither whom I loved—
Divine Achilles, and the wise old king
That ruled o'er sandy Pylos; do they still,
Chanting the pæan, fight with gods and men,
Or are they nothing but an empty name
For wandering bards to sing of? Oh, for me
No famous exploit, mighty deed of arms
Shall ever show me worthy to have held
His weapons, who, from oft the sacred pile
That flaming far on Œta lit the sea,
Rose to his place among the mighty gods:
Nor even may I in paternal halls
Dwell, mated with a loving wife, whose smile
Might cheer my hearth, and train a race of sons
To keep alive the glory of their sires.
    But yet if patience, and to suffer pain
With firm endurance, meet a due reward,
For me, who all these years have dwelt alone
And suffer'd daily from a grievous wound,
Far higher glory may I reach than they
Who fight, whirl'd on amid a multitude
That praise them, and exhort to noble deeds,
And half-inspire the valour they applaud.
    And still, however little, there is hope:
There yet may come a time when I shall see
The faces I have loved in olden time,
And with the spring my hope buds fresh again.
The sea is still, the breeze across the bay
Blows softly, and upon my couch of leaves
May sleep—who drowns alike lost hopes and fears,
Refresh me with the shadow of his wings:
Perchance a ship may touch the coast at morn.

                              "H."

DOUBLE HONOURS.

IT was my intention to have submitted to the Editors of
The Eagle, with a view to their finding a place in their
last Number, a few additional remarks on University Studies,
supplementary to, and on some points *corrective* of, those
which have already appeared in Nos. VI. and VII. of
The Eagle. I was prevented from doing so by other duties
which called me away from Cambridge: an interruption
which I the less regret, because the experience of one who
has tried "double reading" may be of service to some
new Candidate for University Honours, who is at present
in doubt as to his future course. I shall therefore endeavour as briefly as I can, to state where I differ from
your previous correspondents, and what are my own views
on the subject.

The remarks of "Ne quid nimis" of course claim
my first attention. I differ with him on three points:
1st, I maintain that it may be laid down as a general rule,
that all "really great works" have been achieved by men
who have made one study, one pursuit, their sole object
and aim. There is more force in his remark, that whatever tends to give a man one-sided views, is prejudicial
to the formation of a sound judgment.

2ndly, I consider the study of Mathematics to be the
best possible training for a man intended for Holy Orders.
At any time he requires the power of sound reasoning
which he may gain from their study, for the arguments

of theoretical Divinity;* and, in our own day above all, he needs the same power to enable him to detect every sophistry and fallacy, that will meet him in his contact with the growing infidelity of our large towns. Practical observation is strengthening this power daily in the mind of the thoughtful mechanic. The constant tracing of the links between cause and effect in the several parts of the machine on which he works cannot fail to develope in him an inductive power which may make him a dangerous combatant to meet, to one who lacks such training.

3rdly, I cannot assent to the theory advanced in p. 36. It appears to me to strike at the root of a belief in peculiar talents, and to an unwarrantable extent to apply the Jeffersonian Canon, that "all men are born free and equal." At any rate, in my own case, and with reference to my introduction to Latin, experience points to a different conclusion.

To all that your second correspondent advances, I can subscribe, save to that which at first sight appeared to myself, and will doubtless appear to many, his strongest argument: I mean that which he derives from the moral value of the fourth or fifth hour's work. My own experience and that of others, whom I have consulted, go to prove that your "double man" does not take up his Horace at the end of a hard evening's work at Mathematics: that on the contrary, with the exception of the necessary preparation for College Lectures, one branch of study or the other will occupy his whole attention. In this sense alone I believe the maxim to be true—"Change of work is as good as play." It appears to me that such a process of "change" as that to which your correspondent alludes, cannot fail to unhinge and unsettle the mind, and cause a man to realise the truth of that other proverb about falling between two stools. The zest and freshness with which a man returns to a branch of study which he has laid aside for a time, is quite a different thing, and has formed one of my own greatest pleasures in my course as an Undergraduate.

Thus much for the opinions of our friends. My own

---

* I have heard it remarked ere now, that we should not have had so much of the mists of German Neology, had Mathematics been more studied in German Universities.

experience points to somewhat different conclusions. With regard to the generality of knowledge of which "Ne quid nimis" speaks, the history and poetry, the newspapers and novels, the "single" reader has decidedly the advantage over his more ambitious confrère. I am convinced that, if a man aims at a high place in both Triposes he must be endowed with very brilliant parts to be able to devote any time to such reading. He may manage a newspaper or a serial at the Union after hall, but the rest of his time is too precious to be spent thus. Even the history which your Mathematician can take pleasure in, and your Classic provide for in his hours of study, becomes irksome to him from the knowledge that what forms *his* light reading must be reproduced on the sixth morning of the final examination. "Ne quid nimis" is, however, somewhat hard on the Mathematical men, in putting them all down in the same Category, as wholly absorbed in their favourite pursuit with neither heart nor head for aught else.

There are two classes of men, as I conceive, who should read for both Mathematical and Classical honours: those whom early preparation or mental capacity assures of a high place in each—and those who, having thoroughly tested their own powers, know that they would be unable to secure such a place in either; men who, unable to achieve a Wranglership or First Class, can attain to a Double Second. Ordinary men will do best to confine their attention to the one branch, to which their inclination leads them.

But though I would check the aspirations of our juniors in University standing, who dream of the double laurels of Senior Wrangler and Senior Classic, I would remind them that they have in our two new Triposes a preventive of the one-sidedness which your correspondent so much dreads. The studies which they involve afford sufficient variety from the severer pursuits of the candidate for other honours, and cannot be accused of any want of practical bearing on life and conduct. At the same time, either party will find, if he prefers them, studies which, while affording him change and recreation, will at the same time by mental training, aid his other studies. The Mathematician may profit by the analysis of Chemistry, the inductions of Geology, the classifications of Botany and Zoology: whilst the Classic can only gain a thorough knowledge of his Plato and Aristotle by a deep study of their moral meaning. Or if it be more consistent with the Student's ideas of preparation for Holy Orders, let him set about divinity reading, and increase the scanty number of those who seek honours in the Theological Tripos.

But these remarks have already extended beyond the limits which I proposed to myself. I hope that the importance of the subject to so many of your readers may be my excuse.

"OCCIDENS."

———————

MY ——.

———

It has a chassic-carven head :
  Young Sleep lies cushion'd on a cloud ;
  His eyes are closed ; his head is bow'd ;
And at his feet grim Care lies dead.

A Snake crawls subtle round the stem :
  The yellow stem is amber-tipp'd :
  And all the bowl is silver-lipp'd :
Each Snake's eye glitters like a gem.

The amber clear shines liquid bright ;
  As when some sunbeam glimmers down
  On shady brook, and makes it brown
And lucid with the lurking light.

And every curve and Serpent coil,
  The bronzed Sleep, dead Care by him,
  The head up to the silver rim
Is burnish'd with the oozing oil.

"W. E. M."

THE TOTAL ECLIPSE OF 1860.

The Posada, Pancorbo.
July 13, 1860.

WHEN in the month of April Professor Chevallier proposed to me to join him in an excursion to the Pyrenees
and the north of Spain to observe the total eclipse of the
sun from some station near the central line, I was not many
minutes in coming to a decision. I was also empowered to
invite a third friend to join us; and in the coffee-room of
the Hotel des Etrangers in Paris, I introduced to him
Hammond, one of the Sixth Form of Rugby School.

I shall say nothing of our tour in the Pyrenees, and
spare my readers the ascent of the highest mountain of
all the Pyrenees, the Maladetta; an ascent which though
not extraordinarily difficult or fatiguing, and offering a view
at sunrise which the Cima di Jazi under Monte Rosa alone
can rival, has been made by few Englishmen. The summit
was first attained in 1842. After spending some days very
pleasantly at Luchon, and making excursions in the neighbourhood, we returned by Pau to Bayonne a week before
the eclipse, and started on Friday the 13th in the banquette
of the diligence for Vittoria.

At the Spanish frontier our baggage was instantly passed
without examination ; the government having ordered that all
possible facilities should be afforded to foreign astronomers.
Now we were in a new land, and the change was instantly
manifest in the style of driving. Instead of six respectable
horses, we beheld eight mules and two horses harnessed in
pairs to our diligence. After infinite shouting and struggling,
the mules were prevented from facing the driver, and were
in some sort of order. A man stands by each. Suddenly
the conductor shouts ' arrè, arrè' (pure Arabic for gee-up) and
a storm of winged words and blows from above, below, and
on both sides, descends on the unfortunate mules. We
start at a terrific pace, swinging round corners and down
the narrow streets of Irun, till all the runners are out-
stripped, and the unhappy beasts are left to the tender

mercies of the postillion on one of the leaders, and the driver. The latter has a complete assortment of whips on the roof of the diligence, and has a very good notion how to make them speak from the box ; but every now and then quietly descends from his high seat, and frantically rushing alongside of the team, who know well what is coming, and do all they know, bastes every one of them, kick as they may and do, with the wooden handle of one of his whips, and placidly remounts to his box, while the lumbering old coach is tumbling and pitching along at some twelve miles an hour. The shouting at the mules is incessant ; " albonero, albonero", shouts the conductor, in a tone of surprised re-monstrance ; " albonero, albonero," shrieks the indignant driver ; " albonero, albonero", the disappointed conductor ; " albonero, albonero", the furious driver, and enforces his ejaculations with the lash, and so on through every tone and expression of all the feelings that can possibly be supposed to arise in the breasts of a driver and conductor in a hurry to overtake a rival diligence. Suddenly we see the rival before us, the driver instantly descends, and we tear down the hill after it. There is barely room to pass, but our postillion is already by the side of their wheelers ; we are gaining rapidly, when their leaders shy almost into the ditch, and get inside the telegraph posts ; and as we pass in a cloud of dust and shouts we see their struggling team in hopeless confusion, a telegraph post in the act of falling, our conductor shrugging his shoulders, and all goes on just as before ; and the driver, without looking round, continues his shouts " hierro, hierro, la òtra, òtra, òtra."

To ascend some of the passes we had twelve oxen har-nessed in pairs in front, and the ten mules in a string behind ; and the shrieks, in the vain endeavour to persuade the beasts that now, now is the time to make an extra effort, were even more varied, and displayed a copious vocabulary of epithets, many of them alluding to the deceased pro-genitors of the animals.

The Bidassoa, Pasages, San Sebastian and Vittoria, recall many a page in Napier. We were proud of our country as we passed over the spot where Joseph's carriage, stuffed with spoil and fine oil paintings secreted in the lining, and all his papers, were taken the evening after the great battle. " Gracias a Dios, soy caballero Ingles" is the correct reply for an Englishman to make if ever he is mistaken in Spain for a Frenchman.

We had had the most alarming account given us of

Spanish cookery ; a lively little Frenchman who had just returned from this part of Spain, gave us an appalling description, garlic in everything, everything cooked with oil, " ugh, ugh," holding his nose, " l'huile mauvaise ! rancèe !! detestable ! ! !" but fifty marks of exclamation would fail to convey the emphasis of his voice and gesture. We must however do the Spaniards the justice to say that we have lived for a week in Spain, most of it in a little village inn, and have not seen or smelt oil ; and had garlic in nothing but salt : and all travellers who repeat sufficiently often the words " ajo no ! aceite no" ! may fare equally well. The cuisine is very good even here ; and everything clean and nice.

Pancorbo is a little village of some fifteen hundred to two thousand inhabitants, half way between Vittoria and Burgos, and nearly half way between Bayonne and Madrid. The line of central totality passes within a mile or two of it, and this was the station Mr. Chevallier decided on selecting. We drove hither on Saturday from Vittoria, meeting one or two English engineers and astronomers at Miranda on the Ebro. Airy, Otto Struve, and others were in the neighbourhood ; and De la Rue had set up a house and complete photographic apparatus. The Spaniards were of opinion that the English had come to make arrangements for bringing the sun nearer to England, where we had no sun and no fruit. The Spanish ambassador in England is said to have reported, that he met with no ripe fruits in England except ginger-bread nuts. A very intelligent Spaniard asked me whether corn could grow in England.

Mr. Chevallier had requested the English consul at Bayonne to write to the Alcalde of Pancorbo to engage rooms for us. We drove therefore first to his house. He received us in all state. Placing us on his right hand, he began to pour forth an eloquent and copious address in Spanish, of which we could so far gather the meaning, as to perceive that he was, after many sentences were completed, still in the preface. Fortunately, however, we discovered that he spoke French very well ; and all our anxieties were over. He accompanied us to the posada or inn, a large building by the road-side. The capacious front-door leads directly into a low roomy stable, after the invariable fashion of houses here. We found ourselves in one of the bedrooms ; we sat in a row, the Alcalde at the head, and opposite us a plain English looking man and his sharp little wife, master and mistress of the posada. The Alcalde is the interpreter. We wish to know what accommodation they have, and at what price. The Alcalde begins "Los Senores dicen," etc., and interprets the reply, seventeen francs each per day. This was absurd; so we explained that we had travelled and knew a thing or two, and thought the charge monstrous. This was evidently expected, and the Alcalde began again. "Los Senores dicen," that they have travelled in Spain, France, Italy, Germany, and England (laying a marked emphasis on England as an outlandish place which few English might be expected to visit), and made our offer to them. After much more talking, and the minutest enquiries as to the diet we desired, and at the end of a scene infinitely entertaining, for by this time the postman and similar important personages were in the room, we finally agreed on our terms, and the exultation and the delighted glances at each other of the master and mistress convinced us that we had not made a very hard bargain.

Pancorbo is the Thermopylæ of this part of Spain. It lies in a valley, bounded in some places literally by vertical rocks, and though very narrow for more than a mile, is in one place not thirty yards broad either at the level of the road, or a hundred feet higher up. The rocks are, I believe, of carboniferous limestone; but I could detect no fossils whatever in any part by which to identify them. The strata are at all inclinations from horizontal to vertical; and strangely contorted the curved broken strata in one place forming a cave with almost architectural regularity and symmetry of outline. Pinnacles, serrated edges, and ponderous buttresses of rock group themselves fantastically round the village. It is a very Pompeii of antiquity. The old castle, occupied for five years by the French till after the battle of Vittoria, was built against the Moors : the caves are of immense antiquity. Thick-walled houses of the quaintest build, and having their internal arrangements more picturesque than I can describe, stand about facing this way and that, as if they had nothing to do with the modern village clustering round them; and their huge old oak-doors, stable-doors of course, are so massively and handsomely carved, and so adorned with finely-wrought iron-work as to show that their masters, once upon a time, were no mean men. But there is no end to the curiosities of the place. Poking about the little streets, one stumbles here on a half-defaced coat of arms, with ALONSO GOMEZ decipherable beneath it; there on some antique symbols over the door of a cottage, with walls of hewn stone a yard thick; here on a massive arch, and there one's eye is caught by the glitter, as it dangles in the sun and twirls about in the breeze, of the very brass helmet which the valiant Don Quixote won with his lance from the peaceful and astonished barber.

There is a school here of some thirty boys, (there is an elementary school, attended by seventy little boys and girls); we saw them lying on their cloaks in the sun in the school-yard, humming away over their lessons. I looked at one of their books, it was a Latin Phrase book, dated 1725, occumbere somno; dormir—sopor irrigat artus; lo mismo—dare membra sopori; lo mismo, &c., &c. 'Membra,' on enquiry was feminine singular, to the horror of the Sixth Form boy who came up at the moment. We went into the school afterwards. It was a plain kind of barn, the master standing in the middle, on a floor not worth speaking of, and the boys ranged all round. They do no arithmetic, no geography, nor history of any kind; and learn nothing but Latin. They could translate Ovid very respectably, and parse and scan, and give the rules with a volubility which infinitely surpassed our power of comprehending provincial Spanish; but as the master seemed recently to have dined on garlic, and thought fit loudly to repeat, in impressive proximity to our olfactory organs, every word the boys said, we were compelled somewhat precipitately to retire. Mr. Chevallier wrote them a Latin letter, inviting the whole school to come to the inn at noon on Tuesday, if the sun shone, to look at the sun.

The agricultural arrangements are most primitive; ploughs that would illustrate Hesiod; mattocks and hoes of oriental shape. The corn is thrashed by mules treading it out on grass covered areas artificially levelled, or dragging after them a board, studded with flints ingeniously fastened in; it is all thrashed as soon as reaped, and winnowed by being flung out of a window into a blanket when a breeze is blowing. With such antiquities, such primitive modes, not of agriculture only, but of everything; such a simple and courteous people, so picturesquely dressed; such a field of geological and also of botanical interest, it would seem that Pancorbo would have been no bad place to spend a week in had there been no special reason for selecting it. For our purpose of observing the eclipse no place could be better.

We started at 9.30 with a couple of mules, carrying tables and chairs, stands, instruments, &c., and wound by a zig-zag path past ruined French barracks, and the site of the battery that breached the castle in '13, up to the top of the hill.

o

The sky was very cloudy, but gave promise of breaking; and it never actually rained with us. By twelve o'clock the sun had gained a complete victory; but over the valley of the Ebro, two thousand feet below us, the struggle was still pending. The people soon came thronging up, the Alcalde among the first. He is a fine old gentleman, who remembers the war of Independence, as the Peninsular war is here called, and is very proud of the Spanish success, admitting, however, that some English, Germans, and Hollanders came here to help them. He has been invaluable to us as an interpreter, and we have turned over our portmanteaus in vain search for some substantial mark of our gratitude, but we can find nothing that would be valuable, and at the same time a suitable present for Englishmen to make, but soap; and that he would scarcely know the use of.

At the very summit of the hill, a steep ridge, are the ruins of a French powder magazine; and its thick walls served admirably as a place for our thermometer in the shade. At 1.15 there must have been three hundred men, women, and school-boys, on the top of our hill. The Alcalde had promised that when we wished to be alone, the soldiers, some half dozen of whom were in attendance, should clear the ground; but there was no necessity for this. For the next half hour we were three showmen. There was an uninterrupted stream of strange rough bearded men, in the broad crimson sash of Spain, whose open shirt fronts showed a skin tanned to a tawny red; of women with heads undefended against the sun, by anything more than their thick jet black hair, and occasionally a bright coloured handkerchief thrown over them: and of boys not a little proud of being able to exchange a word or two in Latin, with the tall Englishmen. The sharpest of them were much struck by the spots on the sun, one of which was large, and remarkably well defined, and I had many questions about them. The people maintained perfect order and decorum; I made a ring of stones round my stand, and they stood in a line outside it, coming up in order to look through my telescope. My telescope was a large cometensucher, belonging to Mr. Chevallier; with a field of nearly three degrees diameter, and giving a well defined image. After the ring was formed, there came up four priests, with long cylindrical hats, a hole being cut in the side for the head, and thick capacious cloaks of black cloth, which justify Sancho Panza's simile more completely than I had supposed possible— "Blessed be the man that invented sleep; it wrappeth a

man about like a cloak." I found by unmistakeable signs,
that the priests claimed precedence of all present, and
accordingly invited them to the telescope, and the stolid
stupidity of their faces, which were not improved by their
having to look up a tube inclined at about 60° to the
horizon, made me long for a photograph of them. As the
time of first contact drew near, Mr. C. called "silence,"
and the soldiers shouted "silencio," and I find in my notes,
1 hour, 48 minutes, 35 seconds, as the time observed. The
moon advanced very slowly on the sun, shewing even with
my small power two or three distinct prominences. We
left our chairs, and the talking spontaneously began again;
and our labour as showmen. The people were highly delighted
at seeing a piece taken out of the sun. The vanishing of the
large spot, a quarter of an hour after first contact, was a curious
sight, and when that was over I left the telescope in charge
of our friend, the clever carpenter, whose aid we had more
than once invoked, and went to make a very straight forward
observation. I had cut in a piece of card-board, some two
feet square, a number of holes of different shapes and sizes;
triangles, squares, circles, parallelograms, &c., and placed it
on a wall, so propped up with stones that the sunlight fell
nearly perpendicularly on it, and placed another on the
ground parallel to it, in its shadow. The spots of light
were, as I expected, no longer circles,* but accurately represented the phase of the eclipse; this delighted the people
immensely, who had before been gazing at the perforated card-
board with unenlightened curiosity. There was not much to
do now; Hammond took the thermometer readings every
15 minutes, in sun and shade. The light on the landscape was rapidly diminishing: at 2. 50. the lower cusp in
an inverting telescope was very blunt, and suddenly like a
flash of light became pointed again. A few minutes before
totality, I looked round; a greenish unnatural light, wholly
unlike twilight, was spread over the vale of Miranda behind
us, and the great treeless plain that extended as far as the
eye could reach before us. A hush was creeping over the
people: a dog plaintively poking his nose up to his master
within a yard or two of me. I returned to the telescope:
the cusps were now rapidly changing; spots of light became
isolated in the upper cusp, and were then instantly extin-

---

* What is the exact shape of the spot of light formed by the sun
shining through an elliptical hole?

guished. I drew off the dark glass, and saw the arc of light
break up partially into fine points and instantly vanish:
I saw no motion of the beads of light. The whole scene was
in a moment utterly changed. Two bright cherry-coloured
flames appeared suddenly at some distance from the point of
disappearance of the sun: they were not very bright, triangular, with the base towards the moon, somewhat lighter
and brighter at the vertex, and of a singularly beautiful
colour. But the corona was splendid; far exceeding all
my anticipations. My telescope was admirably adapted for
observation of the corona. It was very irregular, in one
place near the upper part the light being very feeble, even
close by the edge, for an arc of the moon of nearly 10°; the
dark part being bounded on one side by straight radii of
light; and on the other by similar rays, like fibres of finely
spun glass in a brilliant light, which however at a little
distance from the moon lost their rectilinear structure, and
curved over toward the dark part in fine wavy silky lines.
At the part where the sun vanished was a similar wavy
portion of the corona, its direction on the whole being nearly
radial which extended from the moon, as well as I could
estimate, more than two breadths of the moon. The corona
was very brilliant; and of nearly white light, tinged with a
light pink cream colour. I now took in hand a photometer,
which Mr. Chevallier had contrived, but found that the halo
was so much brighter than we had anticipated, that I could
get from it no superior limit to the amount of light; it
was however by estimation as seen through the darkest part
of the photometer when barely visible, nearly equivalent to
that of a light cirrocumulous cloud about 12° or 15° below
the sun, ten minutes after its reappearance; but somewhat
exceeded it in brightness. It was also not very unequal
in intensity to the flame of a wax candle at ten feet distance,
two or three minutes after reappearance. I now returned
to the telescope, and having computed the zenith distance
and azimuth of Venus relatively to the sun, had no difficulty
in finding it in my large field. It was extremely brilliant;
the cusps appeared as exquisitely fine lines, completing as
nearly as I could judge, but not exceeding a semicircle, and
the dark part of Venus was wholly invisible. The centre
of the illuminated part was so bright as to dazzle the eye,
and I regret that I did not think at the moment of using the
dark glass to examine it. When will such a chance as this
eclipse afforded, (Venus being nearly in inferior conjunction
with the sun and only 5¼° distant from it, at the time of a

total eclipse) of determining whether Venus has an atmosphere, occur again?

I looked round on the people and the landscape. There was total silence, and not a breath of air: a hush and an awe had fallen on all that crowd, and their faces were pale with a greenish light. The very distant horizon over Burgos was quite cloudless: and the most remarkable general effect was in that quarter. I find "lurid olive yellow horizon" in my notes as descriptive of the colour, fading away from near the horizon to a dark purple; in the neighbourhood of the sun the sky had very much the appearance of a clear twilight. Jupiter, Pollux, and Procyon were very easily visible. The mountains of Santa Inez, a fine group towards the south east, were of a rich dark purple; the vale of the Ebro greenish and dark. But there was far more light than I had anticipated. The shadow of a pencil was distinctly visible. I had just time to return to the telescope and find the sun, (for I had called to Mr. Chevallier to come and look at Venus) and see that some more red prominences had appeared, when a single point of light and then several more which rapidly formed an arc, was hailed by the people with enthusiastic shouts of Sol! Sol! A red flame was distinctly visible (as red, not pink) several seconds after the reappearance of the sun; the corona gradually faded away. I glanced down to catch the line of retreating shadow. It was retiring at no very rapid rate towards Logrono and the vale of the Ebro, and our view in that direction was unbounded; it is said to extend two hundred and eight miles. It swept over the treeless plain like the shadow of a cloud, and was visible after nearly two minutes, and four minutes after reappearance, while I was gazing at a very distant well-defined range of stratus clouds far down in the valley of the Ebro, which I had previously taken note of, they received a sudden flush of light. Nearly all was now over, and the people began to disperse; the light seemed the natural light of day. At 3.25 I distinctly saw in Mr. Chevallier's telescope the moon's edge projected as a dark body beyond the edge of the sun, and behind it a faintly radiate structure of the halo. This was at the lower cusp in a non-inverting telescope. It was visible for, I think, not less than eight degrees of the moon's circumference.

By this time we were almost alone. The people had gone down a few hundred yards and were dancing, a couple of fiddlers having presented themselves. We began to write our notes, and then to compare them. Mr. C. will probably publish his account elsewhere. Hammond was provided with a telescope that threw an image of the sun of about six inches diameter on a screen (the top of a band box,) protected from the light by a triangular cone of black calico fastened on canes moving with the telescope. In this Bailey's beads were seen; and the image of the halo was distinctly visible.

Such a sight as we had witnessed is rarely seen twice in a lifetime. A partial eclipse of the sun is scarcely more remarkable than one of the moon, and can in no way be compared to a total eclipse. The sudden shock produced by the *total* extinction of sunlight; the strange discoloration of the horizon, and the atmosphere that instantly follows; the spontaneous silence; the feeling the time fly by making every second that remains so precious; not to mention the singular beauty of the corona, surrounded with planets and stars, conspire to make a total eclipse of the sun a spectacle to which there is nothing " simile aut secundum;" and there is nothing to occupy even the " proximos honores."

This eclipse must have been so ably and so widely observed that the results to Science will probably be of great value. Those who wish to see scientific accounts of the phenomena observed, will do well to consult the monthly notices of the Astronomical Society, and the Transactions.

On our return to Pancorbo we heard that the fowls had gone to roost; that some men had vowed to kill us if we *had* taken the sun away; that the people were excessively frightened, embracing one another, and crossing themselves, and weeping in the streets, and in the midst of all their tears that much mirth was excited by seeing a tall Spanish woman with a certain long straight tube, used by the local veterinary surgeon for the relief of constipated mules, gazing fixedly at the sun. Many other stories are going the round, and I think it likely that our visit and the spectacle that accompanied it will be long remembered by the inhabitants of Pancorbo.

" J. M. WILSON."

ELEGIACS.

Bitter it is to be bound, when the hurt wings struggle to hurry
  Up from the toil and whirl, up to the beautiful heights;
Bitter it is to be worn with the wretched wear and the worry,
  Here in a selfish world, little regarding our rights.

Pity the soul that seeks to be single, true to its duty;
  Netted about its feet draggle the coils of distrust:
Pity the spirit that pines to walk in a garment of beauty;
  Mournfully mixed with sin, bitterly soiled with the dust.

Blest, if spared at last becoming the slave of convention,
  Strong as a god to crush, subtle and sly as a fiend;
Blest, if it carry clear thro' one wish or god-like intention;
  Blest if, tho' but a film, gossamer beauty be gleaned.

I was proud as a king, and strong as an eagle to hover
  Over the gulfing storm, over the mist in the glen:
Now I go humbled and weak, and skulking wounded to cover,
  Sinning a little sin, held in the clutches of men.

Long I stood high on my hill, and boasted of noble endeavour,
  Speaking of better things, over the pit of their fall;
Fretting the feeble hearts, bitter-jealous, besotted for ever:
  Then—O the bitter slip!—slipped in the sight of them all.

They,—with a fiend's delight, with a sneer and mock at the prophet,
  Speaking the speech of God, lipping the words of the saint,—
"Was it his word rang great? and is this all that comes of it?
  Better for pride to fall." O in my climbing I faint.

God, I am dizzy and weak, with a little hope! O I shudder,
  Climbing the weary heights, hovering over the brink!
Sailing a rainy sea in the dark, no canvas or rudder!
  Be thou the pilot, O God! I shall endure, as I think!

"A."

SCRAPS FROM THE NOTE-BOOK OF PERCIVAL OAKLEY.

SCRAP SENTIMENTAL.

(Continued from Vol. II. p. 143.)

POTENT goddess, Self-possession, why failedst thou thy votary this day in his hour of need; why leftest him thus exposed in the bare weakness of his native idiocy? Surely, but for thy inopportune desertion, all might yet have been well. What were easier than to have soothed the she-Cerberus of an Aunt with sops of honeyed compliment, to have crushed that military monster with an avalanche of pointed sarcasms, and last, not least, to have picked up the drawing things, given my arm to the angelic being, and continued, in the course of a homeward moonlight ride, those golden threads of whispering now so rudely snapped and severed.

Such was the form of my reflections after flinging myself on the sofa at our lodgings, on the night of that picnic to Fairbeacon; and then by way of calming my feelings, I pictured to myself what agreeable remarks must have followed my abrupt departure; how the Colonel must have chuckled and grinned and exploded with asinine jokes; how Miss Veriblue and the female Tuggs must have snarled and whined in chorus; how Ernest and Eugenie must have enjoyed and improved on the news when it reached their secluded corner, and as to Seraphina herself, I consumed about an hour in wondering how she got out of it all, and what her views would be henceforward on the momentous subject. "At any rate"—I remarked aloud, and a cheerful conclusion it was, all things considered—"at any rate she *must* think me an 'infernal fool.'"

" I should rather imagine she did," said Saville, entering in time for my soliloquy, " tho' perhaps she don't put it exactly in that same' forcible language. But really and upon my honour, Percy, a more fearful duffer than you made of yourself this afternoon, it's difficult to conceive."

" Let me tell you, Saville," I began in wrath—

" Can't stop to argufy: old McBean is waiting for me to blow some 'bacca: so ' bye bye, Tuppy,'" and he vanished in fragrant clouds.

Bacca! thought I, the very thing: wonder it never struck me before—nerves to be soothed—walk on the sands—possible light in window—hurrah !— *Vamos.*

So out I stepped and began to put my programme in execution through the medium of a full flavoured Havanna. The tide was coming in fast, and washing with faint sibilation against the sea-wall; the sands were covered, that was certain; but I was aware of a certain cove above high water mark, possessing all sorts of pleasantly perilous crags on which to seat oneself. Not a twinkle of a light in *the* window, and the drawing-room shutters grimly closed. Strange to say, not a star was visible, and for a summer night it was curiously dark, so dark that I ran against the coast-guard man on his lonely patrol, and should probably have received some casual blessing from that jolly tar, only being on duty, he was debarred the luxury of speaking, much less swearing. Towards the cove I bent my steps, and scrambling down a rock or two, found myself on my favourite ledge, with a soft stone at my back, and the lazy sea under my overhanging legs. Needless to say, that by this course of treatment my nerves speedily recovered their usual tone, and in natural sequence I fell to composing poetry in my head. Don't you remember, reader, the amiable lion in the Arabian Nights, who is always " falling down in a fit and uttering these verses?" That's just the class of lion I belong to, and thanks to my diary, the following beautiful lines will not be lost to posterity :—

> Calmly the moonbeams smile
>   O'er the calm ocean;
> Billows have lulled awhile
>   Their mad commotion:
> Oh! such a scene and hour,
> Hath it not magic power
> From the full heart to shower
>   Each fond emotion?

Lo! in what dead repose
  Still Earth is lying;
She hath forgot her woes,
  And hushed her sighing;
The world is sunk to sleep,
Save where the wretched weep,
Save where the watch they keep,
  Over the dying.

I had arrived at this point, and was trying to get some substitute for "shower," in the first stanza; wondering whether "pour" mightn't do better, and running through all the words with a suitable termination, when I was suddenly disturbed by the consciousness of being no longer alone, and a subdued duet of male voices penetrated my ears. Perhaps you'll say I had no right to listen: well probably I shouldn't, if I could have stirred; but judging from the sound, the two intruders had seated themselves exactly on the spot, where I must have put my hand to raise myself, and how was I to know whether in a moment of surprise I mightn't receive such a gentle shove as would send me off the narrow platform for a cool plunge into the yawning gulf beneath? The same result might happen if I spoke, or coughed, or sneezed, or groaned, (tho' the last seemed the happiest idea) so—on the impulse of the moment—I kept perfectly quiet, and clung to the rock with all the tenacity of fond affection. But the conversation that I heard, first of all made my hair stand on end, secondly, produced a deep feeling of joy that there *was* a greater fool in the world even than Percival Oakley, and lastly, made me shake with such internal laughter that my ribs were all but agonised.

It may have been for ten minutes that the converse lasted—then the final remark I heard was this:

"No, Muster Saville, for one tenner I could'na do it, but for foive tenners I dunna know but I mout."

That's all I'm going to repeat, so you see my discretion may be relied on; but your penetration must have told you that the speakers were none other than old McBean of the Lively Nancy Schooner, and my fellow lodger: and the result will presently reveal that the subject of their discourse was neither more nor less than abduction,. or (to put it milder) elopement on the High Seas.

As soon as they were safely off I made the best of my way to No. 6. "Mr. Saville come in?" said I to Mary the slavey who happened to be on the door-step. "No, Sir, he isn't," said Mary, "but there's been a man to look for him twice to-day, since you both went out, Sir." "And what sort of a man, Mary?" "Well, he was a very hugly man, Sir, with a shocking bad hat and a yellow handkerchief round his neck, and no collar as I could see, and he was dressed very shabby hall over: but he wanted to see Mr. Saville particular, and said he'd call at ten in the morning." "Well, if he wants to see him in bed that's about the time, isn't it, Mary?" "Yes, Sir, and so I told him, but he said he should come anyways, and I didn't quite catch his name, but it sounded like Hairyun." "Well never mind, but bring me up some soda-water; and tell Mrs. Eton with my love, that she must lend me a little brandy, for there's not been a drop in our bottle since her last attack "of heart complaint;" and, without waiting for reply, I pursued my way up-stairs, and fell to writing.

About twelve Ernest made his triumphal entry, grabbed my pen on the spot, regardless of blotted leaves, pitched my precious diary off the table, then seized my head, and by a series of violent rubbings, ruined my ambrosial curls.

"Well, when you've done," said I, "perhaps you'll enter into some financial arrangement about our bill at these lodgings, for if you start for France to-morrow afternoon, it's time for us to have a settling."

"Start for France," said Saville, and stared in speechless astonishment, "why, what the dev—."

"Now don't: just think of the Lively Nancy, and old McBean, and his passengers, male and female."

"You infernal scamp, what are you driving at?"

"A fair breeze, eh, old boy, and a six hours' run, and five tenners for the job."

"Well, Percy, how on earth you've got hold of that, beats me entirely, unless the Bargee told you; but I've not lost sight of the Bargee since we made our little arrangements, and I left him just this minute at the Crown and Anchor, speechless drunk."

"How I got hold of it don't much matter, but I know it from end to end, so it's no good your trying to keep it dark; and my impression is, that I ought to give old St. Croix the office on the spot."

"You'll never serve me such a confounded turn as that."

"Why you'll be liable to transportation, my dear fellow, not to speak of action for theft, plunder, conspiracy, and arson; and the Colonel an't a man to be trifled with,

mauvais sujet though he be.   Now what will you give
me to let you off?"

Ernest made no reply, but fell to walking up and down
the room.   "Seriously though, old boy," I continued, "do
reflect a little on what your doing, and hold hard before
it's too late—before you've done what you may repent
of all your life long."

"And what concern is this of yours," he said, stopping
and facing me, "what right have you—how dare you interfere?"

"Dare! come, Saville, what d'you take me for?   Am
I likely to look on and see foul play without doing my best
to stop it?"

I said more than I meant of course, but I was foolish
enough to be annoyed at his tone.

"Well! I do call this low of you," said he, "I do
call it treacherous."

"And worming yourself into a man's intimacy, being
his bosom friend for three weeks, and then stealing his
daughter; that isn't low, I suppose,—that isn't treacherous."

"Percy," said he, sitting down again, "you don't know
all, or you'd never talk to me in that style, I'm certain.
You don't know that I have spoken to St. Croix about
his daughter, and been rejected by him point blank."

"Why, when on earth did that happen?"

"To-night, as we rode home: the old scoundrel said
he was much honoured, but had other views for his girl.
The fact is, as Eugenie told me, he has affianced her to
a friend of his own abroad, a Count or Marquis, or something, who was her *parrain*, and old enough to be her
father.   He's coming over here next month, and they reckon
it all settled, tho' Eugenie has been on her knees to the
Colonel, imploring him to spare her.   She always hated
this Frenchman from her childhood, but St. Croix is in-
volved with him in some gambling transactions or other,
(the old, old story) and can't back out of it now, if he
would."

"Well: it's a nice business and no mistake: but go on."

"I fully expected his answer, you know, and have made
up my plans for some days, but I never intended disclosing
them to you, because——"

"Because you knew I should put a spoke in the wheel."

"Partly so, perhaps; but more because I didn't want
to compromise any one else in my own bad luck.   I know
it's a confounded scrape whichever way one looks at it;

but not exactly so bad as you imagine. Look here. The schooner takes us over to the coast of France, and lands us at St. Ambroise. Eugenie has friends there who will aid and abet her. We can be married at their house the day after to-morrow, and when she is once my wife, I can return to England and defy her father to do his worst. When he sees he can't help himself, he'll have sense enough to keep quiet, or else I'm much mistaken in my man."

"But after what has past between you to-day, it isn't likely he'll give you the chance of meeting her again, much less meeting her alone."

"I'm coming to that directly. By the way, after you bolted from Fairbeacon, I did you a good turn, and no mistake, for I explained the cause of your rather peculiar conduct."

"As how?"

"Said you were liable to frequent attacks of neuralgia, in the agonies of which nothing but solitude was bearable."

"'Pon my word I'm much obliged to you for such a flattering account of my state of health."

"So you ought to be. It wasn't the Britannia Life Insurance I was talking to, was it? so what's the odds? I thought it was pretty sharp of me to name neuralgia, for I was just going to call it temporary insanity."

"I commend your design, but the execution is unequal."

"Anyways, you'll hear no further chaff on that subject, unless it be the softest whisper from that pair of lips which—— "

"Now, drop that, will you? and get on with your story, for you're tedious in the extreme."

"Well, you ungrateful dog, you remember the sailing match we arranged; the match old Bompas, the boatman, put us up to—between those two cutters, I mean, which we have hired from time to time."

"Yes, of course, I remember."

"And how you were to sail the 'Sylph', and I the 'Crest of the Wave': also about our lady patronenes to preside on board, 'each to each'—course from Senanus Point round the fairway buoy and back again."

"Aye—but it's likely either of the girls will be allowed now to preside as suggested."

"But they *are* going to do it, old boy, and what's more, it's coming off to-morrow."

"Gammon."

"It is, I tell you; we fixed it all, as we were coming

home—always supposing your health to be restored, of course."

"Granted I believe all this (which I don't), what then?"

"Simply this—the Lively Nancy lies in the offing with her fore-top-sail loose all prepared for flight—two minutes for Eugenie and myself to be taken on board—then crowd on all canvas, and hurrah! for the coast of France."

"And suppose it's a dead calm."

"Why, we can't have the sailing match in that case, and must wait for another day or two. McBean is backwards and forwards often enough, so it's not as if this was our only chance."

"Your scheme's so mad, Ernest my boy, I'll lay a thousand to one against you."

"I know it's mad, but a desperate game wants a bold stroke or two."

"St. Croix won't let his daughter come."

"He promised he would send her with Miss Veriblue, he an't coming himself."

"Well, we'd bother enough to persuade Miss V. to the arrangement before our little mishap of to-day; she's sure to turn rusty again."

"No, she's all serene: a lot of them are coming to Senanus for another pic-nic, and they're to watch the sailing from the beach. And Tugg will be here to-morrow, his mother said, so perhaps he and that Oxford parson will join in the aquatic contest. Bompas and his boy are going to sail the cutters round from the harbour: I fixed that with them to-night."

"Why, you've been as busy as the devil in a gale of wind."

"About—Well! d'you still mean to give St. Croix the office."

I sat and smoked in silence, pondering it all from end to end. The fact was, I felt certain his scheme wouldn't succeed, and I didn't want to quarrel with him needlessly. It was so unlikely to my thinking that Eugenie would be allowed to come and then there were all chances of the weather, and of the schooner not being there, and fifty other things. Besides Saville's explanation had cleared him a good deal in my eyes, and at any rate I didn't like the idea of using information obtained as mine had been. On the whole, I resolved to wait and see what happened: it would be time enough to act on an emergency: little indeed did I think what the emergency would be, and sorely did I repent within four-and-twenty hours of this piece of temporising.

"I say," remarked Ernest at last, "do you *see* what o'clock it is."

"Oh! my gars and starters, it's time to roost and no mistake; but tell me one thing, where on earth have you got the money from?"

"My guardian sent me a cheque for sixty this morning: the post came before you were down."

"And what will he do when he hears of this?"

"Oh! he'll be all right; he can't let me starve: I'm three-and-twenty at Christmas, and then he's rid of me, and I come into my own."

"Well, upon my word, Saville, you're a queer lot, and I don't know what to make of you."

"Anything you please, so you don't make game of me, as the moorhen remarked on the 1st of September last."

. Nothing further passed between us that night; but fancy my amazement when, next morning, as I was dressing, Mary brought me word that Mr. Saville was "took by that 'ere hugly man"; the said prepossessing individual proved to be none other than Hyam's aide-camp, Aaron Brown by name, despatched at the suit of Messrs. Heelam, Shoemakers, with a writ on E. S., Esq., for little accounts running pretty well up to three figures. Oh! dear, oh! dear, how about the Lively Nancy, and how about the lively Eugenie?

"P. O."

(To be concluded in the next Number.)

DUNGEON GHYLL.

O'ER meadows starred with flowers and strewn about
With boulders lichen-crusted, 'neath whose sides
Peeped heather crisp and hardy mountain bells;—
Past hazel-copses, hung with milk-white clusters,
And threaded by festooning autumn berries,
We wandered forth.—Around, the purple hills
Heaved their huge shoulders to the bounteous day,
And every peak was bright; for scarce a mist
Hung o'er the ridge, or, seemed to hang and soon,
Like some pure spirit that, intent on Heaven,
Burst its frail bonds to dwell in kindred light,
Went slowly up and mingled with the blue.

But near us sang the stream; and all the vale
Laughed with a thousand sparkling threads of silver;
And I was glad at heart: and she,—the maid
Who wandered by my side,—I scarce could tell;—
So deep a quiet held her,—but methought
She drank full gladness from the witchery
Of the pure air, bright skies and beauteous earth;
So clear the rose that flushed her cheek, so pure
The light that dwelt within her eyes, and made
A Heaven of blue in Earth's most Heavenly Child.

But, if the spell of silence held us both,
I wondered not, for the full heart, sometimes,
Knowing how weakly words can picture joy
When joy is deepest, bars with jealous care

The gates of utterance, till a moment comes
When the large flood of words, prisoned and pent,
Forces a channel and flows widely on
In eloquent wildness and confusion clear.

But soon we passed into a lonelier vale:
A deeper stillness brooded round, and hung
Along the mountains, barer and more stern
Than those we left: a solitary tarn
Inurned amongst the hills, half-belted round
By a strange semicirque of deep green firs,
Shone like a diamond chased in emeralds.
But once I saw it 'neath a winter moon
With sombre shadows of the mountain peaks
And gray fantastick piles, larger in night,
And then methought it was a silver shield
Watched by a giant knight in that lone vale.

At length we reached the spot, henceforth to me
Crowded with such sweet memories of the past,
That, when I hear its stern name only named,
Through the long years I leap to youth again,
And in a moment live the joyous hours
Of that most joyous day;—for 'twixt the hills,
Split suddenly and furrowed into chasms,
A darkling passage winds amid black cliffs,
Brawled over by a noisy brook, and leads
Where doubtful light, half-barred, still struggles in
Through crevices of the o'er-hanging crags,
And trembles through the quiv'ring birchen boughs,
And darts a rainbow on the waterfall
That, like a delicate silver-tissued veil,
Droops o'er the front of the black cavern rock,
Informing it with such a wondrous grace
That the rapt spirit, centred in the eyes,
Gazes and gazes, while the flick'ring light
That comes and goes with sheen of rainbow gems,
Together with the stillness of the cave,
Chains it with potent charms.—And so gazed we,
Nor noted time, nor noted for a space
Its softer beauties;—how the tufted heather

P

Gemmed the rough stones that other wreath had none,
Save where the hare-bell lent her modest grace
And pensive head, and tremulously hung,
And quivered with the motion of the spray.
And so, I thought, might droop some gentle maid,
So tremble at the whisper that she loves.

What wonder then that there I told my love?
What wonder that, as there love told received
Love's sweetest recompense from maiden lips,
That day, that hour, that spot dwell in mine heart?
What wonder if, as yesterday we found
A withered hare-bell and dead tuft of heather
Betwixt the closed leaves of a cherished book,
The happy rain welled from our hearts and rose
Into our eyes, and we told o'er the tale
Told first beside the fall of Dungeon Ghyll?

                                    "C. S."

EXPERIENCES.

———————— 'Tis but to fill
A certain portion of uncertain paper.—BYRON.

MY experiences! and what right have I to intrude my experiences on the public? Why there is Miss Pinch my next-door neighbour, Corset-Maker, and Ladies' Seminary-Keeper—with her cold grey eye, and colder, sharp, red nose! She, whose life has been one dull round of the same monotonous drudgery—first taught and then teaching,—it is her sister who makes the articles above mentioned. She, I say, has written, aye, and published a full, true, and particular account of all that has happened to her; and her publisher told her that the work would have had a large circulation, but people were tired of that sort of thing; tired of it—and why should Miss Pinch expect otherwise—is it not a twice told tale, and will the cold and heartless world—cold, that is to say, and in a great measure heartless, to those with whom it comes not in contact,—will that world to which Miss Pinch has appealed, read her book; or, having done so, will they buy another copy, or call at the Seminary, and pour balm in the bleeding wounds of the susceptible Pinch; does she want fame, fortune, or friends? why did she write—by what title does she force herself and her woes upon us; and if she does, why may not I?—nay, I will.

You would like to know my name, from mere idle curiosity perhaps, but still you wish to hear it. Turn over the leaves of Webster's Court Guide, and under the head of Smith you will find—my name? not at all—John Smith—

P 2

now if John Smith had written a book and signed his name, would you be better acquainted with him than if he had written anonymously? and so my name shall remain buried in oblivion.

My abode is London—in a narrow but noisy street—up three pair of stairs—and in a close dark room, whose window gives, on to the dead wall of Lord Muchland's mansion, a pleasant prospect when returning from my day's work; to look on this wall, to look through it with my imagination, and wonder how the great folks within it amuse themselves; and when, tired of this, and weary with my work, I am obliged to listen to the ceaseless piano and singing of the few select pupils at Miss Pinch's, worried by some street organ, or the cry of some itinerant vendor of goods: when I say this is the sole break in the monotony of my daily labour, surely I have a right to lay my sorrows before a sympathising world, and claim their pity; and then my daily work. I am a clerk in an office—I go there at 10 A.M. and take my place on a high slippery stool, and whether there is much doing, or little, there I must stop till 5 P.M. How I envy the man in the green coat and brass buttons, who carries messages, fetches bread and cheese and porter for the hungry clerks at lunch time; he, for the greater part of the day, can stand with his hands in his capacious pockets, idly gazing on the passing omnibus, and now and then bestowing a buffet on the head of some luckless urchin who may have come too near his august toes; and, happy mortal, he has the wondrous faculty of being able to sleep always and wherever he may choose. How he looks down on us clerks, with a serene contempt, and yet my salary is £90. a-year and his £20.; what then makes the difference? why is he a happy, and I a miserable man? alas, I had the misfortune to be born a gentleman. Oh! gentility, what a curse art thou to the wretched being who bears thy badge, unaccompanied by thy rightful wages; not that I am in want, for on my salary and my little private fortune I can live without starving; but what a life! a gloomy present, and a hopeless future. Far better is the lot of the poor curate, his indeed is not an enviable existence, but yet he, at least, can live in the country and see the beauties of nature, while I can only live in London, and injure my sight with the deformities of art.

He can look forward at some time or other to a living however small, on which he can afford to keep that necessary luxury, a wife; while I can but look forward to a possible increase of £10. per annum in my salary, with a proportionate increment of duties : he, leading an out-door existence, can enjoy the blessings of health and strength, while I am injuring my lungs by poring over a desk, and my constitution generally by my sedentary occupations. To what end is all this—to none except a warning to others. That which might have been a purple robe for a monarch, is become a tattered coat for a scarecrow; that which God gave me to enjoy, I spend in misery ahd despair, and all because, with the means of a mechanic, I must live the life of a gentleman, or, that being out of my reach, I must drag on the existence I have described. Such are my experiences !

ΠΟΤΝΑ ΣΕΛΑΝΑ.

Queen Moon, I gaze on thy peerless ray
  As it bursts from yon cloud-white veil:
Thou art gliding along thy starry way
  Like a beauty proud and pale!
And steadfast I look to the silent skies
  Thy golden beams to see,
For well I know that my lady's eyes
  Are gazing now on thee:
     She is gazing now on thee, sweet Moon,
      For she loves to see thee shine;
     But her thoughts are of none but me, sweet Moon,
      And her heart is only mine.

Fair Star of Eve, on the brow of night
  Thou art set as the choicest gem,
That shines in the circlet diamond-bright
  Of a monarch's diadem.
Yet, fairest and firstborn of the skies,
  So bright thou ne'er canst shine,
As the luminous depths of those hazel eyes
  That are gazing now on thine:
     That are gazing now on thine, fair Star,
      For she loves thy ray to see;
     But her heart it is only mine, fair Star,
      And her thoughts are of none but me.

For this was her whispered promise sweet,
  On our last drear parting-day;
"Our spirits, my love, at night may meet
  "Though ourselves be far away:
"On Hesper's fires I'll gaze afar
  "While the moonbeam smiles above,
"And gaze thou too on Moon and Star
  "At the hallowed hour of love."
     At the hallowed hour of love, sweet Moon,
      And this is love's hallowed hour:
     And I gaze on the heaven above, fair Star,
      And I feel that the spell hath power.

"P. O."

OUR CHRONICLE.

IT has been suggested to us that many of our readers would welcome the addition to the contents of *The Eagle* of some account of the events of the term, more especially those which affect our own "ancient and religious foundation:" that such an addition would in particular be a great boon to those of our subscribers, who year after year leave these walls, and for the most part sever the ties which connect them therewith; to whom such a chronicle would furnish tidings of what was going on in the place where themselves have spent so many happy hours, and so serve to keep up their connexion with us. And though this would only apply for a limited time, for as long, that is, as the names which they would see should some of them be familiar to them, yet such as these, together with our resident subscribers, many of whom, we doubt not, will be glad to have such a permanent register of events, will generally form a sufficiently large majority of our subscribers to warrant the introduction of a terminal article of this kind.

We propose then in each subsequent number of *The Eagle*, to include a summary of any events worthy of notice in the college in which our subscribers are likely to be interested, accompanied by such note or comment as they may seem to require. Such matters as Fellowship and Scholarship elections, Examination lists, or changes in the government of the college, may be expected to find a place —with such notices as we may obtain of "events" in the boating, cricketing, or volunteer world of St. John's, who pulled in the Lady Margaret first boat in such race, or who in the Lady Somerset, or who is the last new Ensign. At the same time we may advert to any circumstances of more than ordinary interest which concern not only our own college, but the general body of the University, though this should be done sparingly. For the further promoting of the interest of this column of our magazine, we shall be glad to receive from any of our subscribers, and especially from non-resident ones, any suggestions, which, whether accepted or not ultimately, shall always have our careful attention and consideration. "EDITORS."

With the academical year upon which we have lately entered we inaugurate a new system of management. None who knew the overwhelming amount of business and responsibility, which during the past year pressed upon our respected President, can regret that the work, which he bore up against alone, should now be divided amongst three Tutors. The gentlemen selected for these Tutorships are the Rev. J. S. Wood, B.D.: the Rev. J. B. Mayor, M.A.: and the Rev. A. V. Hadley, M.A. The distinctive feature of the new system is the separation of tuition from lecturing, which will do away with the old rivalries between the "sides." Though the Tutors are "ex officio" lecturers, they have not the management and distribution of the lectures, this task being under the superintendence of two Head Lecturers.

The scheme seems a good one, and likely to work well, and, we hope, to raise our entries beyond, or at any rate to an equality with, our former average.

We understand that considerable alterations are to be made in some of our Examinations, but any statement regarding them is as yet premature. Report, however, deals a death-blow to the famous paper, which might more fitly be associated with Magdalen college than with St. John's: so that probably the future historian will find a great blank after the year 1860, which year he will find to be marked by certain strange proceedings in the church of St. George in the East, and by an election for a certain magazine yclept *The Eagle.* Apropos of which, we must acknowledge the courtesy of the present able Sadlerian Lecturer, who in return for the interesting historical notices deduced from these papers in a former number, has thus handed our name down to prosperity.

Another new feature to be noticed is the introduction of a sermon in chapel on Sunday evenings, to supply the place of the morning sermon at St. Mary's, which was discontinued some months ago.

Among the fellows some changes have taken place. We regret to have to record the death of the Rev. W. J. Rees, who has been cut off by the cruel hand of consumption, just as a brilliant and useful career was opening up before him. The following gentlemen also vacate their fellowships by marriage :

Mr. G. D. Liveing.
" S. H. Burbury.
" E. G. Hancock.

Mr. J. E. Gorst.
" H. Snow.

The Lectureship vacated by Mr. Hancock is now held by Mr. H. J. Roby.

The College is represented amongst the University prizemen by Mr. E. A. Abbott, whose exercise obtained the Camden Medal, and by Mr. S. W. Churchill, who won the Browne Medal for a Latin Epigram ; in the Indian Civil Service Examination by Messrs. H. Beverley, H. C. Barstow, and A. Yardley, who have obtained the nomination, and by Messrs. J. Grose, W. S. Foster, and J. E. Armstrong, whose nomination of last year is confirmed.

Subjoined is a list of scholars elected in June last.

Scholars in the third year :

Abbott.
Bushell.
Freeman.

Gabb.
Hiern.
Hudson.

Nicholas.
Sharpe, H. J.
Thomson, F. D.

In the second year :

Graves. | Main. | Taylor, C.

Minor scholars :

Baron, from Caistor School.
Horne, from Shrewsbury School.
Lee-Warner, from Rugby School.
Moss, from Shrewsbury School.

It will be seen from our cover that our two boat-clubs have both been unsuccessful in the Four-Oar Races which have just concluded. This has created some surprise, inasmuch as the Lady Margaret was decidedly a favourite before the race.

The following were the crews of the two boats:

Lady Margaret.

1. T. E. Ash.
2. P. F. Gorst.
3. H. Williams.
    W. H. Tarleton, (stroke.)
    A. Walsh, (coxs.)

Lady Somerset.

1. F. H. Dinnis.
2. Stephenson.
3. O. Fynes-Clinton.
    J. E. Brown, (stroke.)
    C. R. Cooke. (coxs.)

The officers for the term are:

Lady Margaret.

A. W. Potts, Esq., B.A., President.
J. B. Scriven, Treasurer.
P. F. Gorst, Secretary.
W. H. Tarleton, first Captain.
T. E. Ash, second Captain.

Lady Somerset.

Rev. J. R. Lunn, M.A., President.
J. E. Brown, Captain.
W. A. Whitworth, Secretary.

The second Company of the Cambridge University Volunteer Rifles still continues in a flourishing state. A meeting of its members was held early in the term, to elect an Ensign in the place of Mr. J. B. Scriven, who succeeds to the Lieutenancy vacant by the resignation of Mr. E. Boulnois. The candidates were Messrs. H. Godfray, W. D. Bushell, and A. Walsh. The choice of the Electors fell upon Mr. W. D. Bushell.

The chief topics of interest to the University at large are such as will already be known to most of our readers. Considerable excitement prevailed at the beginning of term, owing to the rejection of Mr. G. Williams, of King's College, who was nominated to the office of Proctor. Mr. Williams has addressed a letter on the subject to the Vice-Chancellor.

The cup offered by the Vice-Chancellor as a prize to the best marksman in the C. U. V. R. was, after a contest of five days, won by Mr. Grant-Peterkin, of Emmanuel College.

On the 12th of November, the newly-appointed Professor of Modern History, Mr. Charles Kingsley, delivered an interesting and instructive inaugural Lecture in the Senate-House, to a large audience of members of the University and their friends.

The account of the Colquhoun Sculls, and the Races of the term will be found in their usual place.

St. John's College.
November 20, 1860.

CORRESPONDENCE.

[We have received the following communication from a valued correspondent. Regard for the rule which excludes the technicalities of Classics and Mathematics has caused us to hesitate about inserting it in the body of our magazine: at the same time the value of the letter and its interest to many of our readers warrant us, as we think, in allotting to it a space in our correspondents' columns.—EDITORS.]

SIR,—I have lately had occasion to turn over the papers set in the Examinations for the Classical Tripos, and have made a few notes as I went along, which may perhaps be of interest to some of the readers of *The Eagle*. I may as well begin with a brief history of the Tripos up to the year 1859.

The Classical Tripos was instituted by Grace of the Senate on the 28th of May, 1822. According to the scheme then adopted, the Examination was to continue for four days, during the hours 9½ to 12, and 1 to 4. No one was allowed to become a candidate who had not obtained Mathematical Honors. Translations were to be "required of passages selected from the best Greek and Latin authors, as well as written answers to questions arising immediately out of such passages." There was to be no original composition either in Greek or Latin. There were to be four Examiners, each to receive £10.

By a Grace passed February 13, 1835, the Examination was made to extend over five days, during the hours 9 to 12 and 1 to 3½. Shortly afterwards it appears from the Calendar that the hours were again changed, and that the Examination was carried on between 9 and 11½ and 12½ and 3½. In the Calendar of 1844 it is stated that the Examiners receive £20 instead of £10.

In 1849, the "Classical Emancipation" commenced. By a Grace passed October 31, in that year, it was determined that, besides Mathematical Honour Men, all persons should be admissible to the Examination who, "having been de-

clared to have deserved to pass for an ordinary degree, as far
as the Mathematical part of the Examination is concerned,
shall have afterwards passed in the other subjects for Examination;"` and also all persons whose names shall have been
placed in the 1st class at the Examination for the ordinary
degree: that is, in simpler words, that "gulfed men" and
1st class Poll men were to be henceforward admissible as
candidates for the Classical Tripos. Other important changes
were made at the same time. The Examination was extended
to the morning of the 6th day, on which there was to be a
paper in Ancient History. The subjects of Examination were
more closely defined, the hours fixed as at present, rules
made with reference to the cooperation of the Examiners in
preparing and looking over the papers, and an alphabetical
arrangement adopted for the third class. A day was also
fixed for the bringing out of the list.

In May, 1854, the "Emancipation" was completed, though
the Grace did not come into force till 1857. In October,
1858, further changes were made with reference to the work
of the Examiners, and the alphabetical order of the 3rd class
was abandoned.

The growth of the Classical Tripos is shown by the fact
that there are only 17 names in the class list of 1824 as
opposed to 71 in the class list of 1859.

I now proceed to my notes. Comparing the early and the
later Triposes I find that previously to 1835 there was great
irregularity in the choice of pieces. In one year there was
no Thucydides; Demosthenes is several times omitted, as
also Plato, Aristotle, Herodotus, Æschylus, Sophocles, Euripides, Aristophanes. In Latin, even Cicero, Tacitus, and
Horace are not set uniformly. Whilst at the same time there
are instances of three or more passages being set from the
same author in a single year. In 1827 there were only three
Greek verse and three Greek prose translations, and two
Latin verse and two Latin prose translations. In 1825 there
was no Latin verse composition. Another point in which the
earlier papers differ from the later, is the large number of
questions in the former. Taking the whole 37 years from
1824 to 1860, the number of passages set from each author
is as follows:—

Greek Prose—Thucydides, 38; Demosthenes, 34; Plato,
38; Aristotle, 33; Herodotus, 35; Xenophon, 13; Theophrastus, 7; The Orators (with the exception of Demosthenes), 14; Longinus, 2.

Greek Verse—Homer's Iliad, 22; Odyssey, 19; Æschylus, 28; Sophocles, 27; Euripides, 30; Aristophanes, 38; Pindar, 30; Hesiod, 11; Theocritus, 26; Bion, 1; Homeric Hymns, 2; Greek Anthology, 4; Comic Fragments, 1.

Latin Prose—Livy, 34; Cicero (Speeches) 20, (Letters) 27, (Philosophical and Rhetorical Works) 28; Tacitus, 37; Cæsar, 14; Sallust, 8; Suetonius, 6; Pliny the Elder, 6; Pliny the Younger, 9; Quintilian, 7; Velleius Paterculus, 2; Seneca, 2; Cornelius Nepos, 1.

Latin Verse—Lucretius, 29; Virgil, 21; Horace (Odes and Epodes) 22, (Satires and Epistles) 17; Juvenal, 22; Ovid, 19; Propertius, 13; Catullus, 10; Tibullus, 3; Persius, 12; Martial, 11; Lucan, 14; Statius, 2; Ennius, 1; Phædrus, 1; Plautus, 26; Terence, 9.

Taking each of these in order, it appears that passages have been set most frequently from the 3rd, 4th, 5th, and 8th books of Thucydides, and most rarely from the 1st and 2nd. In Demosthenes, the Leptines, Midias, Falsa Legatio, de Corona, Timocrates, Nicostratus, Androtion are the most popular; passages have also been set from the Olynthiacs, pro Phormione, Aristocrates, Apaturius, C. Stephanum, Aphobus A., Pantænetus, Conon, Onetor A., Aristogeiton, Chersonesus, Dionysodorus. Out of thirty-eight passages from Plato, the Republic has thirteen; then come the Leges, Phædrus, Symposium, Theætetus, Gorgias, Phædo, Parmenides; and, lastly, Timæus, Meno, Crito, Politicus, Sophista, Alcibiades B. In Aristotle, the Ethics has 13 passages; Rhetoric, 10; Politics, 6; De Anima, 2; Metaphysics and Categories, 1 each.

Herodotus—The three first books are the most popular, the eighth has never been set at all.

Xenophon—The Hellenics, Memorabilia, and Anabasis have been set more than once; Symposium, Hiero, de Re Equestri, Cynegeticus, Œconomicus, Vectigalia, once only.

Theophrastus—Characters, VI., set four times; I., VIII., XXX., each once.

Oratores Attici—Æschines, 5; Isæus, 4; Isocrates, 3; Lysias, 2.

Homer—The largest number of passages have been set from Iliad XVIII. and XXI., and Odyssey XVII.

Æschylus—Agamemnon, Choephoræ, Supplices, each 7 times; Prometheus not at all.

Sophocles—Œd. Col. and Trach. 6; Antigone, 5; Philoctetes, 4.

Euripides—most frequently from Helena, Ion, Iph. T., Herc. F., Orestes, Hippolytus, Phœnissæ; also from Heracl.,

Cycl., Alcest., Bacchæ, Medea, Supp., Troades, Rhesus, Electra, Andromache.

Aristophanes—most frequently from Vespæ, Pax, Aves, Equites, Eccles., Ranæ; also from Acharnæ, Lysistrata, Plutus.

Pindar—Pythia, 14; Nem. 6; Ol. 5; Isth. 4; frag. 1.

Hesiod—Opera et Dies, 8; Theog. 8.

Theocritus—oftenest from xxv., xxii., x., vii., xvi., xv.; also from iv., xvii., iii., xiv., xxviii., xiii., vi., ix., ii.

Anthology—Meleager, 2; Dioscorides, 1; Simonides, 1.

Homeric Hymns—In Merc., In Cer.

Livy—oftenest from vi.

Cicero—Speeches, oftenest from Verres, Cluentius, Pro Domo, Sextius; also from Plancius, Balbus, Quinctius, Cæcina, Vatinius, Murœna, Rosc. Com., Rullus. Epistles—ad Att., 17; ad Fam., 5; Q. Frat. 5. Philosophical and Rhetorical Treatises—Leges and De Finibus, 6 each; Brutus and de Divinatione, 3 each; also de Oratore, Orator, Tusculans, Academics, de Optimo Genere Oratorum, de Senectute.

Tacitus—Annals, 24; Histories, 12; Germany, 1, (largest number from Hist. iv., and Ann. vi.)

Cæsar—Bell. Gall. 7; Bell. Civ. 7, (largest numbers from B. G. vii.)

Sallust—Jugurtha, 5; Catiline, 3.

Suetonius—Cæsar, Augustus, Claudius, Nero.

Quintilian—xii., v., iv., vi., x.

Seneca—Naturales Quæstiones, De Beneficiis.

Nepos, Atticus.

Lucretius—most from ii. and iv., none from i.

Virgil—Æneid, 16; Georgics, 5. The largest number of passages are taken from Æn. xi. and Geor. ii. None from Æn. i., ii., v., vii. G. iv.

Horace—Odes, 13, (of which 9 from Book iii.); Epodes, 9; Satires, 9, (of which 6 from Sat., Bk. ii.); Epistles, 8.

Juvenal—most from vi. and vii.; none from ii., iv., viii., ix., x., xiii., xvi.

Ovid—14 from the Fasti; 3 from the Tristia; 1 from the Ibis; and 1 from the De Arte Amandi.

There is nothing marked in the quotations from Catullus, Tibullus, Propertius, Persius, Martial, Statius, Ennius, and Phœdrus.

Plautus—most from the Trinummi, Captivi, Miles Gloriosus, Persa, Aulularia, Curculio, Rudens. Also from the Epidicus, Amphitruo, Mostellaria, Pseudolus, Bacchides, Stichus, and Pœnulus.

Terence—none from the Heauton timoroumenos.

With regard to composition, Greek and Latin Prose have of course been constant. There has been a good deal of variety in verse composition. Iambics have been the sole Greek verse composition on 24 occasions; Iambics and Trochaics have been set once; Iambics and Anapæsts, 8 times; Iambics and Hexameters, 4 times. In Latin verse, Hexameters have been set alone 5 times; Hexameters and Elegiacs, 8 times; Hexameters and Lyrics, 10 times; Hexameters, Elegiacs, and Lyrics, 4 times; Elegiacs alone, once; Elegiacs and Lyrics, 7 times; Lyrics alone, once.

Two other points which strike me as worth noticing, are—1st, the reappearance of the same piece for translation in different years. One passage from Theophrastus has been set 4 times; one from Homer, 3 times; one from the Anthology, twice; and I have no doubt careful examination would discover other cases: 2ndly, the prevalence of fashions for short periods; *e.g.*, the only passages which have been set from Longinus, were set in 1844 and 1846. Pliny's Natural History was set in 1846 and the two following years. Greek Hexameters were not set till 1852, but have been set 4 times since.

I am afraid your Mathematical readers will think I have been bordering rather closely on those Classical technicalities which *The Eagle* repudiates: and there may be others who will accuse me of putting a temptation to ‘cram,’ in the way of the weaker brethren. Where the extent to be covered, however, is so wide, cram must be too much diluted to be very deleterious; and I think I might rather take to myself the credit of assisting the honest reader to steer his own course by the landmarks of former examinations. Perhaps too, my list may be of use in testing the pretensions of some of those youthful prodigies of whom fame reports that they had read all Classics before their first term, and the Calendar relates that they obtained a third class in their last. But, in fact, my object has been chiefly to gratify a curiosity, which it is possible that even Mathematicians may share, as to the actual compass of Classical literature embraced in our most important examination, and I should be glad if any one were inclined to undertake the same task, either for the Oxford examination or for other Classical examinations amongst ourselves.

“Y. Z.”

To the Editor of the Eagle.

BEFORE this Number is in the hands of our readers, most of them will be aware that the post of permanent Editor, held by Mr. J. B. Mayor since the commencement of this Magazine, has been resigned by that gentleman.

The Editors, although aware of the difficulty, as well as the delicacy of such an undertaking, feel that this Number ought not to go forth without bearing with it some tribute from them, and in the name of the Subscribers, whom they represent, to one who has so long watched over the prosperity of *The Eagle*. It is always hazardous to bring a periodical before the public, even when that public is so large as to ensure a certain number of admirers, and to secure, at any rate, the silence of those to whom the Magazine may be distasteful. How much this difficulty is increased, when a serial, such as this, is offered to a limited public, who, from many circumstances, must be either its friends or its foes, we may see from many an abortive attempt to establish the like. To what then is the success of *The Eagle* due? In some measure, we may venture to hope, to its intrinsic merits; in a great measure, we may boldly assert, to the character, talents, and position of its principal Editor. The zeal and ability which Mr. Mayor brought to his duties, as well as the unvarying courtesy and kindness which his subordinates in office have met with from him, will, we are sure, be long remembered by all those, whose good fortune it has been to serve under him on the Editorial Staff. The Editors are conscious of the disadvantage under which they lie in succeeding him, but will use their utmost endeavours to maintain that character, which *The Eagle* has won for itself under Mr. Mayor's presidency.

FELLOW-FEELING.

WE are now at the close of perhaps the severest season this country has experienced during the nineteenth century. Many an anecdote respecting the intense cold of the winter 1860-61 will be told round the blazing yule-log on future Christmas Eves. It has been accompanied with unusual suffering among the poorer classes—such inclement weather following upon a bad harvest has brought famine and starvation for the first time to many a threshold. Political events too have not been without their influence in producing this state of things. The Commercial Treaty concluded with France has brought ruin upon more than one branch of our home trade. Thousands of honest work-people have, for the moment, been thrown out of employment, and the distress of the Coventry weavers will henceforth take its place in history. The bright feature amid all this gloominess is, that the widespread evil has awakened an amount of public sympathy never perhaps equalled in any previous age. English hearts and hands are as open as ever to relieve the sufferings of their fellows, and it has only been necessary to mention cases of distress to call forth adequate assistance. The feeling has been universal—"Is he not a man and a brother?" It is this fellow-feeling that I propose to investigate, not indeed tracing its origin and growth in the soul of man—a task that may more strictly fall within the province of the Moralist—but endeavouring to offer some few remarks that may be practically useful to us in our intercourse with one another.

What do I mean then by *fellow-feeling?* Is it not synonymous with *sympathy?* Not exactly. Sympathy is included in the idea, but will be found to fall very far short of it. Like its Latin equivalent, it has been confined to a fellow-feeling with actual human suffering, and has reference merely to grief, whether silent or expressed. We sympathize with the wretched when we can enter into their sorrows and make them our own. We extend our compassion, when we feel the workings of our human nature, and yearn to relieve their distress. But we can hardly be said to sympathize in our friend's joy, and he certainly is not a proper object of our compassion. There is in fact no single word to express a sympathy in joy—and I suppose it is because this emotion is more rarely excited, that the idea of sympathy has been confined to a fellow-feeling with suffering. We are glad to hear of Smith getting the Craven, but are apt to imagine that Smith's cup of exultation is not large enough for two, and we had better let him drain it himself. We *do* go up to his rooms to congratulate him, and then we think we have done enough. But congratulation is a bare form of words, and expresses no real feeling on our part. It may as often be accompanied by envy or regret, as proceed from a true fellow-feeling. Who is that shaking hands with the Senior Wrangler? "Oh! that's Jones—he was second." Poor fellow! one fancies there is just a quiver on his lip, as he comes up to his friend in the Senate-House, and yet he has himself tried hard to believe his own congratulations sincere. But though, in nine cases out of ten, another's joy awakens no sympathetic response in our heart, there surely are seasons when a friend's happiness does strike deep root into our own soul. I do not for a moment deny the existence of a sympathy in joy— it is perhaps a surer test of true friendship than sympathy in distress.

Is there then a distinction between *friendship* and *fellow-feeling?* Decidedly. Friendship is limited, a fellow-feeling is universal; the circle of friendship is circumscribed, a fellow-feeling can feel with all the world. A man can never possess more than two or three friends, in the truest holiest sense of the word—he may have hundreds of acquaintances with whose troubles he is ever ready to sympathize, and at the same time he may feel with all his fellows. Perhaps he too has passed through suffering and temptation, but his heart has not been thereby rendered callous—he has a wider sympathy for those who suffer and are tempted— his large soul yearns towards erring sinful man.

Such must have been the spirit of those who founded the glorious institutions on the banks of the Isis and the Cam. A nobler idea was perhaps never conceived than that of establishing these holy brotherhoods, to work to-

gether with one heart and soul for the good of their fellows.
Here was fellow-feeling characteristically displayed, uniting
at once internal friendship among the members of the
University themselves, and large-hearted sympathy with
those without. Fellow-feeling to some extent is a necessary
part of our existence here. What a soul the man must
have who is utterly destitute of all pride in his College !
the happy scenes which surround him cannot fail to make
a deep impression on his mind—and it is with a fond regret
that he leaves his beloved University to go forth into the
world—he carries with him a memory teeming with bright
associations, and whether it be our Emigrant in New
Zealand, or our Civilian in Bengal, he is always looking
forward to hear how the Old College is getting on—aye !—
and where the boats are on the river. What gratitude must
we feel then towards those noble benefactors, who have
bequeathed to us these ancient courts and their broad
acres, and who planted these gardens, where, apart *from*
the world, we may—if we will—train ourselves for after-
conflict *with* the world !

But how are we echoing the sentiments which they
entertained? Are we striving to keep up the fellow-feeling
they intended us to exhibit towards one another and towards
the rest of the world? Alas! the civilization of society—
as it has progressed from one century to another—has left
evident traces of its artificial footsteps on these glorious
institutions—and the absurdities of University etiquette at
present only tend to deaden our sympathy and estrange our
hearts from one another. Can we not for instance see
great danger arising from the mighty gulf that is fixed
between the Fellow and the Undergraduate? That there
should be such a gulf is well; that it cannot be too wide,
I emphatically deny. If it is—even if no positive harm
ensue, what advantages to both are lost! The inexperienced
youth is allowed to pass the most critical years of his
existence, without a word of advice from one who is well
calculated to afford it, as having sailed in the same track
before, and discovered where the shoals and quicksands
lie, and perhaps many a one makes shipwreck when a
seasonable word from a skilful pilot might have warned
him of the sunken rock. What errors in speculation, what
errors in practice, he might thus have escaped while his
mind was drinking in strength and vigour from intercourse
with a maturer and more experienced mind! And would
the other be a loser, if the gulf were bridged over? I think

Q 2

not. Besides a youthful freshness, which many would be sure to catch, how his heart would be enlarged and his sympathies extended as he watched with keen interest the progress of some young friend through the snares and temptations of a University life. There are among us men of this sort—men ready to feel and sympathize with all, and silently, it may be, watching the course of many.

Such an one was he who has lately been taken from the midst of us, and whose loss is deplored by every Undergraduate in the College. A man of large sympathy—with a kind word and a fellow-feeling for everyone—our Captain and the hearty sharer of all our pursuits—in the sunshine of whose genial presence we forgot the difference of Academical rank. What a treasure he was to the College, we knew not till we missed him, and there is not a Johnian but will carry the memory of that warm-hearted man down to his own grave.

The great difference between a large and a small College, and one of the many advantages of the former over the latter, consists in the choice of associates. In a large College like this, where it is impossible for any man to have even a bare acquaintance with all his fellow-students, he naturally falls into a particular set. In a small College this choice does not exist—he must go along with the stream. But absolutely necessary as it seems that there should be numerous sets among us, it is to be deplored that they tend to weaken and destroy all fellow-feeling.

Look at that man rushing along the cloisters with shoe-strings flying loose and a coat somewhat the worse for wear. On he hastens, a victim to Mathesis; apparently caring for nothing else, if only he may obtain the object of his ambition and win his Fellowship. Yet I would affirm that under that rusty garb there beats a heart as true to his College, and as fully bent on working for good, as beneath that elaborate Noah's ark! what an exquisite! in the very pink of fashion! watch those lavender kids dandling the tag end of a cigar! Who would imagine *he* cared for his College, so tightly buttoned up as he is in himself? But come to me at two o'clock, and I will shew him to you on the river—he will have doffed that gorgeous apparel, and you will see him display an English pluck and hardihood you may think incredible under that effeminate exterior. His pulse will beat as quickly and his arms work as vigorous, as his seven comrades of the oar, while they pull the old boat over the course in just 8' 15". "Well! you've taken pretty extremes—but I know which I should go to, if I were in a pickle." So do I—but they're both good fellows at the bottom, and both working for their College, though so differently!

It may seem hard then, with so many sets and cliques, to keep alive a mutual goodwill and fellow-feeling—but surely not impossible—if we would only bear in mind that pride in our College which is equally at work, though perhaps not in an equal degree, in the hearts of all. Why cannot we forget individual peculiarities and sectarian differences? If there must be two boat-clubs, let us remember that the same ribbon is the badge of both, and for heaven's sake! don't let us carry our party-spirit into everything else. We must take men as we find them, without criticising them too severely. Let us pull a steady stroke, all together. Why should not the old College be again as it has been of yore, first on the Piece, first on the River, yea! and first in the Tripos, be it January or March?

" H. B."

FIRESIDE MEMORIES.

I.

WINDS raged without, and autumn rains beat loud,
    Dim eve was weeping sore
From eyelids of the dun-wing'd misty cloud
    Low-hanging on the moor.

II.

But I beside an ingle glowing warm
    In dreamy mood reclined,
All heedless of the peltings of the storm
    And wailing of the wind.

III.

For beauteous pictures one the other chased
    Across my musing brain;
Pictures that from the seasons of the past
    Came floating back again.

IV.

I saw fair morning landscapes wet with dew,
    And early rays did shine,
While fleecy cloudlets mottled o'er the blue,
    On green meads speckt with kine.

V.

And high o'erhead beneath the breaking morn,
    With quivering sun-flusht wings,
Larks mounted singing from the upland corn
    Tuned sweet as angel strings.

VI.

For not alone in sight was pleasure found
    From those strange pictures there,
But as I look'd on each, its own fit sound
    Seem'd round me everywhere.

VII.

I saw upon a widespread rural plain
    Trees wind-rockt, slanting showers,
While dimly in the distance thro' the rain
    Loom'd three fair minster towers.

VIII.

Then saw I in a park, green-swarded, old,
    Deer frisking down a glade
Where ancient oaks in pillar'd aisles stood bold,
    O'erarcht with green-leaved shade.

IX.

Anon o'er some vast city heavenward tower'd
    Great spires, and chimneys tall,
While round them wrapt the murky smoke-cloud lower'd
    Like a dark funeral pall.

X.

And then I seem'd, some dewy sabbath morn,
    To gaze o'er fields and dells
Mellow'd with thin blue mist, thro' which was borne
    The holy chime of bells.

XI.

Or in broad meadows flusht with summer dyes
    I heard the low sweet sound
Of flower-fringed brooks that mirror'd the blue skies,
    And bees that murmur'd round.

XII.

Then heavy drifting clouds were rushing fast
    Across a pale-faced moon,
Whilst woods were rocking in the eager blast
    At night's deep shadowy noon.

XIII.

And winter scenes I saw where deep snows lie
    O'er all the fields, when clear
The hills stand out against the frosty sky;
    Or when the lonesome mere

XIV.

Looks very darkly from amidst its reeds,
    And sword-flags stark and keen,
And moonlit waters seem to tell of deeds
    They shudder to have seen.

XV.

Old Ocean, when in some calm bay his face
  With sunny laughter glows,
As, lull'd within the green earth's fond embrace,
  He sinks in soft repose.

XVI.

Or, when grim storms his angry waters lash,
  And crested billows hoar
From headland unto headland roll, and crash
  In thunder to the shore.

XVII.

Fair ruin'd abbeys girt with summer wood;
  Castles, whose crag-built walls
With many an ancient horror thrill the blood;
  And old manorial halls.

XVIII.

And last a tower'd cathedral's solemn gloom,
  Where gorgeous sainted panes
Fling their rich lights on carven shrine and tomb,
  And holy calmness reigns,

XIX.

Save when the mighty organ peals on high,
  And waves of music roll
Far down the vaulted aisles, and soar, and die,
  And overflow the soul.

XX.

So things of beauty, seen, abide for aye
  Treasured in heart and brain:
Forgotten 'mid the toils of every day
  They spring to life again

XXI.

When we sit weary by our fireside gleam;
  And, pleased, we look them o'er,
Till on our senses and our waking dream
  Sleep gently shuts the door.

                                    " H. Y."

SCRAPS FROM THE NOTE-BOOK OF PERCIVAL OAKLEY.

SCRAP SENTIMENTAL.

(Concluded from Vol. II. p. 195.)

LONG and animated was the conference we held with that wily Caucasian, that precious Aaron Brown; but all, alas! to no avail. Vain alike were my own persuasive arguments, or Saville's vehement imprecations: the minion of injustice persisted in his brutal design. "Yer see," he said, "good Mishter Saville, so long as I knowed yer vos keepin' to the quiet, and never thinkin' on a bolt, vy, I vosn't in no hurry to nab yer, none votsumever. But when I heerd of this gammocking across the vater to France, as it may be, thinks I, 'Blow me tight, it's now or never,' so down I comes at vunst, and here yer be cotched alive O!" Such was the creature's diabolical ingenuity, that he had extracted the whole programme of poor Ernest's plans from old McBean himself, having got hold of that nautical worthy the night before, in a highly confidential state of rum-and-water. A keen encounter of wit it might indeed have been, writ-serving Jew *versus* smuggling Scotchman; but continued glasses of 'hot with—' had ruined even Caledonian discretion. The best of it is, that McBean, to this day, persists he never let out a syllable, and has not the faintest recollection of events between his parting with Saville at the Crown and Anchor, and his waking next morning on the deck of his 'own fast gliding craft.'

Well, it was necessary to settle something; and as Aaron positively declined to lose sight of his captive, he was politely invited to spend the remainder of the day at No. 6; Ernest was to go with him to town next morning, hospitable accommodation being proffered in that well-known spunging-house, *not* a hundred miles from Cursitor Street, where the name 'Brown' is neatly engraved on a dirty door-plate of brass. Meanwhile, I was to be off to the pic-nic, and to look sharp about it too: I was to explain the state of affairs to Eugenie, a delicate task which would tax all my diplomatic powers: I was then to report progress at our lodgings, and receive further instructions to suit the emergency, whatever might transpire. In fact this was Ernest's sole object in remaining that night at Weremouth: what use he hoped it would be, goodness only knows; but there *is* a proverb about straws and drowning men, and there *is* also a passage of Shakespeare which declares the difficulty of being "in a moment wise, amazed, temperate, and furious." Some such philosophical maxims· *may* possibly explain his conduct. For myself I was truly sorry for the poor old boy, and only too glad to undertake anything for him: indeed I *may* say I suffered a *little* on his account, not that morning only, but for a longish while after: and so the reader will himself confess, if my natural spirit of digression ever allows me to finish this narrative.

We had seen from our rooms a carriage full of the expected party driving away to Senanus: since then our two horses had, for good part of an hour, been led up and down in front of the house, by that faithful groom whose patience we always tried so sorely. Once I thought that Ernest might have slipped through the window, jumped into the saddle, and left his persecutor's presence at a hand gallop; but on inspecting things outside, I became aware of a second Hebrew who never removed far from the animals' heads, pretending amicable converse with 'Ostler Jem': so that idea was crushed in the bud. It was time for me to be off anyways, the others having got such a long start of me: as for breakfast, I abandoned the hope: lighted a weed, to take the edge off my appetite; shook hands with Ernest—by Jove! I little thought how long it would be before he and I shook hands again;—one parting bit of chaff I fired at Aaron, next minute I was in the saddle. It was half-past twelve when I started, and good six miles to Senanus; but, thanks to whip and spur, before one o'clock I reined in my panting steed on the sandy beach, amid numerous greetings of applause and enquiry. All the people I expected were there, and one or two more I had never before set eyes on. "The top of the morning to you, Oakley," quoth the Oxonian parson; "fine thing, an't it, this early rising?" "What *have* you done with Mr. Saville?" asked Miss V. "Left him snoring most likely," said Mrs. T.

Eugenie said nothing, but looked a good deal. As for myself, my natural modesty kept me at great disadvantage; however, I excused my tardy appearance on plea of 'important business,' Ernest's defaulting ditto, ditto, and the question of early rising I gracefully and playfully adjourned till further notice. A rustic having appeared to take charge of my steed, we all walked down to a little natural pier of rock off which one of the cutters was lying. And where was the other?—Ah, me! in my first confusion I had hardly realized what was in store for me—there, not twenty yards from the shore, was the clever little 'Sylph', creeping along with her jib set, and the rest of her canvass half-furled—there in the stern sheets, snugly ensconced with shawls and cushions, reclined my own, my precious Seraphina—and who was that monster, trimming the sail? who was that fiend in stalwart human form? John Tugg to be sure; any one can guess that much—*Le temps est cher En amour comme en guerre,* and he had made most of his half-hour's start. I'll do the beast the justice to say that he hailed me at once, and offered to resign command; but of course he never meant it, not he. "Oh! pray don't disturb yourselves," I responded, in the bitterness of my soul, "you look *so* comfortable and settled. Miss St. Croix will give me the honour of her patronage, and we'll sail the 'Crest of the Wave' against you for any stakes you like to name. Do come," I whispered to Eugenie, "I have so much to tell you." Miss Veriblue tried to object, of course, but before she could get out six words we were in the boat, and old Bompas was casting her loose. "Pleasant breeze this here, Mr. Oakley," said that ancient mariner, "but don't you run out too far to sea, keep her well under the cliffs, Sir, for I'm afraid it's freshening to blow, and you'll have a job beating back against it." "All right, John," quoth I, "and thank ye for the wrinkle." "Now then, Oakley," said the parson, "I'll see you start fair; set nothing but yout jib till you're level with the 'Sylph,' and then both of you crack on as fast as you please."

If I were only a nautical man, you should have the most glowing description of our aquatic contest: but it's one thing being able to sail a small cutter in moderate weather, and another to describe the same operation in proper maritime terms. I know if I attempted it, half my readers would fail to understand, and the other half would convict me of a myriad blunders, so consideration and prudence combine to forbid my making the trial.

This much I venture to say: the breeze was off shore, and we were to sail along shore; in our course to the fairway buoy, the wind was rather more in our favour than it promised to be for the homeward run; but either way we had to make a succession of tacks, and I knew perfectly well that the science of my detested rival, under these circumstances, would give him a complete pull over a landsman like myself. However, off we went, and in the excitement of setting sail and getting under weigh, of course Eugenie and I had no time for conversation: presently, however, we settled down to our work; the 'Crest' bowling along with all her canvass, and the 'Sylph' not yet having her mizen set, we drew a little ahead, and I felt I must no longer defer my disclosures. A very few words sufficed to explain: and how ill the poor girl could bear it, I need not describe: her face told its own tale, and so did the tone of her voice in the broken exclamations, which were all she uttered. At last, when I came to Ernest's message that, "come what might, he could never forget; that, parted or united, he was her's and her's only; that his own troubles were as nothing to him, compared with the thought of what she must suffer," and much more in the same sad strain, her spirit failed at last, she buried her face in her handkerchief, and I could only tell by the convulsive sobs which shook her bosom, to what agony of tears she was giving way. Deeply pained as I was to see her, I was utterly powerless to console; and silence was the only comfort I could bestow. What a mockery it all seemed; the bright sunshine and the dancing waves; the day we had all so eagerly looked forward to; the sailing match we had plotted and discussed again and again in happier hours; here it was—but oh! how different now; how changed to that fond foolish heart, which was reaping the fruits of ill-fated passion in blighted hopes and sickening despair.

I'm a bad hand at doing the pathetic, and have cut this part of my story as short as may be: still I wished the thorough discomfort of my situation to be pretty completely realized by the reader. Remembering they had telescopes on the beach, and fearing Eugenie's distress might be noticed, I disregarded Bompas' caution, and stood further out to sea; the 'Sylph' had been gaining on us gradually before, and at this point overhauled us with ease. Caring very little now, I steered wide off the course and kept on across till we were near again to the projecting headland, which gives its name to Senanus Bay. The outline of the coast is here so abrupt, and the water so deep right under the cliffs, that a vessel rounding the point close, would be out of our sight till she entered the basin. The spot was so lonely and so little frequented, that its chief use was for smuggling purposes, and I had heard fellows boasting at Weremouth that, "give 'em the right sort of night, and they could land a cargo at Senanus, in the teeth of the sharpest coast-guard that ever used spy-glass or drew cutlass."

I mention this to explain, as far as possible, how that happened which did happen. For truly I am now on the brink of my catastrophe, and even at this distance of time I feel a cold shudder at having to recount it. If I lived to the age of a hundred, I could never forget that hour. Intending to 'go about,' as the breeze was growing much fresher, I put the helm down with one hand, holding the main sheet in the other; the mizen and jib I had furled shortly before; dead under the rocks, as we were, the wind failed us, and so accordingly did my little manœuvre; I let her forge slowly ahead, past the point, expecting a puff to set all to rights from the open sea. At that instant, while she hung in the trough of a wave, a loud shout of 'Boat ahoy!' rang in my ears; and, looking round in amazement, there, by Jove! running into us, amidships, was the 'Lively Nancy', under all her canvass, old Mc Bean's face grinning above the bowsprit, and another grimy old salt roaring out orders to me, which I couldn't understand a word of, and couldn't have executed if I had. It was over in much less time than it takes me to write it, or you to read. By instinct, rather than presence of mind, I got the boat about, and the schooner, instead of taking us amidships, struck our stern, and stove it in. There was a scream or two from Eugenie, and an oath or two from Mc Bean: I was too astonished myself either to yell or swear. We filled rapidly, and were settling down, when one of the schooner's crew hooked a grappling-iron into the ill-fated 'Crest', and drew her along side, smartly as an angler might land his half-pound trout; we had just time to get hauled on board, and then the poor little cutter gave its final lurch, and subsided for good and all.

Bruised, dripping, and breathless, I confronted the skipper: he was one continuous grin from ear to ear; (the favourite expression of every plebeian Scot) "neatly done, worn't it now, Muster Saville?" said the monster, "looked so nateral like, you'd ha' said it wor a ax'dent, wouldn't yer, now?"

"What the (strong expression)—d'you mean," I replied,

longing to throttle him, "what d'you mean, you infernal old scoundrel?"

"Muster Sav— whew!" here he gave a prolonged whistle, and grinned yet worse than before, "by Jakers! it's the wrong un."

More perplexed and wroth than ever, I was about to punch his old head, and probably, get a thrashing for my pains, when he cried out, "Lord a marcy, look ye there!" and turning, I saw poor Eugenie had fainted.

Well: my only wonder was, she had'nt come to that sooner. Old Mc Bean, who wasn't such a bad-hearted fellow after all, rushed down the ladder and got his cabin door opened. I carried the poor girl into the cabin, (heavens! how it did smell of spirits and tobacco!) and, not being altogether unused to the duty, contrived, by the ordinary remedies to bring her to herself again; the skipper and I made up a sort of extempore couch for her better comfort, and, thanks to her natural spirit, I was glad to see her soon grow more composed, though sadly nervous still, and shaken, as the strongest of her sex, in the same plight, could hardly have failed to be. Mc Bean then volunteered his explanations, which didn't mend matters, however, at all: it seems his conscience (?) had warned him that, by helping the elopement he might get into a precious ugly scrape; so he hit on the happy idea of running the boat down and smashing it, in order that this accident (?) might justify him in the eyes of the law for taking the parties on board. As it happened, I had steered the cutter exactly as Ernest intended to have done, and the Scotchman knowing her by sight, (not to mention Saville's flag which was flying at our mast-head) made no doubt that the right people were in her, and carried out his own amendment accordingly.

When could he put us ashore, was my next question, for I waived indignation for the present, and thought it best to be polite. Oh! we should be at St. Ambroise before that evening. That didn't suit at all; wouldn't he stand in for twenty minutes, in which case our friends in the other cutter could come alongside and take us off? No, he was blowed if he would, or could, and he asked me to look out of the port-hole, which formed the window of his cabin. I looked and saw nothing but a sail in the distance. Did I know what vessel it was? No? Well, it was the 'Revenue' sloop, and catch him, the captain of that 'ere schooner, risking his cargo for any living soul: if he stood in, the sloop would have him sure as fate; he'd had the narrowest shave of it the week before; and he wouldn't risk it again, not for a thousand pounds: no: we came on board of our own doing, no fault of his, and there we must stay till he sighted France: there may be a fishing boat would take us ashore, for he dursn't run into the harbour himself, and must lie off till night-fall. At this point of the proceedings there was a call of 'skipper' from the deck, and up the ladder he vanished double-quick.

Strange to say, Eugenie seemed rather relieved at the turn affairs had taken; her friends at St. Ambroise would receive her, she knew, her Aunt being Superior of the convent in that town: and as the said lady was cuts with old St. Croix, she would certainly aid and abet her niece in hiding, and possibly save her from the forced marriage with her *parrain*. At any rate it was a temporary respite, and any change seemed to the poor girl a change for the better. My own thoughts, however, were not so cheerful: what *would* people say of me? what *would* Seraphina think? How *could* I ever explain to the Colonel, or to Miss Veriblue? and what *was* I to do when landed in France, seeing at that moment I had exactly two half-crowns and a fourpenny-bit in my pocket? Well: time would shew, I supposed; and seeing some ship's biscuit and cold junk on the premises, I just remembered I'd had no breakfast, so fell to work with a will, and finished with a glass of contraband brandy. Eugenie, a faint smile dawning on her wan face, declined to share my repast: happily she had escaped the wetting I came in for, so I had not to insist on her restoring nature by the spirit medium of eau de vie.

Food and drink affect the temper favourably, and really, if I hadn't felt so very damp, I should almost have begun to enjoy the situation. We discussed our affairs and prospects over and over again, till finally we got quite accustomed to them all, and prepared for anything and everything. It seemed the vessel was pitching and tossing above one or two, and I proposed to my fair companion to ascend on deck and take an observation; she declined, but begged me to go and see; promising to return immediately and report, on deck I went.

By Jove! what a change there had been in the last hour: the sky clouded over, and growing darker every minute, the wind shifted round nearly eight points, and blowing stiff enough for a landsman to call it a gale; the schooner with nothing set but her fore-stay-sail and reefed mainsail topping the seas as they rose, and taking them just where they melted into one another, but still, buoyant as she was, giving a dip and a roll from time to time, which shewed she needed her skipper at the wheel, and took all his skill to handle her. Soon as he saw me he roared out a request that I'd "go for'ard and help Bill to clap a guy on that 'ere boom," language which was Hebrew and Sanscrit to me, but go I did, and, under Bill's superintendence, improved my nautical knowledge. Besides these twain there was only a boy on board, and he was swinging somewhere about the rigging in fearfully perilous positions, which I could admire, but not imitate. Bill and I were a long time about our job, and by then the skipper had roared out some fresh orders, seeming to take me for a foremastman, and designing I should work my passage across. Truth to tell, I wasn't sorry for something to stop one thinking, and I laid to work with an uneducated zeal, which provoked mingled admiration and curses from my tarry instructor. Sharper and sharper the wind came singing through the ropes; worse and worse got the pitching, and the way I tumbled about was a ' caution to snakes'; we never had a minute's rest till she was ' stripped', as Bill informed me, ' to the storm stay-sails,' adding, by way of consolation, "if this keeps on we shan't see France to-morrow."

We did though, all the same, and were lying off St. Ambroise in the grey dawn of a drizzling misty day. Fifteen hours I had spent in utter discomfort, on deck all the while, except for a few minutes, from time to time, when I reported progress at the cabin door: rain pouring down in buckets, night dark as pitch, all hands hard at work, as our several abilities prompted; my own chief occupation was to look out ahead, and roar ' breakers' if I should happen to see them, which, happily, I didn't. Towards morning the gale came to a lull, and by four o'clock the sea was so far gone down that we could begin to think of landing. A French fishing smack, after exchange of private signals, ran alongside and took us on board. I offered old Mc Bean what coin I had about me, but he declined, with hideous imprecations, to touch it, saying, "I'd paid my footing, and plenty too." We had got quite thick in the course of our night's adventures, and shaking hands all round, parted with vows of eternal friendship.

No further disaster happened; the French fishermen landed us at the pier, and were uncommonly civil all the while. Eugenie, looking dreadfully pale and weary, leant on my arm, and directed the way to the convent: she knew the town well enough, and we were soon there. I wondered inwardly what poor Ernest would have given to be in my place, and what she would have given that it had been his arm to support her instead of mine. The *concierge* stared a little on opening the grated door, but was evidently not astonished at trifles, and accustomed to vigil at any hour of the morning. I pressed the little hand of my *compagnon de voyage*, saw the gate closed, and making my way alone to the Singe D'Or, a tidy hotel I had noticed on the quay, was soon stripped of my wet habiliments, and doubled up in a peculiarly small comfortless bed. It was long past noon when I woke again.

From necessary causes I staid at the little French port for best part of a week: I had written home the first day, told them all about it without reserve, and waited for further advice. In that out-of-the-way place they were used to strange visitors, and neither bothered me for passport, nor asked me what I wanted. The weather was very fine, and there was good fishing in the bay; with the help of that, and some native tobacco, and such company as could be picked up on the pier and in the public, time passed pretty pleasantly. The second day I got a very polite note from the Lady Superior of the convent, thanking me for my attentions to her niece: Eugenie added a few pretty words of farewell at the bottom of the page. They didn't ask me to see them, nor did I care to go. On the sixth day came a peculiarly jolly letter from home, and everything that was satisfactory in the way of remittances. Next morning I left St. Ambroise for Rhine-land.

Not caring to set foot in England, at least before the Long was over, I took a good spell of travel. At Coblentz, whom should I meet but Fluker and the rest of the four? They had smashed their little craft descending some unpronounceable rapid of the Mayn, and looked uncommonly queer in their boating costume, which was *rather* the worse for wear. Their funds running short, they seemed to be travelling mostly on foot, and lodging in the vilest of slums: however, they all looked peculiarly well and happy, and declared they had done an amazing lot of reading: which, under the circumstances, was highly probable.

I needn't sketch the plan of my pilgrimage, which was not a long one, Venice being the goal. Early in October I was back in Paris, and, in the Rue Rivoli, came across my friend Whitechapel, who had started for Russia, but never got farther than the Quartier Latin; his sojourn had

R

added a moustache to his lip, and extra slanginess to his general demeanour; however, his stock of anecdotes was remarkable, and all of them, doubtless, (?) founded on real experience of student life. He shewed me a file of English papers: I had been sadly out of news for the last month: and what I read now astonished me not a little. Rumours had reached me that a great speculation bank, the Grand Central they called it, had broken in August; but I didn't know then that all Ernest's little fortune was invested in the concern; I didn't know it till I read a detailed account of Mr. Saville's proceedings in the Insolvent Court, and of the very inadequate settlement his creditors were likely to obtain. However, thought I, it won't distress him much, for he always looked forward to a chamber in the Fleet, sooner or later; and by that night's post I wrote him such a letter as I could manage of comfort and condolence. Two pieces of news served to cover a second sheet of my epistle, and though I can write them down calmly at this distance of time, I confess, when I read them first, the sensation was like a chilly hand laying its fingers on my heart:

MARRIAGE.

Sept. 3rd. At St. Mary's, Weremouth, by the Rev. M. A. Smith, John, eldest son of Timotheus Tugg, Esq., Cranbourn Lodge, Manchester, to Seraphina Maria, only daughter of the late Francis Hawthorn, Esq., M.D.

DEATH.

Sept. 10th. At Weremouth, suddenly, of heart disease, Colonel Henri St. Croix.

Not very long since, a medical friend was shewing me the Hospital of St. Lazare, at Paris; there were two or three sœurs de charité in the wards as we were passing through, so neat of dress, so soft of foot, and so gentle of hand, as they went about performing their works of mercy, that Scott's immemorial line

The ministering Angel thou,

seemed to have found its perfect realization there. One of the sisters, as she passed me, gave a start and a faint cry, then, concealing her face in her veil, hurried out of the ward. Time and sorrow, and, for aught I know, severest convent discipline as well, had done their fatal work of change, but the memory of a figure, fuller it might be, and rounder once, but endowed with that perfect grace and elasticity of motion, flashed at once across my mind: that thick veil might disguise the small head and the slender throat, but I knew I had seen once more Eugenie St. Croix. I asked my friend about her, but he knew next to nothing: Sœur Marie, he said, was the name she went by there; she lived in one of the city convents, he did not remember which. I had no right to prosecute my search, but I told Ernest (whitewashed at last, and working hard in Somerset House) the tale of what I had seen. Saville has kept his word, "come what might, he has not forgotten," and I know the first three weeks of vacation he succeeds in obtaining from H. M. Civil Service, will be spent by him on the other side the channel. Perhaps the slight clue I have given may enable him to find his hidden treasure. Will my readers wish him, heartily as I do, 'Bon Voyage'?

"P. O."

ZEPHYRUS.

THERE is a dell in Paphos seen of none
Save Aphrodite and one only pair
Immortal, graced by the Idalian Queen
Beyond all others; for, when Zephyrus,
Languid with love and weary of his task,—
To flit unseen around Aurora's car
And fan the rosy-cinctured Hours, or wake
The leafy murmurs of Olympian groves,—
Besought her, she, by favour of great Zeus,
Touched by his prayer, granted his spirit form
Of Godlike beauty;—and anon she breathed
Her influence o'er the maiden of his love,
Waking the virgin movings of her heart
To answer a felt touch, albeit unseen.

Yet, for she loves her power, and loves to see
Her thralls endure their fetters, ere she brought
To that sweet dell, hid in the Paphian shades,
The pearl of all the isle, she fain would hear
Young Zephyr pour his plaint in earnest song;
For she had noted, when Apollo's lute
Lay idle, how with curious unseen hand
He ever strayed among the golden chords,
That throbbed with weird aërial melodies
At his light touch, and quivered into sound.

Therefore she sate beside him in the cave
Herself had chosen.—Thick around it grew
Her glossy myrtles, and the downcast flower
Whereon she gazing had of old bestowed,
In guerdon for its sweetness, the bright stain,
The azure stain of her own peerless eye,
Gleamed through the cool damp moss about their feet.

And in the eager brightness of first youth
And early love he sate, and while its glow
Purpled his cheek, and with impatient heel
He crushed the asphodels, thus Zephyr sang:—

"O maiden, snow-white maiden, by what name
Soe'er ascribed to heavenly choirs the gods
Shall own thee loveliest, hear the air-god's prayer;
Nor deem my love a love of yesterday,
For I have watched thee, maiden, all unseen,
Cow'ring amid the petals of a rose,
Or lurking in the fairy citadel
Of some bright crocus,—when the kindly spring
Wooed thee to Dian's haunts, and all the sward
Crisp with innumerous spikes and bursting buds
Charmed thy attentive gaze.—O, then, 'twas I
That brake the pencilled cups and shed their dew
Gem-like on thy soft hand;—'twas I that played
Viewless among thy tresses, and unheard,
Or with such gentle whisper as awoke
Thy changing colour, for, methinks, my power,
Unknown, wrought in thee a vague joy e'en then
And sweet indefinite longings:—Hear, O, hear,
I am aweary of the blustering winds,
Those my rude mountain-brothers, and no joy
Visits me now to tend the budding shoots,
Or move old Ocean to a dimpled smile,
Or waft sweet odours through the myrtle alleys.
And yet, so thou wert mine, my earliest care,
My latest still should be to tend thee well
As a sweet flower;—and flowers for thee should wear
A brighter purple, and sweet airs, my slaves,
Should ever breathe about thee, and my love
Should dower thee with immortal life, and give
Thy name to men no less to be adored
Than Psyche's,—scarcely less than hers who gave
Me all I have, and fain would give me thee."

So sang he, all enraptured, and the Queen,
Radiant with conscious power, granted his prayer,
For Dian now had risen o'er the grove,
Not with cold glance, but with the mellow smile
She loves to shed on Latmos, and still night
Heard gentle whispers, and the Star of Eve
Sparkled like fire above the Idalian hills.

"C. S."

SHELLEY AND ÆSCHYLUS.

NONE of the legends of classic story have taken deeper root in the hearts of men, since the revival of letters, than the story of Prometheus. It has embodied itself in the phraseology of our poets; it has given a tone to the proverbial colloquialisms of daily conversation; it has engaged the attention of antiquarians and divines. The latter have discovered in it, (whether justly or not it is not my province now to enquire,*) traces of a primeval tradition of man's fall by the agency of a woman, and of a prophecy that the "seed of a woman should bruise the serpent's head."

It is not difficult to see why this should be. There is somewhat in the legend so stirring, somewhat that appeals so strongly to our sympathy with all that is brave and noble in humanity, and especially with that noblest form of human greatness, endurance under suffering,—suffering incurred for benefits conferred on our own race,—that no heart alive to such feelings could be otherwise than roused thereby.

---

* There are two points in connexion with this hypothesis which I have never seen particularly dwelt upon: viz., the supernatural conception of Epaphus, plainly indicated by Æschylus in two passages of the Supplices (vv. 45, 312) where he speaks of his being begotten, by the inspiration, or by the hand or touch of Zeus; and the additional link supplied by the passage in the Prometheus, referred to below, where Zeus is described as wishing to exterminate the whole race of men, as connected with a primitive tradition of the deluge, of which we have other traces. If I were looking in the legend in question for any such meaning, I should find in it rather a reference to One, himself divine, who—made perfect in sufferings—was to deliver man from the wrath of an Almighty and offended God.

That this is the chief ground of its wide acceptance, is, I think, further shown by a comparison of the original legend with that which is generally current. There are parts of that original legend in which the character of Prometheus does not appear to such advantage, and these have been quietly dropped, though in the latter version we meet with expressions, here and there, which have often been referred to the first tradition. My classical reader will perceive at once that I allude to the choice given to Zeus by Prometheus in the division of the victims in sacrifice. The story is told by Hesiod in his Theogony (vv. 535—557). Prometheus as the representative of men set before Zeus—on the one side the flesh and inwards of a fine ox covered with the ox's paunch,—and on the other the bones and refuse enveloped in the white fat,—and gave him his choice, which part the gods should have. Zeus perceived the intended treachery, and in his rage " with both hands chose the white fat, meditating evil to the whole human race, evil which should hereafter be accomplished." Unless it can be accounted for as above, it surely is remarkable, that so strong a feature of the legend should, in the popular version of it, be so generally ignored, and that when it is required to account for the first proceeding mentioned in the common legend, the withholding of fire by Zeus, which led to the daring exploit of Prometheus. It is singular too, as shewing the tendency to exalt the hero's claims to human gratitude, that to him is given the credit of introducing the pleasures of hope into the human breast, while according to another part of the legend, amidst the general dispersion over the world of suffering and disease, by Pandora's agency, Hope alone remained in the cask where she had been imprisoned with them.*

But my object now is not so much to discuss the legend itself, as to view it with reference to the two phases of it given by Æschylus and Shelley, which have generally been held to be distinct. Of the secondary reasons for the wide spread knowledge of the Promethean story, there can be no doubt that we shall find the chief in the noble work of the former poet, the Prometheus Bound. As regards plot, and the accessory elements of tragic interest,

---

* Can any one read me this riddle of Hope's remaining while the rest were scattered abroad? If Hope staid among men, surely disease was banished from them—if diseases were spread among them, surely Hope was kept from them under lock and key.

this play is far inferior to some of the other works which antiquity has handed down to us,—it involves an episode which is worked out to an extent certainly not warranted by its connexion with the main story,—but, after all, the grand poetry which it contains, and the surpassing interest of its central figure have always found a response in those who could say with the poet,

"Homo sum; humani nihil a me alienum puto."

Most of my readers are aware that, besides the play in question, Æschylus produced another, entitled the Prometheus Unbound, which, with the exception of a few valuable fragments, is unfortunately lost to us. We know however how the story was worked out. In the extant play Prometheus is severely tortured to drive him to disclose a secret,—which is several times hinted at, but which he refuses to divulge till he is released from his bonds,—of a marriage by which Zeus would beget a son that should be stronger than himself. In the sequel, he revealed the secret, which was to the effect that the goddess Thetis, who was then looked to as the probable partner of Zeus' throne, would bring forth a son who should be stronger than his father, and consequently Zeus espoused her to a mortal, Peleus, by whom she had Achilles. Prometheus was then released from his captivity.

There can be no doubt that after the loud boastings of his courage which we have in the Prometheus Bound, this is an unsatisfactory catastrophe, derogating greatly from the dignity of human nature as shadowed forth in the great representative of the race. Such was the feeling which induced the poet Shelley to carry on the work which Æschylus had begun, to what appeared to him its legitimate conclusion. The poem thus produced is one of exceeding beauty, though to be read with some degree of caution; for, knowing the scepticism of its author, we cannot but feel that in some of the strongest exclamations against the empire of Heaven, there is a sneer, if nothing worse than a sneer, at all religious belief. The plot is simply told:— Prometheus patiently endures his fate, and by his suffering becomes the redeemer of the race; Zeus is dethroned by his child Demogorgon, as he himself dethroned Kronos; they dwell together in darkness; no successor is appointed to the throne of Olympus; no more are men to be held in thrall by the capricious power of cruel gods, but are themselves henceforth to live as gods, the new era being ushered in by the downfall of Zeus, and the consequent liberation of Prometheus. The accessories of the play form its greatest beauties, and serve well to set off the simpler grandeur of the main plot.

But my object in this paper is rather to show that in this treatment of the subject Shelley, though diverging considerably from the plot of the lost play of Æschylus, does in fact only work out what we have plain hints of in the Prometheus Bound. The points on which the latter turns are, as I conceive, the following: Prometheus is enchained for having stolen the fire of Zeus, and given it to mortals (7*); as their great benefactor he is looked upon as the champion and deliverer of their kind (235): but he has also been on the closest terms with the Heavenly Ruler himself—for it was by his counsels that the latter had consigned Kronos to the murky depths of Tartarus, and seized upon his throne (219 follg). The first cause of quarrel was that Zeus, anxious to secure an unmolested empire, held thoughts of destroying the race of men altogether, and creating a new one (232), and in his division of power, gauging everything by the rule of self-interest, "took no count of hapless mortals" (230). Prometheus alone of all his counsellors ventured to oppose his plans (234), and rescued men from utter destruction. From this his own account, and that of Hermes, who, later in the play, taunts him with bringing himself into this harbourage of woes by his own stubborn and rebellious course (964), it would seem that the theft of fire was but the open accusation, on which the punishment was based, the actual cause being the gratification of Zeus' revenge. He perseveres in his defence of men, and in his contempt for the ingratitude of Zeus, spite of all the tortures which his foe can heap upon him (1003), and the play ends with an appeal to Earth and Heaven to witness the injustice of the sufferings which he undergoes.

Now to turn to our other author. The key-note of Shelley's play is struck in the first scene, where Prometheus from his station in the bleak ravine of the Caucasian mountains, calls upon the "monarch of all Gods and Dæmons, and all Spirits but One," to

regard this Earth
Made multitudinous with thy slaves, whom thou
Requitest for knee-worship, prayer, and praise,

---

* The numerals refer to the lines in Dindorf's text.

And toil, and hecatombs of broken hearts,
With fear and self-contempt and barren hope.
Whilst me, who am thy foe, eyeless in hate,
Hast thou made reign and triumph, to thy scorn,
O'er mine own misery and thy vain revenge.
Three thousand years of sleep—unsheltered hours,
And moments aye divided by keen pangs
Till they seemed years, torture and solitude,
Scorn and despair,—these are mine empire.
More glorious far than that which thou surveyest
From thine unenvied throne, O mighty God!
Almighty, had I deigned to share the shame
Of thine ill tyranny.

(The allusion to the ingratitude of Zeus occurs again,

> I gave all
> He has; and in return he chains me here
> Years, ages, night and day.)

The curse in Scene i. is expressed in language which,
in an author writing in a Christian age, cannot be deemed
less than blasphemous. Still it finds to a certain extent
a parallel in the pages of Æschylus. Take for instance,

Believe me, Zeus, though stubborn-hearted, still
Shall be brought low.   (907)
And stumbling on such woes himself shall learn
'Twixt slaves and sovereigns what a gulph is fixed.   (926)
Pray on!—and court the sov'reign of the day!
For naught care I for Zeus, or for his power
Yea! less than naught. Let Him e'en as he will
Lord it thro' this, his brief career of empire,
For, be assured, not long shall he hold sway
Amongst the Gods of Heaven.   (937)

Prometheus is throughout the champion of mortals, and
not only so, but, as it were, their representative. He is
the one

At whose voice Earth's pining sons uplifted
Their prostrate brows from the polluting dust,
And our Almighty tyrant with fierce dread
Grew pale, until His thunder chained thee here.

He is

The Champion of Heaven's slaves,
The Saviour and the strength of suffering men.

(So Æschylus speaks of him as one

Who helping mortals for himself earned pains.)

He, who when bent by many sufferings and woes was to escape from his bonds (512), escapes them not by the grace and favour of Zeus, but by the final triumph of patient endurance, and by the cessation of Zeus' power. He bids the furies "pour out the cup of pain," and laughs to scorn "their power, and His who sent them." And at last his enemy is cast down from his lofty throne; the triple fates and ever-mindful Furies (516), whose power is to prove his master (930), overtake him with their vengeance: Prometheus having kept the secret, by keeping of which he was to escape from his torturing chains (525),* is triumphantly set at liberty, therein fulfilling the confident expectation of the Chorus that the time would come even yet, when released from his bonds he should become no less powerful than Zeus himself (500). As it was a son of Zeus, who bound him to the "Eagle-baffling mountain," so it is a son of Zeus who delivered him thence,—the former by his mother's side connected with the gods, the latter by ties of blood and feeling sympathizing with men,—while the former monarch of gods and men appeals to him as "monarch of the world."

I think I have said enough to shew that I have some ground for maintaining that Shelley in his treatment of the subject has not departed from the path which his pioneer had marked out. Passages there are, some of which I have quoted, which appear to me quite inconsistent with the catastrophe of the common legend, though it would be absurd in us to accuse Æschylus of such inconsistency, without knowing how the plot was, in the last play of the Promethean trilogy, worked round to the desired end. I wish my commendation of the whole work could be more unreserved. Its poetry, its imagery quite justify Sandy Mackaye's eulogy, "Ay, Shelley's gran"; there is about the play with its combination of classic and modern veins of poetry an inexpressible charm: but there is a dangerous spirit lurking in it which would sap at the root of all religious

---

* I am not certain about the meaning I have put upon this passage: if it be correct, I can only explain it as alluding to the destruction of the power of Zeus by means of the marriage with Thetis, the result of which Prometheus alone foreknew.

.

belief.* Now it takes the form of Pantheism—now it borders
more upon absolute Atheism—but throughout evinces a
stubborn opposition to the will of the Supreme Being,
which justifies the comparison,—which the author to a
certain extent challenges in his introduction,—with the
Satan of the Paradise Lost. But to any one who can
exercise due discrimination in rejecting the chaff, I can
promise a great treat in the reading of Shelley's Prometheus
Unbound.

---

* There is one passage in this play, which will, I think, throw
some light upon the cause of Shelley's estrangement from all belief
in the truth of Christianity.   It is in the first act:

Remit the anguish of that lighted stare;
Close those wan lips; let that thorn-wounded brow
Stream not with blood; it mingles with thy tears!
Fix, fix those tortured orbs in peace and death,
So thy sick throes shake not that crucifix.
    *   *   *   *   I see, I see
The wise, the mild, the lofty, and the just,
Whom thy slaves hate for being like to thee,
Some hunted by foul lies from their hearts' home
 . . Some linked to corpses in unwholesome cells:
Some . . . impaled in lingering fire.

ARIADNE.

1.

She sat upon a mass of cold-grey stone
   Worn with the rough caresses of the wave,
She heard no more the billows' hissing groan
   The vengeful murmur of the sea-god's slave.
Across the deep one bright-oar'd galley drave
   One cloud all-glorious lay athwart the sun;
She heard the sea-mew fluttering to his cave,
   She heard the shrill cry of his mate, alone
She sat unmated,—the forsaken one.

2.

Smooth spread the sea for many a weary mile
   Blue-gleaming far as human eye might reach,
The little wavelets dimpled to a smile,
   And brake in kisses on the sparkling beach.
Above the south-wind muttering did beseech
   And threaten, in low tones o'er crag and scar,
Until it sank at length o'er-powered, and each
   Rude ocean-sweeping blast retired from war,
   And, sighing, died along the deep afar.

3.

Now Silence, loved of Sleep, mild-visaged king,
   Following the footsteps of departing light,
Close wrapped in cloud swept down on noiseless wing,
   And all the earth grew dim before his sight.
White vapours hid the ocean's slumbering might,
   —The veil of Aphrodite soft and warm,
As beautiful as when sun-flushed and bright
   Its folds first wreathed around her rising form—
   Her silver shield—her close defence from harm.

4.

And she—the kingly born, the fair of face,
   Old Minos' daughter, Ariadne,—she
Sat gazing forward o'er the trackless space,
   —The wind-swept bosom of the mighty sea—
Silent she sat, her hand upon her knee,
   Across her face a deepening shade of pain,
Her hair about her bosom floating free,
   Mourning for him who crossed the heaving main
   Departing—never to return again.

"M. B."

STEETLEY RUINED CHURCH,
DERBYSHIRE.

An ivy-mantled ruin, yet still fair,
With carved device and arch of Norman mould,
That mark a structure consecrate of old
To holy offices of praise and prayer:
But who shall say when last was gather'd there
By softly-tinkling bell the scatter'd fold,
Or sacred anthem to the skies hath roll'd
Save from the light-wing'd choristers of air?
Roofless the aisle is left, the altar lone,
Yet let none deem that from this still recess
The God who once was worshipt there is gone.
Still may the contrite heart its sin confess,
Still thankful knees the green-turft chancel press,
And He shall hearken on His holy throne.

"C."

THE QUESTIONIST'S DREAM.

THERE goes six o'clock! no train now till twelve! so I'm booked, it seems, to spend a Christmas Eve in Cambridge. It was with anything but the complacent feelings which are generally supposed to follow in the train of self-sacrifice and the keeping of a good resolution that I made these ejaculations. The prospect was not pleasant. An empty wine-glass reminded me that a friend had just left me to go down by the six o'clock train. It was a miserable night, muggy, misty, unwholesome: it was a surplice night too, and I had just missed chapel. I was one of about seven remaining undergraduates. The others had all gone. How glad Smith was to 'bolt' as he called it! What joys had not Jones depicted in his pleasant home up in the North! How that wretch Robinson would persist in pitying me. Never mind, I shall live to be envied. No, I didn't much mind all that; but there were all Mr. Todhunter's treatises glaring at me and reminding me that I was a Questionist, and that a week hence I should be in the—— well, it was not a pleasant thought, I did not care to continue it, but there was no doubt about it, I was a questionist, and I was miserable.

If the present was not agreeable, still less was the future. To-night, reading a-bed; to-morrow, breakfast, chapel, with holly and all its suggestions: after chapel, a blank till hall; then unpleasant reminders of the season in the shape of mince-pies (not home made), then a blank, then evening chapel, then a final blank, then bed-time. What a succession of blanks: what a violation of all the laws of Christmas time! I never thought to have been so like that fictitious relative of Viola's. Nor shall I be in one respect. She never told her calamity, whereas I do mine, partly; moreover, she had only one blank to complain of, while I had three, at least.

Well, but virtue, and self-sacrifice, and all that sort of thing: would, or could not they come to the rescue? not they: I only staid up because I was afraid I should be plucked. It would have been a much more meritorious action to have gone down, and I knew it, and felt humiliated accordingly. The idea of praising a man who wants to be Senior Wrangler, as Smith did, or wooden spoon, as I did, for sticking to his work! A Senior Op, now, deserves some credit. Why should he have worked for an ignoble mediocrity? He has no conceivable motive, nothing can account for such a phenomenon but an innate instinct of industry. Thus you see I could not console myself by putting my mind on its back, so to speak, for any extraordinary virtue. Then again, as regarded expediency, would it not have been better to have taken a rest? A week? At least a day? what a pleasant day it might have been! what a pleasant Christmas I had spent last year! What a roaring fire! And the old yule-log too, and the country-dance, and the blind-man's-buff, and the forfeits, and the misletoe, and that charming little— oh! good heavens: something must be done: here's Hymers' Three Dimensions.

"The osculating plane at any point of a curve is that which has closer contact with the curve than any other plane passing through the same point." "An osculating plane cuts the curve unless its contact be of an odd order." "The condition for a contact of the third order of an osculating plane is

$$\frac{d^2z}{dx^2}\frac{d^3y}{dx^3} - \frac{d^2y}{dx^2}\frac{d^3z}{dx^3},"$$

"When a curve in space is a plane curve, the plane in which it is situated is the osculating plane at every point."

Very good—I must master this before I read further. Rather odd though, that! an odd number of kisses better than an even! I began to picture to myself an osculating plane. I flatter myself I have a considerable power of concentration, and at last, forgetting the weather, the chapel, the mince-pies, the six o'clock train, and even the approaching New-year's day, I lost myself completely in my subject.

I seemed to see before me a fair and beautiful maiden, clothed in white, bearing in her right hand a sprig of misletoe. On her head she wore a circular coronet: her shoes were delicate white satin ellipses of considerable eccentricity. From her classical hat streamed back two winged hyperbolas: from a white neck her neck-chain streamed down in a curve which, I need scarcely say, was a catenary: her blue sash, pinned by a brooch, in the form of a logarithmic spiral, fell into folds so lovely, that in them none could fail to discern the line of beauty: upon it was written, " Mathematics made easy." She stood before me with her arm flung gracefully round a man, in whom I thought I recognised ——, well, modesty bids me to conceal what truth would fain have me proclaim.

I was gazing entranced on this beauteous apparition, when a chilly creeping shiver made me conscious of the proximity of a new neighbour. Inclined at an angle of about eighty degrees to the horizon, and leaning somewhat heavily on the arm of a gentleman, in whose features I thought I noted a strong resemblance to——, surely there can be no harm in mentioning the name of a gentleman who keeps in the New Court, up two pair of stairs, and is the author of very many compendious Mathematical treatises—but I won't though—for I hate personalities—leaning then on the arm of a gentleman, who shall be nameless, and who stood exalted on a vast volume, on the back of which I caught a glimpse of the word Variations, was an elderly female. Her arms were what is commonly called a-kimbo: but to my mind they resembled those jointed bars connected by an elastic string, spoken of in page 309, of the *Analytical Statics*, and were painfully suggestive in their motions, of virtual velocities. Depending from her two hands was a rigid rod: her shoes were black leather triangles, her long limp robe might be roughly described as a prism, her head-dress consisted of one of those black cylinders usually worn by the male sex: emblazoned on her breast was a diagram of the Pons Asinorum. Her eyes are best described by Mr. Harvey Goodwin as spherical, the front part being more convex than the rest: eyes, whose dull confusive glare seemed to betoken an absence of the " pigmentum nigrum," and from whose " retina" no gleam of compassion had ever been reflected. Before and around the female went a piteous cry, as of the hissing of innumerable geese, forcibly deprived of their plumage. Upon the cylinder supported by her head, was this label, " Mathematics made difficult."

Both figures stretched out their hands to me, as though each was appealing for my sympathy—against her rival—I shuddered as the rigid inelastic rod fell with a thud on the inelastic floor, and as I looked with admiration toward

s

the fairer form, the other faded from my gaze. Describing
the most graceful of parabolas, the lady in white projected
herself through the air toward me, and said, "Dear, dear
Philocalus, you are now under my tuition: my fees are
osculations: my realms the flowers: the clouds and the
seas, my subjects: the mathematical elves and fairies, of
whom, as yet, you poor Cambridge-men know nothing.
You are now reading, I know, for the mathematical tripos,
though that is not exactly the sort of examination I should,
of choice, desire for my pupils; yet I will proceed at once
to fit you for it, to the best of my power. Let our first
lecture be on osculating planes."

I looked whither the maiden waved her hand, and saw
a nymph, the fairest (but one) that it was ever my good
fortune to set eyes upon. If she had a fault, it was, that
she was so lithe and slender and fairy-like, that an over-
critical eye might have almost called her linear ; her ringlets
streamed in a lovely curve through the air; she too, as
well as my new teacher, bore a sprig of misletoe; but there
was a strange wild magical look about her whole demeanour
which I could not account for, till my instructress said, with
a smile, "You see the witch of Agnesi." I looked again,
and up from the horizon peered a strange thin looking
creature, who approached the enchantress: her attraction
was evidently too powerful for him: nearer and yet nearer
he came, till at last, with a laugh and "three cheers for
the misletoe," he kissed her, methought, somewhat roughly.
Be that, however, as it may, his body instantly assumed
a different and more definite appearance. I am not much
of an artist, nor is it, I believe, the custom of *The Eagle*
to allow illustrations: but if the Printer can trace the following lines, this was the appearance of the three limbs which
constituted his body :

$$\frac{x'-x}{\frac{dx}{dt}} = \frac{y'-y}{\frac{dy}{dt}} = \frac{z'-z}{\frac{dz}{dt}}.$$

"Oh," said the big creature, "I must and will have
another kiss." In vain the poor enchantress writhed dissent:
he kissed a second time. A piteous shriek rent the air,
and from a bleeding gash in the poor girl's cheek streamed
a torrent of blood. "This is my sad fate," cried she, "after
the second kiss my plane lovers always cut me." "But I,"
said the old Caliban, "will never cut you." "Oh," said
she, angry at his stupidity, "why not have contented yourself

with a single kiss: but now, at least, let the contact be of the third—" " Ha! shop! I don't allow such words as contact," interrupted my instructress. " Then kiss me dear, plane one, kiss me," said the witch, " a third time." The monster trembled with delight: his body had once more changed at the second kiss, and now his three new huge limbs: {it will be useful for you to recognise them, reader, so I'll draw them: they are something like one another; one was like this,

$$(y'z'' - z'y'')(X - x);$$

the other like this, $(z'x'' - x'z'')(Y - y);$

and the third like this,

$$(x'y'' - y'x'')(Z - z)\}.$$

Each of his three ugly limbs, I say, trembled with pleasure as he stooped a third time to kiss the bleeding maiden, when suddenly my instructress a second time interposed, " Ha!" cried she, " three kisses! then there is a condition." " Any condition shall be fulfilled," bellowed the infatuated old lover. " Done," said the other, " 'tis a hard one, though, see that you twist your ugly limbs till you make that one there $\left(\dfrac{d^3z}{dx^3} \cdot \dfrac{dy^3}{dx^3}\right)$ of the same size as this, $\left(\dfrac{d^3y}{dx^3} \cdot \dfrac{d^3z}{dx^3}\right)$." " Oh! how awkward," said poor Caliban, " but I'll try:" and he did it. But when he stooped with his poor contorted limbs to imprint the third kiss, the witch, evidently affected, cried out, " oh! kiss me not at all, or all in all, why can we not always be kissing?" " Agreed," cried the monster; when, for the third and last time, my mistress interposed. " So be it, my fair lady, provided you are ready, take all the consequences of your union: for know, in order to wed your plane lover, you will have to sacrifice all your good looks, and rumple your charming dress and pretty ringlets, and become perfectly plane yourself: then again you will have to leave your pleasant mountain air and elope with him to some flat country or other, (I should recommend the steppes of Ex-wye or Wye-zed as most convenient): there, and there only, can you enjoy perpetual love : and now," turning to me, " my dear pupil, my first lecture is over: were you to live a hundred years hence, when mathematics will be made easy, just like theology, and all that sort of thing, and everybody will be able to talk about them and criticise them without any trouble, then you would have more fellow-students ; but now, farewell my only pupil, and forget not osculating planes." "And now you two, will you be married or not? You will? Presto!"

It was done: down came the curve and plane together with a clang: the port from my broken wine-glass dripped across my knees, and I awoke, to remember that I was a Questionist.

Reader, good bye, forgive me this amount of shop. If I speak shop in the hope of preventing shop, abolishing shop for the future, is it not well done? May the reign of my instructress soon arrive, may the time soon come when there shall be no other levers but pokers, the oar, and the human arm, (perhaps also we may except the handle of the common pump) when there shall be no friction or elasticity but on billiard-tables, and every screw shall be done away but the cork-screw; when violets, roses, cockle-shells, cirrhus clouds, and waves, shall expel Mr. Todhunter's books. And lastly, reader, remember my dream better than I remembered it myself. How could I think of the pretty white dress when I looked up at that statue of Pitt in the Senate-House? How could I think of the fair enchantress and the devoted Caliban, and those dainty elliptical slippers, when Aldis was close by me, grinding for life and death: when Proctors were looking to see that I was not 'cribbing,' when Stentorian examiners shouted time: or Boning rushed impetuously over the matting, scattering papers and misery around him. Woe is me! I forgot the condition for the third kiss. Else haply I had not now need to subscribe myself—

"THE PLUCKED ONE."

HOMER ODYSS: V. 43—75.

Thus he spake, and attending the slayer of Argus obeyed him:
Straightway under his feet he clasped his beautiful sandals,
Fashioned of gold, divine, that over the watery sea-swell,—
Over the land's dim tracts bare him on with the speed of the
    storm-wind.
Seized he anon the rod wherewith the eye-lids of mortals,
Whomso he will, he seals, or from death's dark slumber awakes
    them ;—
Grasped it in either hand, and in might sped forth on his pinions.
First on Pieria lighting, he swooped from heaven upon ocean ;—
Skimmed o'er the curving waves, as skims the cormorant o'er them,
When in the perilous gulphs of the wastes that know not a harvest,
Bent on its finny prey, it dips thick plumes in the sea-brine ;—
So rode Hermes, upborne on the billows crowding around him.
But when he reached the isle that lies in the distance, afar off,
Forth he stepped from the sea deep-violet-hued, to the mainland,
Wending his way till he came to a mighty cave, where the goddess
Bright with fair tresses dwelt, and he found her abiding within it.
High up-piled on the hearth a huge fire blazed, and the
    fragrance
Breathed afar o'er the isle, of logs of cedar and citron,
Easily cleft by the axe; and with sweet voice warbled the goddess,
Plying the loom, and with needle of gold her broidery wove she.
Circling the cave around had grown a far-spreading forest,
Alders and silvery poplars and fragrant cypress, and in them,
Drooping their trailing plumes, the birds of the air found a shelter,
Falcons and owls and mews, that, with long-drawn shriek, o'er
    the billows
Ply their watery toil; and close to the cavernous hollow
Flourished a well-tilled vine, and bloomed on it thickly the clusters:
There too, in order due, four fountains, one by another,
Flowed in runnels pellucid, meandering hither and thither:
Far stretched the velvet meads with violets bright and with parsley.
E'en an immortal there might gaze and wonder in gazing,
Gladdened in heart at the sight: so, standing, wrapt in amazement,
Lingered the messenger god, great Hermes, slayer of Argus.

"C. S."

OF MAN,

AND MORE PARTICULARLY THAT STAGE OF HIS LIFE CALLED THE FRESHMAN'S.

REApER, if on seeing the heading of these pages your mind awakes to the expectation, that it is some Verdant that addresses you, fresh from the victimisation of his college career; if you conceive a panorama of cups, tandems, plucks, and more of the unrealities of an University man's life; if you expect that I, though veiled in the incognito offered me by the select pages of *The Eagle*, am doomed to take the Addenbrooke Hospital for Trinity, and the University Press for a Church; or, again, if your mind wanders off to the dread visions of my being screwed into my rooms by some jealous rival, or to the thrilling adventures of a long vacation in the Alps—I will answer, I will tell you, that I do not believe in extremes, that I mean to narrate my own homely personal adventures to whoever will listen to them, unpervaded by the odour either of washy sanctity or un-mixed claret-cup. First however allow me to remark that the personal pronoun, I shall adopt, does not extend any further in its experiences, than the pages of *The Eagle*. It was a soft October afternoon, when I stept out on to the platform of the Cambridge station, and having some-what reluctantly consigned my luggage to the opening mouth of a dry torrent—which like the stream of Alpheus, forcing its way beneath waves of steam, and ships that cleave the air, rises to surface again and presents its varied offerings to the goddess Granta—with an air of perfect ease I stept into an omnibus and said "to S. John's." How vain it is to set up as being better than we are! I was a fresh-man, and I knew it; and yet I thought no one else was aware of the fact. The conductor smiled—such a smile have I seen on the face of a master, who hath put me on in a lesson, which I have not known—and said "If you please, Sir, 't'other' bus is for S. John's." I got out, and giving my luggage into the other bus, determined to avoid any further mistake by walking up. I say 'walking' but I rather ran, for I felt that in me which told me I was like to miss my dinner. True that I did not know my way, but I thought one way would be as good as another, as the town seemed all in one direction, and I remembered one or two of the landmarks from a previous visit. I smiled with pity for freshmen in general, as I past the Press, thought of Ruskin as I past King's Chapel which stood like a plumed hearse awaiting the end of Paterfamilias and Matthew Johnson; on I went between the Asiatic luxury of Mr. Beamont, and the European simplicity of Mr. Lightfoot, the Sestos and Abydos of Trinity, till I reached the gate of S. John's, and there for the first time I remembered that I was nude of Academical equipment. How could I dine without them? Impossible, and yet I must confess that I was only partially sorry at having forgotten these indispensables to a freshman's furniture; nay I took it as a proof that I was no common freshman, inasmuch as I was not subject to the usual weakness of wearing my gown at all hours, and on all occasions. Anyhow I lost my dinner and bought my gown. Once more returning I enquired for my rooms of the porter, "No. 20 letter X, new court," he rattled out, without looking off his book, and I started in quest; in about half-an-hour I discovered them, and proceeded to take a survey. They consisted of four walls, as many doors, and a few chairs, also two tables rather the worse for wear, and a bookcase which proclaimed an occupant of somewhat limited researches. All were painted with a fine stone-coloured paint, shewing an utter want of taste on the part of the decorator, and of great patience and contentment on the part of my predecessor. At least so I thought.

My first thought was to discover the object of these doors. The first I opened satisfied all my difficulties; it led to a little room, set round with cupboards, in which I discovered a dapper little man, who addressed me by my name, and asked me if I wanted anything. Now the first impulse of the genus freshman on seeing anything approaching to a bedmaker, scout or gyp, is to expect to be legged and chiselled, or as the Romans elegantly express it, "de-

artuatus atque deruncinatus," to an extent hitherto un-
paralleled; in fact I have often thought that Plautus was
alluding to the word 'gyp' when he used deruncinatus, 'crane'
and 'gyp' being synonymous; however that may be, I politely
declined assistance, and proceeded to unpack box after box
myself, thereby incurring much discomfort, all to no purpose.
My chief care was to dispose views of my late school in
becoming order round my rooms, to hang my foot-ball cap
on the chimney-piece, and to lay a handsomely bound copy
of my School magazine on the table. This done I felt
myself the public school man. And here let me remark
the difference in advantages and disadvantages between
the generality of men who come up from a public school
or from home, or even a private tutor. What for instance
are the feelings of the public schoolboy, as the echo of the
first step that he places on the Cambridge platform proclaims
him a "man"? technically so called? Perhaps it was only
yesterday that he answered to his name in School calling
over, only yesterday that he was leading on his house to
victory in a foot-ball match, only yesterday that he debated
with puny eloquence some question of the privileges of the
sixth over the rest of the school; yesterday he was head
of his house with half-a-dozen fags, obedient to his call
and delighted to speak even to him; or perhaps again it
was only to-day that he attended his last service in the
chapel, the organ chaunt is still pealing in his ears, the
words of his head-master still echoing in his heart, as he
has dismissed him with the thrilling words "Quit you like
men, be strong." To-day he feels as it were a link between
the present and the past, to-morrow he will be as of the
past, and what he feels more than ever, his school will be
judged by him. He has come up with his heart expanded
by school and house feeling, he has had it satisfactorily proved
to him in his miniature Debating Society that Mahomet and
Blue-beard were good men, and has gravely argued the
advantages of narrow-mindedness in an imitation Union.

It is true that he comes up with a certain pride and
priggishness of conversation, anxious to press his own heroes
upon all society, but does not that somewhat argue that the
"spell of school affection has drawn his love from self apart"?
To sum up all the school-boy "by a vision splendid is on his
way attended." "At length a man he sees it die away, and
fade into the light of common day." But how does the
other freshman? He comes up fresh from home, probably
with no independence of sentiment, with a feeling that it

is his object to gain a high degree, or that he will have
failed in his college career. At least this is the only teaching
that will have been imprest upon him by the system to
which he has been subjected; if he has other feelings they
will be accidental to, not consequent upon, his former
education. This is his misfortune, not his fault, and while
perhaps he may be, and often is, superior to a public school
man in simplicity of purpose, and purity of thought; yet
on the whole he is generally, if he works, a slave to his
books; if he is idle, a prey to a weak idea of fastness; in
other words he has not the idea of public feeling to keep
him up. And how, it may be asked, is public feeling to
be kept up? Chiefly by such institutions as the boats, the
rifle corps, and College cricket, for it is seldom that one
finds a good College oar, or a member of a College eleven,
unwilling to rejoice if one of his College have come out
Senior Wrangler or Senior Classic. Witness the shouts in
the Senate-House, when the respective tripos' are read out,
shouts which tell of the union of gown and jersey, chapel
and river. What means "muscular religion"? is a question
I have often been asked, and all I can answer is that certain
men have seen, how public feeling appeals to our hearts,
and how the excitement of dashing along the banks of the
river by the side of our College eight, is wont to evoke that
sentiment.

But to return—these remarks have taken long to put
upon paper, but I can assure you, reader, that they did not
take long to go through my brain, as I past through our
courts early next morning, duly arrayed in cap and gown,
to chapel. I stopt for a moment hoping to find some architectural beauty on the exterior, but not longer. One glance
was enough, and I entered. Ah! why did I not remark,
that the rest wore surplices, I a gown. What hallucination
had seized me? I rushed out and returned to my rooms,
having again unmistakeably pronounced myself a Freshman.
On returning I ate my breakfast, and then proceeded to call
upon my tutor, not aware of the illegality I was committing;
he however received me with great cordiality and informed
me what lectures I had to attend, what fines I might possibly
incur, to what mortals I was to doff my cap, and which of
my co-freshmen I might best consort with. What struck
me most in Mr. Alderman, was the entire falseness and
absurdity of the general notion with regard to Dons. The
real Don as described in *Julian Home* and other nursery
tales is a rara avis in these days, a bird which when seen

is usually shot at, whose only food is bitter chaff, and whose
race consequently has become almost extinct. At least such
is my short experience in this University. In the afternoon
I took care to go out a walk in order that my chimney-piece
might be well filled with cards for the benefit of my co-
freshmen, nor were my anticipations unrealised. There were
the cards of Smith the head of my School, when I first
went thither, and who was now a fellow of Trinity, of
Peterkin who was head of the eleven two years ago, of
Jones, who had systematically punted me, as long as he and I
were school-fellows, and finally of three or four kind members
of the College who are the first to call on every freshman who
comes up, with more than disinterested motives, as I soon
found to my cost. How bitterly I repented my little ambition
as I returned these calls in every direction during the next
week. However not yet aware of such trouble in store for
me, I was pleased at the time, and freshman-like, arranged the
cards on my looking-glass: this done I went to hall, where
I was greeted with the usual amount of tracts on " Indiges-
tion," " The dangers of a young man just entering the
University," and other equally benevolent contributions
both for mind and body. After dinner I was taken by a
benevolent school-fellow to enter the Union, an advantage
which I would recommend every freshman to secure instantly
on his arrival, as it ensures a comfortable perusal of every
periodical one can wish for, and also reminds the enthusiastic
Johnian, that there are other Colleges besides his own. No
less does it keep the other Colleges in mind that our College
is still flourishing, a fact which our friends, the other side
of the wall, are apt to forget.

Why need I attempt to describe my first essay at
rowing? how after waiting a long time at Searle's I began
to think of moving up the river, and happened to light upon
Logan's; how I thought rowing the best exercise ever invented; how I kept looking on the bank at each of my
school-fellows that chaffed me, and was rewarded for my
pains by "Eyes on boat, two;" how after a few days I went in
for some scratch fours, and spoilt the most promising boat
that was in; how finally I did not row in the Races? Why
need I attempt to describe the excitement of the University
fours, the agonies of seeing our boat bumped, and the
numerous explanations possible? Is it not written in *Tom
Brown at Oxford?*

But my title proclaimed a higher object in writing than
I seem to have attained; I was to write of man; I have

given the data, and you must draw your own conclusions of my definition of a man. For myself I would try to give a small sketch of an individual's qualifications to be called a man. "The man" then must have trodden the Cambridge platform, he must have "wet the whistle," to use a slang expression, of every conceivable letter, luggage, beer, or commons carrier in the College; he must have been to Matthew and Gent's, he must have walked along the Trumpington Road, the Via Sacra of Cambridge; he must have learnt to distinguish King's chapel from the church in Barnwell; he must know Dr. Whewell by sight, and he must have joined a boat-club. Then and not till then may he call himself a man, and till he has served his year of probation he is doomed, no fate can avoid it, to remain, (why should he wish otherwise?) a freshman.

" R."

OUR CHRONICLE.

LENT TERM, 1861.

WE are glad to hear of the satisfaction expressed by our non-resident friends and readers at the inauguration, in our last number, of this Chronicle of events passing in, or connected with the College. It is gratifying to us, not only as a token of the success of our efforts to render *The Eagle* acceptable to its Subscribers, but as showing that our opinion of the sustained interest in our doings felt by those who were formerly amongst us, was not un-founded, and that the true Johnian spirit of loyalty and patriotism is still as flourishing as ever. Such a spirit of fellow-feeling, connecting not only those who are simul-taneously in residence, but those also of a previous academical generation, it is the peculiar privilege of an institution such as our College Magazine to sustain. The Boat Club, the Cricket Club, the Volunteer Corps, can necessarily only serve as a link of union between those who are actually together within our walls—but those who are absent from us can through the pages of our Magazine communicate with us and with each other, and each, in his turn, contribute, or receive pleasure, and, we hope, profit also. And we are anxious to lay the more stress upon this feature of our work, to induce those of our contributors especially who pass from amongst us, to remember that *The Eagle* may still be to them a vehicle through which they may keep up a connexion generally inwoven with many kindly memories. Many of them can, by so doing, confer great benefits upon their juniors who are still going through their curriculum. For instance, how much good might some of them gain from such hints on the duties and requirements of men preparing for Holy Orders, as some of the former could give from their own experience; "Advice to Young Curates," not simply theoretical, as viewed from the student's chair, but practical, as gathered from the daily round through the streets and

lanes of our great cities. Or what interest might be excited
in those who are gathered from other parts of the kingdom,
by a graphic description of some of our marts of commercial
industry, by those whose labours have called them thither!—
an article on a Welsh Coalpit which once appeared in our
pages, is an example. Besides which, Johnians are spread
not only over all the United Kingdom, but over all our
Colonies: why should not our offshoots in India, or Australia,
or Natal, follow the example of "Our Emigrant," whose
descriptions of New Zealand have been such a valuable
addition to our pages? And by doing so, they would not
only be conferring good, but would themselves be receivers
as well as givers. Just as No. Two or Three, though
fairly exhausted and ready to "shut up," takes fresh strength
and courage from the thought of those who are beside him
on the bank, and watching with keen interest the issue of
the race, and pulls manfully on till the louder and still louder
cheers tell him that his "pluck" is repaid, and the bump
made; so the Curate, when disheartened by the degradation
which he sees around him, will be nerved afresh for his work
by the thought that his old companions are watching his
course with kindly eyes, and wishing him God-speed. And
as the school-boy's eye is quickened often in his holiday
rambles by the thought of the account he has to give of
them on his return, so the eye of "Our Emigrant," ever
on the watch for something of which he may give an account
to his readers at home, will become more and more acute to
observe the beauties of nature around him.

The first part of our task this term is a melancholy one.
We have to add to the list of vacant fellowships another
vacant by death. Mr. C. J. Newbery, graduated as third
Wrangler in 1853, and was elected a Fellow of the College
in 1854. For some years he acted as Assistant Tutor, and
in that capacity his personal kindness won no less respect
than his able lectures. But the main feature of his life as
a Fellow was his readiness on all occasions to identify
himself with the Undergraduates, and to enter with heart
and soul into every scheme for the promotion of healthy
exercise and relaxation. A Johnian eleven was not complete,
unless he formed one of the number—and when the Volunteer movement spread so quickly over the country, he was
most active in organising a distinct company of the members
of this College, and as Captain of that Company himself,
won golden opinions. His loss has been, and will even
yet be severely felt among us. Mr. Newbery had been

appointed one of the Moderators for the year 1861, but his illness obliged him to relinquish the post, which was supplied by Mr. A. V. Hadley.

Though again denied the honour of heading the list of the Mathematical Tripos, our College has not proved a traitor to its ancient reputation. Of 29 of its members who went in, 12 are Wranglers, (5 of them in the first ten,) 9 are Senior Optimes and 8 Junior Optimes. The result of the Classical Tripos will not be known till after the time that *The Eagle* will be in our Subscribers' hands.

At the public examinations of the Students of the Inns of Court, held this term, the Council of Legal Education awarded the studentship of 50 guineas per annum to Mr. Henry Ludlow of this College.

The list of those who are in the first class in each year at the Christmas Examinations is subjoined:

Third year.

Laing.	Williams, H. S.	Catton.
Taylor, C.	Jones, W.	Fynes-Clinton.
Main, P. T.	Groves.	Cherrill.
Torry.	Whitworth.	Spencer.
Dinnis.		

Second year.

Snowden.	Pooley.	Falkner.
Rudd.	Cotterill.	Rees.
Hockin.	Stevens.	

First year.
(*In the order of the Boards.*)

Lee-Warner.	Moss.	Creeser.
Burnett.	Terry.	Cutting.
Stuart.	Green.	Pearson.
Reed.	Smallpeice.	Proud.
Quayle.	Reece.	Robinson.
Barnes, J. O.	Ewbank.	Sutton.
Stuckey.	Meres.	Tinling.
Newton, H.	Clay, A. L.	Tomkins.
Hill.	Pharazyn.	Branson.
Baron, E.	Archbold.	

The Master and Seniors have given notice that there will be an Examination for Scholarships, commencing on Thursday, June 6th. This year four Minor Scholarships are to be awarded, of the value of £50. per annum, tenable for two years, or till election to a Foundation Scholarship;

and also an Exhibition of £40. per annum on the Duchess of Somerset's Foundation, tenable for four years. Candidates' names are to be sent in to the Master at least ten days before the commencement of the Examination.

We have already mentioned that No. 2 Company of the C. U. V. R. has sustained a severe loss in the death of its Captain. Lieutenant Scriven has also resigned, being no longer in residence. The new officers are Mr. W. D. Bushell, Captain; Mr. W. H. Besant, Lieutenant; and Mr. J. B. Davies, Ensign.

It will be seen by our list of Boat-Races, that our two Clubs have been, this term, moderately successful.

The Officers of the two Clubs for the present term, are:

Lady Margaret.

A. W. Potts, Esq., B.A., President.
R. L. Page, Treasurer.
D. S. Ingram, Secretary.
W. H. Tarleton, First Captain.
T. E. Ash, Second Captain.

Lady Somerset.

Rev. J. R. Lunn, M.A., President.
W. A. Whitworth, Secretary.
O. Fynes-Clinton, First Captain.
J. F. Rounthwaite, Second Captain.

An important Meeting was held in the Combination Room, on Thursday Evening, March 7th, for the purpose of agreeing to new Laws for the regulation of the Cricket Club. The Rev. W. C. Sharpe gave expression to the wish of the Master and Fellows to carry on the work they had begun, in setting apart a plot of ground for a Cricket Field, by promoting, to the best of their power, such schemes for securing healthy exercise and amusement for the Undergraduates, and themselves occasionally mingling with them in such sports. As nothing is yet definitely settled, we are obliged to postpone further details till our next Number, when we hope to give an account of the new constitution. The Club is, of course, to play hereafter on the College Ground.

The University Rifle Corps have met, as usual, for Battalion Drill once a-week, but their musters have been smaller than usual. On Wednesday, March 6th, they had their first march out to Madingley, and went through various skirmishing evolutions.

The University Boat is, at the present time, in hard training. We are glad to hear that we are likely to have St. John's again represented in it, by Mr. W. H. Tarleton, the first Captain of the Lady Margaret Club.

The Cambridge University Musical Society has given one of its best Concerts this Term, in King's College Hall, which was kindly lent for the occasion, the Town Hall being destitute of stairs, and pending its removal. Mendelssohn's music to the "Œdipus Coloneus" was performed, with a second part, the programme of which was miscellaneous. H. R. H. the Prince of Wales was one of the audience.

The University Pulpit has been held, during this Term, by the Rev. Dr. Kennedy, the Ven. Archdeacon France, B.D., and the Rev. T. J. Rowsell, M.A., all of this College.

The Vice-Chancellor has just received a munificent donation of £500., invested in the funds, from some friends of the late Ven. Archdeacon Hare, for the purpose of founding a Prize, to be called the "Hare Prize." It is to be given once in every four years, for the best Essay on some subject connected with the history or philosophy of Ancient Greece and Rome.

The Cambridge University Commissioners have just brought their labours to an end, by publishing the new Statutes of King's, Emmanuel, St. Peter's, Clare, Corpus Christi, and Downing Colleges.

Most of our readers will be aware, before this, of the great loss which the literary world has sustained by the death of Dr. Donaldson. A most able philologist, he was the one of modern scholars who, above all others, maintained abroad the reputation of English Scholarship, and his place amongst us it will be very difficult to fill. He had been appointed to examine for the Classical Tripos, so that the University has this year lost an Examiner for each Tripos by an untimely death. Dr. Donaldson was engaged, up to the commencement of his last illness, on a Greek-English Lexicon, which he has left uncompleted. This, and the re-editing of some of his older works, seem to have proved too much for his strength.

Just as we are going to press, we are able to record the award of University Scholarships. The Craven Scholar is Mr. R. K. Wilson, of King's College. The Porson Scholar is Mr. Arthur Sidgwick, of Trinity College. The Browne Scholar is Mr. W. H. Stone, of Trinity College.

LIST OF BOAT RACES.

UNIVERSITY SECOND DIVISION.

These Races commenced on Monday, the 25th ult. Owing to the recent heavy rains, the river was high and the stream strong, which latter fact must account for the unusually large number of bumps. We subjoin a list of the boats and the bumps made during the three days' racing:—

MONDAY.

20 Caius II.	35 3nd Trinity III. }
21 2nd Trinity II. }	36 Trinity Hall III. }
22 1st Trinity IV. }	37 Christ's III.
23 Emmanuel II.	38 Corpus III.
24 Queens' I.	39 Jesus II. }
25 3rd Trinity II. }	40 Clare II. }
26 Pembroke I.	41 Caius IV. }
27 King's	42 Queens' II. }
28 Corpus I. }	43 Lady Somerset III.
29 Christ's II. }	44 Lady Margaret IV. }
30 Emmanuel III. }	45 1st Trinity V. }
31 Catherine }	46 Sidney II.
32 Lady Somerset II. }	47 Pembroke II. }
33 Lady Margaret III. }	48 Christ's IV. }
34 Caius III.	49 1st Trinity VI. }

TUESDAY.

20 Caius II.	36 2nd Trinity III.
21 1st Trinity IV. }	37 Christ's III.
22 2nd Trinity II. }	38 Corpus III. }
23 Pembroke I. }	39 Clare II. }
24 3rd Trinity II. }	40 Jesus II. }
25 Queens' I.	41 Queens' II. }
26 Emmanuel II. }	42 Caius IV.
27 King's }	43 Lady Somerset III. }
28 Christ's II. }	44 1st Trinity V. }
29 Corpus }	45 Lady Margaret IV. }
30 Catharine }	46 1st Trinity VI. }
31 Emmanuel III. }	47 Christ's IV.
32 Lady Margaret III. }	48 Pembroke II. }
33 Lady Somerset II.	49 Sidney II. }
34 Caius III. }	
35 Trinity Hall III. }	

WEDNESDAY.

20 Caius II.	35 Caius III. }
21 2nd Trinity II. }	36 2nd Trinity III. }
22 1st Trinity IV. }	37 Christ's III. }
23 3rd Trinity II.	38 Clare II. }
24 Pembroke I.	39 Corpus III. }
25 Christ's II.	40 Queens' II. }
26 King's.	41 Jesus II.
27 Emmanuel II.	42 Lady Somerset III. }
28 Queens' I. }	43 Caius IV. }
29 Catharine }	44 Lady Margaret IV. }
30 Corpus II. }	45 1st Trinity V.
31 Lady Margaret III. }	46 1st Trinity VI.
32 Emmanuel III. }	47 Christ's IV. }
33 Lady Somerset II. }	48 Sidney II. }
34 Trinity Hall III.	49 Pembroke II.

It is intended that the account of the First Division Boat Races shall, hereafter, form a part of "Our Chronicle."

FIVES AT ST. JOHN'S COURTS.

A long contest between 32 gentlemen, handicapped by H. Gray in his usual satisfactory manner, was brought to a conclusion by a match between

A. Bateman
H. Y. Thompson } and { H. Jenner
F. N. Langham

which spirited contest ended in the success of Messrs. Bateman and Thompson; each side having won two games, and the score in the last being 15 to 12.

HOW TO DEAL WITH THE BUCOLIC MIND.

No. I. *Village Schools.*

IN several numbers of *The Eagle* Non-resident Members of the College have been requested to send contributions on subjects with which they happen to be practically ac-quainted. The Country Curate even has more than once been invited to relate some of his experiences, for the benefit, I presume, of those now in residence at St. John's, who are intending to take Holy Orders, or to settle down as "County Squires" upon their hereditary estates.

As a Country Curate of seven years' standing, and a grateful subscriber to *The Eagle* from its commencement, I have accepted the invitation, and will, if agreeable to the Editors, forward a few sketches in illustration of the workings, and the proper treatment of *the Bucolic Mind.* First, in reference to *Education.*

My readers will be prepared to hear that the Bucolic mind is *not* favourably disposed towards education. A friend of mine in Nottinghamshire, some little time ago, asked a farmer in his parish if he would do something for the education of the lads employed on his farm, by sending them to school, at any rate, on alternate days. Would he not like to improve their minds and educate them a little? "No," said the farmer, "I'll have no education for 'em—I like my boys to be *strong and silly.*" My friend had heard this kind of sentiment ascribed to South Carolina Planters, but he did not expect to find it openly avowed by an Englishman in the 19th Century. The number of those who would utter such an atrocious sentiment is certainly diminishing, but I fear for some years to come that the greatest obstacle to education in country villages will be the indifference, or the opposition of the small farmers. Heaven defend us from an Education-rate, pared down and doled out by a board of these parochial worthies.

T

The indifference of parents is another most serious obstacle, and their reluctance, not so much to pay the weekly 2*d*. or 3*d*., as to lose the wages which their boys can get. At nine years old a boy is often taken away from school and hired to a farmer, at " a shilling a-week and his victuals;" and it requires great self-denial on the part of a mother to forego this addition to the weekly earnings of the family.

The wishes of the children themselves put little or no difficulties in the way. On the contrary, as far as my experience goes, they come gladly to school, and at eight or nine years old begin really to take a pleasure in "getting on with their learning." I sometimes think with shame how precious little lessons I should have done at nine years old, if I had been as free, as most of them are, to go to school or to stay away, to work or to be idle.

A fourth set of persons to be considered, in reference to the education and improvement of the Bucolic mind, are the rapidly increasing and influential class known, in government reports, as "School Promoters and Managers;" and I venture to hope that some who may soon enrol themselves in this honourable class, will find in my paper a few practical suggestions.

I will first take the case of the *parents*, or rather the mothers of families, for in the labourer class the *mother* is almost invariably the arbitrator on points connected with the education, the food, and the clothing of the children. To "his missus" does the model labourer bring home his weekly wages, and the "missus" decides, without appeal, on their application.

In many villages the mother decides on sending the children to school "to keep them out of mischief," and to prevent their clothes being torn or spoilt. And consequently, as the true way to influence people is to follow up arguments originated in their own minds, the school Promoter will, in such cases, reserve his eloquence about mental improvement, &c., for an address to a Mechanics' Institute, and dwell on the care taken to keep the children out of mischief or danger. The great thing is to get the children sent regularly, si possis recte—if you *can*, on high moral grounds—si non, quocunque modo—if you *can't*, for the reason that comes most home to the Bucolic mind. I have no hesitation in adding that the requiring a small school-fee promotes regular attendance. When the weekly or quarterly payment is once made (of course it is paid in advance), the parent naturally desires " to have his money's worth," whereas, if the school

be entirely free, one little excuse or another is often allowed
to keep the child at home. I know some wealthy land-
owners have an objection to take "children's pence" in their
little village school, but I am sure they promote regular
attendance by taking them, and I would suggest that the
difficulty might be met by giving rewards, equal to the
whole sum received, at the end of the year to each child
who had been constant in attendance. In the majority of
schools, however, the weekly payments form a considerable
part of the income required to support them. The school-
fees (2*d.* a-week) in the village of one thousand people where
I live, amount to £40 a-year, and the total amount of ex-
penditure is about £125, exclusive of government grants
to the teachers and apprentices. But though disadvantages
attach to schools "free" by the liberality of the land-owner,
who keeps them up, they are trivial compared with the evils
that belong to those parochial schools that are "free," by
the existence of some little endowment just sufficient to
support a master. In many schools of this kind, the Master,
having a fixed salary and no inducement to increase his
numbers, is anxious to save himself trouble by keeping the
number of free boys as small as possible. I have heard
of an instance where the master was bound to admit on
the free list all boys of the parish who could read the Bible
in the presence of the church-wardens. His course of proceeding was as follows: each poor little candidate was called
up, and an *old "black letter" Bible* was put into his
trembling hands; of course he broke down utterly, and was
rejected for another twelve months. I know another free
school, a Church of England foundation, but now governed
by three Wesleyan trustees, where the master *threatens* any
Baptist children whom he wishes to keep out, with the
Church Catechism, if they persist in coming, though he
never teaches it to the others.

The endowed school here, of which I am a trustee, was
formerly free. The master had the whole income of the
charity, £42 a-year, but, as of course, he could not live on
this, he used to charge all sorts of extras for books, ink, &c.,
to take in boarders, copy law documents, and in short,
do anything to make a little money, while the interests
of the free-boys were neglected. On his death, about five
years ago, the trustees, with the assistance of the Charity
Commissioners, carried a scheme for imposing a weekly
payment on each scholar, and putting the school in connexion
with the Committee of Council on Education. Of course the

parishioners, headed by their local orator, contested every
step, but now the most prejudiced of them admit the benefits
of the reform.   The school fees, with the endowment, enable
us to have a good certificated master, and to keep the school
well supplied with books and all necessaries, and we receive
Government grants in one shape or another, amounting to
nearly £50 a-year.   One method I adopted to gain our
improved system a fair start, was to call a public meeting
on the Friday evening before the school was re-opened,
and give a plain account of the several advantages to be
gained from Government, with various educational anecdotes
and small jokes, concluding with a caution that, as the then
school-room was very small, we should only take a limited
number, and that those who knew the old proverb "first
come, first served," would, I was sure, be in good time
on the Monday following.   Our mal-contents had said we
should not enter twenty, but we did enter *fifty-two the
first morning*, and refused three as being under age.   Having
thus secured a fair trial for our new system and excellent
master, we went on prosperously.   H. M. Inspector came
a few weeks after to see the alteration, and told me that
a man said his boy had been to school before, for more than
a year, and had only got to m-u-d—mud, *and there he stuck*,
but you, he said, were " out of the mud" already.

Before the end of the first year, with assistance from
government and liberal contributions from the wealthier
parishioners, an excellent school-room was built, and the
only thing required now is a little systematic attention to
those small details which promote the efficiency of the school,
and the regular attendance of the boys.   Among the most
successful means are Prizes at the annual examination, an
Excursion party in the summer, confined to those who have
attended regularly, and a system of Home lessons so arranged
that the most interesting one, and the one most calculated
to promote emulation, is given out on the Friday, to be
brought up on the Monday.   I may instance two that were
very popular, a Description of the village they live in, and
a little History of each boy's own life.

I will conclude my paper with a few remarks on the
manner of keeping up a school in connexion with Government.   The first thing is to engage certificated teachers.
If they come direct from a training college they are called
probationers, and receive, for the first two years spent in
the *same* school, from £20 to £25 a-year from Government
in augmentation of their salaries.   After that time the rate

of their augmentation is fixed by the inspector according to their examination before leaving the training college, and their performance in their school. The teacher also receives from the Council office a gratuity of £5 for instructing the pupil-teacher apprentice. The *Pupil-teacher* is apprenticed at the age of thirteen to the head-teacher for five years, and receives payment from Government, increasing from £10 up to £20, if he passes the annual examination. The *Capitation grant* is a sum of money paid to the managers in aid of the school, at the rate of 6s. a-head for each boy, and 5s. for each girl who has attended one hundred and seventy-six days in the past year. H. M. Inspector for the district visits the school once a-year, and reports to the Committee of council on education as to its efficiency and progress. With regard to correspondence with the Council office, from which many excellent clergymen and school-managers shrink with horror, I will simply give three rules which I have laid down for my own guidance, and which have made my dealings with the Office absolutely agreeable. 1stly. *Be concise.* 2ndly. *Anticipate objections, when they are certain to be made.* For instance, when applying for aid to build our school, I voluntarily stated that it would adjoin the church-yard, but I shewed that the site proposed was *above* and not below it, and that it was in fact almost the highest and most airy situation in the whole parish. 3rdly and chiefly. *Treat them like gentlemen,* and don't worry them by asking things which *their* code of honour, the "Educational Minutes" forbid them to grant.

J. F. BATEMAN.

** Since writing the above paper I have received the report of the Royal Education Commission. Nearly all its suggestions seem to me most excellent and valuable, and though I have neither time nor space to give a summary of them, I cordially commend the Report to all my readers who are interested in the educational question.

SPENSER DESCRIBETH A GRASS-CUTTING MACHINE.

I.

THEN on he pass'd a sturdie Porter bye,
Nathlesse it was no Castle that did frown,
But manie clerkes liv'd here in companie,
And Wranglers were yclad in cap and gowne,
—The College of Saint John of high renown;
And learned deep in Mathematick lore,
The Students hight throughouten all the town:
Within, a spacious court with paved floor,
And squares of verdent sheen uprose his eyen before.

II.

There on the grasse within this goodlie court,
A hideous monster fed with horrid tongue,
Ne knight with such a dragon-whelp had fought,
Ne poet such prodigious birth had sung;
And up and down it pass'd the grasse among;
And still with fearfull sownd its teeth did grind,
That all the bodies nerves and fibres wrung:
Its bellie low upon the earth did wind,
Four human legs before, and eke a pair behind.

III.

And but that it on simple grasse did feed,
And low its bodie trail upon the grownd,
It seem'd that salvage race which bookmen reed,
The Anthropophagi, whose shoulders rownd
To grow above their ugly heads are fownd.
But well I ween that nothing mote compare
With all that mightie Beastes infernal sound,
Save manie feends concerting some fowle ayr
On verie rustie fyles which no man's eares may bear.

IV.

And much in sooth this sownd the clerkes opprest,
And did confound them in their studie quight,
Albeit no fear their bodies e'er possest,
The creature would ne scratch, ne tear, ne bite,
(Certes its sownd would almost kill outright)
And manie a charm they try'd within their ken,
To ease them from its power by day and night;
For well 'twas thought it was three proper men,
Bound by some evil bond which might be broke agen,

V.

Which quickly Geomet perceived trew,
And hasten'd to dissolve the cruell spell,
For gentle pitie mov'd him, when he knew
The creature did no harm, but worken well;
Nathlesse that awefull noyse no tongue may tell;
Then loud he shouted out the magick word,
Beers! Beers! the yron from the bodie fell,
The curse was broke, the monster's corps was stirr'd,
Uprose three goodlie men—the sownd no more was heard.

F. H. D.

A DAY'S RAMBLE IN SOUTH YORKSHIRE.

WE are at home after the Theological. It is a delicious spring morning, loud with larks, and gay with cloudless sunshine. Everything invites a long ramble; but whither shall it be? "The choice perplexes." Westward are the wild moorlands of Derbyshire, beyond whose blue ridges, now shining so clear in the morning sun, are the rich green valleys and the savage mountains of the Peak; the palatial pile of Chatsworth, embosomed in that wooded valley through which the silver Derwent wanders on to be shadowed ere long by the gray crags of Matlock; and Baronial Haddon, with all its romantic associations. We look eastward, and Bolsover Castle frowns from its lofty range of hills, behind which lies the fair domain of Sherwood:—the woods and waters of Welbeck and Clumber, and farther south, the haunted groves of Newstead. But none of these shall tempt us to day: we will hasten over the fields to the nearest station; travel a few miles down the valley of the Rother, and start from Masboro' for a ramble among the quiet hills and dales of Southern Yorkshire.

Inferior doubtless as this neighbourhood is in many respects to several other parts of the county to which it belongs, there are perhaps few districts in England which combine in a tract equally small, objects of interest so many and so varied. Beginning from the mountainous region about Huddersfield, and the wild moorlands familiar to the traveller on the Manchester and Sheffield Railway, and gradually subsiding through a district of limestone—always so productive of the picturesque—until its irregularities all disappear in the levels of Hatfield Chase and the alluvial flats of Marshland, it has every variety of surface. But its history and its associations form its chief attraction. There where

Five rivers, like the fingers of a hand,
Flung from black mountains, mingle and are one,
Where sweetest valleys quit the wild and grand,

lies Sheffield, murky centre of toil and traffic, resounding
with the din of the forge, the hissing of steam, and the
rushing of innumerable wheels, but yet with so many bright
spots of rural beauty, "like pearls upon an Ethiop's arm;"
and with its long 'list of historic lords, the Furnivals, the
Talbots, and the Howards:—there are the noble halls of
Wentworth, Wharncliffe, and Sandbeck, with many another
fair seat of ancient gentry: there are the feudal castles of
Tickhill and Conisboro', the gray abbey ruins of Roche, and
many an old church full of interest to the antiquary, all
included within a district twenty miles in length and never
more than half that in breadth; nor must we forget to
mention that there too the sportsman finds the combined
attractions of the heather and the turf, in the wild moors
of upper Hallam, and the classic stadium of Doncaster;
and occasionally such a run with Earl Fitzwilliam's hounds
as will form quite an epoch in his history. So much for
South Yorkshire generally: it is but over a small part of
this district that our ramble to-day is to extend, beginning
from Masboro', taking a circuit of perhaps six-and-twenty
miles, and ending at the Woodhouse Mill Station of the
North Midland Railway.

Leaving the train at Masboro', we pass through the
grimy village so called, the birth-place of Ebenezer Elliott,
the stern "Corn Law Rhymer," and the Poet who has
described in glowing colours the beauties of the neighbouring
country. We cross the Don, after it has received its tributary the Rother, and wend up through the narrow streets
to the fine old Church of Rotherham, built in the richly
decorated style of the time of Edward IV., but owing to
the character of its stone, (that unfortunate salmon-coloured
grit found in the neighbourhood, particularly in the celebrated quarries of Anston, about ten miles off), much de-
teriorated by the action of the atmosphere.

This church would repay a lengthened visit, but we
cannot stay now; we leave the smoky little town behind
us, and wander for three miles through a country of quiet
rural beauty, till we climb the hill on which stands, with
its hall and spire-church, the little village of Thrybergh;
a place with that air of substantial comfort about it so
characteristic of the rural villages of Yorkshire, and the
neatness and cleanliness which are the surest signs of a
well-fed and contented peasantry. Thrybergh is an interesting village; its fine hall is modern, but it has two old crosses,
and around one of them is entwined the evergreen wreath

of a beautiful tradition. It tells us how in very old times the lord of the manor had an only daughter, heiress of all his lands; how, when a youth of gentle birth had won her love, they made this cross their trysting-place; and how, when the young squire went to win renown in the holy fields of Palestine, by this cross they took their sad farewell. Time passed by, and at last a report reached Thrybergh that the young knight was dead in Holy Land. And so with many another fair maiden doubtless of those wild old times, the heiress of Thrybergh long wept for her lover slain by the hands of infidels in that far off land. But as the months rolled by, her father, doubtless longing to see, ere his death, his daughter united to one who would worthily uphold the dignity of his ancient house, encouraged a new suitor. And in those days a father's word was law; the poor maiden bowed to her fate, and the day was fixed for the marriage. And then the tradition tells us how she went the evening before to that cross, the old place of trysting, where she had so often prayed with clasped hands for her dear knight fighting in those distant lands; how, while kneeling there and weeping bitter tears, praying for strength to bow to her father's will, the stalwart warrior whom she had so long mourned, burst into her presence and clapsed her in his arms! And that night there was joy in Thrybergh.

A walk of four short miles from Thrybergh brings us to still more haunted ground: soon we have before us that grand old keep, familiar alike to the antiquary and the reader of "Ivanhoe," the Norman castle of the great Earls de Warrenne,—the stronghold of Athelstan the Saxon. How calmly defiant it stands there above its belt of trees, a little grayer and hoarier may be, and long ago dismantled, but strong on its firm foundations as when first it frowned over the sylvan valley of the Don! The origin of the place, Konig's burgh, the King's burgh, is lost in the mists of antiquity. A tradition, as old as the days of Camden, points out a mound hard by as the grave of Hengist, and probably several successive strongholds had passed away before the present Norman keep arose within that spacious enclosure, fit abode for that mighty race, of the true old Norman metal, who dwelt in it;—for him who when Edward the First's quo warranto commissioners demanded his right to his broad lands, brought out a rusty sword with the proud declaration that by that sword he had won them and kept them hitherto, and by that sword, with God's grace, he would keep them still. Not perhaps the most displeasing answer to be received from one of his barons by the greatest of the Plantagenets. Verily a sweet spot is the neighbourhood of this old castle to muse and dream away a long summer's day in; but more especially pleasant with a merry pic-nic party to scale that old tower and view the prospect which the great Wizard of the North has painted in such glowing colours, as it was in the far olden time; to go down into that dark suggestive dungeon, and return from its horrors to the sunny day, and the quiet shade of those ash trees, and spread a banquet on the chequered sward. Pleasant to talk over that matchless story, and to wander off in groups or pairs by the pathway which leads up those green slopes, and scramble through the hazel copses beyond; staying ever to catch some new glimpse of the grand old castle, or suddenly, from the edge of a high precipitous rock to see the long sparkling reaches of the sylvan Don;— your companion, may be, no imaginary heroine of romance, but a warm breathing maiden, peerless in her dark beauty as the Jewess, or blue-eyed and fair as the daughter of Cedric the Saxon!

But no such luck is ours to day; so, after a visit to the village inn, we turn away almost at right angles to our old road; we climb the hill, often looking back to take yet another view of the old castle, and from the high ground which we soon reach have an extensive view over a rich though rather flat country, amid which, five miles away, rises the fine tower of the new church of Doncaster. We pass the pleasant seat of Crookhill; turn aside to see the pretty church of Edlington with its fine Norman mouldings fresh as if but yesterday new from the carver's hand, and a short stage brings us to Braithwell, with its neat church, and old ruined cross, bearing an Anglo-norman inscription which an infatuated village mason some time ago attempted to "restore", in accordance with the village tradition. But if the rambler be as lucky as we once were, and his antiquarian studies have not entirely petrified him, surely his will forget those quaint dim letters, in that "phantom of delight" which greeted our vision from the farm hard by:—

> A dancing shape, an image gay,
> To haunt, to startle, and waylay.

From Braithwell, two miles' walk brings us to Maltby, a pretty village lying in a valley, with a little stream flowing

quietly through green meadows, an old market-cross (we
are in the country of crosses), and a neat church lately
restored. We follow the course of this stream about a
mile further, and then, turning down through a rocky grove,
we find a delicious little valley rich in gray rock and
hanging wood, in soft green pastures and spreading waters,
and come first upon an old gateway, through which we
pass, and a slight curve of the valley opens before us the
ruins of the Abbey of Roche. There are monastic ruins
finer, and standing amid grander scenery, but surely there
are none where that sweet peacefulness, that calm religious
beauty, so in harmony with the feelings and associations
which such ruins awake, are found in such perfection as
here. However, a fine and picturesque fragment of the
choir and transepts still remains, and will amply repay both
the architectural student and the lover of the beautiful
for a long and attentive examination.

Reluctantly do we leave this sweet valley of repose,
and follow a path which leads through the copse on the
other side of the stream, and soon brings us out in the
level grounds above the valley, and we have the distant
spire of Laughton-en-le-Morthen in full prospect before us.
Towards this landmark, far seen over a vast extent of country,
we bend our course, winding along through lanes profusely
rich in autumn with the blackberries which the soil of this
district produces in full perfection, till at last we come to
a small hamlet called Slade Hooton, where is one of those
ancient halls, now probably occupied as a farm-house, of
which the parlour is used only on rare occasions of village
or domestic festivity, but where dwelt in olden times one
of what the historian of the district would call "a family
of lesser gentry." No very "genteel" place, some people
of modern notions would say, but look over the door there
at the shield, duly emblazoned with "two lions passant,"
and put there in an age when it was not so easy to "send
name and county," and obtain by return of post a fictitious
symbol of gentility from certain persons who reap a rare
harvest on the ignorance of their self-complacent victims.
Why, as late as 1666, when the last Heraldic visitation
was made, that grand old Dugdale, "Norroy," had power,
which he used too, "to proclaim and render infamous" all
unlawful and proofless assumption of the title or insignia
of a "gentleman"!

Whither have all these old families gone, who lived
generation after generation in these village halls? The

world has been turned almost upside down since then:
some few names have preserved their ancient dignity, but
how few! And many a sturdy yeoman among these secluded
villages, nay, many a humble day labourer is entitled, as
the quaint parchment registers of the parish church could
testify, to bear arms before whose antiquity the shields
of not a few proud peers of the realm would be utterly
thrown into the shade. What an unmeaning mockery is
a modern coat of arms! Heraldry is no longer a living
reality—all its interest depends upon association, and what
Longfellow says of houses is no less true of it:

> We may build more splendid habitations,
> Fill our rooms with paintings and with sculptures,
>   But we cannot
> Buy with gold the old associations!

How empty is the mere device! But what a thrill it can
awaken in us to know that the shield, charged with that
self-same device, was one among the many whose brave
bearers dimmed the lustre of the French lilies at Creci
or Agincourt; or that, still further back, shone victorious
beneath the walls of Acre, or on the plains of Ascalon,
though gashed with Paynim falchions, and dinted by Paynim
spears!

But during all this digression we are supposed to have
left Slade Hooton far behind; to have dropt into its pleasant
valley, and to have climbed the steep hill opposite and
entered the village of Laughton. An old-fashioned place
is this Laughton-en-le-Morthen, or "Leetin-i'-th'-morning,"
as the rustics in far off districts call it, who see its tall
spire bright, day after day, with the beams of the early
sun; a place which has seen better days, but is far from
the noisy thoroughfares of the modern world, and gets on
in the old jog-trot way as well as it can. How finely the
old church stands at the head of the village street! The
ale-house, no doubt, looks attractive just now, but if you
have a spark of noble curiosity in you, you will certainly
go and look at the church first, and then, when you have
come and had your crust and ale in the sanded parlour,
you will willingly return to it again. How gracefully those
flying buttresses soar from the pinnacles and melt into the
spire! How finely tower and spire blend together in those
receding battlements, every particle of masonry in battlement
and pinnacle leading you gradually up the tapering spire

till your eye rests upon its summit, near two hundred feet from the grassy graves below!

On the north side of the church there is a round arch rudely formed of rough stones of unequal size, evidently worked in from a former building; perchance the very doorway under which the great Thane Edwin, the brother-in-law of the Harold who fell at Hastings, has often passed; for that mound west of the church marks the site of his dwelling, albeit that very useful and generally correct institution, the Ordnance Map, informs us, in peculiarly Roman characters, that it is the site of a Roman encampment. A Roman camp forsooth consisting of a huge mound surrounded by a circular vallum! Let us cross the low churchyard wall, and see the place more closely, for this is of all spots the one to rest in. Here may we lie on the soft turf, with that glorious spire soaring above us, golden with the sunshine from the west, and standing clear against the blue sky. Fair green valleys and woods and sloping hills stretch far away beneath us, bounded to the west by those wild blue mountains of the Peak; we are, as it were, "ring'd with the azure world," and dreaming ourselves back into the distant part we seem to be in the hospitable hall of the great Saxon chieftain, while the gleeman sings his tale to the golden-haired daughter of Godwin, and the mead-cup flows, and the revel waxes louder and louder, in the days on the hateful curfew had been taught to ring out its tyrannizing notes from the rude old Saxon tower.

But the day is fast declining: we must betake ourselves with energy to the remainder of our journey. Away then down the hill that slopes from the south side of Laughton. That small spire peering from its valley side about a league to the south-east in Anston, where are the celebrated gritstone quarries; and those woods more to the south grace the domain of Kiveton Park, the estate which came to the ancestor of its present owner, the Duke of Leeds, in so romantic a manner. It was part of the dowry of that rich merchant's only child whose infancy the brave young city apprentice, afterwards Sir Edward Osborne, rescued from the waters of the Thames, and whose hand the grateful father promised should be granted to none before it had been offered to her gallant deliverer. And the old man kept his promise, and Kiveton, though now no hall stands there, still belongs to Sir Edward's descendants, who have since blended with their own the illustrious blood of D'Arcy and Conyers.

We turn away from the village of Todwick, and the next place we enter is Aston, perhaps four miles from Laughton, in some respects an interesting village, for there for many years was rector, a man of considerable note in his day and generation, William Mason, of St. John's College, Cambridge, afterwards elected to a fellowship at Pembroke, the author of Elfrida and Caractacus, and the friend and biographer of Gray. Here he carried into practice, as far as his limited extent of surface would permit, the principles of the picturesque laid down in his long didactic poem "The English Garden," and what is more, gained the affection of his parishioners by a kind and diligent discharge of his pastoral duties. His remains lie in the chancel, where a marble tablet, with a medallion portrait, has been erected to his memory. Stiff and formal though Mason's poetry may appear now, there is much to admire in it, and few readers could fail to derive pleasure from the perusal of an account both of the man and his poetry in Hartley Coleridge's interesting work, the "Northern Worthies."

From Aston a down hill walk of two miles, (our hostess told us it was reckoned two miles down, and two and a-half up again) brings us to Woodhouse Mill, a small station on the North Midland Railway, whence the train soon brings us back to the spot where we availed ourselves of its services in the morning, and our day's ramble is ended.

Thus have we endeavoured to lead our readers on an imaginary ramble in a district where we have more than once spent what Wordsworth beautifully calls—

One of those heavenly days which cannot die—

and, if we have given pleasure to one of our readers; if we have afforded agreeable reminiscences of Old England to our future Governor General, administering British justice to the dusky tribes of India, or to Our Emigrant on his broad sheep-walks far amid Australasian seas; or, if for one half-hour we have transported one victim to the nervous anticipations of approaching June, from the sleepy flats of Granta to the cool valleys and breezy ridges of South Yorkshire; we shall not have walked or written in vain.

"H."

TRANSLATED FROM THE GERMAN OF SCHILLER.

Yours is the world! said Jove enthroned on high,
   Take it, mankind, and share it as you will;
'Tis yours for time and for eternity,
   But oh! remember you are brothers still.

With busy hands, and cunning's varied wiles,
   Men old and young, each sought his share to claim.
The Farmer stored the fruits of Ceres' smiles,
   And through the woods the Lordling chased his game.

The Merchant grasped whate'er his gains required,
   The Abbot quaffed the generous mountain wine.
To bridge and building Royalty aspired
   And loudly swore:—The tithe of all is mine.

And now the world with all its wealth is shared,
   When lo! the Poet comes o'er distant plains.
Alas! the greedy race have nothing spared
   And naught of worth without a lord remains.

Alas! he cried, shall I of all the world,
   Thine own true son, forgotten be, alone?
Thus at great Jove his dire complaint he hurled,
   Which soon was wafted to the Thunderer's throne.

If in thine own sweet dream-land thou hast stayed,
   The God replied—Then quarrel not with me;
When worldly men the world's division made
   Where was my son? The Poet said,—With thee.

Mine eyes did seek from thine a clearer sight,
   Mine ear drank music from the Heavenly Host,
Pardon the soul, that with thy wondrous light
   Intoxicated, earthly wealth has lost.

Too late, said Jove, too late, the world is given;
   The mart, chase, harvest, are no longer mine;
But would my Bard entwine his bower in Heaven,
   Come when thou wilt, a welcome shall be thine.

"BIS."

DISSENTERS AND FELLOWSHIPS.

THE question of the admission of Dissenters to Fellowships has been of late brought with unusual prominence before the notice of the University. The largest and most influential of the seventeen Colleges of Cambridge, after fourteen years of comparative obscurity in the mathematical honour-lists, has at last emerged into splendour only to find brilliant disappointment. Her bright and shining lights turn out to be mere will-o'-the-wisps whose lustre is just sufficient to reveal the future difficulties of her path without giving her guidance. In other words the two consecutive Senior Wranglers of Trinity College will merely bestow on her the reputation of their success, while there seems little prospect of their being able, either as fellows or even as lecturers, to confer on her any other benefit. Both these gentlemen are Dissenters, and as such are unable permanently to hold a College Fellowship.

It may be that hidden deep beneath the surface of the Academic world there lurked a layer of liberality or innovation which has now, in the natural course of things, cropped out for the first time into distinct vision: or it may be that the present crisis has like an earthquake heaved this unseen stratum into its present prominent position: or lastly it may be that, without supposing the existence of such feelings in any greater degree than we were wont, it is merely the magnitude of this present inconvenience which has been working powerfully on the minds of those who have been brought into close contact with it. Be the cause what it may, the effect is plain. Agitation on University matters mostly begins from without: but now, perhaps for the first time, we have a specimen of Academical agitation. The Agitators have not wanted their Advocate or their Champion. The reasonings of the former and the name and influence of the latter have been doing their work in a recent number of *Macmillan's Magazine*.

U

Mr. Fawcett's arguments are not strikingly original. They are such as must have occurred to any man of common sense and must have been duly considered by any one who would venture to express an opinion on the subject in question. " That policy is intelligible," we are told, " which during so many centuries succeeded in preserving an intimate connection between the Universities and the state-church . . . . but the key of this position . . . . has now been surrendered, for Dissenters are now encouraged to study at the Universities." Further, "the one solitary pretext for the exclusion of Dissenters from Fellowships," the fact that to the hands of the Fellows of each College is trusted a large amount of Church-Patronage, we find to be practically " a purely imaginary objection," owing to the " universal custom of appointing to a College living by seniority." As to the various schools and other charitable institutions dependent on Colleges for support, " we have no right whatever to assume beforehand, that a Dissenting majority would be backward in assisting the spiritual and educational wants of those districts in which College property is situated."

So easily is our guard beaten in, so triumphantly does our opponent hit home at each attack, that perhaps it was scarcely worth while to shew the needlessness of all these tricks of fence, by telling us that after all "it is extremely improbable that those who dissent from the Established Church would ever become a majority in any College." This must needs cause one a little hesitation. Not the slightest, not the very slightest inconvenience can be anticipated from a majority of Dissenting Fellows, and lastly—there is no chance of there being such a majority. Can it be that Ulysses is at heart afraid that there may be something wrong about his fence, and that he may as well use his shield to make all safe? A prudent course certainly: but even this prudence is too imprudent for the man of many wiles. He is triumphant, his foes are prostrate, but for fear he may be in some danger that he does not see, for fear the foes he has just killed may not be quite dead, he will brandish over their humiliated heads the shield of Ajax the terrible, and from that safe refuge kill them over again — he will call in the Public Orator to the rescue.

It is here that we meet Mr. Fawcett's strongest argument: an argument the more difficult to meet because it is not contained in the form of a proposition, but consists of three words at the extreme end of the letter, in which no distinctions of object, subject, or predicate can possibly be made. In fact the signature of the Public Orator is in itself no contemptible argument for the truth, or at least the plausibility, of the statements to which it is appended. If only Mr. Clark had adopted that convenient custom of "giving no reasons," while he merely expressed his agreement with the Petitioners, the argument would have been irresistible. But since he does condescend to give reasons, we are bound to examine them.

It would be too much perhaps to expect that both the defenders of the Petition should agree in their mode of defence. As if to shew us the folly of such expectations, our Ajax resumes a piece of armour which Ulysses has just flung away as useless. We were told a moment ago that the connection between Church and University has been "virtually surrendered." Now on the other hand we hear that it "will not be endangered." Further "an immense majority of the students will be, as heretofore, Churchmen, and .... in the governing body of the several Colleges .... Dissenters will form a minority inappreciably small."

Clearly the Public Orator has a sincere contempt for the cautious maxim "It is possible." Yet surely he must be a bold man who, at a time like this, would say that anything is impossible. Thirty-two years ago few perhaps would have thought to see Dissenters studying, even as Undergraduates, at the Universities. While a great nation and a great church loosening themselves, under the glowing heat of public opinion, from the old rivets which once clamped them together, are still fermenting in the crucible of reform and progress, it is hard to foretel the shape in which they will issue. Mr. Clark is a hardy prophet: it is sincerely to be hoped he is a true one.

One must make some allowance perhaps for sponsorial fondness, which may well deceive sometimes the wisdom of the very wisest. This petition, this little bantling of his, seems so innocent, so pretty in its infancy, that a god-fatherly confidence in its future harmlessness is at least excusable. It is scarcely however justifiable. "Please, Mum, it was only a very little one," was perhaps a legitimate excuse for Mr. Midshipman Easy's wet-nurse. At least it had the merit of being both humble and true. But how dares the Public Orator, or any mortal man, with unhumbled exultant mien forcing a living baby on the recognition of Alma

Mater, who betwixt shocked delight and half-pleased anger hardly knows whether to accept or reject the offering, venture to assure her that it will always be "a very little one!" Are we not forced to confess that the more humble wet-nurse must yield the well-won palm of audacity to her less scrupulous rival? True it is that at present the god-child is harmless: there are undoubtedly some neat points about her. But she comes of a bad stock. It was not Principle and Expedience that combined to give her birth: Principle stood aloof and she sprang, a one-parented child, leaping at the sound of the Public Orator's delivering hatchet, from out the brain of spited Expedience. Of such an offspring it is not easy to calculate the horoscope. Her sponsors have told us what the child's destiny will certainly not be: let us more humbly, after careful examination of her phrenological peculiarities, venture to conjecture what it possibly may be.

The remedy proposed by Mr. Fawcett for the present evils (evils which undoubtedly have a real existence) is a petition to parliament for permission to each College to admit or not to admit Dissenters to the number of its Fellows. It may appear at first sight that the effect of this petition will be to allow Colleges to make such elections in certain cases, while in others they might use their prerogative of rejecting a Dissenting candidate, although as qualified in learning and academical standing as other successful competitors, simply because he is a Dissenter. A moment's consideration will shew the fallacy of this supposition. Either Dissenters must, in the event of this petition being granted, be admitted to Fellowships on exactly the same footing as Churchmen, or else All Souls' herself will soon rejoice in her comparative quiet as she hears of the uproar of personal bickering and unseemly contention, which will soon disturb the cloistered quiet of every College in Cambridge. Again, if while one Dissenter is admitted, another of equal learning but more heterodox tenets is to be rejected, it will soon be necessary to establish a new Sexvirate that shall sound the different depths and shallows of Dissent, test the objectionableness and formidableness of respective sects, arrange on their several platforms the Methodist, the Independent, the Baptist, particular or otherwise, the Romanist, moderate or ultramontane, while a still keener acuteness of discrimination will be required in order to assign his rightful place to any learned competitor who may happen to have no particular creed at all.

Such a discrimination is clearly out of the question. It is clear that Dissenters, if admitted, must be admitted on the same footing as Churchmen. But before considering the possible consequences of their admission, it may not be amiss to glance at another supposition.

One who has signed this petition has said that it is his confident belief that, if the petition is granted, in no case will any use be made of it by the important College for whose particular interests it would almost seem to have been originally set on foot. It is hardly necessary to point out that, if this should be the case, the odium which at present attaches to the Act of Parliament will be immediately transferred to the heads of the electors. At present, to use Mr. Fawcett's own words, " even a Senior Wrangler cannot feel that he is personally aggrieved because excluded. He is not excluded by the desire or owing to the prejudices of his College." But it is not pleasant to foresee what may hereafter be felt toward those who conscientiously vote against the election of Dissenting Fellows by candidates whose competition may have been sanctioned, and whose election almost recommended, by the special abrogation of an Act of Parliament.

It is possible however that the petition may not only be granted but also acted upon. It will be well to consider the consequences of such action. At present there appear to be none that can be productive of anything but unmixed good. Those gentlemen who would be immediately bene-fited by it are not likely to make the University regret her concession. Nor is it probable that in any large College great change would ensue. With repect to the smaller Colleges however the case is different. In these the governing body is small. Six or seven resident Fellows, in some cases even less, are sufficient to bear all the burdens of the administration of a small College without flinching. These gentlemen are between them, Master, Bursar, Tutors, Prælectors, Chaplain, Librarian, Steward, and Lecturers. To such a convenient and quiet place of study it is not impossible that two or three well-read Dissenting Under-graduates should repair. In all probability they would in time become Fellows. They might possibly reside as Lecturers or Tutors. Gradually, without any definite attempt on their part, they would attract around them, not unnaturally, men of the same way of thinking and feeling as themselves. As the old Fellows died or married, they would elect, again without the slightest attempt on their part, Dissenting Fellows.

Thus, there is nothing very improbable in the existence of five or six resident Dissenting Fellows in a small College. But such a phenomenon would assuredly present many curious points worth noting.

Even now it is not always an easy matter to obtain a sufficient number of resident fellows to conduct the administration of a small College. If out of the twelve resident and non-resident fellows of Corpus, the nine of St. Catherine's, the eight of Magdalene, the fourteen of Jesus, the nine of Clare, and the nine of Sidney, six or seven were resident Dissenters, the difficulties of their administration would not be diminished. It is not impossible that there might come a time when no resident Fellows in orders could be obtained. The daily service in chapel might then be perhaps dispensed with. Or if the fellows felt it their duty to enforce on the Undergraduates a worship in which they did not themselves join, and for which some of them might feel a conscientious repugnance, a chaplain might be procured from a neighbouring College. Or, because a College chapel which can count none of its officers in the number of its worshippers is an unseemly sight, the service might be transferred to some other chapel, till better times should come, and a fresh race of fellows that knew not dissent. The divinity lectures, if delivered by the authorities of such a College, would at least have the merit of deviating from the common ruts of such lectures, but they too, together with the chapel-service, would probably be transferred to a more orthodox atmosphere.

These changes were not perhaps contemplated by our forefathers, when in the fore-court of each College they built the College chapel. But they are not all. There have been heard lately rumours, true or false, of the omission of a sacred name in the College grace, out of respect to the feelings of a single person dining in the Hall. The mention would be more blasphemous than the omission of such a name in the presence of a governing body to whom that name meant nothing. One need surely not have lived very long up here to learn, that every public act of University life is either attended by some living act of worship or haunted by its spectre. To pass over the daily life in chapel and hall, a man is admitted as a scholar of his College in the name of the Father, the Son, and the Holy Ghost: in the same holy name he is admitted to his bachelor's degree: it is in the chapel that the elections alike of Fellow and Scholars are conducted. An open recognition of certain religious truths pervades all our academical life. In each act of that life is recognised the principle of the connection between the Church and the Universities, which, as we are told by one of the Petitioners, has been virtually surrendered, and by the other will not be endangered.

If these recognitions are indeed mere dead forms: if, despite the efforts of such men as our Professor of Modern History, they are dead without hope of resurrection, if no one any longer believes that as a scholar of his College, or as a graduate of his University, he has certain new duties to do: if there is no man to whom the admission in the name of the Holy Trinity is anything but a joke, or at best, a mysterious eccentricity of our fathers which he cannot understand, then it were well that they too should be swept away down with the current of public opinion, whereon are floating the wrecks of all that makes life liveable. But if there are still up here those who do believe in the connection between worshipping and doing, praying and working, People and Church; it ill beseems them to do anything that may appear to betoken disbelief therein; to surrender a great principle here because it has been surrendered elsewhere.

The consequences of the success of this petition would probably be not unfrequently those above described. The necessity of taking orders after a certain number of years, which is attached to some Fellowships would render a Dissenter's tenure more brief than usual, and, if not abrogated, which in all probability it soon would be, might somewhat diminish the resulting inconvenience. But it is not the results that should cause us most fear. It is that, be the results what they may, the petition in itself ignores that very connection between the Universities and Church which it professes not to endanger. For if men who openly dissent from the National Church are to be recognised as legitimate governors of the Universities, then indeed it will be hard to say what is the link between the two.

It is not true that this connection has been surrendered, for it is not true that the Universities have been thrown open to Dissenters. For those Dissenters who differ so slightly from the Church, that they are not unwilling to attend her daily service,* for those and for no others is the University thrown open. No instance can be pointed out in which the University has recognised dissent. Still, however much

---

* In one or two Colleges non-attendance at chapel has been connived at, but not recognised.

it may be denied in practice, the fact that the University is not a mere learning-shop, is at least recognised in theory. Still, if nothing else, at least the weekly bidding-prayer in St. Mary's church, reminds the men of the University that they are not to consider themselves individual students connected together by the bonds of present interest and convenience, but that, as members of a College, a University, and a Church, they are bound to one another by the stronger ties of religion and brotherhood. But if among the very governors of the University were men who dissented from her church, this solemn prayer would become a most jarring mockery.

Yet, though the University is not responsible for them, the present anomalous system is certainly not without its evils. It is hard that a man who has taken the very highest honour here, should be unable to devote himself to those studies for which he feels himself adapted, studies which might tend to the good alike of himself and of his college. There are, and every right-minded man will be glad to know this, many Dissenters who, so far from feeling repugnance toward the National Church, attend her services with sincere pleasure and respect: there are some who so nearly approach her pale, that they would soon cease to be Dissenters, were they not deterred by the prospect of gaining something from the change. It is a pity surely, that such men should be forced to quit the University at once for the School or the Bar, while their less learned but more orthodox competitors fill the lectureships which they could fill more ably; that any man, above all such a man, should have to leave Cambridge without having had opportunity for study. No one is ignorant, that during the three years of preparation for the Mathematical or Classical Tripos, little can be done that deserves that name. A man during those three years must read to shew what he can do. Afterwards he may read in order to do. Such reading requires much leisure and some little money. A poor Dissenter cannot read thus unaided, and the Fellowships, one object of which is to encourage study, are closed against him.

This is no slight hardship. It is easy to say that the exclusion must have been foreseen by him at the time of his entering the University. Three years of Academic study makes some men unfit for any thing but the prosecution of those studies, and force on them new prospects and new pursuits. The exclusion which appeared a trifle to a freshman presents itself in a different light to one who has acquired a taste for study. Foreseen or unforeseen, when realised and at hand, it is not unlike a hardship, and well deserves such remedy as can be given without abandonment of a right consistency. Now a Fellowship may be viewed in two ways: firstly, as a prize for past, and encouragement to future efforts, and secondly, as a salary for certain duties which the Fellow either performs or may be called upon to perform. By giving Dissenters all the emoluments, privileges and duties of Fellowships, so far as they trench not on the government, strictly so called, of the colleges, their desires would be fully satisfied, and the interests of learning advanced, while no principle would be sacrificed. A certain proportion of the Fellowships of each College might be set apart, to which, under these conditions, Dissenters should be eligible on the same footing in other respects as Churchmen. By properly regulating this proportion, the inconveniences above-mentioned would be avoided. It certainly would be somewhat more difficult for a Dissenter to obtain a Fellowship than for a Churchman, but there would be no longer any necessity for excluding a man thoroughly adapted for Academic life and studies. There might be certain difficulties about arranging the technicalities of such a system, but the Platt Fellowships which till very lately existed in St. John's College, bear witness to its practicability. These Fellowships were prizes and nothing more, conferring on their owners no share whatever in the government of the college. This kind of Fellowship might be revived and extended for a new purpose, and, if it were thought advisable, might receive a different name corresponding to the difference of purpose.

This measure is suggested in the full belief that the reasons for which Dissenters are at present excluded, are not pounds, shillings, and pence, but far more important reasons. It would not be easy to devise a more effectual method of shewing the real nature of the so-called narrow-mindedness and exclusiveness of the University. None could then fail to see that it was not money or even power, but right for which the University was striving; and the nineteenth century would not perhaps be the worse for beholding the extraordinary spectacle of a body of men contending for that from which they cannot expect to derive any pecuniary advantage.

Again, this measure is not suggested as a final measure. But till the present relation of Church and State, anomalous as it is, and transitory as it must be, undergoes its impending change : till either the English people so change as to become members of the present National Church, or the Church so changes as to become once more the Church of the English people, or lastly the National Church sinks into a mere sect, leaving England, which God forbid, without a Church at all, this measure is suggested as one likely to further learning and goodwill without sacrificing that great principle of the connection between Church and State, to illustrate which our two Universities exist.

THE NEW ZEALAND FAIRIES.

Not only in these haunted dells of ours,
Among the green fields where our fathers dwelt,
And in the forests of this older world,
Have lived the fairy people: other lands
Their feet have lightly trod: the Southern Cross
Has seen them gambol in the forest glades
Of isles about whose green delightful heights
The blue Pacific twinkles; and the moon
Has lit their dances on the shining sands
Of coral creeks in Australasian seas.
And there they are a finer race than ours,
Human in height and feature, fairer-hair'd
And fairer-skinn'd than any Maori,
A people always merry, whose bright lips
Are ever gay with laughter or with song.
For many an one has seen them; with the rest
Kanawa saw them, saw them to his cost,
For they had nearly scared him from his wits.
Kanawa was a chieftain of his tribe,
And once was out with certain of his men
And dogs to hunt the kiwi—wingless bird,
Whose feet are swifter than a stormy wind—
And being thus benighted, on a hill
Amid the forest glooms, they found a tree
That spread enormous shadow overhead,
And under, rising high above the earth,
Its huge roots ran in twinings serpentine,
Twisted, and coil'd, and knotted, and deform,
With many a snug recess wherein to lie
Warm and close-shelter'd for a night's repose.
So out some distance from the tree they piled
Great store of gather'd boughs and bushes dry,

And lit it, and the fire shone broad and bright,
And made a wondrous scene beneath the tree
Of rosy lights, and shadows: then they found
Each his own cell among the twisted roots
For slumber; but ere long from far there rose
Voices amid the darkness, nearer still
And nearer, many voices as of men
Women and children singing thro' the wood.
Heavens! how the men were frighten'd! but the night
Was all about them, and the tracks unknown
Amid the darkness of the haunted woods.

And so they hid their faces and were still
Amongst the deep recesses of the roots,
As is the woodland thing that if you touch,
It gathers up and stiffens and is dead.
Kanawa only, tho' he shook for fear,
Dared let his eyes go wandering in the dark;
And then he saw the fitful firelight flash
On fair white faces of the fairy crowd,
Who singing thro' the darkness came, and peer'd
Into the shadows. By and by they crept,
Now one and now another, lightly climb'd
The huge arms of the roots that circled him,
While he lay still and held his breath for fear.
But merrily they circled round and sang;
And when the fire flash'd brighter, off they flew,
And peer'd about from distant crevices,
Returning ever when it flagg'd again.

And at the last he thought a happy thought—
He took the little image that he wore
Carved of green jasper, from about his neck;
And took the jasper ear-drop from one ear,
And from the other one of ivory,
Made of the white tooth of the tiger-shark,
And thought 'perchance if he should offer them
As gifts, that they would go;' and on a twig
He hung them, frightened at their very touch.
And lo, the fairies, singing merrily,
Pick'd up the shadows of the jewellery,
And pass'd them each to each admiringly;
And there the trinkets hung all shadowless
Between the lighted tree-bark and the fire.

So did they: and when now their merry song
Was ended, pass'd away into the wood,
Nor touch'd the chieftain's jewels, well content
To have the shadows.—O amongst us men,
Amid the noisy bustle of the world,
Are there not many of us, all content

To leave the fair reality untoucht,
So we but have the shadow? So they went.
But soon as morning glimmer'd thro' the wood,
And the gray parrot scream'd his earliest scream,
Kanawa left the mountain with his men,
Nor stay'd to hunt for kiwis; glad enough
To see the thatcht roofs of the village huts,
And dusky faces of his tribe once more.

MUNICIPAL DEVELOPMENT IN THE 19TH CENTURY.

How spake of old the Royal Seer?
(His text is one I love to treat on.)
This life of ours, he said, is sheer
Mataiotes Mataioteton.

TRULY our age is an age of iron: the broad expanse of
country with its happy villages and their heavenward
pointing spires, the ancient city with its stout old burghers or
Society of Merchant Venturers, are not the England of to-day;
still indeed, from ten thousand steeples as of old float up into
the summer air the praises of a happy peasantry, and many
an old town or cathedral city still lives its sluggish life with
no more outward evidence of the lapse of time, than is
shewn by the hands of its old church clock as they come
back day by day at noon to the same old place, to start once
more upon the same old journey. But be it for better or
worse, the smart young England of our time is something
different from these things. The great cities of the country
with their smoke, their noise, their bustle, and their stinks,
their kings of iron or of cotton and their myriad workmen,
joined to one another, and to their great metropolis, the
largest and best representative of them all, by hard lines of
railway where the song of the birds is lost in the scream
of the locomotive, as it dashes through the tunnelled hill;
these certainly now constitute the most prominent feature
of the nation. We do our best to justify the Pacha's description in *Eothen*. "Whirr, whirr, all by wheels!—whiz,
whiz, all by steam!" Most of the old towns have changed with
the changing times, and accepting the new conditions of prosperity have retained their position as vigorous constituents
of the national life. Some, indeed, which scorned to suffer
themselves to be trampled down under the encroaching
wheel of the locomotive, have passed out of the notice of
their more enterprising sisters, and live their hermit life at

a distance from the haunts of men, happy in the calm contentment which reigns throughout their grass-grown streets. The majority, however, have opened wide their gates to the advancing civilization of the day, emancipated themselves as they fondly hope, from the last superstitious trammels of a semi-barbarous feudalism, and grasped with alacrity the iron hand of progress.

So it is with Slowbeach:—dear old Slowbeach, how well do I remember the time when I wandered along your shady streets, or amid the grey ruins of your mouldering castle, reading, with boyish zest, some wondrous tale—the woes of the " Fayre Una," or

> the golden prime
> Of good Haroun Alraschid,

whilst the rooks were cawing peacefully o'er the crumbling walls, and the shadowed elms were dancing 'neath the breath of summer on the sunny lawn; when I fished for trout, which I seldom caught, in the limpid water of your little river, or floated idly across your clear blue bay; or, glorious privilege, sat in awful silence in the parlour of the Slowbeach Arms whilst the burly Aldermen enjoyed, in dignified repose, the fragrance of the soothing weed, and mingled with the curls of smoke which eddied from their senatorial lips sage opinions on the rights of farmers, and the state of politics. Ah, well! this was a long time ago. I had never met Matilda then—poor Matilda—she used to say she should like to be a student's wife, to cheer him in his lonely hours of thought, and soar with him in spirit through the realms of fancy. She's Mrs. Jones now, and a very rising man Jones is too; a trifle hard in money matters perhaps, but a rising man. I met them in their carriage the other day with two fine children on the front seats—God bless me, how old it made me feel—she is really getting quite fat and matronly, who'd think that she had once the smallest waist in the county? It's a fact though, for I remember one day,—but what has a working architect to do with such things as these? It was just before Mrs. Jones's marriage that I left Slowbeach, and after a dozen years of constant and not unsuccessful exertion am a great deal happier, I dare say, than if I were the proprietor of those two red-cheeked young Joneses—happier!—of course I am; I'm sure I can't tell what people can find to like in the children, two more vulgar boys *I* never saw ; and as for Mrs. Jones, why every one knows poor Jones's weakness, and they do say that—but

whatever they say, no one shall call *me* uncharitable.—
I had always a longing though after the old place; there
was something about the rooks, and the elms, and the bright
bay, which I have not quite found in any thing else since:
I used to fancy it was boyish imagination, and all that sort
of thing; but I almost think now there may have been
something real in it after all. I have changed my opinion
about some of these things since my unfortunate connection
with the Orkney and Norwegian Submarine Telegraph Company—I lost a good deal of money by that scheme. Slowbeach, however, has long ceased to be what it was: a great
change came over it soon after I left; large coal-fields were
discovered in the neighbourhood, iron-works erected, docks
excavated, and a vast export trade established. Curious to
see the changes which had taken place I was much pleased
one morning at receiving a letter from an old friend at
Slowbeach, who told me that having had his fair share in
the prosperity of his rising young town, he wished to acquire
increased facilities for trade by adding some additional
buildings to his already extensive workshops. A most
favourable opportunity now offered itself for erecting them,
but there would be great difficulty in getting the plans
ready in time to have them approved at the next meeting
of the local Board of Health: would I, knowing the premises,
see what I could do for him, and so save him from waiting
another month, which he assured me was a matter of considerable importance in a town of such commercial activity and
business-like habits as Slowbeach now was; he added also
that I should find the town much changed and improved
from the dull old place which I formerly knew. I readily
accepted the commission, and in the few days which inter-
vened before the meeting of the Board managed by dint
of considerable personal exertion, and the aid of some
suitable drawings which I luckily had ready, to work up my
plans into a satisfactory condition. This done I forwarded
them for the preliminary inspection of the local surveyor, and
on the day before the Board meeting placed myself in the
train with an express ticket for Slowbeach. On approaching
the town I found every thing much altered; a forest of
masts extended over what had formerly been a moor: my
little trout stream had been applied to the perhaps more
useful purpose of supplying water to the numerous docks;
and instead of the coach-office with which my latest re-
collections were connected, a handsome station in the most
approved style of railway architecture had planted itself in

the centre of the main street. O my honest friend, director of the West Grimington Extension, well is it for you that a great authority has laid down that railway travelling is a process so intrinsically obnoxious as to make any well meant attempts to soothe the harassed minds of your poor passengers by architectural display a mere mockery of their sufferings : were it not for this, how agonizing would be your remorse as you lay tossing on your sleepless bed, and the undigested remnants of the last directorial feast evoked before your eyes a long and ghastly train of weird uncouth stations, which you had forced upon the public gaze, poor long straggling stations with impossible platforms and rows upon rows of weak minded looking iron pillars, fat bulky stations which had tried to be respectable and failed miserably in the attempt, gloomy looking stations which appeared to swallow up incontinently every train which fell in their way, Barbaro-Gothic stations, Greco-Manchester stations; O what an awful procession it would be!

From such reflections as these I was soon roused to a vigorous struggle for my carpet-bag by the harsh voice of the guard shouting " Slo'beach, Slo'beach junction, change here for Struggleforth, Grimington, and Smashwell," and having at length successfully asserted my claims to my property, and ignominiously defeated two old ladies, who had lost their own luggage, and with painful moral obliquity were about to carry off my bag as a compensation for their misfortune, I drove through the somewhat noisy and not particularly well pitched streets to the Slowbeach Arms, which still retained its leading position among the Inns of the town. The first face which I saw here carried me back at once into the early times; just inside the door of the Hotel was the old waiter whom I remembered from my boyhood:—there he was, not a whit older than when I left him: just the same amount of baldness about his shining head, and the seams of his well-worn coat; and under his arm as it seemed to me was the same identical napkin which he had held there when he viewed with pitying interest my departure from the same spot a dozen years before. I glanced down for a moment at my own expanding form (I am getting just a trifle corpulent I own) and thought of the slim young man whom he saw drive away from the gate—what right had *he* to be the same as ever? Hang the fellow, he ought to have died long ago; does he mean to insult me with his youth? I went up to speak to the old man, and giving utterance to the thought

x

which his unchanged appearance naturally provoked, I asked him his opinion of the docks and all the new improvements: " Think Sir," said he, "'taint much I think about 'em: I arn't been down to see 'em yet." And such they told me afterwards was the fact: indeed it was notorious that he had not possessed a hat these twenty years.

Refreshed by a night's sleep I took a walk the next morning round the docks with my friend, and then proceeded to the new Town Hall where the sittings of the Board were held. I here found that the plans would not be approved until after the rest of the business had been transacted, and was therefore, as the rain was falling, forced to wait in the lobby in company with an intelligent but thirsty policeman who protected the sacred precincts. By enabling this stalwart guardian of the municipal dignity to drink my health after the termination of the meeting, I at once acquired his good will, and he proceeded to give me many interesting particulars about the various members of the Board of whom we had a good view through the half opened door of the council-chamber. Their faces were for the most part unknown to me; the portly and complacent burghers whom I remembered had given way to a wiry looking lot of men with a generic resemblance to the Scotch terrier; and who were evidently better fitted for worrying out municipal abuses than their easy-going predecessors. Just opposite to me however sat a jolly looking publican of the old school, whose jovial face and goodly circumference contrasted favourably with the diminutive form and spare visage of a gentleman of watery appearance who sat on his right hand, and who was, my friend the policeman informed me, a very successful dealer in marine stores, and one of the leading teatotallers of the town. They were confronted by an energetic man with straw-coloured hair which looked as if it had fallen accidentally upon his head and stuck there: it appeared that this gentleman whose name was Swiper, was one of the most rising men in Slowbeach, a professed friend of the people, and a demagogue of the first water. Just as I arrived, the rosy son of Bacchus before alluded to, was engaged in delivering a fierce invective directed against Councillor Jolter for some futile proceedings which he had taken to repress the prevailing vice of the town, and which had put the Board to considerable expense. The Councillor attacked, either from a natural timidity or a consciousness of his mistake, did not attempt any answer; but the worthy representative of the pump, thinking the opportunity too good a one to be lost, at once took up the cudgels in his defence, and turning upon his assailant told him that the prevalence of the vice complained of was chiefly owing to "those houses where poison was licensed to be drunk. So long as those houses were allowed to sell liquid fire and double-distilled damnation, so long would the demoralizing system complained of be kept up: he hoped the time would come when those houses would be shut up, if not by moral suasion, by the strong arm of the law."* The gallant publican, undismayed by the attack at once retorted, that "he was not surprised at the remarks of his friend, coming as they did from him; he had spoken to Mr. Jolter, but it would appear that his friend was champion of the light weights, and was ready to cut him up into old junk; indeed he was reminded by the way he was met of Balaam and his ass, when Balaam could not speak his ass spoke for him."

Mr. Swiper here burst energetically into the dispute, and being joined by several other members of the Board, the confusion became too great to allow of anything being heard distinctly. At length the contest began to resolve itself into a duel between Mr. Swiper and a gentleman named Crump who sat near him, between whom a special enmity appeared to subsist. The first voice which rose distinctly above the tumult was that of Alderman Crump, who said: As a member of this Board, I ask whether the time is to be wasted in this way?

Mr. Swiper: I want to show the town what you are, sir,————

Mr. Smith: I rise to order. I beg to move that these two gentlemen retire into the other room, and not go into family matters here.

Alderman Crump: I shall be glad to vote an encomium upon you, Mr. Swiper, if you will behave yourself better in future.

Mr. Swiper: I don't want your encomium.

Several members suggested that Mr. Swiper should allow the business of the meeting to proceed.

---

* The speeches are quoted from the Slowbeach paper. Surprised at such a pitiful display of feeling in the council, of what is represented by the author as an important town, the Editors took the trouble to ascertain its magnitude as given by the last Census, and find to their astonishment that it contains upwards of 30,000 inhabitants.—Ed. *Eagle*.

Mr. Swiper: I don't think it is right that Mr. Crump should have such latitude, and I to be put down.

Alderman Crump (with great warmth): I wont have my name mentioned in this matter.

Mr. Swiper: He has put his speech before you all (great uproar and confusion, and several members rose to leave the room).

The Chairman: Now, gentlemen, I hope you wont leave. Here are moneys that must be paid, and I want your consent.

Mr. Swiper: You are all one-sided, like the Bridgnorth election. If I stop here all night I will be heard, and will repeat it at every meeting till the 9th of November.

Mr. Smith: I propose that Messrs. Crump and Swiper retire.

Mr. Swiper: I will make a proposition that Mr. Crump meet me before a public meeting of the burgesses to decide this point.

Alderman Crump: I will give you this promise—a vote of thanks if you'll behave yourself.

Mr. Swiper: I don't want your thanks—my poor father worked hard to maintain you when you were a pauper on the parish.

Alderman Crump: I deny it. I have maintained myself from childhood up till now.

Mr. Swiper: My father helped to support you and gave you an education.

Alderman Crump: You are too contemptible to notice (going up to Mr. Swiper with his hand lifted up). I wont strike you.

Mr. Swiper: You are *afeer'd* of me.

Alderman Crump: (in a tone of contempt): *Afeer'd* of you, indeed—you are too contemptible to notice.

Mr. Swiper: You are the Tom Sayers of Slowbeach. (Laughter.)

Alderman Crump: I wouldn't touch you with my hand, but I might with my foot. (Exit Alderman Crump, leaving the members quite dumbfoundered).

The meeting then broke up in the greatest confusion, leaving the business of the day undone.

And what of the poor plans?—well, accidents will happen in the best regulated and most prosperous towns, and my friend must be content to wait another month. Nothing was left for me but to return to London as soon as possible: but before doing so I hurried off to see the old castle once more. How glad I was to find that the spirit of progress had not burst in upon its peaceful seclusion. I mounted to the ruined keep, and looked around; the sun had burst forth in splendour after the late rain, and every tree and flower and blade of grass was raising its head to meet his genial rays; the birds were singing joyously above, and the lambs were bleating amidst the fragments of the shattered walls; all was peace and beauty, harmony and order:—the whole of nature with ten thousand tongues was singing praises for the mercies of the All Father; and, remembering the mean and petty jealousies I had just left, I bowed my head for very shame lest my presence there should be a discordant note amidst that glorious harmony.

" ENOD."

OWEN'S NEW CLASSIFICATION OF MAMMALS.*

IF Galileo could be dropped quietly amongst us, now in this nineteenth century, he would find public feeling very much altered with respect to scientific matters. No outcry would now greet him from indignant conservative savans; no grim inquisitors would be kindly arranging rack and thumbscrew for his benefit. He would no longer be denounced as a fool by one party, and anathematised as a heretic by another. No longer would he be requested to go down on his venerable old knees and to solemnly swear astronomical lies. But Philosophical Societies, and Scientific Associations would be delighted to hear him; Mathematical Journals would be rejoiced to print his papers; and a discerning public would gladly receive and honour him, if the sages to whom they looked up and their own common sense approved his doctrines. There is an honest candour pervading society now-a-days which is peculiarly favourable to the development of science, and which has already produced fruit in the shape of numerous improvements and discoveries. Among the latest of these is a new Classification of Mammals introduced by Professor Owen.

For some years past there has been a decided tendency on the part of Naturalists to forsake the old school of Artificial Classification for something more natural and comprehensive. This has been pre-eminently the case in Botany, where the old Linnean system has now quite succumbed to the labours of De-Candolle and others; the result being the almost universal adoption of the "Natural System." In Zoology too we can trace the same change,

---

* *Classification of Mammals.* Reade Lecture in the University of Cambridge, by Professor Owen. J. Parker and Son. 1859.

though we find perhaps fewer Naturalists of original genius in this department of science. From the time of Aristotle to that of Cuvier (above two thousand years) very little had been done by naturalists towards obtaining a satisfactory system of Mammal Classification. Aristotle included in this sub-kingdom all viviparous animals, calling them Zootoka; and with his wonted acumen selected the formation of the extremities and the dental structure as the chief marks for arrangement. After him Ray and Linnæus endeavoured with doubtful success to improve upon his plan. The principal advance made was the substitution by the latter of Mammals for Zootoka; and this is an important change, as the act of suckling is always a mark of a warm-blooded animal, whereas Aristotle's term would erroneously include some species of genuine fish which bring forth their young alive. It was reserved for the famous Cuvier to propound that Classification which has for many years been generally adopted throughout the whole scientific world. This great Naturalist selected as characteristic features the jaws, the teeth, and the extremities. Starting with three sub-classes of Mammals, viz., those with nails, those with hoofs, and those whose hinder extremities are imperfectly developed, as the whale; he proceeds to sub-divide. The Unguiculate (with nails) he separates into orders according to their dental organization; the Ungulate (with hoofs) according to the peculiarity of a thick hide or that of chewing the cud; the Mutilate (maimed) he makes into one order, the whale-tribe. The outline at least of this system is pretty generally known, and its defects have latterly been a common subject of complaint. Its faults are various, the chief being, perhaps, that in this scale of mammal life, our old notions of superiority and inferiority among the brute creation, are quite upturned. Few of us would, for instance, be likely to place a mole in a post of honour above the dog, or a kangaroo above the elephant or horse. Yet such is their relative position according to Cuvier. We at once see something forced and unnatural in this; we condemn the arrangement as not according to the general character, and particularly not according to the individual sagacity of these creatures.

Now to us who recognise an Author of Nature, and see design and final cause in the works of Nature around us, the reflection is not at all out of place, that there is an accurate balance between the organised structure of the bodies of animals, and the sagacity or intellect which is destined to control those bodies. The human hand for example, beautiful machine as it is, would be useless to a hedge-hog or a seal; and again, the tusks of an elephant or the fangs of a tiger would be superfluous to man whose ingenuity and skill enable him to procure his food without those engines of violence. Now, from such thoughts we should conclude that a Classification, like an Examination list, according to the intellectual powers (if I may use the expression) of the members of the Mammal kingdom, would probably be at once systematic and natural. Assuming therefore the brain as the seat of mental power or sagacity in man and beast, it would follow, if we acted upon our theory, that the brain would be the starting point for a good sound classification.

And this is precisely Professor Owen's starting point. He proceeds however not on theory but on fact. He finds by actual dissection in the course of his Anatomical labours at the Zoological Gardens, that there is a close connection between the cerebral and the general bodily developments of the creature, and that dividing the Mammals into four great classes, taking the brain for his guide, he has also marked out four distinct degrees of advancement in bodily structure.

The characteristics of a highly developed brain are, two large lobes, complicated and numerous convolutions, a complete covering of the cerebellum, and a conspicuous presence of that fibrous link of union between the two lobes called by anatomists the Corpus Callosum. These are all present in the brain of man, and in his alone. Man therefore forms a sub-class to himself named Archencephala.

Going downwards, we next find brains with convolutions more or less complicated and partially extending over the cerebellum and olfactory lobes. Of such are the Carnivora and Pachydermata of Cuvier—the dog, monkey, elephant, whale, &c. These are named Gyrencephala.

Still descending we meet a marked decrease in the size of the brain, so much so that it no longer covers the cerebellum or olfactory lobes. We see here no convolutions, all is smooth, with the corpus callosum in a very rudimentary state. This marks the third sub-class, Lissencephala; of which the Edentata and Rodentia of Cuvier, the bat-tribe, &c. are members.

Lastly, we arrive at the lowest type of brain; lobes very small, no corpus callosum, olfactory lobes, optic ganglions, and cerebellum totally uncovered, and altogether the whole apparatus in a very incompact state. This marks the sub-class, Lyencephala, containing marsupials (animals with pouches) such as the kangaroo, opossum, &c.; and the monotremata, such as the duck-mole, so called from their peculiar abdominal structure.

These are the four great sub-classes. A further division into orders follows according to the extremities, teeth, food or other characteristics; the whole forming an almost perfect scale of Mammal nature from man down to the implacental beasts who scarce deserve to be called viviparous. What is here given is of course merely a sketch of a system at once natural and precise. It agrees with our well established notions of the relative superiority of the various animals, and proceeds from a principle which, at the very outset, acknowledges the unity of design in the works of Nature.

" λαβυρίνθειός τις."

THE WOUNDED KNIGHT.

———

PR'YTHEE unclasp the casement: let me hear
Once more the ruffled waters of the lake
Surge on the castle's base: their wild unrest
Vexes me not as heretofore;—I feel
Fresh pulses stir within me, and new life
Dulls in mine aching ear the too keen sense
That knew a torture in all sound, and stills
The feverous impatience, born of pain,
That dwelt about me. Surely there is joy
Even in weakness and in weariness,
As after a fought field, or else this hour,
So passing sweet, by its own witchery
Hath poured a seeming sweetness into pain.

The cloud hath left my mind. I am again
E'en as I was before the blinding blow
Of that fell battle-axe crushed through my casque;
And, as I reeled and sought with aimless hand
The unsupporting air, the mingled noise
Of conflict and fierce clang of struggling hoofs
Grew hollow, and before my sick'ning eye
Spread a broad blackness, and I knew no more.

E'en as I was?—'Tis but an idle boast.
This trembling hand but ill, methinks, could rein
A war-horse pawing at the trumpet-call:—
This arm,—whose sheer and unresisted force
Clove through steel harness and drave back good knights,
As I have sometimes seen from yon hill-side
Start a huge mass, and crush the plume-like fern
And snap the saplings, driving ruin down

Into the seething lake,—might scarcely brook
The burden of the sword it used to wield.

   'Tis strange,—this calm of new-returning life:—
Hast thou not seen me, if some paltry hurt
Hath let me from the field, chafe fretfully,
As chafes an anchored skiff, and strains and tugs
Its anchor, if a wind hath stirred the bay
And o'er the bar and on the jutting ridges
Dashed the white foaming billows;—so have I,
If any note of battle touched mine ear,
Fought with a wound that held my sluggard arm,
Struggling in impotent impatience.
And yet from this more deadly-seeming wound
I rouse me, and find pleasure but in rest,
And joy to be delivered from the thrall
Of the wild dreams and shapes fantastical
That thronged the wayward paths of sense distraught:
For now I seemed to lie on desert sands
And fain would rest me ere the morning strife;
But ever, through the canvass, troubled me
The pale malignant moon, and the hot dust
Filtered through every joining of my mail:
Or else fierce treacherous faces of the foe
Glared on me, and a leaden weight weighed down
My arm, and death seemed terrible if slain
By coward hands I perished, from my peers'
Dissevered. Then, anon, I was at sea,—
A shoreless sea and death in every wave;—
For, in the mad confusion of my soul,
The ocean-floor became a battle-field,
And every angry surge a crested knight
Hissing a shout of onset in mine ears.
And tossed, and overborne, and stricken down,
I sank before them, and the blood-red west
Flashed on my fading eye and blinded me,
As one who falling feels the flag he bore
Droop, muffling him in darkness ere he die.

   But now 'tis o'er.—The weary laggard hours
Slide by on quiet pinions, and I feel
Thy gracious touch and ministering hand,
And hear remembered accents of sweet tone
That are to me as angel utterances.

   O lay thy gentle hand in mine, and while
Day softly melts in evening, sing once more
The melody that broke my deadly trance,

That I may feel and hear thee nigh, and know
A blessed calm, as of some ransomed soul
Shadowed by wings of guardian spirits, that hears
Sounds of unearthly sweetness, and forgets
The pain and grief and turmoil of the world.

SONG.

High o'er yonder rugged fell
  Stars in holy light are steeping,
Lake and cave and silent dell,
  And the dews of night are weeping
  Over petals drooping, sleeping.

And I weep at this still hour,—
  Weep for thee. O may'st thou borrow,
E'en from sympathy's sweet power,
  Strength to battle with the sorrow
  That may find thee on the morrow.

Yet sweet dews the flowers repairing
  Vanish when the mid-day burneth;
But my love, thy sorrow sharing,
  Toward thee still in sorrow yearneth,—
  To thee evermore returneth.

"C. S."

ON THE ADVANTAGES OF BELONGING TO THE LOWER ORDERS OF SOCIETY.

A Fragment.

Plures nimia congesta pecunia cura strangulat.

I LIKE to stroll about Portland Place or Belgravia when the sun shines and my clothes are new and my person got up for the occasion. It makes me feel rich to be in the neighbourhood of so much material wealth! The flunkeys in gorgeous apparel pass me by with a quiet respect. Flunkeys know but two frames of mind, courage and scorn; between these poles they acknowledge no possible mesothesis. The policeman does not watch me—the old ladies with their poodles seem to regard me as one of themselves, and being idle for the nonce and on the stroll, I am open to be considered even a rich old lady. But the flags of Belgravia pall on a man after a time—and playing at being rich is an expensive game—even though it be confined to walking about in dandiacal fashion, and impressing errant flunkeys. Moreover, there is no spot where the sun always shines, and even the west has its rain and mud and concomitant sorrows—and then comes the rub—when a man has to cast about for an object and finds himself ofttimes puzzled to know where he shall turn or what he shall do.

I have more than once been in this frame of mind myself, with just enough in my purse to make me "careful," and no more. I am not a theatre-going man—our English actors shock me—the second characters seriously jar against my nervous system—the cant of the best stars afflicts my soul—in music I am fastidious, and I have no box at the opera—or put the case (a not unfrequent one) that I should find it inconvenient to buy a stall ticket—meanwhile it rains!—or it snows—and parliament is prorogued—and I am at my hotel, &c. &c. &c. In the name of all that's dreary what *am* I to do?

The cause of all this desperation of perplexity is, that I am a miserably respectable outcast. Ten years hence, perchance, I may be an honoured member of the University Club, or a don at the Athenæum: who knows? ten years hence Salathiel may have chambers in the temple, into which I may drop when I choose; or Sallustius may have a bachelor's room for me in his palace in Westbourne; or Hippocrates may be in vogue and welcome me to physiological splendour in Saville Row; all that *may* come, but it has not come yet, and now?—

In such a grim frame of mind I have more than once looked abroad and cursed my stars which ordained that I should belong to the "gentilatres" of this world. Brethren of the upper middle ranks—there's no use denying it—we are a pitiable lot. We comfort ourselves with our bath in the morning—with our daily shave, with our coffee and chops—with our best of tailors and our dilletantism—but we're a pack of finnikin jackanapes after all, and if you would not call me one—if you only wouldn't call me one—I should like to be an out-and-out-cad!

Compare the gent's resources to our's, and how jovial a life is open to him. He has a soul above (or below—which is it?) tailordom; he roams the streets with easy jaunt; in the careless glee of a spirit at ease he whistles aloud at his own sweet will, and is unconscious of the gaze of the multitude; if his hat be a bad one he careth nought, he is not bound to wear a hat at all; if his boots be other than clean he maketh his bargain with the next urchin at the corner, and chaffeth the operator or tosseth up with him for the fee. He is at home in every billiard-room, even supposing he hath never been there till the present hour: who would strive to 'trap' him of the seedy paletot?

Doth he long for Cremorne or Rosherville? there goeth he, and is 'hail-fellow' with the nearest, and at his ease with the fairest; he hath no difficulties at finding his element, his element is to be found everywhere, and if any presume to observe him he asketh thee—"What are ye a staring at?" You and I would be strange in a skittle alley. He is joyous even there, and standeth a pot with yon sharper a-straddle of the railings.

Just look at a gent outside a 'bus' and see him in his glory; you and I hate a 'bus' I suppose, I know I do; outside is dreadful, inside is overwhelming. I am myself subject to a nightmare after a heavy supper, and the vision of that nightmare, as I call it up to my mind, brings the big drops of horror on my brow; my vision is a vision of a ride inside a 'bus' with a woman in black on my right hand, and a woman in red on my left, and two women in yellow in front of me, with each a baby in her enormous arms, and two children, warranted under three, particularly requested to keep quiet, standing by my unhappy legs,-and all the women and all the children with colds, and all strongly and decidedly objecting to the windows being opened, and I there—and I got in at the Eastern Counties Railway, and have to be carried to the Great Western Terminus, and I mayn't get out, and no body else has any intention of doing so either: that is my night-mare, and no wonder that when I awake I am exhausted! And yet I like children; I am partial to the fair sex; I had rather ride than walk any day; I hate being in a draught! How is it that such a vision as this should be so unspeakably abhorent to me?

Why, only because I, and such as I, have educated ourselves to a morbid sensitiveness! The lower orders of society would find such a ride from Shoreditch to Paddington in the highest degree exciting, and your gent would have been invited to tea by all your females before they had got as far as the Bank. What lots of hard cake those precious three-year-olds would have been promised before Holborn Hill was reached! *We* ride in cabs, we do! We get mercilessly imposed upon; we get ruthlessly slanged by cabby if we pay him less than twice his legal fare; we smoke ourselves into convulsions of coughing; if a Hansom do not chance to be on the stand we run all sorts of hideous risks of cholera and scarlet-fever and small-pox and heaven knows what else. While there, high above us, kicking his happy heels, paring his nails in the sunshine, humming a Negro melody, smoking his short clay, and surveying the world from his eminence, sits the enviable cad, whom you and I would be horribly ashamed of as-sociating with, and who cares as little for us as we do for the Emperor of Japan!

I used formerly to hold it as an axiom that soap and

water cost nothing. I have lived to see the outrageous
fallacy of the diction. I begin to see that cleanliness, dependent on soap, is a terrifically expensive luxury. In
the first place it is almost impossible to say how far you
may carry your love of soap!

In our youth we seldom advanced beyond the wrist in
our soapy ablutions, save few of us favoured our feet once
a week with a visitation: as years went on the domain of
soap was ever advancing: and think of a man soaping his
very head every morning of his life. It is terrible to think
of the next step being internal administration. But think
of the laundress and her bills; think of the future of soap
when we are householders, and the steps have their daily
scrub, and the stairs and the floors and the chairs and
the tables. Why the thought is enough to make my next
nightmare turn into a procession of soap-boilers bent on re-
forming the world with old brown Windsor. All this is
quite unnecessary. Our forefathers were happy men, and wise
ones, learned men too, and holy; they lived long and they
laboured stoutly; yet if they lived among us now we should
certainly call them a dirty lot. James I. very rarely washed
his hands; Queen Elizabeth eat her beef with a chop-stick;
Henry VIII. wore particularly greasy breeches, wiped his
fingers, reeking from the venison-pastry, on the dogs that
crouched at his feet, and if they were out of the way, on
the lappets of his jerkin. With all the talk of our age,
I often think there's a great deal of stuff in it all. I think
it was in Mr. Petherick's delightful book that I was reading
the other day, how certain little Africans dress in Nile
mud: they blush at complete nudity, so they roll themselves
in the sluice of the Nile and bask in the sun, and lo! they
are clothed! By and bye they become out at elbows,
and their anxious parents are distressed at their shabbiness,
whereupon the urchins are sent with shame to the river
bank and commanded to mend their attire; they obey—
roll themselves again in their native mud, and return bright
as new pins! Are they clean or dirty? Miss Nightingale
could say, 'disgustingly': I am sorry to differ from that
lady, but I think there is much to envy in that easy supply
of garments.

So to return to our cad; he is not embarrassed by the
craving for an exaggerated purity; happy in his independence, he may be as dirty as he pleases; he can do
very well without that luxury. He has never known the
joy, and he does not pine in the absence of it; his gain

is a real and solid one. Is it nothing to be able to repose in a third class carriage with two man-of-wars men, one singing "The Bay of Biscay O!" and drinking rum incessantly? Nothing to find pleasure in a cheap train to Margate, or an Isle of Man excursion boat?

I own I have tried low life at times, but found myself unfit for it. *I* didn't like it, and I attribute it to a moral or intellectual defect in my constitution; but I stand up for the freedom of the lower orders on principle, and I despise myself for my inability to throw myself into it. It is with a melancholy sense of weakness and shame that I confess myself deficient in that greatness of soul which allows of my throwing myself into. hearty sympathy with vulgar enjoyments: I contemplate them reverentially at a distance. Intellectually I admire the cad; practically I fear I loathe him! It is the loathing of a deep rooted envy perhaps, but it is there! It is not the entire admiration which I accord to the heroes of Arctic discovery; rather is it the sort of contemptuous envy I award to the eccentrics who climb high mountains for no other purpose than to stand in uncomfortable positions.

But I have once or twice tasted the real sweetness of the life of the lower orders.

Not when I've wandered through Belgium in a ' welveteen' jacket, trying to pass for a snob, and failing, by persisting in weakly washing myself, and consequently being treated with most irritating homage: not when I've paid a visit to a small tradesman in Wales, and insisted on being considered one of the family, and found myself unearthed on Sunday by the parson sending his compliments and requesting me to read the lessons. Not when I've attended a sixpenny ball in Liverpool, and danced with the fair daughters, whose Argus-eyed mothers looked on, and as I gallantly led the damsels to their seats, persisted in addressing me as my lord. Not here, not here! but in that paradise of the lower orders of society, those innocent—cozy—private—cool—and very vulgar tea-gardens on the Avon, which any one who knows Clifton ought to know, and if he's wise, ought to resort to; there surrounded by exceedingly frowsy parties of four or six, waited on by very shabby maidens; drinking execrable tea; but bringing your own tobacco; sung to by the nightingales over head, and below the Avon rolling its waters to the sea; you may for ninepence have an insight into the really bright and purer side of our small tradesmen's life, and learn to see that they have resources you and I can only very rarely catch a glimmer of. Such a place as those Clifton tea-gardens we respectable people have not. Nay, we have no real places of amusement at all; we have no billiard tables, no cafés, no bowling greens, no skittle alleys, no innocent casinos, no nothing! In all these matters we are at an immense disadvantage as compared with the lower orders of society.

OUR SEVENTH JUBILEE.

WE cannot allow the Commemoration Services of the three hundred and fiftieth Anniversary of our College's existence, as a corporate body, to be passed over with a merely casual mention among the subjects of our Chronicle. The event in itself deserves separate notice, but more especially so with reference to other circumstances.

It may be as well to mention for the information of those of our graduate readers who associate the sixth of May with feasting only, and the Commemoration Service with the receipt of shillings in chapel on the day after the end of each term, that the three Services are now thrown into one, which is held on the sixth of May, the day set apart in memory of St. John's miraculous deliverance before the Latin gate. The length of the Service is relieved by the help of the choir, who chant those portions of the Service which are appointed to be said or · *sung*. The Sermon on this occasion, being a special one, was preached by the Rev. the Lady Margaret Professor of Divinity: than whom no worthier representative of the good old College could possibly have been found. The learned Professor based his discourse on the words found in Haggai ii. 4—9. He alluded to the hindrances experienced by the Jews in building the house of God, "then ceased the work of the House of the Lord which is at Jerusalem"; (Ezra iv. 24.) and to the effect of the prophesying of Haggai and Zechariah: "then the prophets Haggai, and Zechariah, the son of Iddo, prophesied unto the Jews, in the name of the Lord, ...and then rose up Zerubbabel the son of Shealtiel, and Jeshua the son of Josedech, and began to build the house of God which is at Jerusalem, and they prospered through the prophesying of Haggai the prophet, and Zechariah, the son of Iddo, and they builded and finished it." He then went on to remark on the principle of the Prophetic

Scriptures, how nearer events are made the symbols and pledges of Messiah's coming and kingdom, instancing Isaiah's prophecy of deliverance to Hezekiah, which had its perfect fulfilment in Christ the Virgin-born, (Isaiah vii. and ix.) and the visions of Zechariah, (iii. and vi.) which clearly pointed to Christ the Prince of Peace. After referring to erroneous views of Prophecy lately put forth, and to the unfairness of the Edinburgh Reviewer in citing Bishop Pearson as a voucher for Rowland Williams, the preacher proceeded to remark on the foundation of our own College as somewhat similar in its attendant circumstances to that of the later Temple. We were now celebrating our seventh Jubilee—for the Charter of Incorporation was first sealed in 1511. Many difficulties and hindrances were thrown in the way, the plan being cut short of its original dimensions by the death of the foundress, the Lady Margaret, before the completion of her designs. But Fisher, Bishop of Rochester, and then Chancellor of the University, aided by Ashton, fought his way through all, and the College was opened with solemn religious ceremony in 1516, with a number of Fellows and Scholars diminished from the original intention,—viz. thirty-two Fellows instead of fifty, and twenty-four Scholars instead of fifty. The College prospered in its work, so that its members in a Petition presented Nov. 21, 1547, to the Lord Protector Somerset, could say :—" Primum alimus optima ingenia optimis disciplinis et moribus, deinde ex nostro cœtu proficiscuntur qui reliqua fere singula Collegia explent et ornant. Deinde in Vineam Domini mittimus plurimos operarios, in Rempublicam aptos et idoneos viros." And Roger Ascham, in his " Scholemaster" says, " He," (Dr. Medcalfe) " at his departing thence left such a companie of Fellows and Scholers in S. Johnes College, as can scarcely be found now in some whole Universitie: which, either for Divinitie, or for Civil Service to their Prince and Countrie, have been and are yet to this day, notable ornaments to this whole Realm: yea S. Johnes did then so florish, as Trinitie College, that princely House now, at the first Erection was but *Colonia deducta* out of S. Johnes, not onely for their Master, Fellowes, and Scholers, but also, which is more, for their whole, both order of learning, and discipline of maners: yet to this day, it never tooke Master, but such as was bred up before in S. Johnes: doing the dewtie of a good *Colonia* to her *metropolis*, as the auncient cities of Greice and some yet in Italie at this day, are accustomed to do." (p. 55).

But are we not now, as it were, witnessing the beginning of a new House? We have just received a body of Statutes by which the benefactions, which have been liberally bestowed upon us since the foundation of our first House, during a period of three hundred and fifty years, are consolidated. We are beginning under a new system inaugurating a new period of our history. May we not apply to ourselves the prophet's exhortation to be strong, remembering that the LORD of Hosts is with us? May we not hope and pray that the "glory of the latter house may be greater than that of the former;" that it may extend its front to the street, and spread forth its branches to the River, by enlarged buildings? But first of all, and above all, we must think, like David, of a "house for the LORD." Is not the time come for a new chapel? Many said of old, "The time is not come, the time that the Lord's House should be built;" but can it be said now? The ancient Labyrinth, once a chapel of St. John Baptist, is longing again to be devoted to its original uses, and joined to God's house—the place is too strait for us. When Dr. Powell, near a century ago, gave £500 for the stone front of the south side of the first court, many felt, "that a new Chapel would have been a real ornament to a flourishing Society that were crowded to death in their too contracted one," (Nichol's *Literary Anecdotes*.)

Surely we have not lost the public spirit which animated our College of old:

> Privatus illis census erat brevis,
> Commune magnum — :

when Dr. Wood gave £2000 for the new Court beyond the Cam, and every Fellow the fourth part of his dividend, each receiving for several years £120 only, instead of £160. Let us take to ourselves the words of the text and say—"'The silver and the gold are thine, O Lord;' we will not rest until we have raised a Chapel more worthy of the College, more answerable to the bounty of our benefactors, and to Thy manifold blessings."

But, as Fuller says (History of Cambridge) "The glory of Athens lyeth not in her walls, but in the worth of her citizens: buildings may give lustre to a college, but learning giveth life."

We must cherish hopes of still larger numbers to be trained here to serve God in all the offices of Church and

State, in all walks of learning and science, in study of the word and works of God. Much rests upon us, and our successors, if the glory of the latter house is to surpass that of the former—we have a high standard of achievements to attain to. We must have forty Senior Wranglers in the next hundred and fifteen years. We must have in the next three hundred and fifty years better Divines than Becon, Whitaker, Sibbs, Beveridge, Cave, Wilson, the unanswered and unanswerable opponent of Socinianism, and the last two occupants of the Lady Margaret's chair, Marsh and Blunt; better Preachers than Pilkington, Ashton, honest Lever, (who procured the endowment of Sedbergh School,) Powell, Balguy and Ogden; better Bishops than those four of the famous seven, who went to the Tower in triumph rather than in mourning, Lloyd of Norwich, Lake of Chichester, White of Peterborough, and Francis Turner of Ely, sometime Master of the College. We must have better scholars than Sir John Cheke and Roger Ascham his pupil, the famous tutor to Queen Elizabeth, than Pember, Gataker, Bentley, "prince of Critics," and Butler, with his numerous pupils; better Hebraists than Chappelow and Edmund Cartell; nobler benefactors of mankind than William Wilberforce, the champion of the slave, and John Hulse the endower of the Hulsean Lecture and Essay, and the Christian Advocacy; defenders of ancient foundations more sturdy than Earl Powis; wiser statesmen than William Cecil Lord Burleigh, and Strafford, and Falkland; braver warriors than Fairfax and Cornwallis. We must have physicians more talented than Linacre, Denny, Gilbert, Browne, Gisborne, and Heberden; better naturalists and botanists than Nicholson, Glen, Jenyns, and him who now lies peacefully resigning his soul to God, and even as life wanes, telling with brightening face what flowers are peeping from the ground, what trees are putting forth their buds;* better poets than Sackville, and Herrick, and Churchill, and Akenside, and Matthew Prior, than Kirke White, so soon snatched away from us, and the poet of nature, whose proudest boast was that he had "never written a line which dying he could wish to blot;" better astronomers than Fallows, and the younger Herschel, who was content to spend years in voluntary exile that

---

* Professor Henslow, who we regret to say, has since passed away to his rest.

he might complete the Catalogue of the Stars, and Adams, who cast the line of his analysis into the depths of space and brought to view another member of our system. And last, not least, we must have nobler missionaries than Henry Martyn, who gave up his splendid prospects of advancement here, that he might do his Master's work elsewhere, and Haslam, and Whytehead, than our pair of Bishops in Africa, Cotterill and Colenso, or that other pair who, first fellow-oarsmen in the Lady Margaret boat, have since traversed the southern Pacific in the same Missionary ship, the bishops of Newcastle and New Zealand, Tyrrell and Selwyn. Better men than these must we have, or if not better, more like them, and in more continuous supply, every year adding to their number. We must have more University scholars, more University Prizemen.

And have we not hope of more peace, that we may be more united, and work together, heartily and earnestly endeavouring to maintain the former reputation of our College? "Wherefore be strong, O Master! be strong, O President! be strong, O ye Fellows and Tutors! and be strong all ye Scholars and Students! and *work!* cultivate all manly exercises; let the Lady Margaret be, as of old, head of the River, but let her sons, by their own diligence in study, be also at the head of the Tripos lists."

We regret that this imperfect sketch is all that those of our readers, who did not hear the sermon, will have of it. The Professor will only consent to its publication in one way; by a lithographing process, to be done not by Messrs. Day and Son, but in solid stone and mortar. And there seems to be some hope of this being accomplished, for the interest of our resident members is already excited. We shall be amply satisfied if these reminiscences of the ἔπεα πτερόεντα of the Preacher induce any to give a helping hand to that object, should it be found to be feasible.

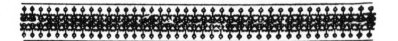

OUR CHRONICLE.

Easter Term, 1861.

———

THERE are, I should think, but few men who have spent
their three years at Cambridge, who do not look back
upon their May Terms as the pleasantest part of their time
here.

An interesting essay might be written on the elements
which make up this pleasure. Of course first and foremost
is the great charm of female society of which so many of
us are temporarily deprived, and the pleasure to those who
do not enjoy that, of meeting among the usual haunts of
familiar faces of town and gown, faces before unknown,
but all lit up with enjoyment: but there are other constituents too of the pleasure in question. There is the idea
of being at the head of an establishment, so to speak, and
doing the honours of it to your visitors: there is the pride
which a man will naturally feel in introducing parents or
sisters to his friends in College. It is well for us to have
once in a way these gentle reminders that there are slight
rules of polite society, that there are ladies to whom we
owe our devoir of respect and attention. Those of our
readers who are at present in residence, have had a fair
amount of this during the past week, and I doubt not there
are some hearts feeling somewhat novel sensations at the
sudden termination of the few moments of bliss they have
enjoyed, especially if it be succeeded, as in some cases it
is, by the pains and perils of the Senate-House. And doubtless some Mary Porter returned to some country vicarage,
feels some little pang at the separation from that dear Tom
Brown.

The transfer of the congregation for the conferring of

Honorary Degrees and the reciting of Prize Exercises, which has always been associated with the somewhat late Commencement, to the middle of the May Term, has formed a nucleus for a week of festivities, in which Oxford, by its Commemoration Week, has always heretofore had the advantage of us. The gaieties were ushered in as usual by the Boat-Races, an account of which will be found later in this Article. On Tuesday, May 14th, Cambridge was honoured with a visit from its Chancellor, on the occasion of the Rede Lecture, delivered this year by Professor Willis. The subject of the lecture was very interesting, "The History of Trinity College, Social and Architectural, from the Foundation of King's Hall and Michael House to the present time." The Professor, however, confined himself almost entirely to the latter, which rendered his lecture less interesting to the mass of those who heard it, to say nothing of those who could not hear, and who formed a large proportion of those present. The Chancellor's visit only lasted for a few hours.

On Saturday, May 18th, the town was the scene of a great martial display. The Volunteers of the Inns of Court in conjunction with our own Corps, were reviewed on Parker's Piece by General M'Murdo, in the presence of H. R. H. the Prince of Wales, and a numerous body of spectators. The details of the review our readers will have seen elsewhere—suffice it to say that the whole was quite a success. The members of the Inns of Court were entertained at dinner by the different Colleges, and seemed highly gratified with the hospitality they received. Nearly seventy of them dined in the hall of St. John's, with the Fellows of the College, and those Volunteers of No. 2 Company, who had joined in the Review, all the Riflemen being in uniform. In-the evening the Procession of the Boats took place, and was better attended than we have seen it for some time: the band of the C. U. V. R. C. playing during the time in the grounds of King's College.

The hundredth Concert of the University Musical Society took place in the hall of Caius College on the evening of Monday, the 20th. The first part of the programme consisted of Mendelssohn's Music to the Antigone of Sophocles, Professor W. Sterndale Bennett conducting, and Professor Kingsley reading the dialogue: the second part was of a miscellaneous classical kind. The room was very much crowded; indeed the applications for tickets considerably exceeded the available space.

Tuesday was the day fixed for the conferring of Honorary Degrees. Seldom has our Senate-House witnessed such a crowd as were assembled then within its walls. The admission to the body of the building for persons not members of the University, was by tickets. The Undergraduates' gallery was crowded to suffocation within a few minutes of the opening of the doors; many having been attracted by a rumour that the Chancellor was to be present in person. The following degrees were conferred: that of Doctor of Divinity, honoris causa, on the Rev. Frederic Gell, B.D. of Christ's College, Bishop Designate of Madras; that of Doctor in Civil Law, honoris causa, on the Earl of Elgin; Vicount Stratford de Redcliffe; Sir W. R. Hamilton; Sir Roderick I. Murchison; Major-General Sabine; Dr. Robinson of Trinity College, Dublin; Mr. John Lothrop Motley, author of the History of the Dutch Republic; and Mr. George Grote, the Historian of Greece. At the conclusion of this ceremony, the following gentlemen recited their exercises:—

Henry Lee Warner of St. John's College, his Exercise for the Camden medal; subject: "Alpinæ vives."

Arthur Sidgwick, Trinity College, his Greek Ode; subject: "Tantalus."

Augustus Austen Leigh, King's College, his Latin Ode; subject: "Padus Flavius."

Henry Yates Thompson, Trinity College, his Greek and Latin Epigrams.

Charles Edward Graves, and Henry Whitehead Moss, of St. John's College, their Exercises for the Porson Prize.

Frederick William Henry Myers, Trinity College, his English Poem for the Chancellor's Medal.

On Wednesday afternoon the Horticultural Society held their annual show in the grounds of King's College. H. R. H. the Prince of Wales was present, and the concourse of people was, if anything, larger and gayer than usual. This was the close of the festivities.

But we must come to our chronicle of Johnian events. On Monday, March 18th, the following gentlemen were elected Fellows of the Society:—

Joseph Hirst Lupton, B.A., bracketed 5th Classic and Junior Optime, in 1858.

James Webster Longmire, B.A., 3rd Classic, Senior Optime, and 2nd Chancellor's Medallist, in 1859.

Walter Baily, B.A., 2nd Wrangler, 1860.

George Richardson, B.A., 3rd Wrangler, 1860.

John Vavasor Durell, B.A., 4th Wrangler, 1860.

Joseph Merriman, B.A., 5th Wrangler, 1860.

Robert West Taylor, B.A., bracketed 17th Wrangler, and 5th Classic, 1860.

On the Thursday following, the list of the Classical Tripos showed E. A. Abbott, B.A. of this College, Senior Classic: the Senior Chancellor's Medal was also adjudged to the same gentleman.

Our readers will have seen that out of seven names of those who recited exercises on Tuesday the 22nd of May, three were those of Johnians.

Subjoined is the list of the Voluntary Classical Examination :—

April, 1861.

First Class.	Second Class.	Third Class.
Evans, J. D.	Bateman.	Green-Armytage.
Falkner.	Evans, A.	Carey.
Graves.	Hickman.	Davis, J. W.
Gwatkin.	Pooley.	Valentine.
Ingram.	Rees.	Willan.
Spencer.	Rudd.	
	Snowden.	
	Taylor, C.	
	Thompson, J. C.	

The Boat-Races, which began on Wednesday, May 8, have been this year subject of greater excitement than usual. We subjoin a list of the Bumps in the First Division :—

May 8.

1 1st Trinity I.
2 Lady Margaret I.
3 3rd Trinity I.
4 Caius I. }
5 Trinity Hall I. }
6 Emmanuel I. }
7 2nd Trinity I. }
8 Christ's I. }
9 1st Trinity II. }
10 Trinity Hall II.

11 Magdalene }
12 Corpus I. }
13 Peterhouse
14 Lady Somerset I. }
15 Sidney I. }
16 1st Trinity III.
17 Jesus I. }
18 Clare 1. }
19 Lady Margaret II.
20 Caius II.

May 9.

1 1st Trinity I.
2 Lady Margaret I. ⎱
3 3rd Trinity I. ⎰
4 Trinity Hall I.
5 Caius I.
6 2nd Trinity I.
7 Emmanuel I. ⎱
8 1st Trinity II. ⎰
9 Christ's I. ⎱
10 Trinity Hall II. ⎰

11 Corpus I.
12 Magdalene ⎱
13 Peterhouse ⎰
14 Sidney I.
15 Lady Somerset I. ⎱
16 1st Trinity III. ⎰
17 Clare I.
18 Jesus I. ⎱
19 Lady Margaret II. ⎰
20 Caius II.

May 10.

1 1st Trinity I.
2 3rd Trinity I.
3 Lady Margaret I.
4 Trinity Hall I.
5 Caius I.
6 2nd Trinity I. ⎱
7 1st Trinity II. ⎰
8 Emmanuel I. ⎱
9 Trinity Hall II. ⎰
10 Christ's I. ⎱
11 Corpus I. ⎰

12 Peterhouse
13 Magdalene ⎱
14 Sidney I. ⎰
15 1st Trinity III.
16 Lady Somerset I. ⎱
17 Clare I. ⎰
18 Lady Margaret II.
19 Jesus I. ⎱
20 Caius II. ⎰

May 11.

1 1st Trinity I.
2 3rd Trinity I.
3 Lady Margaret I.
4 Trinity Hall I.
5 Caius I. ⎱
6 1st Trinity II. ⎰
7 2nd Trinity I. ⎱
8 Trinity Hall II. ⎰
9 Emmanuel I. ⎱
10 Corpus I. ⎰

11 Christ's I.
12 Peterhouse ⎱
13 Sidney I. ⎰
14 Magdalene ⎱
15 1st Trinity III. ⎰
16 Clare I.
17 Lady Somerset I. ⎱
18 Lady Margaret II. ⎰
19 Caius II.
20 Jesus

May 13.

1 1st Trinity I.
2 3rd Trinity I.
3 Lady Margaret I.
4 Trinity Hall I.
5 1st Trinity II.
6 Caius I.
7 Trinity Hall II.
8 2nd Trinity I.
9 Corpus I.
10 Emmanuel I.

11 Christ's I. }
12 Sidney I. }
13 Peterhouse }
14 1st Trinity III. }
15 Magdalene }
16 Clare I. }
17 Lady Margaret II.
18 Lady Somerset I.
19 Caius II.
20 Pembroke

May 14.

1 1st Trinity I. }
2 3rd Trinity I. }
3 Lady Margaret }
4 Trinity Hall }
5 1st Trinity II.
6 Caius I.
7 Trinity Hall II.
8 2nd Trinity I.
9 Corpus I. }
10 Emmanuel I. }

11 Sidney I.
12 Christ's L
13 1st Trinity III.
14 Peterhouse }
15 Clare I. }
16 Magdalene }
17 Lady Margaret II. }
18 Lady Somerset I.
19 Caius II.
20 Pembroke

May 15.

1 3rd Trinity I.
2 1st Trinity I.
3 Trinity Hall I.
4 Lady Margaret I.
5 1st Trinity II.
6 Caius I.
7 Trinity Hall II. }
8 2nd Trinity I. }
9 Emmanuel I. }
10 Corpus I.

11 Sidney I. }
12 Christ's I. }
13 1st Trinity III. }
14 Clare I. }
15 Peterhouse }
16 Lady Margaret II. }
17 Magdalene }
18 Lady Somerset I. }
19 Caius II.
20 Pembroke

May 16.

1 3rd Trinity I. }	11 Christ's I.
2 1st Trinity I. }	12 Sidney I. }
3 Trinity Hall I.	13 Clare I. }
4 Lady Margaret I. }	14 1st Trinity III.
5 1st Trinity II. }	15 Lady Margaret II. }
6 Trinity Hall II.	16 Peterhouse
7 Caius I.	17 Lady Somerset I. }
8 Emmanuel I, }	18 Magdalene }
9 2nd Trinity I. }	19 Caius II. }
10 Corpus I.	20 Pembroke

We have received the following report of the Matches played by our Club during this term:

1. St. John's First Eleven *v.* Emmanuel.
   St. John's 189.   Emmanuel 185.

2. St. John's *v.* Ashley.
   Ashley 232.   St. John's 57.

3. St. John's *v.* Christ's College.
   St. John's 130.   Christ's 113.

4. St. John's Second Eleven *v.* Caius Second Eleven.
   St. John's 193.   Caius 120.

5. St. John's Second Eleven *v.* Christ's Second Eleven.
   Christ's 171.   St. John's 108.

END OF VOL II.